The Orphanage Girls Reunited

Mary Wood was born in Maidstone, Kent, and brought up in Claybrooke, Leicestershire. Born one of fifteen children to a middle-class mother and an East End barrow boy, Mary's family were poor but rich in love. This encouraged her to develop a natural empathy with the less fortunate and a fascination with social history. In 1989 Mary was inspired to pen her first novel and she is now a full-time novelist.

Mary welcomes interaction with readers and invites you to subscribe to her website where you can contact her, receive regular newsletters and follow links to meet her on Facebook and Twitter: www.authormarywood.com

BY MARY WOOD

The Breckton series

To Catch a Dream
An Unbreakable Bond
Tomorrow Brings Sorrow
Time Passes Time

The Generation War saga

All I Have to Give
In Their Mother's Footsteps

The Girls Who Went to War series

The Forgotten Daughter
The Abandoned Daughter
The Wronged Daughter
The Brave Daughters

The Jam Factory series

The Jam Factory Girls
Secrets of the Jam Factory Girls
The Jam Factory Girls Fight Back

The Orphanage Girls series

The Orphanage Girls
The Orphanage Girls Reunited

Stand-alone novels

Proud of You
Brighter Days Ahead
The Street Orphans

The Orphanage Girls Reunited

Mary Wood

PAN BOOKS

First published 2022 by Pan Books
an imprint of Pan Macmillan
The Smithson, 6 Briset Street, London EC1M 5NR
EU representative: Macmillan Publishers Ireland Ltd, 1st Floor,
The Liffey Trust Centre, 117–126 Sheriff Street Upper,
Dublin 1, D01 YC43
Associated companies throughout the world
www.panmacmillan.com

ISBN 978-1-5290-8968-4

1 3 5 7 9 8 6 4 2

A CIP catalogue record for this book is available from the British Library.

Typeset by Palimpsest Book Production Ltd, Falkirk, Stirlingshire
Printed and bound by CPI Group (UK) Ltd, Croydon, CR0 4YY

Visit **www.panmacmillan.com** to read more about all our books
and to buy them. You will also find features, author interviews and
news of any author events, and you can sign up for e-newsletters
so that you're always first to hear about our new releases.

For Julie, my beautiful sister.
Rest in peace, darling.

Chapter One

London, 1910

Ellen looked back from the landau her father had dragged her to. Through her tears she could see her beloved friend Ruth standing on the pavement and could hear her desperate plea: 'Write to me, Ellen! I live at number three, Little Collingwood . . .'

'Ellen, turn yourself around now! I don't want you to even look at that girl, and I forbid you to write to her. That life is behind you. I want us to make a new life. Today is your birthday treat. I cannot believe you are eleven already and I want you to enjoy our time together. We can only heal everything by forgetting it all and making a new beginning.'

As the horses trotted on, Ellen felt her father's hand take hold of hers. It was a mystery to her why he didn't want her associating with Ruth – lovely Ruth who'd been like a big sister to her and Amy, when they were all in the orphanage together.

Ellen pondered on that time, trying to understand why her father had taken her to the orphanage in the first place. Why couldn't he have stuck up for her against the hatred of her stepmother, who'd never called her anything but 'your father's bastard'?

And why to such a place? Didn't he love her? But then,

he must do as he hadn't callously walked away when he'd left her. She'd felt the wetness of his tears as he'd held her in a hug. Heard the sob in his voice when he'd told her, 'It's all so complicated and shouldn't have come to this but Daddy will come and fetch you one day. Hold on to that, my dear Ellen . . . and I'm sorry, so very sorry.' And he had kept that promise as soon as his wife had died, hadn't he?

But as much as she tried to justify and reason it all out, painful memories and the reality of all that she'd been through shuddered through her. She tried to block them by listening to her father. She hadn't taken in all he'd said, but now he was saying, 'Promise me, Ellen . . . Look, I have something to tell you . . .'

With this, a new fear gripped her. Was he going to send her away again?

'You look cold. You shivered just now . . . Driver, take us to Bond Street, please.'

Turning to her once more, he leaned in and said, 'We'll get you a lovely present there, dear, and we'll buy you some new winter clothes, but all that will be after we have a nice warm drink.' He held her tightly to him for a moment.

When the landau pulled up and her father lifted her down, Ellen's fear gave her the sensation of being transported to another world, where she could feel nothing and didn't want to.

The glittering shops, the hustle and bustle, and the noise of the traffic hardly impacted on her as her mind focused on what she would be told.

'That's the shop we need, dear.'

The imposing building of J. Moffat, Milliner's and Costumier's had a window displaying many hats on the left-hand side of the door and ladies' fashions in the right-hand window.

'They have a department for children. They'll be able to kit you out. But come on, dear, let's cross the road and go into that teashop. We'll get you a hot drink to warm you up and then do our shopping. And, like I said, I need to talk to you.'

As they walked towards the teashop, Ellen thought her father's voice a little too jolly. 'Look, doesn't it look nice? They make lovely pastries; we'll have one with our drink.'

The teashop with draped net curtains, huge flower pots each side of the door and window boxes full of pansies did look pretty, but to Ellen it held a dread of what was in store for her.

Tentatively sipping the hot milk, she looked around at the ladies in big hats gossiping whilst drinking their tea out of delicate china cups. All calm and proper until a little boy suddenly began to cry loudly. The ladies turned and stared at his mother. She hurriedly stood and with her now screaming son in her arms, fumbled in her purse. On impulse, Ellen left her seat and went up to her. 'Can I hold him for you, while you pay your bill?'

The lady gazed down; her eyes seemed to hold love. She put out her hand and Ellen felt it gently stroke her hair. But then, when she spoke, her voice shocked Ellen as it didn't go with the way she was dressed: 'Ta, luv, but he might be too much for yer.'

There was something about her that Ellen felt drawn to. She looked and talked like Ruth, only she was older than her.

'Ellen! Sit down at once!'

Ellen ignored this snapped instruction from her father and touched the child's hand. He stopped screaming and looked at her quizzically, then smiled a watery smile, making Ellen feel warm inside. Her father's hissed whisper broke the moment. 'I'm doing all I can!'

Ellen froze as the lady whispered back, 'It ain't enough, you promised. You got me into this bleedin' mess. And for the second time, I might add! No self bleedin' control!'

'Shut up!'

The noisy women, who had started to chat again, hushed. Ellen waited. She felt caught up in something she didn't understand, and yet knew was about her as much as the little boy. She looked at the lady, caught her eye, saw a look of love as she spoke. 'I'm sorry, luv, sorry to the heart of me, but I can do nothing about anything. He's to blame. Everything that happens to you is on his shoulders.'

'Matilda, please!'

'Tilda! Why can't you call me Tilda like every bleeder else does, eh?'

Ellen felt a sudden pressure on her arm. 'Go outside, Ellen, stand by the wall and don't move. I'll be out in a moment.'

Something about her father's voice made her obey.

The door opened when she got to it. A gush of cold air seemed to cocoon her. A nanny carrying a small suitcase brushed past her and went inside.

Ellen stood leaning on the wall, wondering what was going on, feeling even more afraid, and yet the warm feeling the lady and the little boy had given her hadn't left her. She somehow knew that in some way they were very special to her.

When the nanny came out carrying the little boy, and got into a cab, Ellen's curiosity got the better of her. She stepped back towards the foyer but then stopped as voices came to her.

Her father and the lady were standing outside the closed cafe door. The lady was crying. 'I can't bleedin' well go

4

through this again, Albert, I can't. Me 'eart breaks with each one. Why don't you support me to take care of them meself, eh? Look what happened. That bleedin' wife of yours put one of me kids into that orphanage – well, I'm glad she's dead, good riddance to her . . . Though it didn't take yer long to get another fat cow to keep yer 'ow yer like to be kept, did it?'

'Shut up! . . . Look, Matilda, I can't let you do that. You wouldn't bring them up properly. My children should—'

'You what? So, a bleedin' orphanage where horrific stuff goes on is better than I could give me own kids with you giving me the money I need to care for them, is it? You're a bastard! I ain't never going with you again, never!'

'Ha! It isn't just me, is it? You'd already put one brat into that orphanage before I met you.'

The lady sobbed. 'I didn't, I left her with the priests. I thought they'd find her a home.'

'Huh, you knew full well what would happen. You're nothing but a filthy prostitute!'

The lady stepped out of the foyer; tears streamed down her face. She stopped, looked longingly down at Ellen, and whispered, 'I luv you, don't ever forget that,' and ran off down the street.

Father appeared then. His hand shook as he took hold of hers, but his voice was calm. 'You must forget all you saw and heard, Ellen, it does not concern you.'

In his other hand he was carrying the small suitcase.

Without another word, he took her to Moffat's. There, he sat on a chair whilst a shop assistant kitted her out with a new thick coat with a fur lining and thick white stockings with elasticated tops. Long woollen skirts and fluffy knitted twinsets. The suitcase was open. She could see her night attire and clean underwear neatly folded in the bottom of it. Each item Daddy purchased, the assistant folded and put into the suitcase. Neither spoke much.

Once outside, a cab pulled up at the kerb. Hearing her father tell the driver, 'Paddington station, please,' brought Ellen's dread rushing back into her – her heart sank.

She wanted to ask what was happening but was afraid of the answer.

The station was crowded with folk who pushed and shoved their way to where they needed to be. Smoke billowing from a stationary train smarted Ellen's eyes and clogged her throat.

It felt to her as if she didn't exist as no one seemed to see her but barged into her rather than step aside as she followed her father.

Feeling battered and bruised, she filled with relief when he picked up another suitcase from the left luggage office. They were going somewhere together! She caught hold of her father's hand and looked up and smiled. 'Where are we going, Daddy?'

He didn't speak until they reached a platform where he indicated for her to sit down. Sitting beside her, he said, 'I am taking you to your grandmother in Leeds, my dear. She is going to care for you. I will visit you from time to time. You'll be very happy there.'

'What grandmother? And I don't want to go. I want to live with you, Daddy . . . Don't you love me? You said you did! You said you would never leave me again.'

'Things have changed . . .'

'Has that lady changed it? Who was she? Why did that nanny take her little boy and make her cry? Why did you call her a prostitute?'

'Be quiet! Look, I told you to forget all of that. That la . . . woman, is nothing to you and never will be. Your grandmother is my mother, she . . . well, she didn't know about you until I wrote to her. She's happy to have you and wishes that I had sent you to her in the first place. You see . . . well, you knew that Rosamond – my wife – couldn't love you . . . Look, there's things about grown-ups that you don't understand . . .'

Suddenly Ellen knew what he was talking about. It all fitted with everything that had happened to her and she blurted out, 'I do! I had that awful thing done to me that men do to women. So did me mates, Ruth and Amy, and Hettie. It makes you have babies when you're big enough and . . . you did that, didn't you, Daddy? You did that to that lady . . . Did it make her have me . . . and that little boy?'

Sobs wracked her body as a train pulled into the empty platform. Her arm was grabbed, and she felt herself being dragged along. Others on the platform gaped at the spectacle they were making and went to protest, but her father smiled at them and, as if nothing awful was happening to her, told them, 'She doesn't want to go to school, you know how wilful children of this age can be. She will be fine when she gets on the train . . . Now, come along, dear, you have to go and that's that!'

One tug that was too strong for her and they were in a carriage. Ellen landed heavily on the bench seat. Her father slammed the door and sat down opposite her. Out of breath, he mopped his face, and then wiped his eyes, before bending his head and sobbing into his handkerchief.

Ellen softened. The hate she'd felt for him dissolved. She went to him; he took her in his arms.

7

'I'm sorry . . . so sorry, Ellen. I tried; I really did. You would have ended up in that orphanage anyway . . . if I hadn't begged for you to be given to me. Forgive me, I'm so sorry.'

Through Ellen's own sobs, she asked what she had to know. 'Is that lady my mum?'

She watched the different expressions on his face. It seemed an age until he answered, then he nodded his head. 'I – I was weak . . . I – I can't explain. But I love her, and yet, cannot love her. She . . . she is paid by men to . . . well, look, this talk is too much for you, my darling Ellen. One day when you are older, you will understand.'

Despite her young years, Ellen did understand. But she instinctively knew that she should not pursue this but accept it. All she said was, 'One day I will find her and take care of her. Will you do that till I can, Daddy?'

'It isn't that simple. I have my standing in the community to think about.'

His standing, Ellen had come to realize, was because he was rich. She didn't yet understand how. He wasn't a lord or anything, but he did have a huge house, maids, a butler, a cook, all of whom lived upstairs in the attic, and she only saw on very few occasions. And she remembered that before she was banished to the orphanage, she had a nanny, and a tutor. How her father afforded all of this, she didn't know. But how he had it all and yet had allowed her to be in that awful place was even more of a mystery – one that even the knowledge she now had didn't solve for her. She only knew at this moment that she longed to be with the lady in the cafe, to tell her it would be all right and she'd make her daddy take care of her.

'I don't care about your standing, Daddy, she's me mum.'

'My mum! Or even better, my mother! How many times do I have to tell you? I know you spoke like a cockney in that home, but you're not in there now. Haven't you learned anything in the months you have been back with me and having elocution lessons?'

'I'll try harder, Daddy, but will you help me mum . . . my mum, please?'

He was quiet for a moment, then said, 'Look, I'll make a payment to her. Just the one, and that's it. Not that I haven't done so in the past, but she just squanders it away and comes back for more, which she bloody well must earn . . . I mean . . . Oh dear, I should not be having this conversation with you. I'm tired, I'm saying far more than I should. I'm going to rest now, and I suggest you do the same. We'll talk later. I will put you in the picture as much as I can, my dear, I promise, but my head is throbbing now.'

Ellen sat back. Her feet stuck out in front of her like all children's do, but she didn't feel like a child. She knew more than children ought to know and had been through too much to be a child. And now, more bad things were happening. Her father was giving her away again.

As the train chugged along, Ellen's thoughts gave her no peace as such a lot became clear to her. The little baby boy was her brother, she was sure of that. And Daddy had said the lady had had more children. Where were they?

It was all too much for her young mind to take. She stared out at the passing scenery as blackened walls turned to equally blackened houses as they left London, and then fields and cows, sheep and trees – so many trees – became her landscape. Feeling lost and more alone than she'd ever felt, the tears tumbled down her face as the man she loved so very much rested beside her, snoring as if he hadn't a care in the world.

She thought of Ruth and wished with all her heart that she could be with her now, and Amy, who'd been shipped off to Canada with a lot of other orphans taken to a new life, and as her eyes closed, she thought again about her mum, of how beautiful she was, and how very like Ruth she was too.

Chapter Two

1912

The view from Ellen's bedroom window was a beautiful kaleidoscope of colours as she stood gazing out at the rugged hills and fields that seemed to stretch into eternity. The golds, yellows and browns of autumn shone in the low sun.

A voice behind her made her jump.

'My, that were a big sigh, Ellen, lass.'

Ellen turned and smiled at Dilly, her grandmother's housekeeper, who carried the load of not only running this large ramshackle house set on the edge of Leeds on the road to Wakefield but taking on most of the tasks herself, from bedmaking to scrubbing floors, with only Cook and a once-a-week laundry maid to lighten her burden.

Though Ellen helped her as often as she would let her.

Older than Grandma, Dilly was a little woman with a round face and a mop of black curly hair that was peppered with grey. Ellen loved her – sometimes more than she did her grandma, who was a strait-laced woman stuck in her ways. But despite these traits Ellen somehow knew her grandma loved her, even though she never really showed it.

Her reaction to them meeting for the first time was to lift Ellen's chin and say, 'So, you're my son's bastard? One of many, I don't doubt. Well, hold your head up high, girl. I was a bastard too, and it hasn't hindered me, and so is your father, and it certainly hasn't hindered him! Married well, I did, and you can too. Though you can fall again as I did, as now I have to rely on this son of mine who follows in his grandfather's footsteps – whoever his grandfather was. You see, Ellen, I wasn't as lucky as you. I didn't find my family and bad things happened to me that resulted in your father being born. But though I may fall short, I'm yours, girl, and we look like we're stuck with each other. Not that you're not welcome, you are, but it's up to you. Behave and don't disrupt the peace I've found, and we'll get along.'

And that was that and it had set the tone for life as it was to be.

Grandma's revelations had shocked her but had made her love her with all her heart for she knew what 'bad things' were. But Grandma hadn't ever shown her any affection. It had been Dilly, a spinster, who Ellen had learned had never married because her fiancé had been killed not long before their wedding day, who'd hugged her when she'd felt sad or was hurt in any way. And Dilly who cheered on the rare occasions Ellen heard from her father or soothed her when she suffered any ills. She had been the one to help her when her monthlies had begun. And who had taken her for walks, told her stories and kissed her goodnight.

Sighing again, Ellen said, 'I was just thinking, it's months since my father wrote and it's my birthday soon.'

'Aw, lass. Your thirteenth birthday and growing more beautiful by the day.'

Ellen just smiled at Dilly, not having anything to say to this.

'So, why that face, lass, eh?'

'I – I just feel . . . Oh, I don't know. I want my father to love me enough to at least write now and again.'

12

'It ain't going to happen, Ellen. I don't reckon as your da has any respect for us women.' Dilly clucked her tongue. 'I'd not even think about him! He ain't worth it.'

Ellen didn't imagine there could ever come a time when she would feel that her father wasn't worth her loving him.

'I tell you, Ellen, lass, you only have to look how he allowed you to be dumped in that orphanage you told me of. You, his own daughter!'

Ellen flinched but had no protest she could make as Dilly was speaking the truth.

'If that ain't proof enough, look how he treats his own ma. Naw one who can feel justified in taking ownership of his ma's house and profiting from selling the land that was rightfully hers is worth a pinch of salt. Look at this place. It's cold and damp. The boiler only works when it feels like it. The whole house is falling down around our ears, but will your da spend money on it to give his ma a few comforts in her old age? Naw! So, he ain't gonna bother about you either, me little lass. You've to make your own way in life. And you can. You've passed all your school certificates. I would keep studying while he's willing to keep paying your way as a salve to his conscience. Get yourself a good start.'

Ellen knew the truth of what Dilly said but didn't want to acknowledge it.

'Think on, lass. Your grandma hasn't got that chance. God alone knaws what she'd do if I left. I've felt like doing so, many a time. I'm fair jiggered. But I keep going cos she needs me.'

Ellen couldn't defend her father. He'd done nothing that proved Dilly wrong. Sometimes she hated him, and at others longed for him. He'd never visited since he'd left her here and though the few letters that he wrote were affectionate, always he urged her to do as Dilly had just said – study hard

13

and equip herself for one day being faced with the outside world. No hint that he would be there for her to help her to face the future.

A fear of what this would mean made Ellen's heart race. She turned away from Dilly hoping she wouldn't detect this. She picked up the laundered clothes Dilly had placed on the end of her bed. Busying herself putting them away helped her to control her emotions. *Thirteen? I feel more like thirty! Lonely, abandoned by my father who should love me, and unwanted by him.*

Swallowing hard, Ellen turned towards the large oak wardrobe that dominated her room, glad to have the task of hanging her grey serge frock – one of three bought recently; the other two were navy and light blue. This last was for Sunday best. They had replaced the woollen skirts and twinsets she'd now grown out of.

'Reet, lass, I've to get on and your tutor will be here soon. I've lit the fire in the schoolroom for you.'

Keeping her back to Dilly, Ellen kept her voice even as she said, 'Thanks, Dilly,' knowing that if Dilly got a hint of the emotion flooding through her at this moment, she would want to comfort her. If she did, the floodgates would open, then she'd never be able to stop crying.

As it was, as soon as the door closed on Dilly, Ellen flung herself down on her bed and wept. It seemed to her this lonely existence would never end, living her life as she did with two elderly women, and a cook who she rarely saw. Her time was spent mostly in the garden, the schoolroom or this, her bedroom – a large room with faded pink flowered wallpaper and huge dark oak furniture.

She longed to go out, other than to church and for walks around the garden. She longed for her father, and to find her mum and to be in the life of her little brother, who she felt sure now lived with their father. Would she ever be allowed to know him? And how her heart ached just to be able to see Ruth and Amy once more. They were still so special to her.

Ellen tried to remember the address Ruth had shouted out to her on that day that the landau had taken her away from her. Still she could see the desperate plea in Ruth's eyes and hear her shout something like Collingwood, but had she heard right? And where was that street? London? How did you find one street in the vastness of London? That's if she ever got back there. Maybe she would rot here – become old, like Dilly and Grandma, and never see the outside world again.

A bang on her door woke her. Shocked and disorientated, her nerves jangled as a sharp tone came to her. 'Are you going to waste my time much longer! I'm only here for another hour! It's hard enough teaching you, without you not turning up!'

Ellen turned and looked at the clock. She couldn't remember falling asleep but had been for almost an hour! Her mouth felt dry, her eyes clogged and crusty. Rubbing them, she jumped off the bed. 'Sorry, Miss Parkin. I'll be there in a moment.'

Gathering herself, she rushed over to the closet – a curtained-off corner of her bedroom that hid a commode and a dresser with a marble top on which stood a bowl of water. Next to this was a shell-like dish with her soap, and then a box of talcum powder and a hairbrush. A towel hung on a rail on the side of the dresser, along with a dolly bag that contained the clean rags she needed every month.

Relieving herself, she swilled her face, pulled the brush

through her dark hair which immediately sprang back into soft curls around her face, and surveyed herself in the mirror. She could do nothing about the red rims around her huge dark eyes that evidenced her having cried herself to sleep, but she pinched her pale cheeks to bring colour to them and forced a smile onto her face before bracing herself to face Miss Parkin's wrath.

'How dare you keep me waiting!'

Ellen's heart fell at the sight of the cane Miss Parkin swished through the air.

'You shall be punished! Bend over your desk!'

'No! No, I – I'm sorry. I fell asleep . . . I—'

'That's no excuse. You know what time I am here every weekday to try to get a modicum of knowledge into your thick skull! And you dare to insult me by sleeping at the very time you should attend me! Bend over at once!'

Left with no choice, Ellen bent over the desk. Flashes of the spiteful matron of the orphanage came to her and Ruth's screams permeating the thick stone walls as she was thrashed to within inches of her life!

Quivering, Ellen whimpered, 'Please don't. Pl-e-ease.' The last word said on a sharp intake of breath as the stinging, cutting slash of the cane sliced across her buttocks. Before she could release the breath, another blow had her wailing out loud, 'No-o-o! Stop, please!'

Her buttocks smarted with unbearable pain, tears mingled with her snot as she gripped the edge of the table, but on once more hearing the cane swish through the air and knowing she couldn't bear it slicing her again, she moved, turned and flew at Miss Parkin, knocking her over and falling on top of her.

The room filled with hers and Miss Parkin's screams as they tussled, rolling this way and that. Ellen was conscious of her nails digging into the woman's cheeks and hearing a brash cockney voice that she knew came from her but she couldn't stop. 'Yer'll not bleedin' well hit me again, you bleedin' bitch!'

'Ellen, eeh, me lass, what're you doing? Ellen, Ellen! Stop it! Get off her! Eeh, lass, lass.'

Dilly's voice penetrated Ellen's hysteria. She turned. She knew spittle was running from her slack mouth, knew she was still screaming and moaning, but could do nothing.

Caught off guard, a blow knocked her backwards. The light faded, Dilly's protests went into a muffled garble, and the shadowy room spun around as a black curtain descended over Ellen and took her to a place of peace.

'Ellen, Ellen!'

The shaking of her body gradually registered with Ellen. She had the feeling of wading through spiders' webs to reach Dilly's kindly voice so that she could be hugged and soothed, but every time she felt she was making headway something tugged her back – fear. If she left this peaceful place, people would hurt her again.

The shaking persisted, as did the calling of her name, which now sounded a desperate plea. 'Please, Ellen, please wake, lass.'

Opening her eyes, she felt a tear plop onto her cheek. Dilly was crying. She hadn't meant to make lovely Dilly cry. She went to raise her arm, but it felt like it was made of lead. She tried to smile, but something restricted her face from moving.

'Eeh, me little lass, you're going to be all right. I promise.

Don't be afraid. You've a bandage covering most of your face, but it will come off when the cut has mended.'

Ellen tried to say she couldn't move her arms, but she couldn't even mouth the words. The horror of this must have shown in her eyes.

'You'll be reet, lass. Try to lie still. You're in a jacket that keeps you from flailing. You've hit out at everyone who approached you.'

Dilly's hand stroked her hair, but the gesture didn't help to quell the terror that had risen in Ellen. *I'm in a strait-jacket! No! I can't be . . . Why?*

Memories of this garment being used on a girl in the orphanage, who'd gone into an uncontrollable rage, and of her being carted off never to be seen again, flooded Ellen. She remembered the fear she'd felt that such a thing could ever happen to her.

She turned her head trying to see where she was. Then was relieved to see the walls of her schoolroom.

'Take that bloody thing off my granddaughter!'

'But, madam, she had to be restrained and should be transported to the asylum. None of you are safe! When I was called, your granddaughter's screams were filling the house. By the time I got up here, Miss Parkin had managed to knock her out but told me that the young lady had been attacking everyone. That behaviour and the hysterics I heard are displayed by those who are mad and there is only one sensible course of action.'

Grandma looked from one to the other. Still wearing her outdoor cloak and bonnet, she leaned heavily on her stick. Lastly her eyes settled on Dilly. 'And you sanctioned this?'

'Naw, I didn't! I was trying to calm Miss Ellen, madam, as she'd knocked Parkin to the ground and was beating her when suddenly Parkin reached for the doorstop and hit Miss Ellen and knocked her unconscious.'

'And where did you come from, Doctor Ainsworth?'

'I had been called to see Cook. I heard everything.'

'Ha! A likely story. There's nothing wrong with Cook as far as I know. I know your little game. You've got a wife and five children, man! You shouldn't prey on vulnerable women!'

The doctor spluttered. Grandma ignored his protests.

'Where did that monstrous thing come from? Take it off at once!'

'I – I carry many items of apparatus around with me. I – I never know what I might need, and this was needed, I assure you. And by the look in your granddaughter's eyes, it still is!'

Dilly's distressed voice telling how she begged them not to strap Miss Ellen into the jacket was cut short as Grandma commanded, 'Take it off, man, take it off right now! If you don't unstrap my granddaughter and tend to her, I will write to the medical council, or whoever it is you are answerable to and tell them of your . . . your *other practices!* And you, Parkin, are dismissed. I never bloody liked you. Now I see my mistrust was well placed and I should never have taken you on!'

'She beat Miss Ellen, madam. Caned her, she did. No wonder the child went for her!'

'What? You dared to hit my granddaughter? Leave my presence at once!'

Ellen should have felt gratified as the snivelling Miss Parkin left the room, but she was more relieved that strap after strap was being unfastened and with each one, she could gradually move her arms more freely.

'Can you get up, miss? I need you on a bed to examine you.'

Ellen winced as she rolled over onto her stomach. A gasp came from her grandma.

'My God, is that blood on her frock?'

'Aye, madam, she's been cut to ribbons by that cane.'

'No! Oh, my poor Ellen. Help her, Dilly. You're strong. Help Ellen to rise and get her to her bed.'

With Dilly holding her on one side and the doctor on the other, Ellen at last completed the painful journey to her bedroom. Her head throbbed and her buttocks smarted but at least her grandma had saved her. A love of a different kind flooded her for the little woman. It was a powerful emotion and one she knew she'd only felt for four others in her life – Ruth, Amy, the woman she knew was her mum and the little boy she knew was her brother.

She loved Dilly too, although in a different way, but her love for her grandmother had deepened and did more so as she sat by her bedside.

'I'm sorry, Ellen.'

Her small knobbly hand stroked Ellen's hair, not only soothing her but filling her with the warmth of being loved by one of her own kin.

'My dear, I had no idea Miss Parkin could behave in that manner. And though I cannot sanction your retaliation, I understand it, and am glad that you have enough spirit to fight back when oppressed. You are going to need that. And a lot of other gumption too as time passes.'

Though she didn't at all feel like doing so, Ellen managed a smile.

'I'll get Dilly to tend to you. The doctor is leaving creams for you and something to deaden the pain, but I wanted a few moments with you to tell you where I have been today. I've been trying to secure your future. I have – had – some very expensive jewellery that your father didn't know about. I told him I'd sold it long ago to keep this place going. I was protecting myself with this lie, but now I find I have no need to do that, as although he took ownership of my house and land, he has paid my way. Oh, I know it's only enough to help him sleep at night and make him feel his duty to me is done. Not that I wanted duty. Like you, I long for him to love me enough to visit me and show me affection.'

Grandma let out a huge sigh. 'So, in that we have a bond. Anyway, something in me made me keep anything else I had of value from him, hence my lie to him. But apart from one brooch that I want you to keep in memory of me, I entrusted my solicitor to sell everything else and to put the proceeds into a trust for you. There is no age stipulation, only that the trustees are satisfied that you need the money to further yourself in life, or to get you out of a dire situation that wasn't of your doing, or for something the trustee considers money well spent. To that end, my dear, I'm delighted to tell you that the amount for you to access is one thousand pounds!'

Ellen gaped at her grandma. She'd never heard of such a sum. It was a vast amount of money – enough to buy three houses the size of this one! She just couldn't take it in that it was all at her disposal. She immediately thought of how she could help Ruth and Amy with it and she filled with happiness at the prospect.

Taking her hand from under the covers, she found her grandma's. 'Thank you, Grandma. I – I want to tell you how I love you, but you may think it's because of the money. It isn't, as although I was wary of you at first, I did know I loved you very much and that you loved me.'

'Oh, my dear, I know. I felt it the moment I saw you, but I too am wary of giving and accepting love, just in case I am hurt as I have been so often in the past. I love my son and want him to love me, as you want him to love you, but he doesn't seem capable of the same kind of love, only duty – even that he measures by what he considers is enough.'

Feeling she had a friend, confidante and loving grand-mother, Ellen told her, 'He has a son, too. But I think he is keeping him with him, I'm not sure.'

'Really! How old? Tell me about him, as I must look out for him. I know my son. If the woman he married does not want the child, then his son's fate may be to be sent away as he may not want to put on me once more.'

Ellen told all she knew about her mother and brother.

'My God! He is evil! Your poor mother . . . Look, I will do all I can. I will make it known to your father that I know of his new wife and of my grandson and will tell him that I am willing to take my grandson in if need be. And that, if it happens, he can hire a nanny for him and extra help for poor Dilly.'

'Can't you get that help for Dilly now, Grandma? She gets very tired. You can do that with the money you have put aside for me. I would like that.'

'No, my dear. That is for your future. You are going to need it. But I will write to my son today regarding my grandson. I will have to as speed is of the essence to ensure the child is safe, and I will tell him that he will need to find another tutor for you, and ask him to provide more help around the house.'

Ellen felt a little squeeze on her hand. 'Now, my dear, I must send Dilly in to you, and you must rest. I will come and sit with you later. I have something else that I want to share with you.'

The happiness that filled Ellen with the lovely smile her grandma gave her far outweighed the pain she was in.

Dilly came in as Grandmother left. 'Aw, that's a lovely glow you have – a happiness glow. I take it your grandmother has at last bent to let you knaw how she feels about you, eh? By, she's a one. Stiff upper lip in all circumstances. But she don't fool me. I've heard her sobbing into her pillow and it breaks me heart. Maybe now that her defences are broken down, she'll find some happiness again. You've done that, me little lass. You've brought happiness to this house. And by 'eck, it needed it.'

Ellen's pain had once more taken over from the warm feelings she'd had, so she could only give a weak smile as she thought, *Well, it only took me two years to do it!* But though she was glad to have found her grandma truly loved her, she wished it hadn't been by way of being hurt so badly.

'Eeh, me little lass, I'll soon have you comfortable. Your grandma soothed your heart, now I will soothe your body and you'll be all set for a better future, eh?'

This resonated with Ellen. Yes, she was set for a better future. One where she had the love of one of her own and would never be alone and poor again. And one day, she would find her mum and little brother and look after them as well as her grandma and Dilly – and, as was always in her heart and she longed to do, she would find Ruth and Amy too. And then, she knew she would be the happiest she could ever be.

She didn't question why her father didn't come to her mind as someone she wanted to be with, as now he'd become someone to hate rather than to love.

23

Chapter Three

Ellen clasped the letter that arrived from her father two weeks later.

Telling herself she didn't love him hadn't worked. Her heart had flipped when Grandma told her he'd enclosed a letter for her with his reply to the one she'd sent to him.

It seemed her father had consented to employing more help for Dilly and had said that the agency he dealt with would be sending a maid, who was to be given her own room in the attic, two days off a month, and allowed to befriend Ellen. To this last he'd added that she and the maid were of a similar age and that she was very level-headed and, he felt, it would be good for her to have the companionship of a young person.

This thrilled her as she did long for someone of her own age to talk to.

But as she ran downstairs clutching her letter, she found from what she overheard that grandma had taken this as an insult.

'What does he think? That his daughter is only good enough to mix with servants? Oh, I'm sorry, Dilly, I didn't mean you, nor do I look on you or any of my staff as servants, but the implication of this suggestion of my son's

24

seems to be saying that's all his daughter is worth . . . How did I give birth to such a monster?'

Not letting this way of thinking affect her, Ellen grabbed her coat, hat and scarf from the stand in the hall and called out that she was going into the garden.

Kept beautifully by Percy, yet another retainer of Grandma's and just as ancient as she and Dilly were, the garden was divided into a lawned area with a bench seat under a huge oak tree and flower-filled borders – at least in the summertime. But as with the leaves of the trees, the flowers had succumbed to autumn and had faded and died.

To the left of her, there was a walled kitchen garden, which kept them supplied with vegetables and fruit all year round.

Sitting on the bench, Ellen excitedly tore the envelope open but then her heart sank as she read the opening lines.

Ellen, yet again you have disappointed me!

I forbid you to discuss my private business with anyone! You have embarrassed me and prevented any pretence my wife and I have been able, so far, to enjoy.

I had planned on visiting soon with my new wife, who you haven't met yet, and telling my mother that Christopher is our son. How dare you discuss my affairs. I am very angry with you and will not now be visiting.

I trust that you will behave yourself for your new tutor. I have chosen a male tutor for you as I feel he will be able to control you because I was appalled to learn from the agency how you attacked Miss Parkin. Any further behaviour of this nature and I will have to take measures to prevent you from ever being associated with me again.

*This will pain me as much as you, because despite it
all, I do love you. I just cannot show it as your presence
would insult my beloved wife, who was willing to meet
you at your grandma's house before you let us down so
badly by sharing our private business.*

*I beg of you, Ellen, to do your very best in the
next two years, during which time I have my wife's
permission to pay for your tuition, to equip yourself for
your future. I cannot promise to always be here for you.
I am doing what I can now, but a time will come when
you will have to make your own way in the world. For
that you will need a good education! Do not waste this
opportunity that I am affording you.*

I remain, your dutiful father.

The damp patch on the letter made Ellen aware of the
tears streaming down her face. Her heart felt as though a
knife had been stabbed into it and then twisted to leave a
scar she knew would never heal. *So, this new wife has accepted
my brother as her own but wanted me banished?*

But above realizing this, the knowledge that her father
didn't want her and never would hurt so badly that she felt
sick.

Grandma's voice in the distance was the only thing that
stopped her from physically throwing up.

She swallowed and wiped her face on her skirt before
blowing her nose hard into her delicate lace handkerchief.

'Ah, there she is. No matter what the weather, she likes
to be outside.'

Then a male voice. 'A girl after my own heart, for I, too,
like the fresh air.'

The conversation panicked Ellen. Was this the tutor Father

had spoken of? So soon? She turned and saw her grandmother with a man not much older than twenty, weedy-looking, with sandy-coloured hair. They were coming towards her. *It must be!*

Standing, Ellen patted her hair, and hoped that the anguish she felt didn't show in her face.

'Ellen, my dear . . . Ellen? Are you all right?'

'Y-yes, Grandma, thank you . . . Ju-just cold.'

'Well, I'm not surprised, sitting out here, it's very chilly today. The wind cuts you rather than going around you . . . Well now, this is Mr Vale, your new tutor.'

'How do you do, Ellen? I am pleased to meet you and I'm sure we'll get along well together. I'm not one for rules, so there aren't any to worry about or to be broken. I like to help you to learn by what you already know, but don't yet know that you do.'

Ellen hadn't a clue what he meant by this. If she knew it, why did she have to learn it? But she liked his gentle voice and his lovely smile. He just looked as though a puff of wind would blow him over. She smiled as best she could and nodded, but couldn't think of anything to say other than, 'Pleased to meet you, sir.'

'Oh, there'll be no "sirs". I think I can gain your respect without you having to be subservient to me. I wonder if you would like to go for a walk with me? It might warm you up and give us a chance to become acquainted.'

This seemed such a strange request that Ellen didn't know what to say. Mr Vale was so far from what she expected by the tone of her father's letter that she didn't know how to be with him.

Grandma saved her from having to reply. 'I think that's a good idea. You can cross the fields to White Hall Farm. Take

27

a jug with you and get young Bothamwaite to fill it with his ale.' Grandma turned towards Mr Vale. 'The Bothamwaites came to the farm some five years ago now. They soon got the brewery up and running, and it's the best ale you'll ever taste. They even grow their own hops over there.'

'That sounds interesting. Would you like to join me in fetching the ale, Ellen?'

Not feeling she had any choice, Ellen nodded.

They were halfway across the first field walking in the direction of the farm before Mr Vale spoke. 'It's colder than I thought now we are exposed to the winds. Are you all right, Ellen?'

As she looked at him, Ellen realized he was shivering. His lips looked blue and his nose was red with cold. He only wore a jacket and lightweight black slacks. Taking off her scarf, she handed it to him. 'I'm fine. Here, have this; I'm used to the weather here.'

'Thank you, that's very kind. Thank goodness it isn't pink as I'd still be compelled to wear it but be looked on as a fag!'

Ellen hadn't a clue what he meant by this – how could anyone think he could be a cigarette? But he laughed at himself, so she giggled too.

'You have no idea what I mean, do you? A fag is a man who prefers the company of his fellow men . . . well, a bit more than that, but it isn't something that will come up in our biology lessons, so I needn't embarrass you by going deeper.'

Gedberg, the night manager of the orphanage, came to her, and with the thought the repulsion of what he did to the boys immediately connected her mind to what she'd endured. And then Belton, another man who worked nights at the orphanage, flashed into her mind. His ugly face and the stink of him seemed to hover over her, grinning a sickly grin. She gasped in rejection of the horror he put her through.

'Oh, I am so sorry. You are more of a tender mind than I had thought. Please forget that I mentioned such a thing . . . though, well, I am a progressive thinker and do believe that young people, even young ladies, should know about the world and how it ticks – or rather, the people in it, of which there are many diversities. To that end, I think languages are important too and hope you are open to learning them?'

She wanted to tell him that her ex-tutor had been a stickler for her speaking French and German, but she didn't want to converse with him further. He spoke in riddles. However, she did want to scream at him that she knew what he was talking about! That she knew only too well. That even the mention of such things gave her unimaginable pain and sent her reeling back to a time she'd never have got through but for Ruth and Amy.

'I've upset you. And that's unforgivable of me. Please don't worry about such things, they are of no concern.'

Unable to take this, Ellen marched at a quicker pace, wanting to get away from him and the lightness he treated such matters with.

'Hey, wait for me. I – I cannot keep up . . . I . . . cannot walk fast.'

Alarm set up in Ellen. Mr Vale was gasping for breath. She turned to see him bending over, his hands on his knees to steady himself. She ran back to him. 'Are you all right? What's wrong? Can I do something to help you?'

He couldn't answer as he was fighting for every breath and even though the grass was still damp from the morning's heavy dew and the persistent mist hanging around the hills, he sank down onto his knees.

'I'll run to the farm to get help. It's only across the next field. They have a tractor and trailer; they can come and give you a lift back to our house.'

Even nodding his head in consent seemed too much effort for the poor man.

Leaving him, Ellen ran like the wind. 'Mr Bothamwaite! Mr Bothamwaite!'

An astonished Mr Bothamwaite stood from where he'd been bending over a bucket stirring liquid. He pushed his cap back from his forehead. 'Ellen, now then, what makes thee in such a hurry, lass? Is thee house on fire or sommat?'

'No, it's my new tutor. We were coming to buy ale and he collapsed.'

'Collapsed? Will he be an old gentleman?'

'No, he's only young, but he doesn't look well. He can't breathe. Please help him, please!'

Mr Bothamwaite, a jolly man in his late thirties with a huge moustache and a lovely grin, hurried towards the house calling back to her, 'I'll fetch Mrs Bothamwaite, she'll knaw what to do, lass.'

Mrs Bothamwaite undid her pinafore as she came out of the house. As she took it over her head and dropped it on the floor she said, 'Fetch the tractor round, man . . . Top field, you say, Ellen?'

Ellen didn't know if it was called the top field or not, so she turned and pointed. 'The second one that leads to my grandma's.'

'Oh, aye.' She turned and took a blanket off the back of a cow as she told the animal, 'You can do without that, Betty, get yourself inside.' She slapped the cow's rear end and it dutifully walked into the barn. 'I can see you've a jug with you. Leave it on that wall, lass. I'll fill it later and bring it to your grandmother. Now, take this and get gone and cover the young man over to keep him warm. Hurry! It'll take us a few minutes to get to him and he could freeze to death if he's unwell.' As Ellen turned to go she heard Mrs Bothamwaite call out to her younger son, 'Go and fetch the doctor, tell him to come quickly to Shredwell House. A young man there is very ill.'

This put a fear into Ellen that gave her an urgency as she ran for all she was worth across the field.

'Mr Vale! Mr Vale! I'm here. Wake up!' There was no response. Ellen felt his face. It was icy cold, but she could see he was breathing, if only in a funny wheezing fashion. Wrapping the blanket over him, she thought it too thin to do any good so took off her coat, a thick woollen, flared coat that hung to her ankles, and wrapped this around him too. Still concerned, she began to rub his body, using the coat to cause friction. 'Wake up, please wake up. Help is coming.'

Her heart fell to see the deep blue of his lips and how his nose looked redder than ever. It stood out against his deathly white cheeks and dark, sunken eye sockets.

Panic gripped Ellen as memories of a girl in the orphanage came to her. She'd collapsed in this way, but she never regained consciousness. They were told she'd had an asthma attack.

'Don't die, please don't die.'

Her plea was more than fear for him, as she realized that in the few minutes she'd had with him, she really liked him. He was strange, yes, and annoying, but he'd tried to be friendly and put her at her ease, and he'd piqued her interest in a way that told her she would enjoy learning from him. He was different to anyone she'd ever known before.

By the time they had Mr Vale back in her grandma's house and laid on the bed in the room allocated to him, the doctor had arrived. His glance towards her held distrust. She felt certain that he still thought she might be a lunatic and wanted to shout that this wasn't her doing and nor was the last time he came to attend her tutor.

What followed seemed like an endless wait and yet, Ellen felt that she mustn't pester anyone who came from the bedroom on errands to fetch whatever the doctor needed. Even Dilly, who always seemed to have something to say, just rushed past her into the kitchen, coming out a few minutes later with a steaming kettle and hurrying back to the bedroom with it without a word, leaving Ellen feeling even more afraid.

Not ever having prayed much, Ellen found herself praying now. Once more, Ruth came to her mind and how she used to pray to the Holy Mary – a Roman Catholic thing to do, though Ruth didn't know for sure she was of that faith, only that she'd been left outside a priest's house. But she'd loved the thought of Mary being a mother to Jesus and imagined she would have a special place in heaven and be able to ask favours of her son. Ellen found herself pleading, 'Please, Holy Mary, help my tutor to get better.'

A noise on the stairs drew her out of the intense prayers. 'Now, Annie, I want you to keep the room humid for at least twenty-four hours. Lots of steam. It's good that the fireplace in there has a grate plate so you can keep a kettle boiling on it. And every two hours or so get him to breathe in over the bowl of steaming water as I did, in which you put just two drops of the liquid I have left on the side. No more, and no more than every half an hour till you notice his breathing is normal and he can converse with you without panting for breath. However, he is on the mend for now, but asthma sufferers are likely to have an attack at any time, so be aware. I will drop in later to check. I'll leave my bill on the hall table as I go out but would appreciate early settlement. Mrs Ainsworth and my five children have to eat, you know.'

Grandma coloured. Ellen felt cross at the doctor. Why had he spoken as if Grandma might not pay his bill?

As soon as the door closed on Doctor Ainsworth, Ellen rushed to her grandma. 'How is he? Oh, Gran, he looked like he would die!'

'You heard the doctor, dear. Mr Vale is going to be all right. But . . . you called me Gran?'

'Sorry, Grandma, it just slipped out.'

'No. I like it. It's somehow less cold, more loving.' She opened her arms.

Ellen went gladly into them and hugged her. 'I do love you, Gran. You won't ever abandon me, will you?'

'No, of course not, my dear. Not even on my death. Didn't I tell you that I have put in place a security for you? Well, when the time comes, think of that as me still loving and protecting you . . . Oh, I know I seemed crotchety at first, but that was because I was cross at your father, and mine. Oh, yes, it never goes away – that feeling of anger at them for their callous disregard for you. But I have learned to live with it, and you must do so too.'

'Oh, Gran, his letter is awful.'

'I thought you'd been crying when I brought Mr Vale to you. Tell me about it, my dear.'

After the telling, Gran held her closer. 'I cannot change any of that, Ellen, you have to be strong, but what I can do is to help you to do as he says – to further yourself. He has promised his support of you for a further two years. Together we will make those years pay. By the time they are up you will be fifteen. I will squirrel away what I can to add to the fund I have started for you – there are still a lot of pieces and paintings that I could sell. We'll then go for a higher education, maybe abroad even. You must think what it is you would like to do. There aren't many opportunities for girls, but they do exist for those who are determined, clever and have the means. We will look at your options and you can choose a path.'

Her gran held her at arm's length. 'Of course, you could go for marrying well. You are very beautiful and have some connections through my husband's family whom you haven't yet met. I was going to tell you about them but forgot all about it. They are landed gentry and owners of several mines. You aren't related to them, but if they take to you, they will help you. I am long overdue a visit to them. I will take you along and see how we fare.'

It seemed strange to Ellen not to have heard of this connection of her gran's before, and also that they didn't help her but allowed her to be at the mercy of her son. As if Gran had read her thoughts, she said, 'My son – your father – caused a rift between me and them.'

Ellen listened to how her father had procured Gran's house by tricking his dying step-grandfather into signing the house and land over to him. And how this greatly upset his family into whose hands all should have gone. This realization didn't surprise Ellen, but it did sicken her to her core.

'You see, we had no children of our own. My husband

34

took your father in and treated him like his own and, being so ill, he must have thought it was the right thing to do to protect me.'

'But instead, he left you at the mercy of my father.'

Gran sighed. 'Yes. It took a long time to get even on speaking terms with my in-laws again . . . Maybe now that I am they will help me to help you find someone of worth to love and take care of you. But in the meantime, let's hedge our bets and make sure you are educated and have enough means to carry you into a good future, whether you marry well or not.'

Once more Gran drew Ellen into her arms, and Ellen thought she'd never been loved so strongly as she was by her gran. It had seemed to take a long while for it to happen – or maybe it was as she'd said, that she'd loved her from the beginning but had been wary of showing it. None of it mattered now. She was safe – safe and loved by her gran.

Chapter Four

1913

By the time Ellen's fourteenth birthday came around, she already felt like a young woman rather than a young girl.

'Eeh, lass, I don't knaw where the time goes to. Here's you growing up, and far before your time if you ask me.'

'Dilly, you make Ellen's birthday sound like an accusation. It's good that she is growing up into a strong young woman and you've had a hand in that and should be proud. I've heard you many a time counselling her wisely.'

'Aw, I'm sorry, Mr Vale, I didn't mean it like that.'

Ellen blushed to think Mr Vale looked on her in that way. But she knew it wasn't because she was growing up that had upset Dilly but rather that she was feeling her own age. Hugging Dilly, she told her, 'But I'll always be the same and will always love you, no matter how old I get.'

Dilly giggled. 'Aye, but I won't be. I'm old and wrinkled already, without piling more years onto me . . . Now, where's that Aggie? I can never find that lazy madam!'

Aggie, Dilly's helper, wasn't lazy at all. Ellen loved her. She was funny and caring, and took it in her stride that Dilly hadn't been pleased to have the help she'd been moaning she needed for a long time, but rather resented Aggie and found fault with her all the time. Aggie handled it all well and seemed to Ellen to be slowly winning Dilly over.

'I'm here, Dilly. I've done all the fires and swept the carpets, not to mention giving a lick of polish to the furniture. So, can I join Ellen in her lesson now?'

Dilly hmphed. Aggie learning to read and write didn't go down well with her at all. She didn't think it was the place of a scullery maid to have such skills.

'I've a new book I can read to you, Dilly. You like that, don't you? Well, this one is about four sisters, Jo, Beth, Meg and Amy. Their dad's away at the Civil War and they're struggling, but, eeh, it's sad as little Beth—'

'Don't spoil the story before you even start to read it to me, Aggie, you daft ha'peth!'

Ellen laughed. She knew that, despite Dilly's objections to Aggie receiving an education, she loved how it meant Aggie could read to her each evening. 'Oh, Dilly, we do love you.' The squeeze she gave Dilly brought a smile to her face.

'Aw, Aggie, I suppose you have your good points, lass.'

Aggie beamed. Ellen knew she loved Dilly dearly and any snippet of praise could send her soaring.

From a large family living in Leeds, sixteen-year-old Aggie had been like a breath of fresh air when she'd arrived at the beginning of the year. Ellen had taken to her immediately and now they were the best of friends. Something at least that her father got right, as having a companion nearer to her own age had changed Ellen's life.

As Dilly left, Mr Vale took charge. 'Well, ladies, I want you to both go to the woods and bring me back anything that depicts a title of Mr Charles Dickens's work.'

Neither of them thought this strange as they were used

to Mr Vale's quirky way of – as he put it – getting the knowledge they already had to come to the fore.

He'd grown stronger with living here and breathing in the clean country air and Ellen's first impressions of him hadn't changed. She still liked him very much. He was thoughtful and interesting and had opened a world of knowledge to her – especially in their biology lessons which she loved, having made her mind up that she wanted to be a nurse.

But he also scared her as he talked of the troubles in the world and how he thought that one day soon, it could all erupt. His stories about the Greeks' and Turks' battles and a Bolshevik activist in Russia with a name she couldn't pronounce, but who was becoming known by the name he used to publish articles – Stalin. And of the troubles in the Balkans which all seemed to give weight to Mr Vale's theory.

But then, there were exciting things to learn about the goings-on in the world as aviation was going from strength to strength and pilots were flying further and further, which Mr Vale thought meant that one day they would all be flying to different countries. Something Ellen couldn't imagine.

As they walked across the field the blustery wind caused their coats to billow around them and played havoc with Aggie's mop cap. Ellen was glad of her bonnet with ribbons tied under her chin to keep it secure. She offered it to Aggie, worried at how cold she must feel.

'Eeh ta, lass. But naw. It would be more than me life's worth. If you catch a cold and Dilly hears of me taking your hat, she'll have me guts for garters!'

They both giggled as they huddled together and entered the wood.

'I ain't a clue what to look for and I can only remember *A Christmas Carol*.'

'Well, that one should be easy. We can find cones and holly to depict Christmas.'

'Aye, and hold them and sing a carol to him. By, he's as daft as a brush setting us the lessons he does, and yet there's sommat in it, as I've learned more from him than I've ever learned in me life!'

'Me too, and he makes it fun. I'm going to find dead leaves, branches and an old nest. The nest is a house, and the dead things are bleak – *Bleak House*!'

'Eeh, I wish I had your imagination, lass.'

Ellen had no time to answer as a loud crack made them both jump. A dead bird landed in front of them, blood seeping from a ragged wound in its stomach.

They both froze. Ellen felt her heart break as she looked at the poor defenceless creature. But a rustle of the bushes ahead made her instantly aware of danger.

He came swaggering through a gap in the foliage. A scruffy individual of around forty years old with blackened teeth, grinning as if proud of his prize. 'Who we got 'ere, then? A toff and her maid, eh? Bert, come out 'ere. We've won ourselves a bigger prize than a fat wood pigeon.'

Another man, just as scruffy but with tangled ginger hair rather than the black mass of the first man, emerged through the bushes.

'You try it, man, and I'll kick you in the balls!' Aggie stepped in front of Ellen as she said this.

'Ha!' The ginger-haired man spat on the ground. 'I'm having the lady, you can have the trash, Victor.'

'You're welcome. I bet this feisty maid has some go in her.'

Aggie stepped backwards; her arms came towards Ellen even though she still faced the men. She clutched Ellen's skirt. 'Stay close to me, lass, I'll deal with them . . . Come on then, just try it!'

The man with the ginger hair raised his rifle. The blast deafened Ellen. She felt Aggie slump down, her weight heavy on Ellen's feet, leaving her unable to move. 'No! No! Aggie, Aggie . . .'

Wet sticky blood penetrated Ellen's skirt. She stared down at the wound in Aggie's side. A movement had her looking up. The ginger man had borne down on her. His arm clamped her in an iron grip. Her body was wrenched away from Aggie and landed on the ground. Her breath left her. Fear stopped her from screaming as if it had a stranglehold on her throat as she saw the huge bulk of the man in the throes of undoing the buttons of his trousers. Her 'no' came out as a whimper.

'Get on with it, Bert, as I'll have to have her after you. That one ain't no good to shag now. What did you do that for, eh? Bloody maniac!'

The ginger man turned his head. His face looked like that of a gorilla as he snarled at his companion. 'Don't call me that, or you'll never shag another lass in your pathetic life, man.'

With this he lowered himself and tore at Ellen's clothes.

Held in terror, she didn't resist – couldn't. Her past came at her in a red swirling mist. Belton was lowering himself onto her child body, her screams were echoing down the years – *It can't happen again, please don't let it* . . . 'Ple-e-e-ase!'

'Huh, she's begging for it! Well, here it comes, lady!'

It was over in seconds, leaving Ellen in a stupor as the ginger man, squealing like a stuck pig, rolled off her and lay panting beside her.

After a moment he sat up. 'God! She's good, man, and she's no virgin, I'll tell you. Get yerself a slice of that.'

Bert didn't move towards her.

The ginger man let out a laugh that sounded like a bellow. 'You've shot it, ain't you? Call yerself a man, look at your wet trousers. Ha! Well, I'll just have to do it for you, won't I?'

As he rolled back on top of her and tried to enter her again, Ellen saw a light that almost blinded her. It lit her rage. Bringing her hands up, she clawed at his eyes, gouging them. Screams rasped her throat. Vile words spewed from her, leaving her spittle to run from her mouth and down her cheek.

The shock of the attack had the ginger man reeling backwards. Ellen took the moment and drew up her knees. With all her might she kicked out at him. Her feet squelched into his private parts. His gasp heralded a loud, agonizing holler. At the sound of it, the other man scarpered through the bushes and was gone, leaving his heaving, sobbing friend curled up in a ball.

Ellen, spurred on by her rage, stood and kicked him again and again, until he begged for mercy.

A moan from Aggie finally brought her to her senses. She rushed over to her. 'Aggie, oh, Aggie.'

'Help me, Ellen . . . h-help me.'

Aggie's stomach looked a mass of blood. Her face, ashen white, seemed more like a mask than the real Aggie.

'Aggie, Aggie, love, don't die. Hold on. I'll run for help.'

Not stopping to adjust her clothing but allowing her skirt to fall over her naked lower body, Ellen ran faster than she had in all her life. Her screams brought Dilly and Cook rushing through the back gate that led onto the field. But then she saw Mr Vale push past the women and run towards her, his voice full of anguish as he called out to her, 'Ellen, my dear. Oh God, what has happened?'

Hardly able to speak, Ellen could only gasp, 'Aggie! Aggie!'

'Take care of her, Dilly. I'll go and find Aggie.'

'No, I'll come. I can take you straight to her . . . and you mustn't run . . .'

But this last fell on deaf ears as Mr Vale left her standing.

Finding she was too weak to move, she just shouted, 'That way!' before her legs gave way beneath her and the world went black.

'Aggie? Aggie?'

'Shush, me little lass. Shush. Rest yourself. The doctor's been and left you a powder. Take it now and it'll make you sleep.'

'No, Dilly, I've got to go to Aggie, she's bleeding.'

Dilly's sob froze Ellen's heart.

'Aggie?'

'The Lord took her, me little lass. She couldn't have survived. Her injuries were too bad.'

'No, Dilly. No . . . not Aggie. Not lovely Aggie!'

The door of the bedroom opened. Gran came in, looking years older than Ellen had ever seen her. 'My darling Ellen. The local police are here. They say they have the men.'

'You know . . . Gran, I – I . . .'

'Yes. Well, I know what I think happened, but the men are telling a dreadful tale.'

Ellen lifted her aching head. 'What are they saying, Gran? They attacked us, they shot Aggie, and . . .' She couldn't say the word. Her stomach churned at the memory.

Gran sat down in a chair next to Dilly. She sighed heavily.

'My dear, I know what it is like once . . . well, once it has happened . . . once you've had a taste of . . . well, what men have to offer, so I don't blame you.'

'What! Gran . . . no! Gran, you think it's my fault? How . . . I – I . . . they attacked us, that ginger-haired man raped me!'

Dilly had her head down.

Gran's voice shook as she said, 'You've been asleep for three days, my dear. The men have spoken to the police. They've told the same story even though they couldn't corroborate it. The ginger-haired man was still on the ground in agony when the police arrived after Mr Vale brought poor Aggie's body back here. He said they came across you and that you started to goad them. That you . . . well, they said you asked them to do it. You said you'd had "it" before and . . . oh, my dear Ellen. It's awful, but the police believe them as when they found the other one, he said the same. He said that Aggie said "no" to you and that she couldn't believe you could suggest such a thing. That she threatened them that if they touched you, she'd kill them, but that you still wanted it so . . . anyway, in her attempt to stop it, Aggie lunged at the one who still held his gun, and it went off. He said he left then, but that his mate was already on top of you.'

Ellen couldn't speak. A fear entered her on seeing that her gran doubted her without even asking her side of things.

'The one who did . . . well, he said that you went mad when it was over. He described how you were when—'

'No! Gran, no! I'm not mad, I'm not! I attacked him as he was going to do it again . . . I – I didn't want—'

A knock on the door stopped her.

At that moment she knew she was doomed as her father walked into her room. His face held disgust and hate. 'Blood will out! I should never have taken you in. You're a whore, Ellen, just like your mother!'

'No! It didn't happen like that, it didn't! Please listen to me, please!'

'Get up out of that bed! I'm taking you to a convent, where you'll stay till you learn the sins of your ways!'

'No, Daddy, no. Please, please listen to me . . . they attacked us. We couldn't do anything . . . Oh, Aggie, poor Aggie, she tried to save me.'

'As I have done since you were born. But you seem beyond saving from what you truly are. Well, let's see if the nuns can do any better. No doubt you are with child. Well, I shall instruct them to take it away at birth and do what they will with it as I'll never let it, or you, darken my doorstep!'

His look of hate shrivelled Ellen. She turned her head away from the strength of it as it withered the last of her spirit. There was nothing she could do. Once more she was alone, as those she loved most in all the world were rejecting her.

Dilly stayed with her after her father and grandmother left the room. 'Don't worry, lass. He ain't taking you yet, you ain't well enough. He'd have to get by me first.'

Wanting to be held, Ellen reached out her hand to Dilly. Dilly clutched it with both of hers.

'I loved Aggie, Dilly. I wouldn't put her in the situation they are saying I did. How can they believe those ruffians over me? Gran's been through this, why isn't she on my side?'

'She is. By, she ain't said owt, but I knaw she desperately wants to help. She was only trying to get you to deny it, as you did. She'll do something, I'm sure. Now, I'm going to bathe you and get you comfortable, eh?'

It was as she was washing her down that Dilly said, 'Your gran's hardly eaten since it happened . . . She's battling for you. You see, well, it ain't me place to tell you this, but that father of yours went for her over the legacy your gran has put aside for you. It seems the lawyer your gran trusted, and whose firm has seen to her husband's family business for generations, is in your dad's pocket and has been told about it. He's furious and has threatened to get it transferred to his son. Your gran isn't sure she can stop him. She's trying, but, well, I don't like saying this, but your dad is wicked, ruthless . . . Oh, I knaw you love him, but he don't deserve your love, he's the devil himself.'

'The money means nothing to me, Dilly. It's losing my gran's love and trust and never having my father's that hurts.'

'You haven't, I told you. Your gran loves you . . . Your father? Well, he ain't capable of loving anyone. Look how he treats his wives – he drives them into the grave.'

The truth of this hurt. But it was there for her to see. She'd only ever been a 'duty' to him. Not even that when he wanted something, and she got in the way. Look how he allowed her to be put into that orphanage, and now . . .

'Dilly, what's this convent like. Will you visit me?'

Dilly hung her head. 'Me little lass, they won't let me. They run a strict order and once a girl goes in there . . . oh, me lovely, I would help you if I could but . . .'

'Please try, Dilly. If I can get out of here before they come for me, I can go to London and find me friend. She'll take care of me. I – I have her address. Her name's Ruth Faith and she lives on Collingwood Road in London.'

'But . . . Eeh, me lass, I would worry meself sick about you. You've naw money or owt.'

'Please, Dilly, don't let me be locked up, please.'

'Look, I'll speak to Mr Vale. Now you're a bit better, I can leave you a while, lass. Only up till now I ain't had a minute with anyone, and only knaw stuff from when Cook comes in to bring us food. She says that after poor Aggie's funeral, Mr Vale is leaving. He asked Cook to ask me to give you his regards and said if there was ever anything he could do for you, he would. And another thing, he believes you, lass, he told Cook that and she said that he won't hear of a word said to the contrary. So, I'll have a word with him, eh?'

'Do you think he'll help me? Oh, Dilly, go now. Please go and see him.'

A little bit of hope lit inside Ellen as Dilly left the room. If Mr Vale would help her to get to London, then he surely could help her to find Collingwood Road.

The hope this lit in her died when her bedroom door opened. Her father came through it with a giant of a woman who stomped around to the other side of Ellen's bed.

Ellen looked from her to her father. 'Daddy, no, no, please.'

Ignoring her pleas, her father spoke as if she was nothing to him. 'I'm informed by the doctor that you will be well enough to travel tomorrow. Miss Partridge will look after you from now on and accompany you to the convent . . . This is goodbye, Ellen. I tried, God knows I tried, but in the end, you are what you are, and I can't change that. I do not want my family tainted with another like you and your mother.' He turned and left the room without another word. Ellen's heart split in two as the door closed behind him.

To her it was as if her world had come to an end. Her head burned with the agony of all she'd been through. Scenes of when she was just ten years old and abandoned in the orphanage came to her and she saw again the wicked, filthy

Belson, holding her down, touching her, hurting her, doing that thing to her! And then pictures of the ginger-haired man doing the same . . . the gunshot . . . Aggie . . . poor, poor, Aggie, falling, bleeding . . . Oh God, Aggie!

A scream pierced her ears. She knew it had come from herself, but she couldn't stop it.

Hands grabbed her. The feel of them was as if a man had hold of her and this fuelled the terror burning inside of her. Her own screams didn't lessen the fear gripping her; they compounded her horror as her thoughts became confused . . . She knew it must be Miss Partridge who had hold of her, and yet, was it? Was it happening again? That thing? She had to fight. She had to escape.

Suddenly it was as if she'd been given a power – a strength beyond anything she'd ever possessed – and she knew she was clawing, kicking, pulling hair, but couldn't stop herself as all the rage of the pain inside her erupted. But then, one of the hands let go and a forceful punch on her cheek sent her reeling backwards. Her head struck the iron bedstead and the darkness she'd known before enveloped her, taking her away from the hate, the bad things men did, and the pain of not being loved.

Chapter Five

Struggling, Ellen found, didn't help. Not against the strait-jacket that she came to realize she was once more encased in.

Nor did the voices soothe her. Her gran telling her she loved her. *Huh! What is love? Where was she when I most needed her? Standing over me, questioning me as if she didn't believe me!*

Dilly's voice came to her . . . 'Me little lass, naw!'

Mr Vale's voice, imploring, 'Please, don't do this. The child is afraid, that's all. Stop this!'

Then her father's voice that only held hate: 'Get out of the way, Vale! My daughter is mad. It's clear to see. She belongs in an asylum, and good riddance. You don't know the half, man!'

Then came the sensation of being lifted and laid on what she knew must be a stretcher. It began to move. 'No! No, don't send me away. Love me, Daddy, love me and believe me, please, Daddy, please . . .'

'This is wrong. For God's sake, how can you treat your own daughter like this?'

'She is no longer my daughter. And it is none of your business, Vale. Pack your bag and get out of my house!

You've clearly been a bad influence on Ellen. Did she cajole you to let her loose in a wood, eh? Did she give you favours? Is that what this is about? It is, isn't it? You can see what you had, the pleasure you took, being taken away from you . . . Get out! Go now, or I'll have the police on you, man!'

'No . . . no, Mr Vale, no . . . I'm sorry . . . sorry.' Ellen wasn't even sure whether the words were coming out of her mouth or were just inside her head, but then Mr Vale answered.

'Don't worry, Ellen. Hold on and have faith.' Then his voice took on a different note. 'You're disgusting! Disgusting! You judge others by your own standards. Well, we aren't all the same. I could never behave like you or in the manner you are accusing me of. I will go, but I will never forget Ellen, and someday I will find a way to help her.'

Ellen opened her eyes. Saw the tears falling down her gran's cheeks. 'Gran, help me, I love you.'

Gran stepped forward, but then the harsh voice of Father stopped her. 'Mother! Do not hinder me! How my father stood by you, I do not know. Your behaviour is disgraceful!'

It was as if a new person jumped inside Gran then. 'Your father did not stand by me. You don't know your father. Neither do I. I was raped by a stranger! You are a bastard, as I am, as my father made me by paying for his pleasure as you made Ellen. Only, you are a bastard by nature as well as by birth!'

'Mother!'

'Don't you "Mother" me. I am doing the same to you as you are doing to Ellen – I disown you! You are not my son and will never be again – have never been. Not in real terms. All you've ever done is take from me . . . My home, my rights and now my granddaughter. And you have another bastard child who you have never given to me, and so you have deprived me of him too!'

'Shut up! How dare you say such things in front of strangers? Or at all?'

'I dare, because they are true. What you are doing to Ellen is inhumane. She has been wronged, but you choose to believe two murdering rapists over your daughter because it suits you. Because you want to rid yourself of her. Those men who did this wicked thing to your own flesh and blood and an innocent maid have got off scot-free because it suited you! Gave you the chance you were looking for. You've regretted your decision to take Ellen in as a baby from the moment you made it. Why else would you consent to having her put into an orphanage, eh? But at least you did show you do have a modicum of conscience as you fetched her out and brought her to me – where she should have been in the first place!'

'Mother, I do not know what has got into you! I have taken care of your affairs—'

'Stolen them! I have nothing now. Why? Why? And now you're trying to take what I put by for your own child, knowing you would not provide for her once she reached sixteen years old. You're wicked – evil – and I never want to see you again!'

Held in a sort of trance as she witnessed all of this going on, Ellen no longer fought against the restrictions of the jacket, but just stared at the two players in the drama that was unfolding in front of them all. But then, she could not believe what happened next. Her father sank to his knees. Tears rolled down his face. 'Mother, no. Don't do this. You're my mother . . .' A sob shook his body.

'Then stop this . . . this horror from happening. Do something decent for once in your pitiful life and be worthy of being my son. Allow me to adopt Ellen. Stop the action you are taking to take away her inheritance. Give me some financial independence back and visit me with my grandson from time to time.'

Her father shook his head. 'I cannot do that. My wife has taken my son as her own – adopted him. He is not mine to bring to you without her consent – nothing is. I – I am bankrupt. All I have is hers. All I've ever had is through my marriages. When widowed, I had enough to see me through, but . . . I – I . . .'

'What? Gambled it away? That was your weakness when you were at home – paying off your debts to keep you out of prison almost drained my dear husband! Is that what is happening? Is that why your succession of wives have a hold over you? Has all the money you took from me gone? Is that why you need what I put aside for Ellen?'

'I'm sorry, Mother . . . I – I . . .'

A gasp came from her father, then a bubbling sound as he clutched his chest, before falling forward.

The men holding the stretcher put it back down on the bed and rushed to him.

'Daddy, Daddy, no! I love you. Don't die, Daddy, don't die!'

Another gurgling sound came into the silence that followed Ellen's words and then nothing but her Gran's sobbing voice: 'Oh, Dominic, Dominic, no, please, no . . . I'm sorry. I didn't mean . . .'

'Annie, love, come on, lass. He's gone. Let's take care of Ellen now, she needs us.'

'Oh, Dilly, I didn't mean those things, I didn't.'

'They had to be said. Him being dead don't make naw difference. He was what he was. Eeh, he must've taken after whoever it was who took you down as he didn't take after you, lass.'

Mr Vale, who'd only got as far as the door and had stood captivated, stepped forward and spoke to the two stretcher bearers. 'Take that horrendous thing off Ellen at once!'

None of them objected, nor did Miss Partridge, who'd stood in the corner as if turned to stone. Till Mr Vale turned on her. 'And you, madam, pack your things and go.'

No one objected to his instructions.

As soon as Ellen was free, Mr Vale gently helped her off the bed. 'It's all right, Ellen, nothing will happen to you now.'

Nothing? She looked over at her dead father. A sob escaped her. It seemed to her that the worst that could ever happen to her had.

Still supporting her, Mr Vale guided her towards where her father's body lay. Her gran, looking frail and shaking from head to foot, held out her arms. Ellen went into them, but rather than her gran holding her, she held her gran and they cried together, tears that maybe weren't deserved by the dead man at their feet, but then, despite everything, he was her father and her gran's son, and they both loved him.

Dilly's coaxing voice helped them to move away. She took them towards the door. As they reached it, Mr Vale said, 'Dilly, get someone to go for the doctor.' Then he turned to the two stretcher bearers. 'Kindly lift the gentleman's body onto the bed, please.'

One of them replied, 'He weren't no gentleman from what I heard, sir.'

Mr Vale didn't object, though Ellen wanted him to, but then neither did she. She just walked away with Dilly.

When they reached Gran's sitting room and were sat together on the sofa, Dilly said, 'I'll be back in a mo with some tea, madam.' The informal use of 'Annie' had now gone and Dilly was back to being subservient, though Ellen did wonder at what the relationship between her gran and Dilly really was, as after the death of Father, Dilly had spoken affectionately to Gran, in terms that a servant never would.

Gran hadn't missed it. 'Not madam, Dilly. Annie will do fine. Let this day change many things – well, it will naturally anyway, as where our income is going to come from, I do not know.'

'Eeh, don't worry about that now. You'll sort sommat, Annie. You allus have.'

With this Dilly left. Ellen put her arm around her gran's shaking body. 'I'll help, Gran, everything will be all right.'

Gran sighed. 'But will it? I know I shouldn't be talking like this or even thinking of such things, but I don't think Dominic's . . . your father's wife is going to continue my allowance and I don't own this house, it will belong to her – if it doesn't already. All I have are a few paintings in the attic and one or two bits and pieces that might fetch in about one hundred pounds and that's it.'

'That's a lot of money, Gran. It's plenty. It will rent us a decent house for a good few years, and I can get work. Girls of my age work in the factories, I could too.'

'No, my dear, never! Oh, Ellen, forgive me. I didn't believe that of you, I didn't. I just wanted to hear your side of the story. It was so confusing – the police, then your father telephoning in a rage. I was just trying to get everything straight in my head. How could I have questioned you in that manner?'

'Don't worry about it, Gran. I know.'

'It – it brought it all back to me, Ellen. I found myself in a bad place. I couldn't think logically. I – I . . .'

'Hush, Gran, I understand. That's what happens to me. I get confused and all I see is to fight like an animal to stop what is happening, but it doesn't stop it, it makes things worse.'

'It does, darling. Always use reason to get yourself out of trouble. Deny the rage that boils up inside you. I had to. It used to happen to me too.'

A small moan came from Gran. 'How could I have said those things to my son?'

Although it hurt Ellen to admit it, she said, 'Because they were true, Gran, and they had to be said. Daddy deserved every word. He had to be made to face up to what he has done. He ruined your life, mine, my mum's and . . . well, I haven't said, Gran, but when Daddy picked me up to bring me here and I met my mum as she handed over her son – my brother – to Daddy, he said that she had two other children. He said they weren't his, but mum blamed him for them, saying he could have helped her to look after all of her children, not take them away from her, so there are more lives he has ruined too.'

'And all in the pursuit of his gambling. Why? Why did he need to do that? He would lose hundreds of pounds a year. My husband did his best to pay off his debts, but it was ruining us.'

With this revelation earlier, Ellen understood what had motivated her father to take all that her gran had. Suddenly, she felt not only a disgust, but something akin to hate for the man lying dead upstairs and it was a relief to do so. An unshackling of her which was more than the relief of the straitjacket being removed.

'That was a big sigh, my darling, I'm sorry not to be supporting you. I – I feel so . . .'

'Trapped? Don't, Gran, think about it. My sigh wasn't anything other than a feeling of being free. That dead man upstairs has had a hold on me all my life. I believed he loved me. I adored him, but that made me like a prisoner. Just as you were, Gran, but now you're free too. You no longer have to rely on him. You no longer have to be hurt or insulted by him. He can do no more to us.'

Gran turned her head towards Ellen. She had a look of astonishment on her face. 'You are wise for your age, Ellen, but then, what life has dealt you has made you grow up before your time . . . Strange, but just then, you sounded like my dear husband. He wanted me free of my son. He told me to break all ties, or he would break my heart. He was so right and so are you. I am sad, but I realize it is only for what could have been – what should have been – not for what I had. I had a bully for a son – a selfish, manipulating bastard. There, I have said it!'

Gran, too, let out a sigh. Ellen could see that she had the same feeling – of being freed from shackles.

'We'll get by together, Gran. We will. And Gran . . . well, Dilly said my father had taken the inheritance that you had put by for me. Could he do that?'

'He was trying. He did say he could. He said my solicitor was a good friend of his and was arranging it.'

'Maybe it hasn't happened, and you can get it back?'

'But if it hasn't, it is yours, my dear. I wouldn't touch it.'

Ellen was stopped from saying more as the doctor arrived.

The next hour was a strange one as her father's wife was contacted, and screamed hysterically down the phone at Gran, who kept magnificently calm throughout. Even when it was obvious that she'd been told she must vacate the house, as with dignity she said, 'I have no intention of staying in the house a moment longer than is necessary, thank you,' which made Ellen boil with rage. But as her gran had asked her to always do, she suppressed it. Only to vent her emotions in another way as her father's body was taken from the house.

She hadn't thought to cry, not after the revelation of feeling such freedom, but her heart broke at this final goodbye.

Mr Vale held her. As he did, she felt that she was being supported by a good friend. Dilly held Gran, who wept too. Ellen understood. Knew that Gran's emotions were like her own: tears for what might have been – should have been.

As soon as the door closed on the coffin, Mr Vale, as if he was now head of the household, said, 'I think we need a meeting – a chat to sort out what to do, madam.'

'Annie, call me Annie. I am no longer mistress of this house and don't even know where your final salary is going to come from, Mr Vale, so I cannot retain you.'

'Don't worry about me. The agency is committed to paying my salary until my contract ends, and therefore your son's estate will foot the bill. As I haven't had a formal dismissal, I shall carry on in my post until I do. How long it will take for your son's wife to realize that the money is going out from her bank, I do not know. But the agency is my employer. All contracts have to be ended with them by the person who signed the contract with him or the administrator of his estate.'

'I see. Well, I must say it will be a comfort to have you around, thank you . . . A meeting, you say?'

'Yes. Forgive me if that feels forward of me and not my place, but I see you all swimming against the tide with no plan and no one to guide you to safe ground. If you will permit me to, I would like to help you all.'

'We would be very grateful to you, thank you. We are, as you say, lost.'

'Yes, and in shock, but nevertheless, if I have interpreted the snippet of conversation I heard of your telephone call with your daughter-in-law correctly, then you need to act swiftly.'

They all made their way into the dining room – Gran, Dilly, Mr Vale and Ellen. Ellen felt out of herself, as if all of this was happening to someone else.

'Now. The first thing we have to deal with is funds. Have you any, Annie?'

'No, only assets.'

'If you're talking about the furniture belonging to you, then you do have quite a few pieces that will fetch in a nice sum. I am a bit of an antique buff. Always have been interested in history, and a lot of your furniture dates back to Elizabethan times and is very much sought after. Especially in the lovely condition it has been kept.'

'Really! Good gracious! Yes, it does all belong to me, but it's just been furniture – practical, nice to look at, but I had no idea that it was of any value.'

'Eeh, and nor did that son of yours, Annie, as by 'eck, it would've been out that door by now.'

'Dilly! I know now, and have always known, what my son was like, but out of respect for the dead, and for me and Ellen, we don't need it spelling out to us at such a time!'

'Sorry, Annie, I were just saying.'

Ellen thought how true Dilly's words were, but she didn't say so. She had a feeling of excitement that Mr Vale could sort out their worries and fears.

'Carry on, Mr Vale, please.'

'Adrian. Call me Adrian as we are all on first-name terms and, I hope, friends.'

Ellen smiled at him. She thought the name suited him and liked the way his position had changed in the short while since her father's death.

'Now, I think time is of the essence here. Do you have anything else that might be of value?'

'Well, there are a few paintings in the attic. My husband used to buy them and then store them – I never knew why. And I don't know if they have any value. There may be a few other oddments up there too. Bits that I didn't like, or that outdid their use.'

'Hum, this may be better than I thought. I know a few dealers as I have frequented auctions, though never had the money to buy in those days, but one in particular I was at university with. We were friends and still have contact now and again. He works for Sotheby's in London. If I may use your telephone, Annie, I will ring him and get him up here. I think you will be pleasantly surprised at what you are offered. And even if there is a sentimental value to anything, I would say sell it and make a deal as soon as you possibly can, or you might find that it is taken from you. It can easily be made to look as if your daughter-in-law holds the right to the furniture in recompense for what your son spent on you. Especially as we can now surmise that money came from her purse.'

'Do it, Adrian. Do it right now.'

The phone call didn't take long, but Ellen knew that like her, her gran and Dilly held their breath till Adrian came back into the room.

It was a relief to see him smiling.

'Well?'

'He is leaving immediately, Annie. He will arrive tomorrow, so we need to get everything ready for him – drawers, ottomans and wardrobes emptied as he will want to check every detail for damage or signs of woodworm. And I will go up into the attic and bring down anything I think worth putting before him. I believe your fortunes are about to change, my dear Annie.'

Gran went into a bit of a flap. 'Oh, but what will we sit on, and eat off? And where will we put all my things?'

'We need some strong men. Do you know anyone who would come and help? Only you do have a lot of nice furniture that is practical but of no value in the drawing room with which we could furnish your sitting room very comfortably for you, and then we could bring all the beautiful pieces of antique furniture you have from there to this room which is already dripping with valuables, from this table and chairs to the ornaments adorning the wonderful cabinets and the sofa in the bay of the window. The same, I am sure, will go for the bedrooms. There will be plenty of unused furniture in them that can be utilized for storing what you normally store in the almost priceless chests of drawers that are in use at the moment.'

Gran clapped her hands. 'I will ring the vicar. He will send the village lads to us. When should they come?'

'As soon as possible. Have you any money to pay them with?'

'I do have a little cash.'

'And I've got some in me pot, Annie. You can have that, and it'll be more than enough.'

'This is excellent. Are there any trunks or cases in the loft, Annie?'

'Yes, there should be several.'

'And I have a small case that I brought with me, Adrian.' It felt funny to Ellen to call him this and yet nice too.

'Right, you run up and get that, and Annie, you empty your bureau into it. Have you another bureau somewhere?'

'There may be one in my husband's study. It's been locked for years, though. Dilly, can you open it and take Adrian in there for me?'

When Ellen came down with the suitcase in which her father had brought her things to this house, Adrian stood inside the study exclaiming with joy. 'Oh, that desk, it is exquisite! And the bureau! It is worth ten times the one you have in your sitting room, Annie, so keep that, but empty this one and sell it.'

'Am I really going to be all right, Adrian? Will it all fetch enough to keep us?'

'Yes, you are, my dear. You will have enough to buy a cottage, which you can furnish from the pieces you keep, and still get some money from those that aren't valuable, but worth something second-hand, besides put a tidy little sum into your bank. I can act for you with all the transactions if you want me to, but I know that my friend will give you a fair deal.'

'Yes, I would like that. And right now, I am going to telephone my solicitor – or rather the traitor that posed as mine – and see how the land lies with something I put aside for Ellen.'

Gran explained what had happened.

'You might be in time to save that. It depends if your son had signed the papers, which to my mind are illegal anyway. That money was yours to give and nothing to do with your son. Look, I don't want to appear as if I am interfering, or big-headed in my knowledge, but I do have a fair grasp of the law – especially inheritance law. You see, it was my chosen career, only, well, I have been where you are. Three years into my law degree, my father died, and I found he was penniless and in debt. I had to leave law school and found that teaching was my only option. I have an aunt who I'm very fond of and who could have paid for me, but I didn't want to put on her. When she found out she wanted to help me back into law school, but by then I found I loved teaching. So, if you wanted to, I will tackle your solicitor, though you will have to trust me enough to make me your trustee and able to speak on your behalf.'

'I do, Adrian, thank you.'

'It will only be for this one instance. I won't draw up papers that say you have to relinquish anything to me or give me any power over further aspects of your life, or anything in the future.'

'Thank you, Adrian.'

'Initially, you ring him and tell him you have someone to represent you in the matter. That may be sufficient for him to come clean and revert everything to you. Now, where is the loft and do I need a ladder?'

'No. You go up those stairs that lead to the top floor – it's where the maids slept in the old days, but one of the doors up there leads to the attic space. I hope you find a treasure trove. I'll go and telephone the vicar and the solicitor.'

'As soon as I am down, I will give you all jobs to do. But we need the trunks for the packing.'

'I'll come with you, Adrian.'

Adrian's smile warmed Ellen's heart. As they went up the stairs his voice was kind as he said, 'How are you, really, Ellen? Your poor face. That horror of a woman must have given you a real punch.'

61

'I'm sore and feel as if I'm not in this world. That all this is happening and though I am taking part, I'm not. Does that sound silly?'

'No, it doesn't. You've had a massive shock, my dear, as well as a nasty injury. You should really be resting, but that might give you nightmares. You will be better off helping and being amongst people.'

'Thanks for everything, Adrian.'

He was quiet until they were inside the attic. 'Ellen, I want you to know that you will always have a friend in me.'

Ellen smiled at him, but inside she felt comforted and knew that it was so. Adrian would always be her friend.

Chapter Six

Two days later, Ellen shivered as she stood with the other mourners around the gaping hole that contained a cask holding her dear friend Aggie.

She couldn't cry. It all seemed too sad to cry.

With the ritual of throwing dirt onto the coffin over, they turned to go when a voice said, 'Ellen?'

Turning, she looked into a face so like Aggie's that it took her aback.

'I'm Aggie's sister. Me name's Gwen. There's a lot of us, but I were nearest in age to Aggie. I wanted you to knaw that she loved you.'

Ellen drooped her head. 'I'm sorry about what happened.'

'Did they . . . well, you knaw . . . do that thing to Aggie?'

'No. She tried to save me. I – I loved her too.'

'She were brave like that, Aggie were. Eeh, she saved me many a time, taking the blame for sommat I'd done. I miss her.'

A tear plopped onto Gwen's cheek.

'I know, I do too, so I can't imagine how you feel. That man should hang.'

'But the police say it were your fault.'

Ellen gasped.

'Not that none of us believe it. We knaw you through Aggie and would've known if you were a hussy. Aggie said you were lovely and kind to her and treated her as if you were equals.'

'Thank you. I couldn't bear you all to think that of me.'

'How old are you, miss?'

'Fourteen.'

'You seem a lot older, but I thought Aggie said you were her age.'

Ellen knew she was older. Not in years, but what she'd been through had aged her.

'Your face looks sore. Did they do that to you?'

Ellen nodded. She didn't want to talk about the morning her father died, but it seemed she must as Gwen said, 'They say your dad died. I'm sorry. Were it the shock?'

Ellen just nodded once more. She found her throat tightening and was afraid to let go.

'I can hold your hand if you like.'

Ellen put out her hand and felt the warmth of friendship through the feel of Gwen's. They walked together out of the churchyard but didn't talk any more until they were outside on the pavement, when Gwen said, 'Me ma's having a wake at home, you're welcome to come.'

'Thanks, Gwen, but I think me Gran will want to get back. She's had a few shocks recently.'

As she said this Ellen thought, not least coming into a small fortune of seven hundred pounds from the sale of all of her good bits of furniture and finding that the legacy she had put by was safe.

But that, of course, paled in comparison to her losing her son. As it all did for Ellen when she thought of her father gone. It felt as though everything was unfinished.

'Well, I'd better go. I hope to see you again sometime. Ta-ra.'

On the way back from Leeds, where the funeral had been, everyone was quiet until Gran said, 'Well, they don't blame you, Ellen, and that has put my mind at rest.'

'I know.' She told them about her conversation with Gwen.

After a moment, Gran spoke again. 'My dear, we won't be invited to your father's funeral. Are you prepared for that?'

'Yes, Gran.'

Adrian cleared his throat. 'May I change the subject, Annie?'

'Yes, of course, Adrian. What is it?'

'It's the urgency of your situation. I read in *The Times* that your son's funeral will take place at the end of the week. Once it has, there will be the reading of the will and then things may happen very quickly. I think you should throw yourself into settling your future. Would you like me to look at properties for you?'

Beside her, Ellen felt her gran stiffen. She reached for her hand. As she took it, her gran smiled at her. 'We can do this, can't we, dear? You and I are made of the same strong stuff.'

'We can, Gran.'

'I suggest that once you have chosen the place where you want to live, you go away for a holiday. I know winter is on us, but there are still some nice places open. I love the south – Margate is wonderful and has a mild climate. While you are away, I will organize the move so that you are all settled by the time you return.'

'Eeh, I reckon that's a good idea, Annie. You and Ellen go away together. I'll help Adrian as I knaw how you like everything, and by, me old bones don't take to these journeys.

This carriage is shaking me to pieces as it is, and we've only been into Leeds.'

'Well, Dilly, it might be that we can afford a car in the future. I still know how to drive one, you know.'

'I don't doubt, but by 'eck, you'll not get me in with you till you've had some practice, lass.'

'Ha! We'll see. But yes. That sounds like a good idea, Adrian. Goodness knows what we would have done without you, thank you for everything . . . Driver! Stop off when you reach Thomas Cook's, please.' Looking pleased with herself, Gran told them, 'I'll get it all booked for two weeks' time. That should be long enough for everything as I have the cash to buy a house outright.'

Adrian spluttered. 'Well, I'd better get my skates on then. There's an estate agent's next door to Cook's. I'll go in there and get all the brochures they have, then you can peruse them tonight. We'll set up viewings for the rest of the week and see how it all goes.'

'Good man . . . Ah, we're here. Come along, Ellen.'

By the time they reached home, Ellen felt as though she'd been hit by a whirlwind. Not only had she had the heartbreak of attending dear Aggie's funeral, but they had booked a guest house in Margate for herself and Gran, and Adrian had a pile of houses for sale for them to look through.

They'd only gone through a few of the brochures when they came across an adorable cottage, aptly named 'Rose Cottage' as its frontage was covered in a climbing rose – the picture obviously taken in summertime. It was situated a few miles along the Wakefield Road, where they already lived, but nearer to Leeds.

'That's the one. Do what you can to get it. Four bedrooms,

a kitchen, a scullery, and two reception rooms, plus a dining room – it's perfect. You and Cook can share a room, Dilly. Then, if Adrian will do us the honour of continuing his tuition of Ellen, there will be a bedroom for him too,' Gran said.

Dilly hmphed, prompting Adrian to say, 'There's no need to accommodate me. Of course I will continue in my post, but I can lodge nearby.'

'Well, we'll see. That barn it mentions may be ripe for conversion. Let's get that viewing set up and then we can make our minds up.'

Ellen was thrilled her schooling would continue with Adrian. She had so much to learn and exams to pass to even be considered for a place in the London School of Medicine, which took women as trainee doctors – her dream now, since she'd learned more and more during her biology and science lessons.

And yet, despite thinking all this and being involved in the planning of everything that was taking place, still Ellen felt as though it was happening to someone else. She liked the feeling as it stopped the pain in her frozen heart.

But then, it was when night fell and she was snuggled up in bed that everything crowded in on her and the invisible protection cracked.

Different emotions attacked her – fear as she heard again the crack of the rifle and saw the gaping, burning hole in lovely Aggie's side and her life's blood seeping over the ground. Then disgust, as the image and the feel of the bulk of the filthy ginger-haired man catapulted into her mind, blocking out everything else. But only for a moment as the agonizing pain of seeing her father slump to the floor and hearing his last breath shuddered through her, triggering the hot, burning tears to flow down her cheeks and giving rise to a need to lie where he had lain in the hope that she would gain some comfort – maybe feel his presence.

Throwing the covers back, she swung her legs out of bed only to find that when her feet touched the floor there was no strength in her. She couldn't stand. It was as if the torrent of tears had drained her.

Afraid now, she called out, but nobody came. Her heart felt heavy with the cloying loneliness that enveloped her; the terrible gulf inside her at the realization that those she loved were taken away from her – Ruth, Amy, her mum, Aggie and her father.

'I want them back! I WANT THEM BACK!' The words came from her over and over and although she was aware that they had become screams, she couldn't stop them.

Into these exhausting, hysterical feelings came the awareness that the room was now flooded with light and that there were others around her, trying to calm her – Gran and Dilly. Both were crying, both were imploring her to calm down, and Adrian, too, telling her it was all right. Everything would be all right. But it wasn't and it never could be for they would all leave her, and she would be in a dark hole – left, unloved and unwanted. An object that men did things to, whenever they wanted.

'Filthy, dirty things – don't let them . . . please, don't let them.'

'Who, my dear? It's all right, you've been dreaming. You've had a nightmare. You're awake now, my dear, and it's all over.'

'Aye, that's what it is, lass, and not surprising with all that's happened.'

Then Adrian's voice. 'Maybe take her downstairs and make

her a nice milky drink, let her awaken properly and be able to put it all into perspective?'

His male voice repulsed her. She shrank back. Would he one day do that thing to her? Did all men do it when they got the chance?

She tried to tell herself that no, that wasn't the case. Adrian was good and kind, but a new fear had set up in her and she turned on him. 'Don't touch me! Don't come near me. I HATE MEN!!'

'Oh God! Oh, Adrian, I'm sorry. She doesn't mean it. I know how fond of you she is.'

'It's a natural reaction. No one has tried to help her or to understand what it was she experienced in that wood. The focus has been on everything and anything but that. Ellen needs help, Annie. She needs treatment. She is mentally sick.'

'No! No! He's trying to put me away. Don't let him, Gran. Don't send me away, please don't.'

The begging brought more tears. It rasped her throat. The pain of everything was too much. She wanted a different pain to take it away. Something that wasn't in her heart or her head that would break this terrifying fear she had.

Her hands went to her hair. Grabbing fistfuls of it, she began to tear it from its roots – the stinging, smarting pain helped.

'Stop it . . . Oh, Ellen, my darling girl, please stop.'

'You must get help for her, Annie, you have to.'

Ellen felt her lonely, agonized body being taken into a loving hold. 'Eeh, me little lass, I've got you. I won't let owt hurt you, I promise. You're safe. All the bad folk in your life have gone. We love you and will protect you.'

Some of the fear left Ellen as she clung on to Dilly. 'Help me, Dilly, help me.'

For a moment a peace settled in her, but then her gaze

fell onto the patch of carpet where her father had died and she had the urge to beat it and so to beat her father. Pushing Dilly away, she flung herself off the bed and pummelled the carpet with her fists as she cried, 'Why couldn't you have loved me? Why? Why? You gave me life! You did that thing to my mum. You took me from her when she would have loved me. You broke her heart. YOU WERE A BEAST AND I HATE YOU . . . I HATE YOU!!'

Into the screams that tore at the soreness of her throat came Gran's sobs. 'No . . . no, my darling girl, no.'

Two strong arms lifted her, and she smelled the familiar smell of Adrian's aftershave. A repulsion shuddered through her. Wriggling from his grip, she turned on him and snarled, 'Don't touch me! All men are filthy!'

Adrian plonked down on the chair. His look of shock and hurt meant nothing to Ellen.

After a moment, Adrian said, 'My dear, we are not all the same. I think you are unwell. It isn't surprising after all you have been through. And I understand how you feel. Will you let me find a nursing home that will care for you and help you to get better? I will make sure it is a really good one and that you receive nothing but kindness while you are recovering. And that your gran and Dilly visit often . . . I won't come until you are ready to receive me. I would never hurt you or cause you distress.'

His face held the honesty she knew him to have. And what he said gave her the feeling of a sanctuary where she might find peace. She nodded her head.

When they had calmed her, they called the doctor who immediately said she needed more than the kind of home they had planned.

Gran stood against him, telling him that no granddaughter of hers was ever going into an asylum and that she agreed with Mr Vale on this, that Ellen was having a breakdown and wasn't insane.

With this, the doctor told them of a private nursing home on the outskirts of Leeds. He said it wasn't cheap but was renowned for the care given. 'I know the lady who owns it. We studied together. She wanted to be a doctor but couldn't get into medical school – it's always been nigh on impossible for women and a travesty in her case. Anyway, she then became a nurse and eventually, after inheriting her father's wealth, set up this excellent facility.'

As Ellen listened, she warmed to this lady and her fears of going to her home settled.

She took the medication offered by the doctor and felt all her terrors leaving her as she drifted off to sleep.

On waking the next morning, she felt so much better and knew she could cope once more. But Gran wouldn't hear of it.

'Only until the next thing triggers you, my darling. We telephoned the home and I spoke to Miss Roland. She was very sympathetic and kind. I told her everything, even about your ambition to become a doctor. She said she would help you all she can and if, and only if, you want it, she will accommodate Adrian coming in to continue your schooling once a week.

'But most importantly, she told me that she has been recently studying the illnesses of the mind with the intention of opening a specialist unit and is excited to be able to work with you as your symptoms are classic of someone who has been traumatized.'

'But what about the cost, Gran, and the holiday we booked?

I don't want you to lose anything because of me . . . I know, why not use the money you set aside for me?'

'We will see. I will do what I can until the time comes when I need to do something else, but my dear, you have taken the first step as Miss Roland said the first thing that she learned about traumatized people is that they have to accept they have a mental illness for them ever to benefit from the treatment, and you just did.'

'I do realize it, Gran. I was never a person who stood up for myself or caused a fuss. Ruth was the one to look out for us all, she was strong. Oh, Gran, I would so love to see her again.'

'I know, dear, Dilly told me everything about what happened in the days when I distanced myself from you – but you know, I have come to realize that I too have been traumatized. Not in any way as gravely as you as I was much older when I was used so badly – well, apart from experiencing, as you did, the awful feeling of not being wanted. So, when you appeared it was like you triggered all that in me . . . feelings I had suppressed. And all I could think to do was to keep you at arm's length. I'm so glad that has changed for me. Now all I want is for you to be well.'

A love for her gran surged through her. She stood and opened her arms. Gran came forward and they hugged.

'I love you, Gran, with all my heart. Thank you. I will get better and then we'll live together in Rose Cottage . . . You are still buying it, aren't you?'

'Yes, I am, my dear. But the holiday is on hold. I telephoned Cook's and they have cancelled it for me. I have told them to transfer the funds, less any forfeited deposit, to a hotel near to where you are going to be, for Christmastime, for me and Dilly. So, we will spend Christmas together as

Miss Roland has said that as long as you are well enough, she would release you for Christmas lunch and would invite us back for the afternoon as that is when they put on a concert for the patients.'

'Oh, Gran, you've thought of everything!'

'Not just me, my dear. You can guess who is behind all the plotting and planning of it, but we won't talk of him until you are ready.'

At this, Ellen felt a shame wash over her. How could she have tarred dear Adrian with the same brush she did all the other beasts? But then, even saying this, she knew she wasn't ready to welcome any man into her world – not yet and, maybe, never.

Chapter Seven

Miss Roland was a joy, and yet a stickler for rules at the same time. Ellen found it surprising that a lady so small in stature, like Miss Roland was, had achieved so much in her life as she must have had to stand up for herself in a male-dominated world.

She wore her thick black hair coiled into a huge bun on the top of her head, which Ellen was sure was designed to give her height. In contrast, her eyes were a piercing blue and gave the impression that they missed nothing.

Everyone loved her even though she didn't show any affection but was fair and ready with a lovely smile and plenty of encouragement.

And Ellen found the home to be a peaceful place, mainly decorated with whitewashed walls and many pictures, though the common lounge – a large room with French doors leading to the perfectly manicured garden – was painted a pastel blue with huge comfy sofas in a royal blue and a wooden, highly polished floor. The rug in front of the roaring fire was mainly cream with a pattern of small blue flowers woven into it. Ellen loved this room, but she loved the activity room more, where she found easels, paints, brushes and paper. She spent hours painting scenes of the garden, winter birds and bushes with frosty cobwebs on them.

She was in this room, a fortnight after she'd arrived, when Miss Roland came in and called her name. 'I want you to come to my office, dear.'

The office looked more like a sitting room than a formal place and was very feminine with its pink sofas and armchairs.

As soon as Ellen sat opposite Miss Roland, who sat behind a small desk placed in the window, Miss Roland asked how she was.

'Much better, thank you. I haven't had a nightmare for two nights.'

'Yes, I know. The night staff informed me and that is why I have brought you in here to discuss the treatment I have in mind for you, Ellen. It will require you to be very brave.'

A nerve twinged in Ellen's stomach.

'No need to look alarmed. What I have in mind will only be painful to your heart and your emotions, no physical pain. I want you to agree to talk. You see, there is a school of thought prompted by Mr Freud that if we face our demons by talking about them, they will lose the power they have over us. I do know you have demons – horrible, unimaginable ones – but hiding from them is only a temporary cure. You have to face them, get strong despite them and the way to do that is to talk to a trained counsellor. Someone who can guide you through the awful path that revisiting them will take you along.'

None of this made sense to Ellen. But she had heard of Freud and his theories from Adrian, and she did trust Miss Roland, so she nodded her head.

'You are agreeing?'

'Yes. I want to get better. You see, I want to be a doctor.'

'Ah, yes, I remember, your grandmother told me. A noble profession. Well, my dear, I will help you all that I can to achieve that, but first we must heal your mind.'

After a few days, Miss Roland summoned Ellen again.

'My dear, I have had to change my plan. The only trained counsellor who is free is a man, and that wouldn't do, and so I am to undertake the work myself. Come on in and we will begin.'

As she said this she closed and locked the door behind Ellen. 'Lie down on the couch, Ellen, and I will pull up a chair.'

This all felt very strange and frightening.

'Now, I want you to just talk. Tell me memories – happy ones and sad. Start at the earliest you can remember. And, Ellen, cry if you want to, scream if you need to, but don't hold back – not on a happening or an emotion. I am here for you and will keep you safe.'

An hour later, Ellen felt drained. She had cried, she had wailed, she had visited many memories and replayed many scenes and yet she'd only reached the time she was taken to the orphanage.

She'd felt again the nasty pinching of her body inflicted by her stepmother, and the pulling of her pigtails by one of her daddy's maids who had taken advantage of the situation and knew she wouldn't get into trouble. Her loneliness as she spent hours alone in the nursery, sometimes not fed all day until her father came home but afraid to come out even to visit the lavatory.

'You have done so well, Ellen. Sadly the mind is selective and can store the major events that have influenced our lives and we then dwell on them, good or bad. Before the end of our session, I want you to now tell me some good memories from that time.'

'Daddy coming home from work and playing with me.

Twirling me in the air, giving me freedom from the confines of the nursery and fear. The walks he took me on through the park. Me skipping as I held his hand . . . and making things up. I did that a lot, told him I had a happy day as I somehow sensed that if he thought I was unhappy, then it wouldn't be good, that he might get cross with my stepmother and then she would treat me even worse. How I had this perception at such a young age, I don't know.'

'You are a special person, Ellen, never forget that. You are wise beyond your years. You can beat these demons you have. Let us see things from your stepmother's point of view. You were a daily reminder of the hurt that she suffered through your father's infidelity – and not just a discreet affair, but her husband had actually paid another woman to pleasure him. The impact on her must have been devastating. That doesn't excuse her, but she, too, deserves some understanding, as we all do for our actions. As you do for yours.'

To Ellen, this was a revelation. She had never thought of the pain she must have caused by just being there. *Maybe inflicting pain on me helped her, just as it did me when I attacked my tutor and that disgusting man in the wood and then Adrian, poor, undeserving Adrian – and yes, when I pulled my own hair out.*

An understanding of her stepmother came to her and with it some peace surrounded that part of her life.

'They look like different tears to me, Ellen. Your emotions are not anger now, but empathy. Does that feel better? Can you now look back and forgive?'

Ellen knew she could. She nodded her head.

'That's good, my dear. Now, I think a hug is what you need and then a rest.'

To Ellen's surprise, Miss Roland came towards her with

her arms open. The hug she went into soothed the remaining pain associated with her early life and gave her hope that she would be able to deal with all the bad things of the past. She didn't know how yet, but with this lovely lady's help she might.

With Christmas in two days' time, there was a feeling of excitement throughout the nursing home. Those who were well enough were rehearsing a pantomime for those who weren't and for visitors.

Ellen was to be Snow White and loved the activity around getting ready – learning her lines, the laughs they had as they rehearsed, helping to stitch the costumes, and to paint the scenery.

'Eeh, that looks grand, Ellen.'

Ellen giggled. To listen to June was like having Dilly with her. A young woman of twenty-four, June had had what she called 'a funny turn' after her baby son was born. She'd run screaming from her home after having thoughts of wanting to kill her child. At first when she'd heard of this, Ellen had recoiled in horror, but as she got to know June, she found her to be a lovely person, who just wanted to be accepted back in her son's and husband's life. Ellen prayed that would happen one day and was hopeful as June's husband had made an effort to find the funds to get her into here instead of into an asylum and had made one visit and was coming to the concert too.

They stood back together and surveyed the backdrop several of them had created by painting squares which were now fitting together like a jigsaw puzzle on a screen that would be wheeled out for the scene when the prince kissed Snow White. The kiss was to be planted on her cheek and she was fine with it as it was June who was to play Prince Charming.

'I think we've earned a break, everyone.'

Miss Richards, an artistic lady who lived locally and volunteered her services, looked around at their handiwork. 'Well done! Now we just need to leave it all to dry properly, and then I think it will be perfect.'

'By, I could do with some fresh air, lass. I knaw it's freezing out there but are you game?'

'I am, June. The smell of the paint gets down you after a while.'

As they walked huddled up in their coats, scarves and bonnets, June said, 'You look well enough to leave here, lass. Have you finished your sessions with Miss Roland?'

'Not yet, and I don't know that I want them to end. They are helping me so much.'

'So, how do you feel about men now? Are you still hating them all?'

'No. Adrian, my tutor and friend, is coming at Christmas. He'll be at the concert. I – I, well, I feel afraid of how he'll be with me after the way I treated him.'

'The fact that he's coming, lass, is a measure of his understanding, so don't worry. Though I knaw how you feel. Me Arthur's coming with me son and I'm so afraid that he'll be different with me. And me little boy won't knaw who I am . . . or . . . well, he may be afraid of me . . . I mean, I never hurt him, but I did cry a lot and leave him crying. I just don't knaw what came over me, only that, well, Miss Roland says it can happen after any trauma and a birth is a traumatic event.'

'There then, so you've no need to be ashamed. You suffered something a lot of women suffer, that's all.'

'I've never met another who has been like I was, have you?'

'I have never had dealings with anyone when they had a baby – not anyone I knew – so I don't know. I've no friends or acquaintances of that age group, but if Miss Roland says so, then it is so . . . If I was you, I'd just be grateful you're getting better and will soon be home. Don't feel guilty about something you couldn't help.'

As she said this, Ellen felt a bit of a fraud as she still felt guilty about how she'd treated Adrian, but June saying that he must have forgiven her to even be coming to see her helped.

'Has your husband forgiven you, June?'

'Aye, he said in his letter that he has. He said that after reading the letter Miss Roland sent to him that he understood, and that he just wanted me home.'

'That's wonderful, June. So now we must heal the guilt, and we'll be fine.'

June put her arm through Ellen's. 'I like talking to you, lass. You're going to make a fine doctor, you knaw.'

Ellen knew a warm feeling of friendship flood her. She liked June. It brought Ruth back to her, as Ruth had been three years older than herself and would be seventeen now.

'Aw, that were a sigh and a half, lass.'

Not wanting to drag up memories and longings, Ellen just smiled. 'Come on, let's get in. Me lug'oles are like icicles, as me lovely Dilly would say.'

'Ha, we'll make a Yorkshire lass of you yet between us.'

Gran and Dilly arrived on Christmas Eve. The hug Gran gave her went on and on.

'My darling, you look so well.'

'I feel it, Gran, and I am getting well, really well.'

Gran's smile faded as she stepped back and held her at arm's length. 'Are you sure? Will you be all right with Adrian tomorrow?'

'Yes, I will. We have been writing to each other and the air is cleared between us.'

'Yes, I know and that is good, but when you actually see him?'

'I've been around a lot of men here, Gran. I've been helping on the wards. I love it and I've been fine with them.'

Gran sighed. 'That's good to hear. And how have you been . . . ? Has everything been functioning . . . ? Are you . . . ? I mea—'

'Eeh, Annie, stop fannying around the bushes.' Dilly looked at Ellen. 'Come here, me little lass, and give me a hug.'

Going into Dilly's arms, Ellen felt mystified and had no idea what Gran was worried about. But Dilly's next words soon put her in the picture. 'Now, then, me little lass, have you been seeing your monthlies since you've been here?'

Shock zinged through Ellen. The last time she'd seen her bleeding had been the week before her rape – that was eight weeks ago now!

'Aw, me little lass, you haven't, have you?'

'No. Oh, Dilly . . . Gran! No, I don't want . . . No!'

Gran took her from Dilly and held her close. 'Keep calm, my darling girl. Let's go and have a word with Miss Roland, shall we?'

Ellen felt her heart beating fast and her body began to shake. Miss Roland's coping mechanisms, as she called them, came to mind. 'Take a deep breath,' she would say. 'This is a panic attack, nothing more.' Just thinking this helped Ellen. She took the deep breath, pleased with how she was now in control.

'I – I'm all right, Gran, I just don't want that to happen.'
Her tears flooded her face.

'Now then, what is all this? I thought you would be so
happy today, Ellen, and I can see those aren't tears of joy.'

'It's our fault, Miss Roland . . . well, mine. I'm so sorry.
I was anxious to know if . . . I mean . . . Oh, I'm so sorry.'

'You're talking in riddles. I suggest you all come to my
office and tell me what has upset Ellen. She has been doing
so well, so I have to say, I am not pleased that what should
have been a joyous time for her has been spoiled by whatever
this is.'

Gran was red in the face. She looked so ashamed and
flustered that Ellen felt sorry for her. She put her hand into
Gran's and found it was shaking as much as her own was.

As soon as they were seated in the office, in an informal
manner, herself and Gran sitting on the sofa and Dilly and
Miss Roland in an armchair each, Miss Roland said, 'I can
guess what it was you wanted to know. Well, we are moni-
toring Ellen, and the fact that her menstruation has stopped
has not worried me. It often happens when a young girl is
traumatized – her reproduction system can shut down. The
brain is a powerful organ. It has to protect the body, the
mind and the emotions. The normal cycle of things can
interfere with that and so, often when someone presents with
symptoms of hysteria and on the verge of a breakdown, this
can be a trigger to use all the energy they have to help them
to get well and that entails shutting certain things off from
working as normal.'

Gran sighed with relief.

'I must caution you all that this is what I think may be
happening, but of course, the trauma that triggered Ellen's
breakdown was the fact that, yet again, the poor dear had

82

been raped and, as we all know, that can lead to pregnancy, but I don't think it is something we should be worrying about. If, now she is recovering, she doesn't start to ovulate, then we will have to go down the route of examining her for a pregnancy, but I have every hope that hasn't happened.'

This all seemed so matter-of-fact to Miss Roland, but inside Ellen was screaming against it, and praying for all she was worth. To her, Christmas was now spoiled. She dropped her head.

'Ellen, my dear, I am extremely sorry this has happened. I am to blame. I should have written to your grandmother and put her in the picture. Now, I want you to listen to me. I am not concerned that you may be pregnant. At this stage, if you were, there would be changes to your breasts. Matron tells me there are none as she has observed you in the bath with the other girls. You will also have felt nauseous in the mornings, when you are up bright as a button and helping on the wards. So, now is the time to use your coping strategies. Remember, there is good in everything and hope in everything. If you are pregnant, we will take care of you.'

'And we would look after your baby, we wouldn't let it be taken away from you, my darling girl.'

'But I don't want to be, I want to be a doctor.'

Gran smiled reassuringly. 'And you will be. Your study would continue.'

Miss Roland nodded her agreement. 'And will begin again very shortly as soon as you say you are ready, because I think it is time that you took up your study again. And that can be twofold, as I will teach you many things you will need to know. We will have one half day a week together, Ellen. I will be your medical instructor!'

Everything seemed as if it would be fine to these folk she loved. But . . . Stopping the doubt that threatened her, Ellen decided to take on the same positive way of thinking. She was thrilled by Miss Roland's suggestion. It took away the pain of doubt, and the fear too. There was nothing Miss Roland couldn't fix.

'You are going to be me – for me, Ellen. I couldn't progress to become a doctor, but I am going to make damn sure that you do!'

This made Ellen giggle. She'd never heard Miss Roland swear before. The giggle broke the tension. Miss Roland beat her chest. 'Ha, now I will have to go to confession.' Her laugh was a lovely tinkly one and it set off Gran's chuckle and Dilly's cackle till they were all laughing together.

Dabbing her eyes in the precise way Miss Roland had of doing everything, she said, 'Now, it's Christmas! So let us enjoy it, shall we?'

They were all looking at Ellen, and she beamed back at them. 'Yes. I'm so excited. Merry Christmas, everyone!'

The fear had lifted completely. She trusted Miss Roland with her life and if she said all would be fine, then it would be.

The next day Gran arrived in a taxi to pick her up to take her to the hotel for Christmas lunch.

Before leaving, Ellen had visited the ward that gave her the most sadness, where the women who couldn't recover from their illnesses were. She'd wished them all a happy Christmas and been rewarded with a few weak smiles.

If they could face what they had to face, Ellen knew she could go forward to the next step in her recovery.

This new resolve was put to the test when Gran said, 'Now, are you sure, my darling, that you are ready to meet Adrian?'

'I am, Gran. Very sure.' And she knew she was. 'I cannot wait to tell him how sorry I am and—'

'Now, now, no apologies. You do not have to say sorry for being ill. Just be yourself with him and that's all Adrian wants . . . Driver, take us back to my hotel, please.'

The hotel was a plush affair, with a rich decor of blues and golds. A huge Christmas tree stood in the foyer, giving Ellen an excited zing through her body. At the home, they had put up a few streamers in the lounge area, but Miss Roland had said that was all she could allow as they were dust collectors and therefore unhygienic for her more sick patients.

When they went through the foyer into the dining room, Adrian was there. He gave her a huge smile. On impulse she ran towards him. He put out his hands to her. Taking them, she leaned in to kiss his cheek.

'My, is that appropriate behaviour from a pupil to her teacher?'

'Well, you shouldn't have stood under the mistletoe!'

He put his head back and let out a roar of laughter.

Ellen laughed with him but had the feeling he was changed – more handsome, with the effect of the extra weight he'd gained, but mostly it was his confidence.

'I can see you've noticed what these last few weeks have done to me, Ellen. Well, you can blame these two. I've done more manual work than I've ever done in my life since I have been at their beck and call.'

'Oh, the move and everything! How did it go? Is the cottage lovely? Is there room for us all?'

Gran came nearer to her. 'It went very well, and we found more valuables as we packed, my darling, so Gran is richer even than she was when you left.'

And Dilly added, 'Aye, and the cottage is grand, though why it's called a cottage, I have naw idea. It's not as big as the house was, but it's bigger than any cottage that I've ever come across.'

'Yes, and the barn at the bottom of the garden, that is big enough for Adrian. He is going to oversee converting it into a schoolroom with apartments above for himself . . . well, I'll let him tell you all about it, but first, let us get to our table and order an aperitif.'

When they were settled, Adrian told her that he'd discussed with her grandmother about him renting the barn and opening a private school for local children whose parents could afford education and for adults in the evening. His enthusiasm shone from him as he warmed to his theme. 'And I will reserve one day a week to school those who cannot afford to pay, and besides all this, there's a field behind it which is owned by your gran, so I hope to take a section of that to use as a playground. I am so excited about it all.'

'Me too, just to know you'll be there so near to us.'

'Yes. But my first project is to begin your lessons once more. The moment you say you are ready, then I will set up a time to come to the home on a regular basis. Miss Roland is a gem, and together, we will help you to get all the right exams to get you to university and then to medical school.'

'It all sounds wonderful. And I am ready, I am.'

It all seemed so natural, as if nothing had happened between them. This filled Ellen with happiness as she really liked Adrian. He was like a big brother to her.

Chapter Eight

1915

Ellen sat looking out of her bedroom window. The view was ever-changing. Today flurries of snow landed on the already covered ground and on the branches of the bare trees that bent under the weight of the previous heavy fall.

They'd hoped for a white Christmas, their first spent in Rose Cottage, but it hadn't come until the new year came in.

Now it was mid-January and Adrian's school had opened.

The schoolchildren had arrived about an hour ago and soon, Ellen would go down to the schoolroom to help, which she often did, sometimes reading a story to the younger ones while Adrian took those ten years old and over for a subject that needed his undivided attention and, at others, organizing everything for his next lesson or joining in with a painting class, which she loved.

Today was the nine-month anniversary of her return home.

She could have been discharged earlier. Her periods had restarted and she understood and could rationalize a lot of what had happened to her, but she hadn't felt ready until after June had left, happily holding her husband's hand as she waved goodbye. This gave Ellen the courage that she needed to take the next step herself. So, she'd come home for Easter as a trial run, and had found that she didn't want to go back.

She loved everything about the cottage and felt at home as soon as she'd walked through the door into the small square hall with its beamed ceiling, stairs going off the centre, and a door off each side wall and one facing the entrance that led to the kitchen. The one on the right led to Gran's sitting room, and through that the dining room with its French doors opening onto the large garden. Through the left-hand door, there was a drawing room which also had a door leading to the kitchen.

As you could also go through another door from the kitchen to the dining room, it meant that you could complete a circular tour of the whole of the ground floor of the cottage.

Ellen often did just for the fun of it, having a word with each occupant in each room and then giggling to herself.

Gran's personality was woven into the cottage by the pieces of furniture she'd brought with her, and in the colours – the blues and silver-greys of the wallpaper, curtains and cushions.

It was home.

For Ellen, if the weather wasn't good and she'd finished her lessons, or wasn't needed in the schoolroom, her bedroom was her sanctuary, as here, under the window, had been placed the small desk Gran had once used in a corner of her late husband's study.

Ellen loved it and liked to sit with the medical books that Miss Roland had given her. She would peruse them for hours as they fascinated her – *The Human Anatomy* in particular.

In a way, learning about the sexual functions of men and women gave her a little understanding as to why what happened to her did. Though trying to equate that with not fearing Adrian wasn't easy. If those others followed their basic instincts, then why not him? In the end she'd concluded that not all men were led by their need, that many more weren't and were respectful of women, and she began to feel better about life.

Why she hadn't become pregnant was a source of both mystery and great relief to her. Reading about a woman's cycle and reproductive system had given her the knowledge that she surely should have done, but then, she'd also read that besides a natural cycle having to be in place at the time of the act taking place, there were things that could be wrong, though not all were known and research into the subject was ongoing.

Whatever they were, she was glad they might be part of her as she didn't know how she could cope with having a child; and worse, having that child remind her every day what had happened – something she didn't want to think about. Though she thought of poor Aggie often and wished with all her heart she was here now.

Gran had never replaced Aggie with another live-in maid. Dilly still did what she could and both she and Cook had daily helpers coming in.

Ellen so wished that at least one of them was nearer to her age. But despite being lonely for a friend, all in all, with her new frame of mind and ways of coping with her demons, she was the happiest she'd ever been – or would be if it weren't for the awful war going on.

It threatened to disrupt life as she knew it and was hitting home now as only yesterday Josie, one of the part-time dailies, was crying on Dilly's shoulder because her son, at only sixteen years of age, had lied about his age in order to be accepted and had signed up.

Her thoughts went to Ruth and the young men with her

on the last day she saw her. They, and Hettie too, had stayed in the landau. Had those young men gone to war? And Hettie, what of her? She'd been assistant to the cook at the orphanage and had helped them all she could. Had she gone to do war work? Had Ruth?

This thought had her slamming her book closed and running out of the bedroom and down the stairs. 'Gran, Gran, where are you?'

Gran appeared from her sitting room. 'My dear girl, where is the fire?'

'Ha! Gran, there's no fire . . . Why did you ask that?'

'Well, your shrieks made me jump and I thought there must have been – not really, it is just a saying when someone makes a lot of racket to draw your attention. Now, what is the matter? What made you scream out like that?'

'I want to go to London! Please say yes. I have to find Ruth. She may go to war! She is the kind who would. She always wants to make things better.'

Gran was quiet for a few moments.

'Come into my room and sit down, my dear.'

Ellen followed Gran and sat on the sofa while Gran sat in her favourite chair by the side of the roaring fire.

Ellen waited, hoping Gran would agree to her making the trip. When she nodded her head, Ellen's hope soared.

'Yes, I do agree, my darling, that you should go and try to find your friend. Not doing so has been eating away at you for years now. I will arrange for Adrian to take you one weekend. How would that be?'

'Wonderful! Thank you, Gran. I still have the address – well, part of it and I know London is huge, but Adrian will find it, I'm sure.'

'Yes. He'll look on his ordnance survey maps, he always

has the latest ones . . . My dear, there is a possibility that Adrian will volunteer to go to war. He has been talking to me about it.'

'Oh no! No . . . he can't!'

'He can, Ellen, you must prepare yourself.'

'But what about the school?'

'It will be put on hold, like many other things have had to be. We all have to do our bit and you must be proud of and encourage Adrian in this.'

'Yes, Gran. I am and I will, but it's just so frightening. I don't want him to get hurt . . . or worse – killed.'

The thought sent shivers through her. She wanted to scream out against such a thing happening.

Gran bowed her head but didn't deny the possibility. Ellen could see that she looked troubled and for the first time noticed that she'd aged so much since they had moved here.

'Are you missing your old home, Gran?'

'What? Where did that come from? Well, yes, I am dear . . . the memories at least. Though I am still haunted by my beloved son's death.'

Ellen gasped. She hadn't expected that! It shot the scene into her mind. Panic rose inside her, but she breathed deeply.

'We should talk about him, Ellen. He did many things wrong, and his wife has done a lot more since, but we cannot deny people who are intricate to our lives – even evil ones. It isn't good for us.'

Ellen knew she was right.

'Let's remember the good things, Gran. I do have good memories of Daddy.'

'Yes. And let's add prayers for his soul on the end of our usual night ones. I will feel better then. It has been lonely grieving alone.'

'You haven't grieved alone. I have grieved too, but it will be good to talk about how we feel. Miss Roland always encouraged it.'

Gran smiled. 'I think you are truly healed, my dear. To be able to talk about one of the traumatic events in your life is a massive step forward for you. And it has helped me too.'

'I – I, well, I often think about the boy I told you of. He will be about three now . . . my brother. And my mother. Always I'm thinking of my mother and wondering how she is.'

'My poor darling. Well, I can't fix everything, but I can try to help you find Ruth.'

The door burst open then and Adrian stood there waving his weekly magazine – *The Bystander*. 'Forgive me barging in, Annie, I just had to come and tell you both and Dilly told me you were together – just look at what is in my paper!'

'What is it, dear boy? Tell us before you burst!'

'Prepare yourself, Ellen.'

Ellen was mystified and yet Adrian's excitement had her holding her breath.

He opened the magazine with a flourish.

'Miss Ruth Faith's acclaimed performance in *This is Paris* at the Prince of Wales Theatre has set London alight!'

Ellen released her breath. 'Oh, Gran . . . Adrian! Is it really true? My Ruth, a famous actress? We've found her! Gran, we've found her.'

'Oh, Ellen, my dear. Wipe away your tears, this is a happy moment for you.'

'It is, Gran. At last . . . at last.'

But Ellen couldn't stop her tears. In the loving arms of her Gran, she cried her joy, but also her sadness at all that had happened. The crying, prompted by talk of her father and by the best news she could possibly have of knowing she could now find Ruth, emptied her heart and soul of the pent-up emotions she'd denied. She'd pretended they'd gone; now they truly were.

When she looked up, Adrian had left the room.

'Is that better, my dear? Sometimes it is better to let it all out. I, too, feel like doing so, but then becoming the comforter helps me. Now, let me ring for Dilly to bring us a cup of tea.'

'Eeh, just look at your puffy face, me little lass. And I thought Adrian was the bearer of good news.'

'He was, Dilly. Such wonderful news.' She told Dilly what had happened.

'That's grand. So you'll be going back to London, no doubt?'

'Only for a visit.'

'Well, you're braver than me. I'd not want to go out of Yorkshire . . . You don't think being back will make you talk funny, do you? Only, we had one of them cockney women as a helper, many years ago, didn't we, Annie? By, she'd got some rattle and all in this funny accent. I didn't knaw where I were with her.'

Ellen smiled to herself, thinking that she could understand the cockneys better than she had Dilly when she'd first met her.

'You will come back, won't you, lass?'

'Of course she will, Dilly! Why wouldn't she? That's a stupid question, Dilly.'

Gran's irritation crackled in every word. Ellen knew it was through fear. She took her hand. Still, she could feel the slight trembling of it. Poor Gran. She really was upset by her thoughts taking her back to losing her son.

'Don't mind me. I were thinking aloud, Annie, sorry. Eeh, lass, sommat's upset you. Drink your tea, love.'

Gran smiled and nodded. Ellen sensed that Gran wanted to be alone.

'You look tired, Gran. We'll leave you for an hour or two, shall we? I need to go to see Adrian. He must think me mad breaking my heart when he must have thought I would rejoice.'

'That's a good idea. I do have a headache, my dear. Dilly, would you close the curtains for me? The light is hurting my eyes. I'll ring when I want you.'

Dilly began to fuss. Ellen could see she was as worried as she felt.

'Come on, Dilly, Gran will be fine. She just needs time on her own. We'll all be on hand if she needs us.'

Gran smiled gratefully.

'Shall I leave your tea here for you, Annie?'

Gran didn't seem to hear this. She'd put her head on one side and closed her eyes. Ellen motioned to Dilly to draw the curtains, then held the door open so she could find her way out.

'Eeh, I've never seen your gran like that afore, lass. Should we get the doctor? I don't like the look of her.'

'No, she's just grieving. She spoke of my father this morning and was overcome. I think she really does just need to be left a while and will surface later when she feels better. But we will keep coming quietly and listening in at the door to make sure.'

Ellen had to admit to feeling very worried herself as she ran down the garden pulling her shawl around her shoulders to ward off the cold.

When she opened the door to the classroom it was empty.

She called Adrian's name up the stairs that led to his apartment. He appeared immediately.

'Where are the children?'

'I sent them home. The boiler is on the blink again and it became too cold down there. I have a fire lit up here. Come on up.'

Ellen hesitated.

Adrian looked upset as he sighed, 'Very well, I'll come down. We'll go into the drawing room as we need to chat.'

Once in there, Adrian asked, 'So, was that good news, or not?'

'Oh, it was, Adrian, thank you.'

'But it upset you.'

She explained that she'd been told that she still would have triggers. 'Hearing this news seconds after talking to poor Gran about my father was one of those – joy and sadness all mingled together.' She told him then how she was worried about Gran.

'Oh dear, poor Annie. But you know it is expected. We grieve those who were bad to us as much as those who were good – sometimes more as we want things to change, and they can't . . . So, are you going to London?'

'Yes, but I don't want to go on my own.'

'You would like me to take you?' At her nodding, Adrian's next words were a shock. 'Well, that will suit me as I do want to go myself. I want to visit my aunt. You may remember I told you about her living down there? And I can also look up a friend whose father is a training officer at Sandhurst. I want to speak to him – see if he can recommend me as a candidate.'

'The military school for officers?'

'Yes.'

'You are thinking of volunteering? What about the school? And the children?'

'Yes, I need to do my bit and think that I would be best suited in command rather than in the trenches. My knowledge of languages, and of mathematical planning, will be of more use in helping strategy. As for the school, I have been approached lately by a retired headteacher. He said that if I need to release myself from the school for a bit, then he would be willing to run things for me. I will meet with him when I come back . . . It was embarrassing really as I had the impression that he was hinting that I should have volunteered before now.'

Ellen didn't know what to say to this. Part of her had thought the school would stop Adrian from going, but now . . . 'I – I just didn't imagine you going. Though Gran did say something. I just wish that I was old enough, but maybe I can volunteer in a hospital as they say they may become overrun with casualties.'

'Not up here, I wouldn't think, though they may take overspill, but in the south, yes.'

'You didn't object. I thought you would.'

'No. Despite you only being fifteen, from what I have read about what is happening and what I have deduced is possible to happen, I believe every able-bodied person will be needed to combat the threat to the world's freedom.'

This seemed like a different Adrian to the one she knew. But talking to him about the war had fired her imagination as to how useful she could be. She had her studies, of course, but they needn't be interrupted. Maybe . . .

Suddenly Ellen was gripped with excitement and anticipation as the idea came to her that maybe she could lodge with Ruth so she'd be where she might be needed!

Warming to these thoughts, she justified them by thinking that after all, many thousands of young girls of thirteen and over worked full time, so why shouldn't she?

'I can see your mind ticking over, Ellen.'

Ellen shared with him what had occurred to her. 'But then, would Gran allow it?'

'I believe she would. She is worldly wise. Probably some of her upset is thinking along the same lines as you are, that maybe you will have to go eventually to do some war work. She may be trying to prepare herself. But think about it first. Perhaps while we are in London you can look at the possibilities. Then you can tell your gran when you get back.'

All of this coming so suddenly left Ellen with mixed feelings. She didn't like the idea of leaving Gran and Dilly, but at the same time wanted so very much to be out in the world where others of her age were living their lives – having and making friends, doing things other than studying, but most of all, she wanted to be with Ruth.

Chapter Nine

Two weeks later, Ellen stood outside the orphanage in Bethnal Green watching the children play. They looked happy. Ruth had done that. She'd brought an end to the abuse she, Ruth and Amy and the other kids had suffered.

A shudder passed through Ellen. The abuse may have stopped, but the memory lived on. The stinking smell of Belton's sweaty body, his pawing hands, his foul breath and then . . . Ellen turned away in a desperate bid to block the rest from flooding her memory. How difficult that was.

She had been just ten years old! The physical pain had been bad, but the emotional pain had scarred her for ever, even though she was now master of how it affected her.

Ruth had been her saviour, her friend, her most loved person in all the world. And tonight, when she went to the theatre, they would be reunited as she'd wanted them to be for so long. She wished it could be with Amy too but knew that she might have gone from her life for ever. For as far as she knew, none of the orphans who'd been shipped off to Canada had a hope of returning.

Her mind went back to her last encounter with Ruth, and she could hear again Ruth's desperate voice, shouting out her address. How many times she'd tried to recall it, but now she needn't do that.

Excitement clenched her stomach as she walked away. She didn't know why, but she had the urge to retrace her steps. Find the tearoom her father had taken her to. Relive the moment when she'd met her mum for the first time ever. Not that she thought for a moment that she would see her again as she didn't think her mum would frequent Bond Street. But it would mean so much just to be where she had been.

As the taxi she'd hailed pulled up and Ellen alighted, she saw the tearoom door. Her own plea came to her, and her stomach turned over. *I want to live with you, Daddy . . . Don't you love me? You said you did! You said you would never leave me again.*

It was all as if it was yesterday.

As she stood gazing at the plant pots outside the door, she saw again her mother and her little baby brother. And yet, was it her mother's face or Ruth's that she was seeing?

A thought shot into her head. Why did her mother resemble Ruth so much? Could it be . . . ? Her father's accusations about her mum having got rid of two children before she was born came to her. Hadn't Ruth been left at a priest's house and that's why she'd been given the surname of Faith? *My God!*

Ellen needed to sit down.

Making her way inside the cafe made the incident even more vivid. She found a seat, ordered tea, though she didn't think she could stomach one sip – her mind and body were in a turmoil.

A voice startled her. 'Excuse me, are you feeling all right, miss?'

She nodded her head.

The young gentleman smiled. 'If I can be of assistance, please say.'

Others looked around at her. She managed a smile. 'I – I'm just cold, thank you. I'll be fine when I have had a hot drink.'

The tea steadied her and went down better than she'd expected. The action of pouring it had helped too as it gave her something to focus on rather than the door where she'd stood and her mum had told her to remember that no matter what happened, she would always love her.

But it didn't work as the little boy crying came to her and seemed so vivid. And how he had stopped when she'd held his hand. Suddenly, she wanted to see him again and wondered if her father's widow still lived in the same house. The house she remembered so well. The house of pain.

'May I? Look, I'm sorry to intrude, but you really do look as though you need help. My name's Frederick Holbeck. I'm going into the army next week and feeling very nervous about it. What's your name and why are you on your own?'

Ellen cowered away from him, afraid.

'Hey, I'm not going to hurt you. I'm just worried about you. I'll leave, I'm sorry.'

'No . . . it's all right. I – I'm just retracing my steps. I mean, well, my father brought me here four years ago and . . . he died.'

'He died here?'

'No.'

'Oh, I see, you are going down memory lane. Not always easy. I'm sorry. But there really should be someone with you. London isn't safe for a young lady on her own.'

'I am with a friend. He's gone to his aunt's today.'

Ellen didn't know why but she felt at ease now with him. He looked to her to be in his early twenties. Tall, with blond hair and a gingery coloured moustache that was trimmed neatly to his lipline. He had amused-looking blue eyes, as if he was used to teasing everyone. She found herself telling him, 'My friend is looking into going to Sandhurst.'

'Oh, well, there's a coincidence as that is where I am going. I'm in town buying my uniform and the many things they require you to take with you. What's his name? If he is successful, I can make myself known to him.'

'Adrian Vale.'

'Good lord, I may know him. I went to school with a chap of that name. Sandy hair. Puny-looking.'

'He's not any more – not puny-looking . . . Look, I have to go. I have to meet him at four at the hotel we're staying at.'

'Is he related to you?'

'No, my tutor.'

Frederick looked quizzically at her.

She felt herself colour as she realized that didn't sound good – a young girl with her tutor. 'I live in Leeds, and he has an apartment at our house. I needed to come to London and so he said he would bring me when he came to see about joining up. My gran approves of him doing so.'

'Well, it's a strange arrangement, I must say, and for him to go off and leave you to your own devices too. May I take you safely back to your hotel?'

'No!' The word came out too hurriedly.

'You're afraid of me? Please don't be. I am an honourable gentleman. I am just concerned for your welfare, as Adrian should have been. He should have taken you with him, not left you alone.'

Ellen felt her temper rising. She jumped to Adrian's defence. 'He couldn't take me with him and it's none of your business.' Lifting her hand, she indicated to the waiter to bring her bill.

'I'll see to that and see you safely into a taxi . . . no buts.'

Outside, Frederick hailed a taxi. As she stood by the open taxi door, he said, 'You tell Adrian Vale that he will have me to answer to for leaving you alone.'

As he went to close the door, he hesitated. 'Look, I'll give you my card. Pass it on to Vale, will you? Be good to see him again, if only to give him a piece of my mind.'

He closed the door, turned and walked away. Ellen sighed as she thought, *Just who does he think he is?* But she watched him till he was out of sight. Something about him fascinated her.

Adrian was full of his news when they were in the taxi going to the theatre, when all Ellen wanted to do was to savour the excitement that tickled the muscles of her stomach at the prospect of seeing Ruth once more. They had left early to try to catch her at the theatre door before the performance.

'I cannot believe how smoothly that went, Ellen. My aunt was very pleased to see me as she had a lot to discuss with me, but the outcome is that I can afford to pay my way through Sandhurst. On top of that, my friend's father was a very jolly, welcoming chap. He made a couple of phone calls and I have an interview on Wednesday.'

'I'm glad for you, Adrian, I know you will pass. And I know someone you will meet up with, but he may give you a ticking off.' She pulled Frederick's card out of her bag.

'What? How can you know that?'

Ellen told him about Frederick. His expression went from

embarrassment to complete joy. 'Well, well, Frederick, eh? Freddie Holbeck! I lost touch with him years ago. Be nice to see him again . . . and well, yes, he is right. I shouldn't have left you to roam London on your own, I'm sorry. I'll be with you from now on.'

'There's no need. I'm fine. Anyway, I'm hoping to spend time with Ruth . . . Ooh, I cannot believe I am on my way to see her! Do you think she will recognize me?'

'I'm sure she will. I'm looking forward to meeting her myself, I've heard so much about her.'

The theatre looked magical lit up like a Christmas tree, or so it seemed to Ellen, and there it was – the huge poster that pronounced MISS RUTH FAITH STARRING AS LOLITA IN THIS IS PARIS.

'It's a comedy, you know. It's about the German soldiers having their first taste of Paris. It can be a bit raunchy in places, I believe.'

Ellen didn't care about the play, only seeing Ruth. She could hardly breathe with the tension that gripped her as she looked towards the side of the theatre.

This area was badly lit with just one gas lamp throwing a dim light, but there it was, slightly ajar – the stage door with its sign 'No Unauthorized Entry' seeming to bar her from what she most wanted in all the world. 'Now what do we do, Adrian? What if Ruth is already inside?'

'Well, I think we should just walk in as if we are allowed and see what happens.'

They crept up the stone stairs. At the top they were met with a maze of activity – half-clothed actors calling for attention, needing a costume fastening at the back, or bending to fix a suspender, others stretching themselves while what they assumed were dressers were flitting from one to another carrying out all their demands. Everyone glanced towards her and Adrian but none seemed to take heed of them.

One girl gave Ellen a lovely smile, relaxing her enough for her to ask, 'Can you tell me where I can find Ruth Faith, please?'

'You a fan of hers, duckie?'

'A friend.'

'Well, I ain't seen you before. What you doing up 'ere, anyway?'

'I'm sorry, I just need to see Ruth.'

'Who's this with you? Dishy, ain't yer, mate? What yer doing after the show, eh? I'm at a loose end.' The girl winked at Adrian.

Ellen had never thought of Adrian as 'dishy' or ever heard anyone called that, but it made her giggle to see Adrian blush.

'Ha, I see you've got a sense of humour, girl, you'll do. Come on, I'll take you to Ruth. Lucky cow has a dressing room – she don't have to get changed in this stuffy corridor where all and sundry can see your bits.'

Ellen giggled again. This girl was so funny and outspoken. She reminded her of Hettie. Lovely Hettie. It would be good to see her again, too.

The picture of Hettie standing up in the landau that Ruth had alighted from on that day when Ellen last saw them came to her.

Hettie was going mad. Standing up and swearing at Ellen's father for taking her away from them and not letting them speak to her.

The cockney ways came flooding back to Ellen. It was hard to believe how quickly she'd become one of them as a child, dropping her posh accent and talking like them, and yes, finding love amongst them.

''Ere we are, mate.'

The girl tapped on the door they'd arrived at and opened it. 'Ruth, luv, you've someone 'ere to see you. Says she's a friend.'

Ruth, beautiful, elegant Ruth, stood up and turned, pushing her lovely, thick dark hair from her face. Her so-remembered huge, dark eyes opened wide, then filled with tears as recognition made her mouth drop open.

'Ellen! Oh, Ellen.'

They were in each other's arms, hugging, crying, laughing.

Ruth smelled of the cheap make-up that was caked on her face. But she was Ruth! The Ruth Ellen remembered, and to be in her arms was like coming home.

As they withdrew and stood at arm's length, tears streamed down their faces.

'Where did you come from, mate? Oh, Ellen, I've thought about yer every day, luv.' Her hand brushed Ellen's dark curls. 'You haven't changed, luv. How've yer been? Where've yer been? Every day I hoped there'd be a letter from you. I don't live at the address I gave yer any longer, but with Bett, me friend . . . well, she's more like a mum to me really. She knows the folk who live in me old 'ouse and asks them often if there's any post for me.'

'I couldn't remember your address, Ruth – well, not all of it. But I've thought about you every day too, and Amy. Have you any news of Amy?'

'No, nothing, luv. I just pray she's all right.'

'And Hettie?'

Ruth's face dropped. 'Hettie ain't with us no more, luv. Look, I've so much to tell yer. Can we meet after the show?'

Ellen's throat had tightened with sadness. She nodded.

Ruth looked towards Adrian and smiled at him. 'So, who are you then, mate? Thanks for bringing me Ellen to me.'

'This is Adrian. He's my tutor and friend . . . Oh, I've so much to tell you too, Ruth.'

Ruth hadn't taken her eyes off Adrian. And he stared at her. Ellen felt that she was seeing the coming together of souls, but didn't know why she felt that way, only that she was glad that even though they hadn't spoken to each other it was plain to see that each liked the other.

Adrian coughed, looked uncomfortable, shifted on his feet, then without taking his gaze from Ruth, said, 'Pleased to meet you, Ruth. I've heard a lot about you.'

Ruth took his outstretched hand and held it longer than was normal. 'And I'm pleased to meet you, Adrian.'

The show was so funny, Ellen's sides ached. Ruth was magnificent as the raunchy Lolita, making fun of the German soldiers who hung on her every word, and Ellen loved the scene where Ruth danced with two soldiers, a Russian in front of her and a German behind her, in a kind of goosestep way as she sang in a French accent:

> '*Monsieur, you think that I am yours*
> *And your comrade thinks it too*
> *But we French have come through many wars*
> *And will show you how we do*
> *They will kick you far and wide*
> *Bringing you to your knees*
> *And you will have nowhere to hide*
> *As we all laugh at your pleas.*'

With this she pushed them both and they tumbled and rolled away behind the curtain to an uproar of cheers and a standing ovation.

Ruth took so many bows that Ellen, though bursting with pride, just wanted the audience to stop clapping so that Ruth could step off stage, get changed and be with her once again.

At last Ruth came through the stage door amidst a flurry of kissing and hugging her fellow performers, signing programmes for her fans and calling out, 'I'll be with you in a mo, Ellen, luv.'

The girl who'd first spoken to Ellen called out, 'Hope you enjoyed the show, Ellen. See you later, luv.'

Ellen waved and hoped with all her heart that she really would see her again.

'That's Katie. She's lovely. So, come on then, let's get going.' Linking arms with Ellen and Adrian, who once more looked awkward but glowed with happiness at the same time, Ruth said, 'I'm taking you both to supper.'

Ellen giggled from sheer joy but did wonder what kind of place Ruth would take them to.

She needn't have worried. The supper bar was only a short walk away. When they entered the bright room, Ellen could see Ruth properly. Her pan-stick make-up had gone and her skin glowed with the beauty that Ellen remembered.

But there were differences in Ruth. She was now a woman – there was nothing about her that said young girl of thirteen as she had been when they were last together. But then, five years had passed.

The waiter swept up to them. 'Ruth, how did it go?'

'Very well, Ramon, thank you.'

'I have your usual table ready for you. Three for supper, is it?'

'Yes. This is me mate from a long time ago – we've been reunited at last – and this is her friend, soon to be mine. The table in the corner will be fine, mate, ta.'

When they were seated, Ruth said, 'It'll be pie and mash for me, but I expect you will go for the cheese and port, Adrian, but you, Ellen, I'm not sure, luv.'

There'd been something wistful in Ruth's voice.

'Why did you think me a cheese and port man, Ruth?'

'Oh, it was something from my past. A friend of mine, his name's Abe. We were worlds apart, and him saying that the other way around, to me – that I were a pie and mash girl and him a cheese and port man seemed to endorse that. I've never forgotten it.'

'Well, I'd much prefer the pie and mash.'

'You would?'

Adrian nodded, though what he'd said had surprised Ellen, as she knew different. But she didn't expose him, just smiled at Ruth and said, 'And pie and mash for me, too, Ruth. I haven't had that since we left the ho . . .'

'The bloody rotten orphanage, you mean, Ellen. Never be afraid to talk about it, mate. It was what it was and it shaped us into what we are – strong women who no one can knock over. And that's good. Good always comes from bad.'

Ellen didn't say that it had knocked her over. But then the thought came to her that it hadn't, not really. It had tried but failed, as she too was now a strong woman. Yes, she had the age of a child still, but inside she was a woman with all the knowledge women had. She'd left childhood many years ago.

Chapter Ten

Ruth

Ruth stood outside the supper bar holding Ellen's hand. She felt drained as her story had taken so much out of her, and yet elated too. She still couldn't believe that Ellen had turned up like that out of the blue, and now that she had, she vowed that they would never be apart for long again.

She'd told them about the late Rebekah, the lovely woman who'd taken her in when she'd run away from the orphanage and become like a mother to her, teaching her to make hats which she had sold on the market.

And about Robbie, who had run away from the orphanage before herself, and who she'd met when he was sleeping rough in the market and who'd also moved in with Rebekah. And about Abdi, Rebekah's nephew, and his wife Ebony who now ran a restaurant in Stepney and their son, Horacio, who she adored and who was now away at school.

And then she'd told them about Abe, the posh son of the people of the house where she'd found work, and how both he and Robbie were now fighting in France, having left last month.

Abe was an officer while Robbie was a private, though Robbie, a dancer, had already written to say that he was on cooking duties most of the time and the camp entertainer at night. This made her feel that he at least was safe.

Abe, though, who she knew Robbie was in love with, was in the most danger as Robbie had told her that he regularly led charges on horseback. She feared for him.

She loved them both dearly. Robbie as a brother; Abe, well, he'd meant more to her, but she'd come to realize that they were confused over their feelings for each other and that she would always be loved in the way a sister would be, by both of them.

And she'd told them about Bett, the market trader who'd also helped her and who she now loved like a mum too.

She'd tried to get Ellen to talk, but she told her very little. Only that her father had abandoned her again and had since died and that she lived with her adored gran and her gran's companion named Dilly.

Ruth sensed there was a lot more and hoped that one day Ellen would open up.

Adrian cut into this thought: 'Well, we'd better get back to the hotel, Ellen. You must be tired after your adventures today.'

'Why, what did you do today, Ellen, luv?'

Ruth listened to how Ellen's day had gone.

'I do that often. I go and stand outside and watch the kids play, looking for signs of any of them being unhappy. I check up too. Cook went back there after Matron left. She couldn't settle in the big house, not after Hettie died. Anyway, that's all another story. But, well, I visit Cook and she lets me know that all's well there and I make donations too, when I can. That makes me feel good. It's like I'm really helping in a practical way. And I'm planning on doing a concert there when the season ends.'

'Oh, Ruth, that's good to hear.'

'You should do something like it, luv, it helps. It's like a healing.'

'I will, now I know that you can.'

Still that guard was up, and Ruth felt it like a division between them. That and how far apart their lives had been – she living in the slums of the East End, and Ellen living with monied folk and sounding as if she'd had a good education.

This gulf between them saddened Ruth. She didn't want it to be like that. This Ellen was pensive, unsure. Though at first she'd been gushing and loving, now she was in a kind of shell as if protecting herself. On a whim, she asked, 'Ellen, would you come and stay with me while you're here, luv? I just don't want to be parted from you.'

Ellen's face lit up. She turned to Adrian. 'Will that be all right, Adrian? I really, really want to.'

'Yes, I think you should. It will do you good.'

Ellen turned towards Ruth. The pensive expression was gone, and she held out her arms. Ruth's relief as she went into them spilled her tears. Ellen meant so much to her, she didn't know why. Amy did too, but not as much as Ellen. It had always been like that and was a mystery to her.

Adrian's voice sounded thick with emotion as he told them he would hail a cab for them. As they waited, he took a card from his pocket. 'I think I'll look Frederick up; the name of his club is on his card and then I can get my telling-off out of the way.'

Ruth looked mystified, but Ellen giggled.

'So, who yer in trouble with and why, mate?'

'A friend from the past. He found Ellen in a cafe on her own and took it on himself to become her protector, much to her annoyance. Anyway, it turned out that he knew me and I'm to be the subject of his wrath for leaving her on her own.'

'Oh, yes, the man you met. Well, I reckon you deserve what's coming to you, Adrian. Good luck.'

Adrian laughed as he left them, telling Ellen to make sure she came to the hotel to have dinner with him the next evening.

'I've never known him so relaxed, Ruth. You have a good effect on everyone.'

Ellen snuggled into her when they were seated in the taxi, and it felt good.

Ruth squeezed her.

'Oh, Ellen, I can't tell you how happy I am to have you back.'

When they reached Bett's house all was quiet.

'Bless her, she's gone to bed. You'll love Bett. She's the salt of the earth. But she's getting on in years and gets tired easily these days . . . She's still not one to be crossed, though. She'd skin anyone alive who hurt any of hers, and she considers me one of them, and she will you when she meets yer.'

Ellen giggled; it was a lovely sound. None of them had giggled much when they were last together.

'We'll creep through the living room, Ellen, as that leads to a door to mine and Robbie's flat upstairs – well, it did used to be Robbie's too, till he made a name for himself, as I was telling you. Robbie Grant, he is now – always the lead singer and dancer in any production he appears in and sometimes actor, and the best mate in all the world . . . This way, luv.'

When they were upstairs, the tiredness that Ruth had felt washed over her. She slumped into one of two big comfy chairs that stood each side of the fireplace.

'I'll put the kettle on, Ruth. All that dancing and excitement must have worn you out.'

'It does take it out of you but reliving all those events in me life drained me, luv. A cup of tea would be lovely. Thanks. Yer'll find everything in me little kitchen through there.'

When Ellen came back with the tea, she said, 'It does. I've done that in a nursing home.'

This shocked Ruth. 'Have you been ill, luv? What happened?'

It was one in the morning when Ruth and Ellen slipped off the chairs onto the rug to be close to each other. Both had emptied their souls of all that had happened to them since being little girls and both sobbed as they clung on to one another.

'Ruth, can I come and live with you?'

'Oh, Ellen, what about yer gran? And yer studies, luv?'

'I think Gran is expecting it. She became very withdrawn for a week before I came, then the night before she held me and stroked my hair and said, "Ellen, you're to make your own way in life eventually and I will never stand in your way. If you find after this visit that your path leads away from here, then all I want for you is to be happy." Then she said, "I know in years you are only fifteen, but what has happened to you in your lifetime has made you much older than that, and I think you are ready. All I will need is to know that you are well, happy and safe."'

Ruth was quiet for a moment. This was a lot to take in. She'd forgotten that Ellen was still that young as, like her gran had told her, she was much more mature than that and came across as a young woman. 'Look, luv, I want that. I want us to be together, but I'm turned eighteen this year, and there's something I haven't told yer yet . . . I've been working with the Red Cross for months now and have put meself forward to go to war as a volunteer – a help to the medical staff, an orderly who does a little first

113

aid. I want to do me bit and try to be near to Robbie and Abe.'

'Then I'll do that too. I told you that my ambition is to be a doctor. I already have a lot of knowledge which will stand me in good stead.'

Ruth listened to how the lady who had started the nursing home had taken Ellen for lessons in medicine practice and taught her everything about the human anatomy, and how she took lessons in biology and science with Adrian. 'I can join the Red Cross and learn more. We can go together, Ruth.'

'But, your age, luv. Yer have to be in yer twenties. I'm lying about me age, but—'

'You said yourself that I could pass as the same age as you. I don't have a birth certificate. I wasn't registered. My father told me that once. He said that he thought my mum had done it and that he would get around to it, but when he died Gran's solicitor enquired about my papers, but my father's wife told him that Father hadn't ever registered me as his daughter and so I needn't think that I had any claim on his estate.'

'I'm sorry, luv, that must hurt.'

'It did, but it wasn't unexpected. I'm the child he didn't really want – the one he tried to forget.'

'That makes two of us then as I've no birth certificate and everyone just seemed to have forgotten me. I even made up my birthday and took it as the day I was left at the priest's house.'

Ellen went quiet for a moment but then shocked Ruth to the core.

'Ruth, Mum has never forgotten us . . . I – I mean, well, I think we may be half-sisters.'

'What? What do yer mean, luv?'

As the amazing story unfolded of Ellen having met a woman that she knew to be her own mum and how much she looked like Ruth, and how this woman had had two children before and had left them, and at least one had been left at a priest's house, Ruth's heart swelled with love. When the story came to an end Ruth held Ellen to her. 'I always knew there was a strong connection between us. Now I know why . . . My sister! My little sister!'

The hug ended in a sleepy but happy yawn from Ellen. She tried to suppress it, but it changed her grin into a creased-up face with tears running from her eyes.

'Come on, as yer big sis I'm telling you, it's bedtime for you, mate. You're whacked out and so am I. We'll sleep together tonight then I'll make Robbie's bed up for yer tomorrow.'

Ruth had never known a happiness like she knew as they snuggled up together. To have a sister – as she, like Ellen, was convinced it was so – was the most amazing thing in all the world.

A banging on the door of her flat – and hearing Bett call out, 'I got yer a cup of tea, Ruth. You were late last night, weren't yer? What did yer get up to, luv?' – woke them.

The bedroom door opened. Bett's 'Bloomin' heck, what's this?' made Ruth giggle though she could hardly open her sleepy eyes.

Pushing the covers back, she said, 'Meet me sister, Bett, luv. Me real-life sister!'

Bett looked astounded. 'Yer've got a skin and blister? Well! Would yer Adam and Eve it!'

'Ha, Bett, it must be the shock, as yer don't usually use as much rhyming slang!'

'It is a shock, mate! Where did yer find her . . . ? 'Ello, luv.'

Ellen was sat up now. She grinned a sleepy grin at Bett.

'Gawden Bennett, she's yer double! How yer could have lost her in the first place, I don't know . . . You two, get up. I'll take this tea back down and make some fresh. I want to hear all about it.'

Ruth looked at Ellen. 'That was Bett!'

'I gathered that. I loved her curlers in her hair and her lovely round, shiny face. She looks like a proper mum.'

'Don't be fooled, luv, she's a matriarch and she's got two huge sons who are gangsters and would kill anyone if she asked them to. Did you ever hear what happened to Belton and Gedberg?'

'Yes, everything got better after that . . . Was that Bett's sons?'

'It was.'

'Well, I for one would like to thank them. There was no other way to stop what was happening.'

'You're right, luv. I've never had a moment's guilt over either of them . . . Robbie did, though. He cared for Gedberg. He said it made him feel better to forgive him.'

'Yes, I've been taught that, and sort of did it, but couldn't altogether.'

'I've never tried. I hate the guts of them both. Anyway, we'd better hurry or Bett will have our guts for garters. I'll go first, I'm dying for a pee.'

'Eek, so am I!'

'Right, the lav's downstairs in the backyard. You go, and I'll use the chamber pot.'

Ellen laughed as she scampered out of bed. 'No, I'll use the pot. I've got nothing to put on and you have your warm dressing gown.'

'Blimey, I can't stay here arguing, I'll do it in the bed!' But as she ran down the stairs, Ruth was full of joy at having had her first sisterly tussle – something she never thought she'd ever have in her life.

Chapter Eleven

Ellen

When Ruth came back, Ellen was washed and dressed as she'd found the bowl that she thought Ruth used for the purpose and filled it from the tap in the tiny kitchen. She'd shivered from the coldness of it but nothing could really take the warmth out of her today.

A little giggle had escaped her as the joy of everything had surged through her. She didn't think that she'd ever giggled as much in all her life as she had since she found Ruth. She never wanted to leave her side now but knew she must be fair to her gran and go home with Adrian. She needed to make proper arrangements. She couldn't not do so as she loved her gran with all her heart, and she hoped she'd be a gran to Ruth too, as Ruth had no one of her own – well, until now.

Ruth was washed and dressed too, as she'd done her ablutions downstairs. It appeared that Bett had the luxury of a bathroom which Ruth shared.

Downstairs two steaming mugs of tea stood on the kitchen table for them beside a mound of toast, which smelled delicious.

'Now then, luv, let's 'ave a proper look at yer. I'm still in the dark as to where you came from, but like I say, yer very welcome, and my, you're a pretty thing. You're the sister that got the curls, then? But yer eyes are Ruth's.'

This thrilled Ellen. To have a sister and to look like her was heaven to her. And yes, she knew it was all speculation, but it was all more likely than not from what they looked like – how the woman she'd met had looked so like Ruth too, and with Ruth being left at a priest's house.

'I wonder who yer poor mum is. It's hard to think of her out there without the pair of yer, but no doubt she had no choice but to leave yer, bless her. Not all who take her game up are wicked or callous, yer know. They have feelings. Most are good girls. I know a few. They just fell on hard times and into that way of life.'

This made Ellen feel comforted as she wouldn't like anyone to think badly of her mum. 'My mum told me that she loved me very much. And she said to my father that it was his fault, that she didn't want to give up her babies and that he should help and support her to care for them.'

'There yer go, luv, she sounds like a decent lot, poor sod.'

When Ruth spoke, her voice shook with emotion. 'I can't bear to think of her on her own. I've always known that whoever me mum were she loved me and couldn't help giving me away. I think we should try to find her, Ellen. There's some well-known places where prossies hang out.'

The word grated on Ellen. She didn't like to think of her mum in that way.

'So, she looks like Ruth, yer say?'

'She does, Bett. So much. It was like looking at Ruth when I saw her.'

'Well, that's a start. Leave it with me, girls, I've got a scrapbook full of pictures of Ruth. Some are from when yer were younger, Ruth, and that bloke used to come around the market with his camera, but most are recent since yer struck it good in the theatre. I've folk I can show them to. And some have prossies on their books. I'll put a few around and see what happens. I don't want the pair of yer going anywhere near where these girls 'ang out. Do yer 'ear me?'

They both nodded. Ruth winked at Ellen. Ellen felt warm inside, as if she belonged. This was her true home. She could feel it in her bones.

'Are you standing market today, Ruth, girl?'

Ellen didn't know what Bett meant. Surely Ruth wasn't still a market trader?

'No, but I'm taking me hats down. I'll arrange them next to Ruby's stall and she'll sell them for me. It's been good since she came out of retirement and set up again. I've always got her to rely on.'

'She's bleedin' daft if yer ask me, but then, if you need the money, what else can yer do? I'm lucky to have me boys – they keep me in clover. So, what you going to be up to then, girl, if yer not standing market?'

'I want to spend the day with Ellen before I have to be at the theatre.'

'You didn't say that you still traded your hats, Ruth. How exciting. Where are they? Do you still make them yourself?'

'I do. Theatre wages aren't that good, even for an acclaimed leading lady, luv. I have them all in Robbie's bedroom and me hat-making stuff too. I used to have a store at the back of a cafe that was across the road from the market, but it changed hands and the new people needed the room. Like yer said, Bett, everything's changing . . . Anyway, I'll show you me wares and me equipment, Ellen, when you've finished filling yer face.'

Ruth laughed out loud at her own joke. Ellen couldn't

help but join her. So many of hers and Bett's sayings were taking her back to her childhood – not the bad bit, but the nice bit, as Hettie and Cook used to use the same phrases. Though as for this one, it wasn't said often as they never had a lot to give you to fill your face with.

It felt good to be able to see the good bits of her past now – the times when Ruth, Amy and herself had sat on the stone veranda at the top of the steps that led to the playground and dangled their legs through the railings just chatting, and yes, sometimes giggling. And how after dark she would sometimes creep into bed with Ruth and snuggle up to her. And as she remembered, the feelings visited her again of the complete love that she had for both Ruth and Amy, but mostly for Ruth.

Ruth brought her handcart out of the backyard around to the front. Their giggles filled the street as they stacked the hats in the cart and passers-by called out a cheery word to them. On the walk to the market, they took it in turns to push the cart, only their giggles became belly laughs when it was Ellen's first go as she found she couldn't control it and a couple of times almost tipped it over, blaming the cobbled streets.

The smells hit them first as they turned into the market-place – a heady mix of food cooking, and fresh fruit and vegetables all mixed with the aroma of tobacco as every man and woman seemed to have a cigarette hanging from their lips, and most squinted from the effect of the curling smoke stinging their eyes.

All around them was hustle and bustle, permeated by voices calling out their wares and having a joke with one another.

Their first port of call was for hot, sweet tea from the stall Ruth told her had once belonged to Bett.

Then when they got to Ruby's stall Ellen thought it looked lovely with shiny apples and pears displayed next to cabbages and carrots. But she was sad to notice the empty boxes next to these that she guessed would have held fruit and veg from across the sea. These brought home the stark reality to her of what Adrian had read aloud from his newspaper of how they were to expect shortages of food supplies.

An inward shudder passed through her as she thought of the horrific stories of merchant ships being sunk by the Germans at a terrible cost of young lives. Her heart went out to them and their families.

Another broad cockney voice that sounded the same as Bett's brought her out of these thoughts.

'Mornin', Ruth, girl. Who we got 'ere then?'

'Me sister, Ruby. Ellen. We were in the home together, only we didn't know then that we were sisters.'

'Well, that's a tale and a half. Pleased to meet yer, Ellen. A kin of Ruth's is a kin of us all.'

Ellen smiled, feeling a little intimidated by Ruby's abrupt way of speaking, even though what she was saying was nice to hear.

'You setting up today, Ruth?'

'Only if yer think yer can cope with selling me hats, Ruby. Usual ten per cent?'

'Where you off to then? Blimey, I don't know why yer bother with this hat game when yer've got your stage work.'

'I have to, Ruby. Me stage work can dry up at any time, as you know. But if it's any trouble . . .'

'No, you know it ain't any bleedin' trouble. Ten per cent would be welcome as yer hats sell better than me carrots these days – bleedin' rotten they are by the time I get them. Bloomin' war!'

As Ellen helped Ruth to empty the boxes of her lovely hats, she was mesmerized by them and amazed at them being Ruth's own handiwork. Mostly they were bonnets made of felt, but all were different. Some had intricate patterns stitched on the side, others roses made of silk, and yet others had huge silk bows. The colours ranged from dark red to navy blues, browns and greens. Three of them weren't bonnets, but works of art. Too good for a market stall. Made of a stiff netting with their curved brims edged in satin and a trim on one side of feathers and pearls, they were beautiful. So much so that Ellen had to remark on them and asked, 'Do hats like these normally sell here, Ruth?'

'They do, luv. The rich women often send their personal maids to me stall to find something for them. I've even had commissions from them in the past.'

'It were a pity that hat shop you used to supply closed down, Ruth. Yer should have had a go at taking it over. Bett would have 'elped yer out. She's loaded is Bett.'

'You know me plans, Ruby. I can't take anything on yet.'

'Madness, I call it. What do you want to give up what you have to go to bleedin' war for, eh?'

Ruth just sighed.

Ellen was relieved to hear Ruby change tack. 'Have you heard from Robbie, or Reg, luv? And 'ow's Ted doing, eh?'

'I've had one letter from Robbie, luv.' Ruth told Ruby what Robbie had to say.

'That's good news. Got himself a cushy little number then? Nothing from Reg?'

Reg was the man Ruth had told Ellen about – a vagabond when she first met him, but he'd fallen from a great height and had climbed back by finding himself a rich widow. And now he'd gone to war and was reinstated as a captain in the army.

'No. I ain't heard from Reg but see Ted every night at the theatre. He's doing all right, Ruby, and sends his love. He says he'll drop by one of these days.' Ruth turned to Ellen. 'Ted was one of them who were living rough. I met him with the others when I first ran away. He's a musician who was down on his luck. He used to earn a bit of money playing on the street corner over there and then treat the others to a jug of ale and a butty. Now, he's part of the orchestra.'

'It sounds like you fell on your feet with so many friends looking out for you, Ruth.'

'I did in a way, luv, though it wasn't all plain sailing.'

With the last hat on the stand, Ruby made Ellen laugh as she called out, 'Hats to keep yer lug'oles warm! Come and get them! When they're gone, they're gone!'

'I'd like to buy three hats, please.'

'Three, Ellen? Yer not just being kind, are yer? What do you want with three hats?'

'One for me – the green one with the rose on. And one for my gran and one for Dilly. I'll take a brown one for Dilly as her Sunday-best winter coat is brown and a dark red one for Gran as one of her coats is a floor-length wool coat in that colour. She'll like the one with a bow, but Dilly would best suit one of those that you have stitched a pattern on – Dilly doesn't like anything fancy.'

'Thanks, mate. That's given me a great start to the day. Put them underneath for Ellen to have later, Ruby, luv.'

'I'll put mine on, thanks, Ruby. The wind's a bit cutting. It'll keep me lug'oles warm.'

They all burst out laughing at this. But though she laughed with them, Ellen had the thought that the words had come so naturally to her as that was the way she spoke from being put in the orphanage. At first, just to be like the others, but in the end, it had been a comfort to express herself in the way that the cockneys did.

There were more giggles as the first one she tried on was too big for her.

''Ow you going to know what size to put away for yer gran and Dilly, luv?'

'Dilly will need large. She's round all over. And Gran a small as she has a tiny frame and is skinny.'

'Right, but you can change them later if you get it wrong, luv. You can even measure them and bring me the proper size and I'll make them especially for them.'

Ruth didn't offer for her to do the purchase that way round now which made Ellen have the feeling that Ruth was a lot worse off than she appeared to be. She didn't say anything but thought to try to find out in ways that wouldn't embarrass her.

When they left the market, it was to many stallholders calling out to Ruth. It was obvious that they all loved her. This made Ellen feel happy, as to be loved, in her eyes, meant the world.

'So, luv, what would yer like to do? I thought to show yer some of London. I bet you ain't never seen anything like the palace, or did your dad take you there that day I saw you in the landau?'

'No . . . He couldn't wait to get rid of me. He had it all planned.' Ellen filled in the details of that day that she'd left out the night before when they'd had their chat.

'He sounds like a pig.'

Ellen didn't remark on this, but was surprised to feel the pain of it, but then, Ruth would only see him in a bad light – why would she see him any differently? *She doesn't have the memories that I have of the times when he was loving and kind.*

Not that she'd seen that side of him for many years, but still, she did have the memory of them to keep for ever.

'I'd like to go to my father's old house, Ruth. I just want to try to get a glimpse of my brother.'

'He'd be my half-brother, then, wouldn't he?'

'Of course, I never thought of that. Oh, Ruth, we're a family, a real blood family.'

'Will you be welcome at the house, Ellen?'

'No. I'm sure I won't, but that won't bother me. I just have this burning desire to catch sight of him and to make sure he's all right. I've worried about him from the moment I met him. He was such a lovely little boy. He warmed to me immediately. He has dark eyes too, and dark curly hair like mine.' She fumbled in her bag. 'Here's the address. Sardinia Street, West End.'

'That's a long way from here but we can get the Underground. Come on, luv. Have you ever been on the Underground?'

'No.'

'Well, you're in for a treat. It's like you're going down into the bowels of the earth.'

'Isn't that where Hettie . . .' Ellen could have bitten her tongue off when she saw the pain on Ruth's face. 'I'm sorry, Ruth, I shouldn't have mentioned it. It just slipped out.'

But Ruth said, 'Don't worry, luv. It's just such a horrific memory that I don't like to think of it.' And then brightened her voice and added, 'Come on, slow coach.' Ellen felt her distress. And more so poor Hettie's. She, like Ruth, had known the same deep despair; the terror of thinking that you might have been made pregnant through a disgusting and painful rape was awful enough, but for Hettie it had been a reality. And one she just couldn't face.

Hettie's round, smiling face came to her and how she seemed happy with everything, taking the stance that it was better to just put up with Belton's disgusting abuse of them than to make a fuss, as it hurt less then. But in the end, she'd broken.

It only took a few minutes to reach the Underground. Ruth didn't speak the whole way and Ellen could sense her upset – knew her thoughts would have been along the same lines as her own.

Poor Hettie, though I have walked the path you trod, I've never reached the desolation you must have done to do such a thing as to jump in front of a train. I send my love up to you and remember the many kindnesses you showed me. Rest in peace, dear Hettie. Ellen quickly wiped away the tears that had filled her eyes and was glad that Ruth was walking a few paces in front of her and would not have seen her heartache.

Forcing herself to think of other things, for Ruth's sake and her own sanity, Ellen allowed the exciting experience of her first venture into this different world of underground trains to come to the fore.

She'd never been anywhere like it and was partly scared, partly exhilarated by the noise, the rush of people going up and down the hundreds of steps, and by the train appearing like a snake out of the tunnel.

The house was just as she remembered it. White-fronted, its four storeys seemed to almost touch the sky. She held her breath as they stood outside the black iron gate and gazed at the brass knocker on the shiny black door.

'Do you know any of the servants, Ellen? Maybe it'd be an idea to go down the steps to the kitchens and talk to them first.'

'Yes, I know Cook well and Florrie, the upstairs maid. Cook used to give Florrie treats for me as they knew I wasn't being fed during the day.'

'It was that bad? Oh, Ellen, I had no idea, luv.'

'It wasn't my father's widow who put me into the orphanage. I've never met her. It was his first wife. She did a lot of bad things to me. She's dead now.'

'You're trembling, luv . . . Are yer sure this is what yer want to do?'

'Yes, I have to know how my – our – brother is . . . Oh, look, the door's opening!'

A child's voice could be heard complaining. 'No, Nanny, it's cold. I don't like the cold.'

'But you have to have your walk, Christopher. Come on, now. Be a good boy and put your best foot forward. You know Nanny loves you and will only make you do what is good for you.'

Ruth grinned at Ellen.

At that moment, little Christopher spotted them. He looked directly at Ellen. His face creased into a frown, then lit with a lovely smile. 'Hello.'

'Hello. How are you?'

'Nanny is making me go for a walk and I don't want to.'

'Walking is good for you. Do as Nanny says, there's a good boy.'

'Who are you . . . Christopher, you must not speak to strangers!'

'But she's nice.'

'You don't know that, now come along.'

Ellen turned towards Ruth. She knew her face was beaming, but shock zinged through her to see that Ruth had tears streaming down her face.

'Why is that lady crying, Nanny?'

'It's none of our business. Please, Christopher, come with Nanny, and don't say a word of this to your mama, or Nanny might be made to leave.'

On an impulse, Ellen said, 'We're his sisters – at least I am, but Christopher shares the same mum as Ruth, my half-sister.'

'What? What are you talking about? Who are you? Why are you here saying such preposterous things?'

'I'm Ellen Hartington. My father died two years ago whilst visiting me and his mother in Leeds.'

'This is ridiculous. What do you want?'

'Nothing, only to see that my little brother is all right.'

'How can he be your brother? His mother isn't old enough to have a daughter your age! Please go away.'

'Ask Cook and Florrie, the upstairs maid, about me, they will tell you.'

The nanny took hold of Christopher's hand and turned him back towards the house. 'We won't walk today, Christopher. Come on, we're going inside.' When she reached the top of the three steps she turned, 'You're mad! Mad! Don't come near here again.'

With this she was gone, and Ruth's distress penetrated Ellen as the failure of her quest to be recognized as Christopher's sister sank in.

'Ruth, Ruth, love, are you all right?'

'I am, Ellen. You were so calm. You handled that really well, whereas just seeing the little chap undid me.'

'I don't feel calm. I feel like breaking that door down and grabbing little Christopher and taking him with us.'

'I know, luv, I feel the same. What a lovely little boy. I love him with all my heart. He seemed to recognize you, Ellen, but he couldn't have remembered yer. I think there's a sixth sense in these things. I've always felt it with you.'

'And me with you, Ruth. I have longed to be with you from the moment you left the orphanage. It was like a sore festering in me. Gran knew about it, and it is why she didn't object to me coming to find you. And I don't think she will object to me coming to live with you . . . Oh, Ruth, I so wish you could come up to Leeds to meet her.'

'I can, luv. I get Sunday, Monday and Tuesday off. I could come back with you and stay for them days.'

'Oh, that would be wonderful!' Not heeding that they were in a posh, busy street, Ellen flung her arms around Ruth. It was the best feeling when Ruth hugged her back.

Chapter Twelve

Ruth

The rest of the day went so quickly, and Ruth only had time to take Ellen to see Buckingham Palace, which looked lovely with the low winter sun shining on it. And though the King wasn't in residence as the flag wasn't flying, Ellen loved it and clapped her hands when the guards marched up and down.

The time to take her to the hotel to meet with Adrian came around all too soon.

Adrian was waiting outside the foyer and came up to the taxi door. His smile jolted Ruth. She couldn't believe it was possible to be attracted to someone else after the way she'd fallen so heavily for Abe, but then, Bett had told her she would have many loves before she found the right one, so perhaps this was normal. She smiled brightly back at him, not wanting him to guess what was going on in her head.

'How long before you have to be at the theatre, Ruth? Are you able to have tea with us?'

'Yes, I can. I must be there for five thirty. There's a lot to do before curtain up.'

When they were sat in a small room off the foyer and tea – a plate of sandwiches and a pot of tea – had been served in dainty bone china, they chatted away about this and that, and Ruth felt that she'd known Adrian for years.

'So, did you get your telling-off by that horrid man, Adrian?'

'I did, Ellen, and he really isn't horrid at all. He's a good sport actually, always was. I was bullied a lot at school, and he always stuck up for me. I owe him a lot as it wasn't easy. He often brought the wrath of the others down on himself for looking out for me – the puny one.'

Ruth saw Ellen blush and wondered if it was talking about this Frederick chap or at what Adrian had said. She soon found out.

'Yes, I know I was puny, Ellen, and I know it's what you thought of me when we first met, especially with me having an asthma attack within minutes of us getting acquainted. But I don't mind so there's no need to blush.'

'Well, you ain't puny now, mate, far from it. The country air Ellen's been telling me about must suit yer.'

'Ruth's coming up to stay for a few days when we go back, Adrian. I want her to meet my gran and to see our house and your school.'

It was Ruth's turn to blush as Adrian's look of joy at this news really affected her. A shiver went down her spine – a nice one, but one that confused her even more.

'That will be lovely, Ruth. You'll be made very welcome. I'd love to show you my schoolroom.'

'As long as yer don't try to teach me to talk proper like you two do. I'm a cockney girl through and through.'

'And yet your diction on stage is brilliant. Is it hard to do that when it isn't how you naturally speak?'

Ruth glared at Adrian. 'No, it ain't. Acting's acting, mate. We are trained just as you are in your job.'

'Oh, I didn't mean any offence, Ruth. I'm sorry if it came across like that. I love your accent and you should never change. I was just admiring the way you can sound so completely different for your work.'

Relaxing a little, Ruth told him, 'I can do many accents, depending on the part I am playing. But I love me own best.'

'So you should.'

With Ellen yawning, the subject changed, and Ruth was glad as that had been an awkward moment.

'Yer tired, luv. I'm not surprised after we sat up so late.'

'Well, you still have your room here, Ellen, and all of your clothes. Why don't you go up to it and have a rest, then you can order a bath later and dress for dinner, my dear. I'll take Ruth to the theatre.'

'There's no need for that. But I'd like it if you both came to pick me up again. I liked it last night. Sometimes it can get a bit hairy travelling on me own back to the East End that late at night. And Ellen needs to bring a few things to mine.'

'We'll do that. We'll wait at the stage door for you.'

With this, Ruth excused herself, hugging Ellen before she left. She hated leaving her and found herself wanting to mother her – tuck her up for an hour, and lie on the bed with her – but she knew she mustn't become that kind of sister as she could soon spoil things.

When they woke the next day, Ellen was a lot brighter.

'I have to go to the Red Cross today, Ellen. Do you want to come with me, luv? You can see how the land lies for them believing your age and see if they'll take you on . . . only, well, it costs. And if we've a chance of going, we'll have to pay our way. We'll need uniforms, and our passage to wherever they send us. It ain't going to be easy.'

'Oh, I didn't know that. Yes, I want to come. I really do.'

'Yer might need someone to speak for you too.'

'Adrian would. He's already said that he believes that I should go.'

'He's very forward-thinking. What about your gran? Would she fund yer? I'd help if I could, but I'm struggling to get enough together for meself, even though I'm working night and day.'

'I thought you were. Oh, Ruth, it shouldn't be like this. The soldiers need us, the money should be there to take us to them. But yes, I can raise the money to pay for us both, as Gran has put a fund aside for me and I can access it whenever I need it.'

'That's good, but I'll get mine together, thanks. I want to feel that I did it meself. I'm getting near to the amount and Ruby did well with me hats today, which means I will have to spend a couple of days making more bonnets, so won't be able to take you out much . . . But are you sure yer up to going to war with me? They say it's a hard life, blood and gore, death and disease, and all under the fire of the Germans.'

'I am. The medical side anyway. I won't know about the other till it happens. But getting them to believe that I'm in my twenties is the first obstacle.'

'You would never take you for just fifteen. And I can make yer look older. Yer hair for a start. We'll do it up in a more sophisticated style. And I know a couple of tricks using stage make-up. All you have to do is believe it – that's the first rule in acting. Believing you are the character. And if you act how you did this morning with that nanny, luv, they'll believe you.'

'It was lovely seeing Christopher, wasn't it?'

'It was, though it set up a longing in me for him to know me and to know the love I feel for him.'

'I know. I already knew I loved him, but like you, I want him to know me and to love me.'

Ruth sighed. 'Well, luv, eat yer porridge as we have to go.'

The church hall was buzzing with activity when they arrived. Girls chatted as they took their coats off, and Red Cross officials seemed a lot more agitated than normal as they tried to get some sort of order, walking around flapping clipboards.

'I've never seen it like this, mate. I wonder what's going on?'

'Order! Order, please!'

Miss Jaminson, the senior official, booming out this instruction brought silence.

'Now, can we all please settle down? We have news to share, so please sign in as quickly as you can.'

Miss Jaminson looked in their direction. Seeing Ellen, she came over. 'And who is this, Ruth?'

'Me sister, Miss Jaminson . . . well, me twin, actually.'

Miss Jaminson looked Ellen up and down. Ruth was glad to see that Ellen held her head high and looked every bit a young woman in her twenties. The subtle make-up helped as it took away all traces of the young girl face – not that Ellen had many signs of that, which Ruth found sad.

'Well, you do resemble each other, very much so, but you've never mentioned a sister before.'

It was Ellen who answered.

'We were separated a long time ago, Miss Jaminson. We've only just found each other . . . Well, I found Ruth after she had a review in *The Bystander* magazine. I was adopted by a well-to-do couple but after my adoptive mother died, I was taken to live with my adoptive father's mother in Leeds. I would very much like to be considered for training. I know a lot about medical practices, the human anatomy and blood circulation. I have studied under a Miss Roland, who runs a nursing home, and my tutor made biology and science lessons come alive for me.'

Ruth thought Ellen magnificent and felt almost humble in her presence.

'Well! Chalk and cheese comes to mind – in a nice way, of course, but though you have had the education and upbringing that Ruth missed out on, she has shown a good ability and a natural learning for all we teach her. She will pass her certificate very soon . . . That said, yes, Ellen, we will welcome you. We need many volunteers at the moment, as you will find out today.'

What they found out came in an announcement when they were all sitting down in a circle.

'We have been asked to send nursing help as part of the Voluntary Aid Detachment to both France and Belgium. Even though Germany has invaded Belgium, there are many of our soldiers, as well as Belgian and French soldiers and refugees still in hospitals on the border and the staff are struggling to cope. I am asking for volunteers.'

Miss Jaminson glance towards Ruth and Ellen. 'You must be twenty-three to thirty-eight years of age, qualified to our certificate standard and be able to pay your own way.'

Ruth saw Ellen go to speak then change her mind, then to her amazement, stand.

'May I speak, Miss Jaminson?'

'Yes. What is it, Ellen?'

136

'Ruth and I don't know our true age. Neither of us have a birth certificate to give our exact birth; we were only told that we were left with a priest and that he took us to the orphanage. They counted our birthdate from then. I was adopted at the age of ten and that was at the turn of the century. My adoptive grandmother could testify to that.'

Ruth couldn't believe how Ellen could fib so convincingly and even to back the lie up with offering evidence. Surely her grandmother wouldn't lie for her, would she? It seemed to her that it was Ellen who should be the actress. She was so different to the child-Ellen. The timid, weepy child badly treated by Belton.

She looked at Miss Jaminson's face, saw she was unsure but before she could speak, Ellen spoke again. 'I believe that I could pass your certificate. I have practical experience and extensive knowledge and I can pay mine and Ruth's way.'

'I see. Well, I will have to give this consideration and put it to the board. Thank you, Ellen.'

But Ellen wasn't done. She seemed determined to further their cause.

'Please will you tell the board that if we are allowed to go, then I will sponsor one other to go too . . . That isn't blackmail, but a persuasion tool as we so desperately want to go to help our soldiers . . . I am trying to get accepted into medical school to become a doctor and my learning so far has all been channelled towards that aim. However, that is something I can do in the future. I see this as an opportunity that I don't want to miss to use the skills I have and the desire in me to do everything I can to help our war effort.'

Miss Jaminson looked lost for words. Ruth felt a little embarrassed. Ellen was overdoing it a bit. She glanced around her. More than one of those in attendance had their mouths open in astonishment. She knew how they felt. This was a different Ellen – mature beyond her years, yes, but a statesman-like young woman who had herself and everyone in the room in awe. She thought about Adrian. Had he been the influence that had brought this change about? Or had it been her time in the nursing home that Ellen had spoken of? Or her grandmother? Or maybe all three? But whatever it was, she so wished that she too could be the same.

Being an actress was something to hide behind – a way of being someone else, someone better than herself, and being accepted as that person. She knew this, but now, as she looked at Ellen, she wanted to gain the skills to be like Ellen, her amazing, lovely sister, and not to have to pretend ever again to be someone else. *I want to be proud to be just me.*

She raised her eyes to heaven and saw the beautiful Rebekah's face smiling down on her. She seemed to be saying, *Rebekah wants you to be proud of yourself, girl.*

In her mind she said, *I will be. I'll do me best.*

Not knowing how, she found herself standing too. Now she had to add to the fib. She wouldn't act a part, she would be herself, supporting her sister, doing all they could together to get to go and do their bit. 'There's truth in what Ellen says, Miss Jaminson. We don't know our birthdate, but there's someone still at the orphanage who remembers when we were brought in. I can get her to speak for us too.'

Ruth crossed her fingers behind her back in the hope that if they did want them to evidence their age, lovely Cook from the orphanage and Ellen's gran would stand up for them.

'Very well, both. I commend your fight and determination

and admire your dedication. In everything I have witnessed, I would say that, yes, you are of the correct age to take on the task in hand, but I will have to consult the board members, and you both will have to address passing the certificate . . . Now, are there any others amongst you that will offer your services?'

Two or three hands went up. Ruth was glad to see that Alison put hers up. She knew she couldn't afford the cost of the trip, but there was no one that Ruth would like to benefit from Ellen's offer more than Alison. She really liked her.

A plump girl, who was always hungry, Alison had a jolly nature. She could see something funny in the direst of situations and often lifted them all.

Ruth smiled over at her and nodded. Alison grinned back and Ruth thought she'd make sure that it was her that Ellen sponsored as she knew that Ellen would like Alison too.

'Right, thank you, girls. I would have liked a few more, but please think about it, and speak to your parents as we have a few days to put names forward, and you young men' – Miss Jaminson addressed the five young men who attended the class, all hoping to become orderlies as each had a reason why they were unable to join the army to fight – 'you mustn't feel left out. There will be news for you, I'm sure.' Miss Jaminson turned towards her and Ellen.

'Now, Ellen and Ruth, come with me. The rest of you, I want you to practise bandaging each other. Pick a partner. One of you has a supposed broken ankle, the other dresses it. I will examine your work when I have finished with Ruth and Ellen.'

They followed Miss Jaminson to a corner of the hall where there was a screen, which Ruth knew she often used to section a piece of the hall off to give some privacy to whoever was taking their exam.

Nerves tingled her stomach. If that's what was happening, she hoped with all her heart that she would pass. But what if Miss Jaminson questioned them further and they got tied up in knots? Once more, Ruth lifted her eyes to heaven, but this time she prayed to the Holy Mary. She loved the Holy Mary and trusted that she would help in all things.

When she'd lived with Rebekah she'd gone to Rebekah's chapel and loved it, but in her heart, she'd always believed she was a Catholic – why else would her mum have left her with a priest? And after once seeing a statue of the Holy Mary in her flowing blue cloak, she'd just known that she was special. *I need you to be special for me now, Holy Mary. Please help me to pass me exam and me and Ellen to be accepted.*

'Right, girls. I need to go to the board with concrete evidence that you're both a good choice. You both having your certificate is the best way to do that, besides being able to pay your own passage . . . So, Ruth, I will put an exam paper on this table for you and while you work your way through that, I will put Ellen through the practical side of the exam. Let's get started, girls. I want this completed by the time today's session comes to an end.'

As Ruth worked her way through what turned out to be easy questions for her, she could hear mutterings like, 'Excellent! The best I have seen.' And, 'Very good, well done!' At one point, she even heard Ellen saying, 'May I show you the way that I have been shown to stop bleeding quickly? We had a patient in the nursing home who haemorrhaged, and Miss Roland used a book. She put a gauge pad on first then pressed hard with a book on top of that and it worked.'

'Yes, very good, it is good to know different ways. But, my dear, you will be out in the field and may not have anything other than your own physical strength to apply pressure with, so it is good that you know the conventional way too. And you do, that is an excellent job.'

In this Ruth could hear Miss Jaminson warming to Ellen as if they were kindred spirits, and she knew that in medical things they were. Her pride in her sister swelled even more as she tackled the last question. Sighing with relief, she felt satisfied that she'd mastered all of them.

But as the tension in her released, she began to realize what she and Ellen were proposing to do. For her, it would mean giving up her stage career where she could lose herself in being someone else. *But this will be for me – Ruth Faith. Nothing to hide behind.* She consoled herself with the thought that if it did happen, she'd have Ellen by her side as surely, knowing their story, they wouldn't part them?

For Ellen, it would mean so much more. She might look older and act it, but that didn't make her older. She really wasn't much more than a child. She'd been cossetted for years. Could she really leave her grandmother, who it was clear she adored? Would she really cope with all they would surely face?

These worries were lost in her concentration as she took her practical exam, while Ellen took her written one. Once more, she sailed through it and when they rejoined Ellen, she'd completed the exam paper.

As Miss Jaminson perused their papers, she said, 'Well, my dears, you have both passed with flying colours. Twins by birth and twins by nature. Well done. I am particularly proud of you, Ruth, as you knew nothing of the medical world when you came to me, and I am in awe of you and your

141

knowledge, Ellen. When the time comes you will make an excellent doctor, my dear. Whether you should give that quest up to be an aid to nurses in France or Belgium, I'm not sure, but I do know you are sorely needed, both of you, and I will put your case as favourably as I can. After all, the powers that be are turning a blind eye to boys of fifteen and sixteen who are volunteering and lying about their age, and have no birth certificates, so two girls who genuinely don't know their age should surely be accepted.'

At this Ruth felt the guilt of their deceit and knew that Ellen did as she saw her hang her head.

'Is anything wrong?'

Ellen spoke up quickly. 'No, Miss Jaminson. I just felt humbled for a moment and wished things were different and I could go on to be a doctor as planned, but I am not regretting my decision. I will do all I can to help the sick and wounded and if that means assisting in the way you say, then I will.'

'Good. Well, you can both go now if you like. I need to assess the work the others have been doing, and then class will break up for today. There is so much for me to do, other than teach at this moment.'

With this, she left them.

Ellen looked over at Ruth. Ruth put her finger to her lips to hush her from what she was going to say as she felt sure it was something that some listening ear would pick up on and expose them over.

'Let's get our coats, luv.'

Once outside, she hugged Ellen to her. 'My amazing, wonderful sister. I love you.'

Ellen smiled her lovely smile. 'And I love you, Ruth . . . my twin.'

They both giggled as they hurried away from the church hall. Once out of sight, that giggle turned to an amazed laugh.

'How did you think of them lies, Ellen?'

'I don't know. Anyway, you started it, saying we were twins!'

'I know, but it suddenly struck me that if we were, it would be easier as whatever age I said I was, you would be that age too.'

They giggled together like two naughty little girls who'd got away with something really bad and Ruth thought how much her life was changing with Ellen having come into it. A change for the better that she so welcomed. She took Ellen's hand.

'Oh, Ruth, I hope they accept us. It will mean that I truly can stay with you.'

'It will, me darlin'. It will.'

Silently she prayed it would as a little worry entered her. When she said things like this, Ellen did show her true age. Would she really pull this off? And would she cope if they were separated? *Please don't let it happen.*

Chapter Thirteen

Ellen

The days went by so quickly that Ellen couldn't believe that she was packing her bags to go home already.

Adrian was picking them up in a taxi any minute and poor Ruth wasn't near finished as she flapped about this and that being suitable for her to wear when staying at Gran's.

'Ruth, stop being so daft. Gran isn't a snob, I told you. She, too, was born out of wedlock and knows what we've been through . . . Well, she wasn't put in a home, but she was unwanted so knows what that feels like. She won't judge you, I promise. And I know she will love you.'

A toot on a horn heralded the arrival of Adrian.

'Come on . . . yes, that frock is perfect for day wear. Put it in your valise and do it up. That's your final decision, it has to be.'

Gathering up her own small case and the hat box that contained the hats for Gran and Dilly – she was wearing her own – Ellen made for the stairs. Bett was at the bottom of them. 'Well, me girls, yer off then?'

'Yes, Bett. But we'll soon be back.'

'Yer'd better be!'

When Ruth came out of the flat, she asked, 'Any news on our mum, Bett?'

144

'No, I'd 'ave told you, luv, but don't give up 'ope, eh? You go and have a good time with Ellen and I'll see yer when you get back.'

'You know which hats to let Ruby take to market now, don't you?'

'Go on with yer, darlin', and stop fussing.'

Ruth flung her arms around Bett's neck. 'Ta, luv, I'll miss you.'

'And I'll miss you, duckie. Now get going before I start to blub.'

As they went to go through the connecting door to Bett's flat to make their way to the road at the front, Bett said, 'Hey, you. Aren't you going to give me a hug before you go? Come 'ere, luv.'

Ellen felt warm inside as this big woman enveloped her in her arms. 'Thanks, Bett. I'll be back. But like Ruth, I'll miss you while we're gone.'

Bett patted her back. 'Off yer go, then.'

Ellen felt that Bett was near to tears. She felt her own throat tighten as she doubted that Bett had been parted from Ruth since she'd first moved into the flat upstairs.

They greeted Adrian with a kiss. Ellen noticed that Ruth's was more than a peck. It was nice to see them growing close as she'd had the idea that, apart from her time at the theatre, Ruth was lonely in the way that she herself had been at home – surrounded by older people. Not that Adrian was old, but he'd been an authority over her.

Aggie came to her mind. How lovely it had been having Aggie as a friend.

'That was a big sigh, luv. And you went into yerself again. You often do that. When that happens to me, I think of something funny, or do a little dance, or sing a funny song from one of the musicals that I have acted in. It works.'

Ellen was glad that Ruth hadn't asked her what it was she was thinking about. She had told Ruth about Aggie but hadn't gone into detail. She didn't want to visit it all again.

On the train the talk was all about the war. Adrian had been accepted for the specialist training and told them that he had such a short time to get everything ready that he'd spent the day before at the outfitter's with Frederick and how glad he was that they had met up again.

'He asks every day about you, Ellen, and is mortified that he made you so cross.'

'Oh? I hadn't thought any more about him, so he needn't worry.'

Ruth changed the subject. 'So, Adrian, yer haven't told us yet yer thoughts on what might happen for us.'

'My thoughts are that you are both very brave women, and I am proud of you. However, I'm not sure what Annie – Ellen's gran – will think of it all. She could go one way or the other – back you both and raise no objections, or she could put her foot down and expose Ellen's true age. She isn't an easy woman to read.'

'She is forward-thinking, though. She actively encouraged me to follow my dream to become a doctor. She didn't put any argument as to my age then. I honestly think she is prepared for me going away . . . Sadly, I think that is what was making her so in the doldrums before I left.'

'I do too. But from what I know of her and her spirit, she will have lifted herself out of that state now.'

When they reached Rose Cottage, Gran and Dilly must have been waiting and watching through the window as the door opened almost as soon as they pulled up in the car. Dilly came bouncing forward to hug her. 'Eeh, lass, it's good to see you.'

To Ellen, the hug meant she was home, but as she looked over Dilly's shoulder and saw her gran not attempting to come out, but holding on to the door jam, a trickle of concern tightened her throat. Gran looked so frail.

Smiling as she walked towards her, Ellen's mind settled as Gran held out her arms. Her voice sounded steady as she said, 'Oh, my darling, it is good to have you home. The place has been quiet without you.'

Ellen snuggled into her gran for a moment, surprised to feel how thin she was, but just so happy to see her that she didn't give heed to it. 'I've missed you too, Gran, but, oh, I've had the best of times . . . Gran, this is my sister, Ruth!'

'Your sister, Ellen?'

'Yes, Gran. I'll explain later, but we know that we are sisters even without the overwhelming evidence we have.'

'Well! This is a shock, but, Ruth, I am very pleased to meet you. You have put a lightness into my Ellen . . . And, yes, looking at you, my dear, you do so resemble each other . . . the eyes, and the colour of your hair, you could almost be twins.'

Gran looked mystified as Ruth and Ellen burst out laughing.

Adrian stepped forward. 'Don't mind them, Annie. They have a lot to tell you and being twins comes into it. How are you?'

While Gran and Adrian chatted, Dilly greeted Ruth. 'Nice to meet you, Ruth, lass.'

'And me you. Yer just like Ellen described yer.'

'Ha, a cockney! Eeh, takes me back to the helper I was

147

telling you of sometime ago, Ellen. Nice to meet another. But by, I hope I fare better with understanding you.'

'You will, Dilly. Ruth doesn't use rhyming slang and she doesn't talk the hind leg off a donkey, as I gathered the help did.'

They all giggled at this from Ellen. Then Dilly said, 'Well, that's good to hear. You're very welcome, Ruth.'

Ruth loved everything about Rose Cottage and especially the schoolroom. 'It's much nicer than I even imagined, Adrian. It's a lovely place for the kids to learn.'

Adrian beamed.

Dilly brought them back into the house as she called out that tea was ready.

As they made their way up the path, Ruth caught hold of Ellen's arm and in a frantic whisper said, 'I need to pee first, Ellen.'

'Oh, what am I thinking of! Come on, I'll take you to the bathroom. We'll take your valise up at the same time.'

As soon as they entered Ellen's bedroom, Ruth exclaimed, 'Oh, this is lovely! Yer've a lovely view. Am I sleeping in here with you, luv?'

'You are. There's a shake-me-down under my bed.'

'I won't bother with that, luv, I'll get in with you. Yer bed's big enough.'

Ellen smiled. 'I hoped you'd say that. I've got used to sharing your bed with you.'

'I know. Thanks for not insisting that I cleared Robbie's room. Me hat-making things get strewn all over it, but I know where everything is and that helps me to get on with me work quickly.'

'That reminds me, I've not given Gran and Dilly their bonnets. They're going to love them.'

'Yes, it's a good job I stopped you bringing both hat boxes, luv, there'd have been no room for us in the car!'

When they went downstairs, Ellen thought Gran looked tired. Maybe it was all a little too much for her and she must be thinking that this trip hailed the time when they would stop living together – and she wondered how she would take what was really going to happen.

The tension broke, though, as Ellen said, 'I have a present for you both.'

Handing Dilly and Gran the bonnets she'd chosen for them, she told them how they had been made by Ruth.

'Oh, my darling, it is beautiful.' Gran turned it this way and that. 'The workmanship is wonderful. Ruth, my dear, you are so talented! I love it.'

'And, eeh, look at mine, Annie. It's the exact colour of me winter coat. We'll be the talk of the church this Sunday!'

'We will, Dilly. Now, let us all sit down as I think you have a lot to tell us, Ellen. And I am sure I am not going to like it all.'

Adrian came to the rescue once more. 'Well, I think you are going to be very, very proud of Ellen. We have seen her grow from a very traumatized young child into an assured young woman, and that is your doing, Annie. What it is that Ellen wants to do is all influenced by you.'

'Well, I feel even more worried now, as not only have I the feeling that something ominous is afoot, but that you, Adrian, are not going to champion my cause if I don't agree with it.'

'Gran, I can only come straight out with it and ask you to please not dismiss it on the grounds of my age. I have been through more than most. I don't feel as though I am just fifteen, but much, much older. I have the capabilities of an older person, and those assets will be needed.'

'My, your confidence has grown, my dear, and that in itself is reassuring and wonderful to see, but until I know what it is you want to do, then I cannot agree or disagree with it.'

Ellen took a deep breath. 'Have you heard of the Voluntary Aid Detachments?'

'My God! No, Ellen!'

'Please don't dismiss it out of hand, Gran. I wouldn't be alone. I would go with the Red Cross and Ruth will be going and there will be many more of us. We'll work in field hospitals that are situated way back from the front line and protected from warfare under the Geneva Convention . . . I'm needed, Gran. I have skills that will be needed to help to save lives.'

Gran went quiet. The colour had drained from her face. 'I – I expected you to say you wanted to live with Ruth, but this! No, Ellen, I cannot allow it . . . You are too young.'

Ellen's hopes sank. She looked at Ruth with despair in her heart. Ruth's expression showed she didn't know what to do about the situation, and Ellen didn't expect her to. She felt defeated.

It was Dilly who chimed in. 'I don't agree with you, Annie. Like Ellen said, she's been through so much and one terrible event happened whilst in our care, so how can you even think she is safer here than she would be with nurses, sisters, a matron and doctors, doing her bit in this war?'

Ellen smiled gratefully at her, then told Gran, 'I've already been accepted by the Red Cross, Gran, and I passed all of their exams.'

'You have gone that far? Did they not ask your age?'

Ellen looked shamefaced.

'You lied?'

'Yes, Gran.'

'But they believed you . . . And you lied too, Ruth? You backed up her story?'

Ruth nodded.

Gran hmphed. 'Well, that's a good start, I must say. And what's this about you being sisters?'

Ellen explained.

'Oh, I see. So it is speculation, though I do agree that it is most likely that you are . . . Ellen, everyone, please leave me for a while, I need to rest and to think.'

As they closed the door, Ruth linked her arm in Ellen's. 'That didn't go well, luv.'

'Aw, don't you fret yerself, me little lass. Your gran'll come to a good conclusion for you.'

'I'm not sure about that, Dilly. She may come to one that she thinks is best for me but isn't what I want.'

'Well, lass, life's like that. We don't allus get what we want. Your gran loves you, but in an unselfish way. She'd never stop you doing owt that's good for your future or your wellbeing. She knew she faced losing you when she encouraged you to go and find Ruth, but she didn't put any obstacles in your way. She knaws you'll leave her one day. She just hopes to put that day off.'

Ellen understood and, in doing so, felt torn. Her gran was everything to her, she didn't want to hurt her, but could she give up her dream of doing something now to help those sick and injured and to be with Ruth? She just hoped that her gran wouldn't ask that of her.

'May I say something, Ellen?'

Ellen had almost forgotten Adrian's presence. She knew he'd followed her out of the room but had been so engrossed in her disappointment.

'I think there is a compromise here. On the one hand, there are wounded soldiers who need you and, on the other, your gran who needs you too. This is all such a rush. Do you have to leave her so soon? She was preparing herself for you wanting to spend more time with Ruth but living in London meant you would visit often. France or Belgium is a different matter. She may not see you for years and will worry about you. Couldn't you give her more time to prepare? Do you have to go with this first batch of VADs? The Red Cross will be sending more and more nurses, I'm sure.'

Ellen's heart sank as she knew this was the sensible approach, and the kindest, but so not what she wanted to do. And yet, she owed much to her gran. She went towards the window of the drawing room. It was already dark outside and with the curtains not yet drawn she could see her reflection in the glass. The young woman that she was now looked back at her. Her curls were tamed into a neat bun at the nape of her long neck, made to look that way by the slant of her shoulders. Her curves were accentuated by the fitted bodice of her frock, a light grey, ankle-length dress that she kept for travel or walking out in during the winter as it was of a heavy cotton and kept her warm.

She wondered what other fifteen-and-a-half-year-old girls looked like, and if she was advanced for her years. Then sighed as she realized what a closeted life she had led. Maybe being around older people so much had matured her beyond her years – that coupled with all that had happened to her. What must it be like to live the life of an ordinary girl of her age – going to school, then out to work, but all with others of the same thinking, having fun, doing normal child-like things? Had she ever had fun? Maybe a little when she had Aggie. So now that those around her had shaped her, were they to deny what was her calling and at this late hour try to say that she was a child? Had they ever let her be one?

A hand came on her shoulder. She turned and looked into Ruth's lovely face.

'Will it help you to know that I won't go without you, luv? I'll tell Miss Jaminson that without you I don't feel ready. She'll understand. I mean, it's a voluntary thing, ain't it?'

'Oh, Ruth, I'm sorry this has happened.'

Ruth hugged her. 'Don't be, luv, I understand.'

As they came out of the hug Ellen said, 'But I still want to come and live with you. I can help with your hat-making and maybe volunteer as a part-time orderly at one of the hospitals and have a tutor in the evenings while you're at the theatre, then if the war's still on, Gran will let me go next year.'

She'd turned as she'd spoken and saw Dilly and Adrian visibly relax. They must have been worried that this setback would cause her to relapse into her mental breakdown. She smiled at them.

'Eeh, me lass, you truly are well. And aye, as we've said many times, mature beyond your years. A lovely young woman.' Dilly came towards her with her arms open. 'I'm going to miss you, me lass, but I knaw you'll visit often.'

'I will, Dilly. I promise. And you and Gran can get on a train and visit me too. I'll just go and have a chat with Gran.'

As she went out of the door, she heard Adrian say, 'Ruth, I know it's dark and you won't be able to see a lot, but would you like to go for a walk? I could do with some fresh air.'

And Ruth answered, 'I'll get me coat, as that'd be lovely, ta, Adrian.'

To her knock on the door, Gran's 'Come in' was pensive.

'It's all right, Gran, I won't go yet. I've thought it all

through. You need time to get used to the idea, and I need that too.'

'Oh, my darling, thank you. Come and sit with me. I'll move to the sofa.'

'No, stay where you are. It's been a long time since I kneeled at your knee.' As she spoke Ellen lowered herself and put her head in her gran's lap. Her gran gently stroked her hair.

Her voice shook as she said. 'I – I have something to tell you, my darling.'

The words zinged a realization through Ellen that she hadn't given attention to how Gran didn't look well. She hadn't done so even before she'd left last week, but now, she looked greyer and frailer. 'Are you all right, Gran. Are you ill?'

'I am. It's my heart. Did Dilly say that I've had the doctor attend me?'

'No.'

'Ah, she wouldn't want to put that guilt onto you and neither did I want to, so I am glad that your decision hasn't been influenced by my health, and I don't want it to be.'

'H-how ill are you, Gran?'

Gran trembled. 'Very, my darling. My heart is failing.'

'Oh, Gran, no! I'll make you better, Gran. I won't leave you. I know quite a bit about the workings of the heart, but I'll study more about it. You will need equal measures of rest and gentle exercise, and you'll need to eat a diet high in energy-giving protein. We'll get that bath chair down from the loft and I'll wrap you up warm and take you for walks as fresh air is good for you too.'

Gran laughed out loud. 'Oh, my dear, you're a natural doctor. But no. You won't do any of that. I want you to

154

have a life of your own. I know you want to be with Ruth, and that must happen. I already have the doctor looking into finding me a nurse to hire to do all the things you recommend.'

'No. Gran . . . Look. I did intend to go back with Ruth and to come here for a couple of days every fortnight. But I will do that the other way around. We will hire a part-time nurse to care for you once a week – Saturday to Monday. Ruth has Sunday and Monday off, so I can get to London on Saturday evening and be back here for Monday evening.'

'Are you sure, my darling?'

'I have never been more sure of anything in my life, Gran. I could not bear to leave you when you need me, and I can . . . well, I can keep you well.'

'Thank you. I feel much more hope now. I know you cannot do what you said – make me better – but you can make my last days happier than I thought they were going to be with thinking of saying goodbye to you.'

Ellen so wanted to deny that these were her gran's last days, but she knew she couldn't, so changed the subject to something she knew she must broach.

'Gran, I promised to sponsor a nurse to go to France. You see, we have to pay our own way out there, but there are many girls who are brilliant nurses and willing to go, but who cannot afford to.'

'My darling, I would expect no less of you. We will arrange that, and for the money I put aside for you to be at your disposal. I will also instruct my solicitor on a number of things that now seem pressing. I'll have him attend me tomorrow.'

'Thank you, Gran. There's just one other thing, then we'll get you resting. I think Ruth is struggling. She works at the

155

theatre at night and makes hats on a couple of days and stands market on the other days which should be her resting days.'

'Well then, we will help her out too. After all, I can be a gran to her too. I'll adopt her! Unofficially, of course. Will you fetch her in, darling, and we can ask her how we can best be of help to ease her load. She seems to be a lovely young woman and having her by your side puts my mind at rest as to your future.'

'I can't fetch her in at the moment as she's gone for a walk with Adrian . . . I think there's a romance brewing there, Gran.'

Gran's mischievous look came onto her face. 'Ooh, wouldn't that be lovely? We need to make that happen, darling. And we haven't got much time.'

Ellen laughed out loud. Her gran might be coming to the end of her life – a thought that gave Ellen great pain – but she was still Gran, and Ellen was so glad that she'd made the decision she had. It would be an honour to care for her. She just wished with all her heart that it wasn't something that needed doing. She wanted her gran to live for years and years. But her heart sank as she looked into her gran's face and saw the tell-tale blue tinge to her cheeks. She wanted to take her in her arms and to tell her that she would make her better, but she knew she couldn't do that.

Chapter Fourteen

Ruth

Ruth pulled her coat around her. A thick, long navy-blue wraparound coat that she'd bought from one of the market traders.

'Are you too cold, my dear?'

'No, we Londoners can take any weather. Mind, this northern wind does take the easy route and cut through yer.'

Adrian put his head back and laughed. 'I've never heard it described so aptly. Oh, Ruth, you're a tonic . . . You're a beautiful person – to look at and to be with.'

Ruth felt a thrill zing through her at his words. She didn't know what to say. She wanted to say that he was beautiful too, but that might sound too forward.

These feelings that Adrian had stirred up were unsettling her. Abe had always held her heart from the moment she'd met him.

Theirs has been a chance meeting on the stairs of his home. She'd panicked as maids were meant to be invisible, but he'd been kind to her, and their unlikely friendship had grown from there and blossomed into love. But lovely Robbie, who'd taken care of her from when she'd run away from the home, had come between them – Abe not knowing which of them he loved.

157

She suspected it was Robbie. But with Adrian coming into her life none of that mattered. All she wanted was for Abe and Robbie to be safe, and to be happy as she loved them both dearly.

'Penny for them as that was a huge sigh.'

'It was me letting go of part of me past.'

'Oh, that's a huge thing to do. Can you tell me about it?'

'I have done, partly. On the night we first met and went for supper. I must have bored you silly with me life story.'

'No, you fascinated me, and still do. What particular part of your story have you just let go of?'

'Abe and Robbie. Well, not in not wanting them in me life, but well . . . I imagined meself in love with Abe . . . and, well, Robbie . . . he – he was different to other men . . . he . . .'

'Preferred other men? I do know what you mean, there's a lot of it at boarding school. So, when you said once that Abe was confused, was he in love with you both?'

'Yes. I – I've been sort of waiting for him. Saving meself for him, but now I'm not . . . I mean . . .'

Adrian took her hand. They stood still for a moment. In the dim light of the gas lamp, Ruth could see the intense expression in Adrian's eyes as he looked into hers. His words came out on short breaths. 'Ruth . . . could meeting me have . . . have anything to do with that . . . ? Only, well, I – I would really hope so.'

She could only nod. Holding his gaze had tightened her throat muscles.

'Oh, Ruth, I feel the same, but you're so young. I – I wasn't going to speak of my feelings, when all I wanted to do was to tell you how I feel and ask you to wait for me.'

She waited. His breathlessness increased with the emotion

she could feel between them, but he hadn't yet said that he loved her.

'I – I felt it . . . from the moment we met. I love you, Ruth. I love . . . how you are, who you are, your . . . outlook on life, your values, your talents, I love every bit of you.'

A tear escaped her eye and must have glistened in the light as Adrian cupped her face in his hands and wiped it away with his thumb. 'Did happiness trickle that tear, my darling?'

'It did, Adrian, as I feel the same way about you. I thought meself in love with Abe, but it was different to this. I don't have any doubts. And yet, though I am the happiest I've ever been, I'm heartbroken too, as we'll be going away to war when we've only just found each other.'

Adrian didn't speak for a moment. He seemed to be struggling for breath. Ruth began to worry that this wasn't caused by emotion.

'Are you all right, Adrian, luv?'

'Yes . . . It's nothing. I – I . . . wanted to say that we can write to one another, even when you are a VAD. You will get letters delivered to you and so will I. We can take a photo of each other with us – I already have one of you that I cut out of *The Bystander* magazine.'

'Oh? Well, that one was in me costume. I have me favourite photo of meself in me handbag back at the 'ouse. It was taken outside the theatre on opening day. You can have that one.'

'Thank you. I will give you one of me . . . May I kiss you, Ruth?'

She couldn't answer him but leaned in towards him. And then it happened.

To Ruth, as Adrian's lips met hers it was as if she'd been

159

waiting for this moment all her life – a complete love, without any doubts marring it, something she could never have had with Abe. And with this thought she let go of the last part of the dream she'd had since she was thirteen when she'd first met Abe. A dream she'd stored in a secret corner of her heart. For now, she needed no other dream than to be with Adrian.

As they came out of the kiss, she asked, 'How did this happen to us after just spending a few hours together?'

'It . . . only takes one moment in time.' Adrian kissed the tip of her nose. 'Oh, Ruth, thank you for loving me.'

'It was easy, mate.'

'I love it when you call me "mate". Hey, you're shivering! Now I know that when they say love will keep you warm it's a myth as I'm getting very cold too . . . Let's go back, shall we? I don't know about you, but I'd like a nice hot drink.'

Relief filtered into Ruth. She'd remembered talk of an asthma attack that Ellen and Adrian had spoken about, but now it seemed his breathlessness was due to him being cold.

'Cocoa would be lovely. Does Dilly have any, do yer know?'

'She does . . . and she makes it with hot . . . milk and it's delicious. Come on, my love, we've news . . . to tell them all.'

'Ha! What're we going to say, that we're in love? I think they'll think us dafties!'

'I know, but I have to share the news. I have to! I never thought that . . . anyone would love . . . me.'

'Now yer are being daft. Come on . . . Adrian? Adrian? Oh God, Adrian, what is it?'

From his bent-double position, Adrian tried to tell her

something, but he hadn't the breath to use to speak as he collapsed at her feet.

Fear gave Ruth wings. She ran for all she was worth back to the house screaming out for help.

When she reached the door, she banged on it with all her might. She hadn't thought to stop to get the key out of Adrian's pocket.

As soon as Ellen opened the door Ruth gasped in air to steady herself. 'I – it's Adrian, he – he's collapsed!'

'His asthma! Oh, Ruth, no!'

Ruth had heard of asthma but didn't know it could be this serious, or what to do when someone had an attack, but she had no time to ask as Ellen told her to telephone for the doctor. 'His number's by the phone.'

As Ruth hurried inside, she heard Ellen calling to a couple of neighbours who'd appeared at the sound of the commotion. 'I need your help! Mr Vale is ill!'

Between them they managed to get Adrian into the warmth by the time the call was made. When Ruth went back into the drawing room Ellen was checking Adrian's vital signs.

Ruth could only pray. *Please let me Adrian live. Holy Mary, please hear me prayer.* She was unaware as she did that there were tears running down her face.

Ellen tried to soothe her. 'He'll be all right, Ruth, don't cry.' The calmness in her voice helped. 'The last time we had to have the doctor, love, he told us that it is better if an asthma patient passes out because they panic and that makes things worse. If they pass out, that element goes, and their breathing becomes easier.'

When the doctor had left, Ruth sat beside Adrian as he lay on the sofa. Although he looked pale and very tired, he was relaxed. She found his hand and held it. He managed a weak smile. His breathing still didn't seem right to her, but she thought to keep him calm and not to fuss would be the best approach. Smiling down at him, she said, 'It must have been all the excitement.'

'Yes. Tell them . . . Ruth. I want the world . . . to know.'

Ruth blushed as she looked around at them all. Ellen's gran, looking pale and upset, sat in one of the armchairs next to the roaring fire. Dilly stood behind her, her anxious gaze going from Gran to Adrian. And Ellen stood next to her gran, her arm protectively around her shoulders.

'Me and Adrian are in love.'

Dilly was the first to speak. 'What? Eeh, lass, that's good news in all the bad.'

Ellen beamed. 'Ruth! Oh, Ruth, that's wonderful . . . I knew it! Well, I saw the looks you gave each other and the feeling between you as if you'd known each other for ever. I'm so happy.'

Gran smiled. 'That's good news, my dear . . . Well, Adrian, I didn't have you down as a fast mover, but a slow, think about everything logically kind of person. This is lovely to hear, and I hope you'll be very happy . . . Dilly, let's get that bottle of sherry out, shall we? This calls for a little tipple to celebrate.'

Dilly gave a giggle as she went through to the kitchen.

Ellen came towards Ruth, her arms open. Going into them gave Ruth the feeling of being safe, of Ellen's serenity soothing her. She clung to her beloved sister. Her body shook. 'Oh, Ellen, I was so afraid.'

'Ruth . . . I'm all right, darling.'

'It's the shock, Adrian. Better she cries it out.'

Adrian went to rise.

162

'No! Stay there. You must rest while you recover. Your breathing is still a little laboured, you need to save all your energy.'

Ruth felt in awe of Ellen. She truly was cut out to be a doctor. Coming out of her arms, Ruth kneeled back down next to Adrian. 'I'm all right. You did give me a fright, mate, but it's relief that's making me cry.'

His hand stroked her hair but not for long as his arm flopped down. The effort had been too much for him. Ruth's heart thumped with anxiety. She hadn't known how it had happened that she'd fallen so suddenly in love, but Adrian had become her world in such a short time, and she didn't want to lose him.

The mood lightened with Dilly making them all laugh as she poured the sherry. 'Eeh, it feels like Christmas again! Annie got a little tiddly at Christmas, thou knaws.'

'Dilly! Now don't you be telling any of your tales!'

'Aw, I have to tell them just the one, lass. About that time you had a couple and decided you wanted to dance naked in the garden, and—'

'Dilly!'

'Ha, you did!'

'I kept my petticoat on!'

Ruth was glad to see Gran was laughing now. She looked at Ellen and grinned at the astonished look on her face. Even Adrian laughed weakly, but then began to cough. Not wanting to spoil the moment for him by reacting in the way her heart wanted to and implore him not to laugh, Ruth giggled along with them all. Adrian soon calmed, but didn't have any sherry. He lay back quite peacefully and was smiling as they all toasted and congratulated them on their new-found love.

*

With Adrian asleep on the sofa, and Ellen having helped her Gran, who'd seemed to become weaker by the minute, to bed, Ruth finally got her hot drink of cocoa made by Dilly, before she too retired to her bed.

'I don't want to leave him, Ellen.'

'I know. We'll sleep in the chairs, eh? I need to check on Gran a few times in the night, so this will be good practice for us.'

'Your gran's not well, is she, Ellen?'

'No . . . Oh, Ruth. I've wanted so much to talk to you and was going to the minute you came back in, but . . . well, you see, my gran's heart is failing.'

'Oh no, I'm so sorry, Ellen . . . Does this mean that you won't be coming to live with me, even?'

'Not full time . . . I need to care for Gran. Not that she asked, or even wanted me to, as she said she would get a nurse to tend to her, but we came to a compromise.'

Ellen explained what had been arranged.

'I'm so sorry, Ellen. Your poor gran and you. But you said until I go? That you'd come to me a few days each weekend until I leave with the Red Cross? But Ellen, I told you, I don't want to go and *won't* go without you, and now, I have another reason for not doing so: I don't want to leave Adrian . . . Though we knew we had to part soon.'

'Ruth, Adrian has to face the fact that he won't pass the medical to go to Sandhurst. He'll be so disappointed, but his asthma is on his record, and he won't be accepted.'

'Oh no. He's set his heart on becoming an officer.'

They were quiet for a moment. Both looked over at Adrian. He looked peaceful and as if there was nothing wrong with him as the rest and his breathing steadying had restored his colour.

'Can people die of asthma, Ellen?'

Ellen nodded. 'I read up about it once I came out of the home and I asked Miss Roland about it. It's very frightening and not a lot is known, but sufferers are prone to attacks and . . . well . . .'

Ruth was shocked to her core. How could this be?

'He didn't show any sign of being breathless before. Then tonight . . . I think it was the cold.'

'I know, and that's strange as according to what I have read the patient suffers wheezing and breathlessness on a continual basis, and more especially on exertion, but Adrian doesn't. He seems very fit in between these bouts, and they seem rare too, as I haven't known him to have an attack since the first day that he arrived to be my tutor.'

'Could it be something else? Maybe a specialist could find the real cause and treat him?'

'I did read about allergic reactions and that made me think that what happens to Adrian could be something like that. There isn't a lot that's known about it . . . and, well, there are also other causes – anxiety, which causes panic attacks and sometimes extreme reactions. It's a varied and interesting subject, and one that a lot of scientists study because it can cause sudden shock to the body which may result in death.'

Ruth shuddered. 'He was anxious, Ellen. He didn't think anyone could fall in love with him.'

'Oh? I wonder why he should think that? But come to think of it, he did say he was bullied as a child. And anxiety could have caused his other attack, as coming to my home to meet a young pupil and her family for the first time – and given that my father had told him that I was verging on being classed as mad – must have been stressful for him. He must have felt nervous.'

'There were no outward signs of him being anxious tonight.'

'That's just it. He didn't have any when he arrived here that first time, but that's the worst type, the kind where you don't address it, but suppress it, as it manifests itself in other ways.'

'I'm in awe of you, Ellen. You're so clever. And you've given me hope because if it is anxiety, then all we'll have to do is to avoid him getting nervous over anything.'

'Miss Roland, who I told you about, could help if it is. Look how she helped me. I'm a different person to what I was.'

'I can't imagine you having rages, Ellen.'

'Well, watch out as I turn into the devil when I do.'

Her giggle when she said this cheered Ruth. It somehow felt that if Ellen could giggle, then the situation wasn't so dire.

She looked over at Adrian. If you hadn't known what had happened, you would never guess. How was it that such illnesses existed – Ellen's rages and, if it was so, Adrian's anxiety? And yet both were so clever and logical-thinking beings. It just didn't make sense – or maybe they knew too much? *Being ignorant like me is probably the best thing*.

The next day, Adrian was back to normal and laughed at their theory, but when Ellen said to him, 'Well, if it is asthma and not anxiety, you can say goodbye to becoming an officer, Adrian.'

This shocked him. 'But I only have an attack every now and again!'

'Exactly. Look, I'll lend you my books on the subject of lung conditions and you can read it for yourself. The doctor has assumed you have asthma. Have you ever been properly diagnosed?'

'Well, no. But, well, I was always a sickly child . . . though nothing like this until my father's death.'

'When you not only had to deal with your grief, but Gran told me there were debts too and you had to give up your ambitions to become a lawyer.'

Adrian was quiet for a moment. When he spoke, it was as if a light had been switched on for him. 'It does make sense, as when I came here, I was very anxious. It sounded as though I was coming to teach a monster who might attack me, and I was still reeling from my world suddenly being turned upside down.'

'But when you found we weren't so bad – in fact, needed your help – you never had another attack. Now, you are facing going to war and self-doubts creep in, and you weren't sure that anyone could love you and yet needed to declare your love for Ruth, besides which you knew that she was soon to go away.'

'And you too, Ellen. That has worried me. I felt guilty because I have encouraged you . . . Oh, I can see it all now and I think you're right . . . You're one gifted young lady, Ellen. Your calling could be in psychiatry. You should look into it – especially as you have benefitted from it yourself with Miss Roland.'

'I am interested in it, but I do find the workings of the whole body interesting and love Freud's theory that the state of the mind can affect the wellbeing of the body – that our mental health is just as important as our physical health as they are interconnected.'

'Did he say that?'

'Well, not in so many words, but it is all part of his theories.'

Ruth had listened to all of this with growing wonderment. How could Ellen, who truly had been the forgotten one, as she called herself, know so much? And at such a young age. She was inspirational. *And she's my sister . . . My very own sister!*

Ruth's heart flooded with love and admiration. To her, it was as if Ellen could save them all.

Chapter Fifteen

Ellen

When Ellen woke, she shivered. The fire had died, leaving the room cold. There was no sound but the ticking of the clock on the mantelpiece. She rubbed her eyes, moved her aching body, and glanced at it. Two thirty!

She looked over at Ruth who sat in the chair opposite seemingly asleep, but at Ellen's movement she stirred.

Adrian's whispered, 'So, you're awake?' surprised her.

'Yes. How long have you been awake? Are you all right?'

'I am. Back to normal. Sorry I gave you both a scare. I'll get over to my apartment now. You both get yourselves off to bed.'

Ellen stretched. 'I'll look in on Gran. I'll see you in a bit, Ruth. You know where everything is, don't you?'

'Yes, I'll be fine, luv.'

Leaving them alone together, Ellen crept upstairs and was relieved to find Gran was sleeping peacefully.

When the solicitor arrived the next day, Ruth and Adrian went out walking once more, though Ellen wished they wouldn't as she still worried about Adrian. What if she was wrong and there was a type of asthma that only attacked occasionally?

But she had no time to think about it as she was called into her gran's sitting room.

'Come in, my dear. I want you to know everything that I am arranging.'

Gran sounded breathless.

'There's no need, Gran. I don't want you to go through it all again for my benefit. Nothing's going to happen for a long time, I promise.'

Gran just smiled, a tired smile, full of love.

The solicitor cleared his throat.

'This is unconventional, and I have advised against it. It is akin to having a will reading, Annie, before your demise.'

Gran chuckled. 'I like to be unconventional.'

'Very well. Please sit down, Miss Hartington.'

Once she was seated, he cleared his throat again and began to read:

'This the last will and testament of Mrs Anne Ellen Hartington.'

'I'm named after you, Gran!'

'May I have silence, please. This is a solemn occasion.'

This made Ellen want to giggle. She daren't look at her gran, who she could sense wanted to, too.

The solicitor, a small dumpy man with a handlebar moustache, sighed.

'As I was saying . . . To my grandchild, Ellen Hartington, I leave my house, with the proviso that both Dilly and Cook can use it as their home for as long as they need to and are looked after and with the additional proviso that Adrian Vale may rent the schoolroom and apartment for as long as he needs to. To Dilly Cookson I leave twenty pounds. Any money left in my account after any liabilities to my estate have been settled shall be divided equally between my two grandchildren,

Ellen Hartington and Christopher Hartington. Though as and from today's date, the date I signed this will, the trust fund I set up for my granddaughter, Ellen Hartington, is hers from this day to use as she wants, though I trust she will do so to further her future. My solicitor is the executor of my will and will inform my in-laws of my demise and wishes. Signed, Anne Ellen Hartington and witnessed by the hand of Archibald Franks, solicitor, and dated today.'

There was a silence. Ellen felt that she had to wait for permission to speak, or even to move.

Gran seemed to think the same. Though as Ellen saw the colour draining from her, she did move to be by her gran's side.

'Thank you, my lovely Gran. I love you. And thank you for not leaving Christopher out . . . Oh, I do wish you could see him, Gran, he's so beautiful.'

'Tell . . . tell him that his gran loved him. Make sure he knows that. You . . . you don't have to meet someone to love them. Just knowing they are there and your own . . . flesh and blood is enough.'

'I will, Gran.'

Ellen held her gran's hand. To her, it felt so frail. Fear gripped her but before she could say anything, the solicitor said he was taking his leave. To Ellen's surprise he told her, 'It's been my pleasure to meet you, Miss Hartington. I am at your service.' As Gran moved as if to rise, he said, 'No, Annie, rest. Your wishes have and will be seen to. Good day. I will let myself out.'

When he'd gone, Ellen kneeled with her gran. 'Gran, shall I get the doctor?'

'No, dear. There is nothing more he can do. I have made my peace with God and put my house in order. I am ready.'

'No, Gran. Please don't give up. Please.'

'Ellen, don't give in . . . don't be ill again . . . Go out into the world and do good . . . We prepared you for that . . . Now, please fetch Dilly, my darling.'

When she returned with Dilly, Gran was slumped over the arm of her chair.

'Gran!'

This came out as almost a scream of despair. Ellen rushed forward. 'Gran, Gran, no, no!'

'Annie, Annie, me dear friend. Aw, Annie, lass.'

'Help me to lift her, Dilly.'

'She's gone, me little lass, she's gone.'

Dilly took one of Gran's hands in her own. 'Me best friend in all the world. We first met as young women, thou knaws. Annie were a beauty. I were engaged to be married but then I lost me man and Annie . . . eeh, poor lass, went through what you did and found herself in a predicament. We helped each other. It was a struggle, but then she fell in love. Her life changed, but she didn't forget me.'

Dilly shook her head. Tears streamed down her face. Ellen went to her and enclosed her in her arms. 'And she still hasn't, Dilly. You're to be looked after, you and Cook. She thought of you right to the end, and called for you, but we were too late.'

Dilly sobbed on Ellen's shoulder, but Ellen couldn't cry. It was all too much of a shock and wouldn't sink in. *Gran, gone! My lovely Gran.*

Dilly seemed to sense this and took charge. 'You need to phone the doctor, lass. And while we wait for him, we need to make lovely Annie comfortable. We can't leave her like this. Run and find Ruth and Adrian to help us.'

*

172

After the doctor left, the house became still. Dilly just sat staring at Gran. Ruth stood behind Ellen as she sat on the end of the bed and held her to her. Adrian stood with his arm around Ruth and one hand on Ellen's shoulder.

Ellen could feel no comfort. She couldn't feel anything. It was as if she was turned to stone.

All she could do was to stare at Gran and to think how beautiful she was.

The door opening broke the spell.

'Eeh, Dilly, Ellen, is it all right if I come in?'

Cook, rarely seen out of the kitchen, stood in the doorway. Dilly went to her. 'Aye, come on in, lass. Our lovely Annie has gone.'

Cook, as round as she was tall, dabbed her eyes. Then went up to Gran and tapped her hand. 'Ta for everything, Annie. You've been a good 'un to me, lass.'

With this, she walked around them all offering some comfort. When she got to Ellen, she said, 'You made her happy, thou knaws, lass. You lifted the sadness she'd been in since her husband left this world. I loved serving her and'll do the same for you till I pop me own clogs. Should I make tea, Miss Ellen?'

Ellen sensed that though she felt like saying that Cook had no need to feel subservient to her, Cook needed her to take over from Gran to keep things as normal as possible for her. 'Yes, please, Cook . . . and, Cook, Gran left everything so that you will be looked after and will have a home for life here so please don't worry.'

'Ta, lass. She was like that, was Annie. She could have her moments, but you'd never find a nicer or kinder boss in the world. Nor a better friend than Dilly.' She looked over at Gran. 'We'll carry on looking after the cottage and Ellen, love.'

Ellen wanted to say that it was each other that Cook and Dilly must look after as now she would go with Ruth. But then, the thought came to her that Gran needed more from her so she made a silent promise to the still figure of her beloved gran that when the war was over, to honour her, she would study at medical school, and she would become a doctor one day.

The days to the funeral flew by. Ruth had gone back to London and, like all troopers, had ensured that the show must go on. But as they had arranged Gran's service for the following Monday, Ruth's next day off, it didn't seem a moment to Ellen till she and Adrian were at the station on Sunday evening, waiting for Ruth's train to bring her back to them.

When the train chugged towards them billowing out choking smoke and deafening them with a shrill whistle, before coming to a screeching halt, there was a moment when Ruth alighted that she looked indecisive. Ellen stood back and pushed Adrian forward. Their hug warmed her heart. These two were so special to her and for them to have come together how they had was like a lovely gift.

A warmth swept through Ellen when Ruth came to her and held out her arms. Going into them felt to Ellen as it did the very first time – as if she was home, as home had come to be wherever Ruth was.

'How are you, me darlin'?'

'Oh, you know. It's been a busy week, so I haven't had time to think. Though I'm dreading tomorrow.'

'I know. But we'll get through it, luv.'

When they were sat in the cab to go back to Rose Cottage, Adrian told them, 'I've been busy, too. I made an appointment with a specialist to see if he can determine whether I do have asthma or not. He has said that if not, he will authorize that any record that says I have will be destroyed.'

'Oh, so you ain't given up wanting to go to Sandhurst, then?' Ruth's voice held an almost pleading tone.

'No, my darling, I can't, and I know that neither you nor Ellen will give up on your quest either. We all need to help to put the world to rights for our future generations.'

Ruth looked at Ellen. 'Is that how you feel, Ellen?'

'Yes, it is. And I'm glad you're getting a professional opinion, Adrian.'

'Yes, I told the specialist your theory while I was on the phone to him and he said that you could well be right. He has come across a number of cases where anxiety has caused a panic attack. So, he did say that if this is proved to be the case, that he won't recommend that I go into active service for at least a year but agrees that my training at Sandhurst could go ahead and be part of my therapy. I have also contacted Miss Roland. She said that she will gladly help me cope with my panic attacks if this is the diagnosis.'

'Oh, I'm so glad. I have a lot of faith in her.'

'Will there be many at the funeral, Ellen?'

'Quite a crowd, I think, Ruth, though only one of Gran's in-laws is coming . . . I wonder what they are like. Gran once said she would introduce me to them when I am older, in the hope one of them, or of their circle, would fall in love with me and keep me in clover.'

'Ha, that sounds typical of Annie.'

They didn't speak much for the rest of the journey. Ruth sat in the middle of them holding both of their hands. Ellen still felt as though there was a block of ice inside her that even Ruth's hug hadn't melted. She still hadn't cried. She wished that she could as the feeling was painful. She tried to comfort herself by telling herself that this must be part of the grit that a doctor needed – an ability to quash their emotions. She would need that in the months and years ahead. She couldn't go around showing her feelings, upsetting everyone by crying and wailing when they needed someone strong and capable by their side.

Thinking this, she felt better about her reaction to losing someone so very dear to her.

All these thoughts dissolved, and the agony did break as she stood looking down at her gran's coffin in the deep hole cut into the ground. Sprinkled with earth and with most of the mourners having walked away, it looked a lonely place for her gran to be. Ellen gasped in a huge breath as if to steady herself, but it didn't work. Her legs gave way. She sank to her knees. A painful moan rasped from her dry throat as a burning agony finally melted the icy place in her chest.

Tears wet her face. 'Gran, oh, Gran . . . I – I don't want you to be gone.' The dampness of the ground seeped through her long black skirt and her thick stockings, wetting her knees and increasing the shaking of her body.

A gentle touch on her shoulder helped to steady her as she told her gran, 'I'll make you proud of me, Gran. I promise I will become the doctor you dreamed I would be.'

Another hand came onto her other shoulder. 'She was proud of you, Ellen. She told me not long ago that she couldn't be prouder of you. She asked me if I'd ever known a fifteen-year-old to have your courage, your knowledge and determination. I told her that the only one I had ever heard of was Joan of Arc. She laughed and said, "That's it, Adrian, Ellen is our very own Joan of Arc." But then she asked me to take care of you, to try to stop you being so impetuous as she was afraid for you. I told her that she should never ask that of me as you must follow your heart, that we'd both taught you that and now must live by it. She smiled and said, "Oh, yes, we have raised a free spirit and, yes, we must let her follow her instincts." And that's what you must do, Ellen. What we must all do. The world is in a sorry state and only its people can put it right. Good against evil. You, Ruth and I must be part of the good fighting the evil.'

Adrian's words steadied Ellen. She took the hand he now stretched out to her and stood. As she did, Ruth pulled her into her arms. 'We'll be fine, mate, I promise.'

Ellen couldn't speak. She clung on to Ruth and sobbed. No one stopped her.

When empty of tears, she calmed. The knot had gone. It had been replaced by a deep sadness, and yet a kind of peace.

The ordeal of meeting her gran's in-laws wasn't as bad as she thought. An elderly gentleman stood at the gate of the cemetery. He offered his hand. When she took it, he shook hers in a very formal way. 'I'm Anne's brother-in-law. She wrote and told us about you. We're sorry for your loss. Are you going to be all right?'

She told him she would and that was it. He got into his car and was driven away.

Hugging Dilly and Cook goodbye wasn't easy the next day. Both women were deeply grieving for Gran – their Annie – but now had the added sadness of her leaving.

'Are you sure you're ready, Ellen, luv? It's only one day since the funeral.'

'I'm sure, Ruth. I have to do it now. Make the break. Besides, I want to be with you.'

'I'm glad. We should be together. Bett'll be pleased you're coming. She told me before I left to be sure to bring yer back with me, but I didn't think you'd be ready.'

'I am, Ruth, so ready.'

'Come on then, both of you. Your train goes in an hour!'

Though Adrian sounded light-hearted as he jollied them along, Ellen could see his heart was aching.

Ruth clasped his hand and at that moment, she'd never looked more beautiful as she lifted her head to look into Adrian's eyes. The dark, ruby-red cape she wore over her long grey, woollen frock suited her so much, bringing out the best of her ivory skin. She'd pinned her hair back and wore a beret-type hat with a bow on one side and in the same colour as her cape. Ellen knew she would have made both garments herself.

The talents Ruth had astounded Ellen, though she knew all had been influenced and nurtured by others – the hat-making and sewing by the lovely lady, Rebekah, who'd been like a mother to Ruth, and the singing, acting and dancing by her friend Robbie.

Ellen let her tears flow as she looked back from the cab window and waved to Cook and Dilly. To see them standing at the gate waving and blowing her a kiss undid her. But she took a deep breath. It was time for her to be strong. And she would be. She would take up whatever challenges lay ahead.

Chapter Sixteen

Ruth

As they prepared to go to market two weeks later, Ruth worried about Ellen, since although she seemed cheerful enough, she wondered if she was really settling in London.

She seemed restless and only ever totally happy and relaxed when they were attending the Red Cross training – something that was getting very intense, as soon those chosen to go to the field hospitals of war would be notified.

Their age hadn't been mentioned again. But more and more Ruth felt as though she was the younger sister. Especially when it came to absorbing anything new. Often Ellen, who grasped everything taught to them in seconds, had to help her to really get whatever it was they were learning to sink in.

'Right, luv, have you got both bags?'

'Yes, they're all ready. I'm looking forward to standing on the market stall.'

Ruth could see this really was so. 'Well, it's good to see you smiling, luv.'

'I know, I've been like a wet weekend since we arrived, but I'm feeling better now . . . I wonder if we'll hear tonight whether we've been chosen or not?'

Despite her words of feeling better, Ruth could feel the

tension in Ellen as she said this and felt the same trepidation that she did over the coming announcement.

Their worry was twofold – what would it be like being in a war zone, and would they get to go together or not?

But for now, she had no time to think about it as she hauled the bags and boxes onto the handcart that Robbie had made for her a couple of years or so back.

'Have a good day, me darlin's.'

'We will, Bett, ta. We're starting with a hot mug of tea off your old stall and one of them sausage buns.'

'Huh, sausage buns! Never 'ad them in my day – hot spuds did everyone for breakfast and dinner and snacks in between.'

Ruth laughed. It was always easy to rile Bett.

'Get off with the pair of you . . . sausage buns, my arse!'

For once, Ellen didn't look shocked at Bett's language, which was a sign she was getting used to life with the cockneys, and Ruth was glad of this. She hated any differences between them. It was bad enough that Ellen had a posh accent.

'Now, as we pull the cart, Ellen, we'd better practise you calling out the wares, luv. I don't want you saying, "We have hats for sale for all occasions," but "Cam 'ere and see for yerselves – the finest 'ats in the world. 'Andmade they are, me lavlies.'"

Ellen burst out laughing – a lovely tinkly sound. 'Oh, Ruth, I've never heard you speak in such broad cockney – lavlies? It sounds so funny . . . and yet, homely and nice.'

'Ha, I don't really shout that, though some of the stall-holders do.'

Their giggles helped them to manoeuvre the cart over the cobbled roads to the market square. Ruth's back was aching when they arrived, but Ellen looked as strong as when they'd set out.

Pressing her fists into her waist and leaning back, Ruth's eyes fell on the parkland along the street behind the market. Vivid memories came to her of herself, Robbie and Abe sitting under the tree. How she wished she could turn the clock back . . . but then, did she really want to? They were tough times, and she didn't have Ellen and her adored Adrian in her life then.

'Are you all right, Ruth?'

'Yes, luv. Let's get busy, eh?'

They were nearly finished setting up the stall when Ruby came over to them. As usual, full of bad news and doom to come. 'I didn't expect you girls this morning. What yer bothered for I don't know, there's no trade to talk of.'

'Well, you never know, Ruby, luv, we could be run off our feet.'

'I 'ope so. I'm on near starvation rations now. Mind, we're better off than them Belgians, poor buggers.'

Talk of the war always upset Ruth. She shuddered as she thought of what it must be like to be on the road, trying to get to freedom whilst being shot at, as she'd heard was happening on the borders of Belgium.

'Are you really starving, Ruby?'

'No, girl . . . What's your name again?'

'Ellen.'

'It's just a saying. No need to take me to the soup kitchen just yet, luv.' With this, Ruby let out one of her rare cackling laughs, but then stopped abruptly. ''Ere, get away from me stall, yer ragamuffins!'

With this she was gone, running in a wobbly fashion as she chased thieving kids from her stall.

'Oh, Ruth, those children looked as though they really were starving.'

'They probably are, poor beggars. There's a lot of poverty in London, Ellen. People think the streets are lined with gold, when the truth is that half are near starved to death, especially here in the East End.'

A puffing and panting Ruby returned.

'You shouldn't run like that, Ruby. The sudden upping of your heart rate is very dangerous.'

''Ark at her. You a bleedin' doctor now, young miss?'

Ruth was glad to see Ellen smile and say, 'Not yet, but one day.' She'd thought this might have upset her, but she was finding Ellen was a lot thicker skinned than she imagined as she was now telling Ruby off even more. A brave thing to do in Ruby's case.

'But I do know, for the children's sake as well as your own, you are better to let them get away with it.'

'You what! Look, if I were rich, I'd feed the bloomin' lot of 'em, but I ain't. I work 'ard to feed meself and me own. Ha, even so, if they asked, I'd give them an apple a day, but I ain't condoning them stealing. That'll land 'em in more trouble than they are in now.'

Ruth held her breath, but once more Ellen showed her maturity. 'You're right, of course. And I suppose if they did ask and you gave, you'd be inundated with all the poor folk coming to your stall.'

'Yer've got it, girl. That's exactly how it would be. The problem's too big for one scrimping and saving stall 'older like me. It's them in the bleedin' government that should sort it out.'

Ellen went quiet then. Ruth sought to change the subject, imagining Ellen marching to Whitehall here and now to

182

demand help for the poor. 'Well, that's us all set up, mate. I'll go and get the mugs of tea, then we'll be well lubricated to start shouting out our wares. Do you want one, too, Ruby?'

'No, ta, I've brought me flask. I ain't wasting me money on the ditchwater they serve up. Never been the same since Bett left. I miss her. We used to have a good laugh.'

As she went over to the barrow from which the tea was sold from a huge urn, Ruth thought about those days and knew that for all their hardship, they were good times.

After doing very little trade – the sale of one bonnet and a brimmed hat – it was time to pack up. Ellen had been quiet for most of the day. Ruth knew that the incident with the starving kids that morning had really affected her. How was it that such things happening had become a normal part of life to herself? They weren't normal. But then, what could she do about it all? There were so many pulls on her time as it was. But she wasn't surprised when Ellen said, 'Ruth, I've been thinking about those children, and I want to help them.'

Sighing, Ruth told her once more how massive the problem was. 'There ain't nothing you can do, luv. I know yer heart's good, but think about it. Tomorrow we go to the Red Cross, and will know if we have been chosen. What if we are? How are yer going to continue with whatever it is you're planning to do, eh?'

'We wouldn't go straight away, would we?'

'I don't know. If they need nurses, they need them – not next week, but now. It could be that we're on a train tomorrow! Who knows? Look, luv, I know yer want to help, and you have enough money to make a difference, but it's one thing or the other – go and help the wounded or stay and help the poor of the East End.'

'What if I asked Bett to set up a soup kitchen? You know she could do it. She doesn't have to do the work, just organize it and then oversee it. I would give her enough funds to keep it going.'

'Well . . . yes, it might work. It might serve two purposes. Bett ain't on the scrapheap yet. She just gave up because of the hours standing in the cold and she didn't need to do it, but I know she misses the company. What you're proposing might be right up her street. And I think I know a good venue: the chapel where I used to go on a Sunday with Rebekah. Well, it's like a small church really. Oh, I miss those days. I should have kept going. I'll tell you of them one day.'

'We have so much to tell each other, Ruth. I – I know I've told you some, but there's more about my life. And I want to know every bit about yours. But anyway, you really think it could happen? The soup kitchen?'

'I do, mate. The more I think of it, the more I think it a brilliant idea. The members of our church community would help, I know they would. Abdi, Rebekah's nephew as I've mentioned before, is a kind of leader of them all. We'll go and see him and see what he thinks. If he agrees, then you've got your workers as he'll jolly them all along. They'll make soup and bread, and the chapel – which is used by the congregation for wedding receptions after the marriage service and funeral wakes – has a side kitchen and plenty of bowls, plates and cutlery. It would be ideal, though you may have to donate some money to them as the gas and electric you'd use ain't cheap.'

'I know . . . I can manage that.'

'Blimey, how rich are you, Ellen? Don't forget you have

our passage to pay, and you said you'd sponsor another volunteer too.'

'That's just it. I can do a lot of good with the money my gran left me, or I can keep it and think of myself as rich. I don't care if it all goes, as long as it does a lot of good.'

'Are you sure you were only born fifteen years ago? Ha, yer like a hundred years old in yer wisdom and thinking . . . Well, I'm proud of yer, luv. I couldn't be more proud. Most would set themselves up in clover, but not you. Yer a lovely person, Ellen, and I love you with all me heart.'

On impulse Ruth opened her arms. Ellen snuggled into her. It felt good to hold her young sister, and yet she wondered if she was ever young. A pain shot through her as memories showed her all Ellen had suffered. And how she did so in almost complete silence, trying to support Amy when she was new to the home and became a victim of Belton's too.

'You shuddered, Ruth. Are you all right?'

'I am. I've never been more all right, but well, you know how it is. When you least expect it, a thought will come into yer head and knock you for six. Come on, let's get finished up here, as I have to get to the theatre in a couple of hours.'

Bett loved the idea of the soup kitchen. She seemed to glow. Ruth suspected it was more the thought of having some responsibility over others than the actual charity work, though Bett did have a good heart underneath the hard exterior, so maybe it was a bit of both.

'Let's go and see Abdi tomorrow, Ruth, eh?'

Ruth laughed at her enthusiasm. 'All right. It's ages since I've seen him and Ebony, but are you sure, Bett? It won't be too much for yer, will it?'

'No! I won't do any of the bleedin' work, girl. I'll just see that it's done and done proper, and a proper use of whatever money Ellen can put into it as well. That's the most important thing for me. There's a lot who would rip her off, even when she's trying to do good . . . and this is a good thing yer doing, Ellen, luv. Yer altogether a bloomin' good girl, mate.'

Ruth saw Ellen blush with pleasure and had a surge of love for this lovely sister of hers.

'And I'll tell you another thing, yer'll only need to provide the set-up money, Ellen, as now you've put the idea into me head, I'll get me sons to take over. It's about time they did me a favour. I ain't asked anything of them since they saw to them two rotters at the orphanage. It'll do them bleedin' good to help others, rather than keep taking from them!'

Ruth once more felt the shudder that always sent her cold at the thought of how things were at the orphanage and how it was all resolved by violence – an act that she instigated by telling Bett of the depravation. And yet, she was glad it happened as she could see no other way the situation could have been resolved. No one, not even the police, would have believed that it was all going on. Matron, Belton and Gedberg got away with it for years.

The following afternoon, Abdi's huge smile greeted them when he opened the door of his flat, situated over his restaurant in Stepney. His lovely voice called up the stairs behind him. 'Ebony, my dear, you won't believe who it is . . . Come on in, Ruth . . . And Bett! Good to see you. And who is this young lady?'

Ruth took great pleasure in telling Abdi who Ellen was.

He beamed at Ellen. To Ruth, he looked more regal than ever, and she supposed that was because he was now master of all he owned instead of being subservient as he was when he was a butler and she'd first met him – the great, great-grandson of a high chief, who'd been brought to England as a slave.

When they reached the top of the stairs, Ruth found herself in a profusion of colour as her adored friend Ebony took her in her arms.

'You look beautiful, Ebony, and it is so good to see you. I've brought my sister to meet you. This is Ellen.'

'I can hear the pride in your voice, Ruth, but what is this? A sister? You never said . . . Hello, Ellen, it is nice to meet you. My, Ruth kept you a secret, girl!'

Ruth felt a happiness settle in her as Ebony, clad in a colourful long frock held in at the waist by a wide silk band, hugged Ellen to her. Ellen blushed but beamed with pleasure as she said how nice it was to meet Ebony.

Hugs with Bett followed – though Abdi, always the formal one, only bowed to them all and expressed his pleasure at seeing them. 'To what do we owe this lovely surprise?'

'I'll tell yer everything, Abdi, but first, how is Horacio? I haven't had a letter from him in three weeks, which isn't like him.'

'He's busy doing exams. He must have told you about them? He has been set the entrance exam for a very posh school that we could not afford, not even with dear Aunt Rebekah's legacy, but which has an exam for boys who are very clever and if they pass, then they gain entry that way. He very much wants to go as the friends he has made at the boarding school are going.'

'Oh, I'll write to him and wish him luck.'

Horacio, Ebony and Abdi's son, had stolen Ruth's heart when she'd first met him.

Over a cup of tea, Ruth told them how she came to be reunited with Ellen.

'That's a lovely story.' Ebony dried a tear as she said this.

'It is, my dear. We are very happy for you, Ruth.'

'Thanks, Abdi . . . both of you . . . So, the second thing I'm here to tell you stems from the first. Well, from an idea that Ellen has had.'

After listening to how Ellen wanted to feed the hungry and how they all wanted to make it happen, Ebony said, 'That's a wonderful idea, and I will make some food.'

'Oh, the kids will love your curry, Ebony. It went down well on me stall when Rebekah couldn't make hers any longer.'

Ebony clapped her hands together. 'What do you think, Abdi?'

'I think the whole idea is a very good one. I know our church will love to be involved and I think Reverend Jafari will be more than willing to lend out the chapel and will give all the support he can . . . Though, Ebony, my dear, even though it is a wonderful idea to donate our food, I think the logistics of getting a huge hot pan from here to the church hall may defeat us.'

'You can cook it at the church, Ebony,' Bett said. 'I'd store all the spices you need, and you can shop in the market for the veg.'

Ebony looked at Abdi.

'That's a much better idea. We're not so busy in the restaurant now, so we can both help out.'

This worried Ruth, as put together with there not being enough of the legacy left to send Horacio to the school they'd planned for him could mean Abdi and Ebony were struggling. She so wanted to ask if everything was all right but knew this would hurt Abdi's pride.

'And what it is that you think, Ellen? Would you like Ebony to help in this way?'

'Oh, I would, and may I say how lovely it is to meet you. I've a lot to thank your family for, for taking care of my sister.'

'No, my dear, you have no need to thank us. We all helped each other, didn't we, Ruth?'

Bett put her pennyworth in. 'And I had a bit to do with it, yer know.'

'You did, Bett. My Aunt Rebekah had a happy last few years with you all. It's me who should be thanking them, Ellen.'

'We're cockneys, mate, we all 'elp each other. I got Rebekah her market stall and she made curry for me to sell on me barrow – that's 'ow it works. Only, I'd never seen me own eat curry like they did. Me hot spuds used to go to waste! Bloody young ones, they'll soon not know what it's like to eat pie and mash at this rate!'

They all laughed at Bett.

'I'm telling yer. I bet that 'alf the young we feed'll go for your African food, Ebony.'

Ebony beamed, then said, 'Ruth, girl, why don't you come to the service on Sunday? You used to love it and the Reverend Jafari and everyone is always asking after you. They're so proud of your stage work, girl.'

'Oh, can we . . . I mean, well, I know you said, Ruth, but may I come too?'

'Of course you can, Ellen. All are welcome in our house of God.'

'Thank you, Abdi. I'll look forward to it.'

Ruth felt warm inside. All the people she loved in the world were coming together. She only wished the one she loved the most – Adrian – would be there too.

The rest of the visit went by with chatting about Robbie and Abe, and Ruth's stage work and hers and Ellen's plans to go to work with the Red Cross, though when they asked about hers and Ruth's parents, it became a little uncomfortable explaining how they shared the same mother.

Abdi saved the day. 'I shall pray that you find your mother, Ruth and Ellen. And if you do, we will care for her while you are away, just as you cared for our Aunty Rebekah.'

'Ta, Abdi. We're hoping Bett gets a lead to where she is before we leave.' As she said this Ruth glanced at the clock on the mantelshelf and realized that they must take their leave if they were to get to the Red Cross meeting on time. And today was particularly important as they might learn what was to happen and if they had been chosen.

After hugs with Ebony, Abdi followed them down the stairs. Then, as the other two said their goodbyes to him and went through the door, Ruth hesitated. 'Is . . . well, as a friend, mate, I hope you don't mind me asking, but are you and Ebony all right? Are yer managing?'

Abdi put his head back and laughed the laugh she remembered and loved.

'Oh, Ruth, always mindful of others. Yes, we're all right. We've had to pull our horns in like everyone; business isn't so good and supplies hard to come by. But we'll manage. We've enough of Aunty Rebekah's legacy left to put Horacio through university but won't have if we pay for this higher school, so it will help if he gets a scholarship. But there's nothing like that for him to apply for to go to university – it will all have to be paid for. We're willing to make any sacrifice we must to get him there. He represents the future – the change in this country for my people.'

Ruth sighed with relief. It had been a long road of suffering for these two beloved friends to get as far as they had. It was unbearable to think of them losing it all. Abdi surprised her then and warmed her heart as he bent and kissed her cheek. She smiled at him.

'See yer soon, mate.'

A grin lit his face. To Ruth, it was a wonderful moment and one that was rare for the very proper Abdi.

Chapter Seventeen

Ellen

There was an excited air amongst those of the young men and women gathered in the hall who had said they were willing to go where needed and chatter filled the room.

Ellen kept her fingers crossed that she, Ruth and Alison, the girl Ruth had asked her to sponsor, were chosen.

When Miss Jaminson stood, after ticking them all off on her register, a silence fell. She looked around the room.

'I know that those of you who have put your names forward are anxious for me to announce who has been chosen from my group. But . . .'

Ellen tensed. She hadn't thought there would be a 'but'.

'Well, it is unfortunate but out of the ten of you who volunteered, only three have been chosen. That is if the three can be ready to go next week. If not, then others can take the place of anyone who has to decline. But I want you all to keep your chins up as it is an ever-changing position that our medical staff abroad find themselves in, and it is likely that they will need a steady stream of us to help them. The problem at this early stage is funding. Only those who can pay their own fare are being chosen. This again will change as we raise more money, but sadly, though a unit of much talent, we do all come from one of the poorest areas of

London . . . For the men amongst us, you are now trained enough to volunteer for the Army Medical Corps, and they are asking for you to come forward.'

A cheer went up from the five young men who always sat together.

'I have details here for you all of where you should go to offer your services and your Red Cross certificates. And we all wish you well. Now, if you would like to come up and take a pack each, you may leave as there will be little time for you to make arrangements and spend time with your families.'

Ellen took hold of Ruth's hand and squeezed it. 'Oh, Ruth, could it be you, me and Alison?'

'I hope so, luv. I'm sure we were the only ones who said we could pay, but I have to admit to feeling nervous. Next week's bloomin' quick! I'll just have to hope the theatre will let me go.'

'Is there any doubt?'

'There hasn't been any objection, and they know me plans. It's just if they can do it at such short notice. But if it's us, then I ain't saying anything about that to Miss Jaminson, just accepting the offer. But yer sure yer'll be able to afford it all, ain't yer, Ellen?'

'I will, love. And I'll have enough to keep us going . . . They'll feed us, won't they? So, we'll not want much more than our uniforms and our fares.'

'Yes, that's all we'll need, mate. But next week! That's a bit worrying.'

'It is for me, too. I'll have to make a trip up to see Dilly and Cook, and make sure they're all right. Gran left plenty to keep them going, but I need to say goodbye.'

'I'll come with you.'

'Ha! I thought you would.'

They both giggled.

'Right, settle down, girls. I want you all to stand and applaud the lads as they go.'

This was a moving moment, and yet, one filled with pride too, as the five left them all waving and looking as though they would win the war on their own.

Once they were seated again the anticipation had waned as those who couldn't pay their way were very quiet. Ellen felt sorry for them and wished she could pay for them all.

'Ellen, Ruth and Alison. You are the ones chosen, and I am very proud of you all.'

The rest of the meeting was abandoned for everyone else but them.

As the girls filed out, they wished them luck. Ellen's heart went out to those who'd been hoping to go.

'Now, here is where you are to report to and what you will need, girls. Our hearts all go with you. Good luck.'

Once outside, Alison linked arms with Ellen. 'Ta for making this possible for me, Ellen, mate. You're a diamond.'

Ellen didn't know what to say to this. She wasn't comfortable in the role of benefactor and didn't want Alison's gratitude. But, out of her depth with the older girl, she just smiled and nodded.

'Let's go and get pie and mash at Rosie's caff, eh? She makes the best yer know.'

'Ha, Ali, you're always thinking of your belly, girl. We've to get back to Bett, and we've arrangements to make, so yer'll have to go on yer own, luv.'

'But we'll meet tomorrow at the Red Cross headquarters and get kitted out, eh?' Ellen chipped in.

'Yes, Ellen, luv, and ta again. See you both then.'

Ellen would have liked to have gone for the pie and mash. She wanted to get to know Alison better and to feel as comfortable with her as Ruth and she were together but supposed that would come in time.

They left Alison at the end of Bonner Road. The night had turned bitterly cold, so they huddled together as they walked. Her voice shaking with the cold, Ruth said, 'Let's call in at The Old George Inn and ask if they'll let us use their phone, eh? I'd like to talk to Adrian.'

'They might not let me in.'

'Ha, nothing seems to have been said about our ages by the Red Cross. I mean, I can't believe I got away with it, but you! It's not that yer don't look it or anything, but well, yer really are only around fifteen.'

'I am. My father was adamant he knew my birthdate. But you could be a good few months older than you think, Ruth.'

'Well, we got away with it and it's what we both want to do. I just hope that it leads to me seeing Robbie and Abe. Anyway, going into the pub'll be another test for yer . . . Though, hold on a mo. Yer've got yer make-up on, but I'll add a bit of lippy. I've got some in me bag. We can get under that gas lamp and we can put a bit on, and on our cheeks too, to look like rouge.'

They both giggled as Ruth fiddled in her bag and pulled out a powder compact. The mirror glinted in the flickering street lamp.

Ruth managed expertly, but Ellen had a job to keep her lips tight over her teeth, she was giggling that much.

'Pack it in, you daft thing. I'm freezing.'

Making an effort to keep a straight face, Ellen allowed Ruth to paint her lips and found it a strange sensation, though the taste of the lipstick was even more alien as it had a hint of stale fruit.

When they stepped across the road and reached the pub door, Ruth whispered, 'Act confidently. It ain't done for girls to go into a pub by themselves, and we might be taken for floozies. Just leave the men and their catcalls to me, luv.'

'Floozies! Oh, Ruth, no!'

Ruth took her hand. 'It's all right, luv, nothing'll happen to you, yer'll see.'

'Can't we ring in the morning? Surely you know someone with a telephone?'

'They have one at the theatre, but I just needed to talk to Adrian. He was due to have that test, remember?'

At a loss, Ellen allowed herself to be dragged inside. The smoky atmosphere stung her eyes and made her cough, drawing attention to them.

'Put the wood in the bleedin' 'ole, girls . . . Blimey, it's Ruth. 'Ello, girl, what're you doing in 'ere?'

'Jack! Hello, mate. Yer just the one. This is me sister, Ellen . . . Me long-lost twin sister. We're going to war as Voluntary Aid workers next week and wanted to use the landlord's phone. Will you ask him for me?'

'Anything for you, Ruth. Going to war, yer say? Ain't them VAD nurses? I didn't know yer were one of them.'

Glad that he didn't question her being old enough, though none of them really knew how old she was, she told him, 'We've been training for months with the Red Cross.'

'Well, I'm proud of yer. But what about yer theatre work? We're all proud of that too, yer know.'

'This is more important, Jack. Now, come on, mate, go and ask the landlord, will yer? I need to make that phone call.'

'All right, luv, keep your hat on.'

Within a minute or two they were behind the bar in a little cubbyhole. Lifting the receiver off the wall, Ruth handed it to Ellen. Almost as soon as she dialled the number Adrian's voice came down the line. 'Hello, Adrian Vale here. Who's calling?'

Ellen swallowed. It was so nice to hear his voice, and yet homesickness flooded her at the sound. She thought of the lovely cottage and imagined Gran sitting nodding in the chair – only, she wouldn't be any more.

'Hello, Adrian, it's Ellen.'

'Ellen? What are you doing calling me at this time of night? Is everything all right?'

'It's fine. Ruth and I are going abroad. We set off next week. We're coming home, though, before we go. Here's Ruth. She wants to chat to you.'

Ellen heard Ruth's part of the conversation, sometimes sounding fine but at other times distressed. 'Yes, we're going, we really are going.' 'No, they didn't ask for verification of our age . . . I mean, how could they get it? I reckon they're so desperate they let it go. Yer see, not that many can pay their way.' Then, 'She'll be fine, Adrian. I'll look after her – though it might be her looking after me! Anyway, that's all sorted, but I'm worried about you. How did yer appointment go?'

Waiting patiently, Ellen strained her ears to listen to Adrian's crackling voice coming down the line. Ruth leaned closer to her so they could share the phone.

'Not good, I'm afraid. It is asthma. But he's given me some tips on keeping well. Apparently, a sudden change of atmosphere – going from the warm to the cold – or sudden exercise can bring on an attack. So, I won't be able to go abroad to fight.'

Ellen saw a look of relief on Ruth's face. None of them wanted Adrian to go. But Ruth didn't say this, she just comforted him.

'I'm sorry, me darlin', I know yer disappointed but surely there's other things that yer can do to help the war effort?'

'Yes, there are. I've already been in touch with Sandhurst. They are going to train me in some special work needed; probably at the War Office, I don't know yet, but yes, I can do my bit.'

'Oh, that's good. I almost wish I weren't going now.'

'No, don't say that, Ruth. This is something you need to do . . . We all need to do something about this war. We'll write to each other, darling, don't worry about it now. When will you be coming here?'

'I don't know yet. I think we'll have to go to the theatre first and make arrangements. I'm going to leave them in the lurch a bit.'

'I'm afraid that's true of us all, darling. We're all leaving something behind. They have a stand-in for you, don't they? And they know that you're planning this so don't worry too much.'

'I'll try not to . . . Adrian, I'll have to go as the landlord's making faces as much to say we're using up his phone bill. Love you.'

'Love you too, darling. Make it soon that you come here. Love to Ellen. Bye for now.' The click of him replacing his receiver seemed to echo around them.

Ruth held on to the phone for a little while. Ellen could see her hands were shaking. Her own heart had dropped a little. It had never seemed so bad when they were all going, but now that just her and Ruth were, it somehow didn't seem the same.

Ruth put the receiver down and took hold of her arm. 'Come on, let's get out of here. Let's get home to Bett, she'll soon cheer us up.'

On the way home they chatted about their decision, and both came to realize it was the right one. Many couples were being parted at this time and it was the same for Ruth and Adrian.

'Let's make plans to go up to Leeds as soon as we can, Ruth.'

Suddenly, Ellen knew that's where she wanted to be.

'We'll have to, luv, as we ain't got long. Tomorrow, we'll go to headquarters as planned to get the rest of the instructions and to buy what we need. Then we'll go to the theatre. I'm just going to tell them that's it. I just can't do any more performances. I had warned them so they should be all right with it . . . They'll bloomin' well have to be.'

When they reached Bett's, she was asleep in the chair in front of a roaring fire. She woke with a start.

'Bleedin' 'ell, yer 'ome early.'

As they told her why, her face changed. 'That soon?'

'Yes, luv. We told you we were going to find out tonight and that it might be soon.'

'I know you bloomin' well did, but I still didn't expect it to be in just a few days. You will come to the church with me on Sunday, won't yer?'

Ellen glanced at Ruth. She could see Ruth was undecided so jumped in. 'We'll try. We want to go to Leeds the day after tomorrow, so it depends on how long we stay.'

Bett looked downcast.

Though Ellen didn't think this the moment, she couldn't help herself as she blurted out, 'Bett, have you heard anything about our mum yet?'

Bett looked shocked. Her face took on a few different expressions as she seemed to be pondering her answer, but then Ellen filled with disappointment and heartbreak as she said, 'No, sorry, mate, I ain't. Me boys have asked around, but though they 'ad a prossie on their patch called Tilda, they ain't seen her and no one's 'eard of her for a good while. They'll keep looking, though, luv, and if anyone can bleedin' find her, them two can.'

Ellen's heart sank. Ruth didn't say anything, and Ellen didn't feel like pursuing it with her as she was laden with sorrow as it was, hearing that Adrian was going to be in London, now that she'd decided to go abroad.

After a solemn supper of mashed potato and minced lamb that Bett had made for them, which was delicious but hard to swallow with all that weighed on them, the girls hugged Bett and then went up to their own flat.

Bett called after them, 'I put hot stones in yer bed, me darlin's. They're wrapped in old bits of thick blanket so should still be nice and warm.'

Ruth turned and ran back down and into Bett's arms. 'Oh, Bett, I'm going to miss yer.'

Ellen felt a lump in her throat as she watched from her position halfway up the stairs. Bett held Ruth and gently patted her back. They both dried their tears as they parted, but didn't say any more. Ellen's own tears spilled over, but she quickly wiped them away.

Once they were ready, they got straight into bed and snuggled up together. The hot stone on Ellen's side gave her comfort.

'We won't have hot stones in those tents, Ruth.'

'I know. Are yer scared, Ellen?'

'A bit, Ruth, are you?'

'Yes. I'm frightened out of me wits, to be honest. I don't know if I've got enough knowledge now or if I'm going to be accepted by the others, or even if I can actually help in any way. I can't even remember how to bloomin' well tie a bandage!'

Ellen laughed. 'Really? You daft thing. Of course you'll be up to it and be able to do it. We've had our training – you at the Red Cross and me with Miss Roland, and we both know what we're doing. It will be fine when we get there, I promise.'

'Anyone would think you were the oldest out of us two. I tell you, Ellen, I can't believe that yer the same person as that frightened little girl of the orphanage . . . Oh, Ellen, they were bad days, weren't they?'

'They were. I don't like to think of them.'

'No, neither do I, but, well, if ever you do want to talk, you will, won't yer? Because yer know what yer learned in that home – that talking was the best thing.'

'Yes, you're right, I will, I promise. But I am a lot better now and, like I said, I don't think about it a lot, do you?'

'Not a lot but it never leaves me, and I know it never left Robbie.'

'I'd love to meet Robbie. I hope we do get somewhere near to him. With him being a cook, he might even be in our camp and cook our meals.'

'I never thought of that, but he might be . . . Oh, I hope we do meet up with him as that would help me. And Abe. Remember, yer have seen them as they were both in that landau with me and Hettie the day I saw you in London?'

'Yes, I do remember. I remember every bit of that time. I made myself remember it so that one day I could find you.

201

It was Abe's father who was shouting at you as we disappeared around the corner.'

'Yes . . . Anyway, let's not talk of that.'

Ellen remembered that Ruth had told her that it was this part of the incident that had led to Hettie's death. She felt mortified at mentioning it.

After a moment, Ruth said, 'I'm worried about Abe. Worried he'll take too many risks, wanting to be a hero. I can imagine him leading from the front, trying to prove he's a man.'

'But he is a man.'

'I know, but, well, he's like Robbie in a way.'

'Oh, I see. You did explain about Robbie.'

'Yes, but no one must ever find out, Ellen, because it's against the law and if they did, they might even shoot him or something, I don't know. But, well, please make sure if we do meet up with him that you never, ever let it out.'

'I wouldn't dream of doing so. I don't understand it all, Ruth, and I've never really heard of it . . . except, well, Gedberg . . . But no, I wouldn't tell anyone. I promise I would never do anything that might harm your Robbie.'

'I know, luv. I don't know what's the matter with me. I'm all jittery tonight. I don't seem able to do anything other than moan. Let's try to get some sleep, shall we?'

'You haven't said anything about me asking after Mum?'

'I . . . I find it too painful. Thinking of her. Thinking that she might be out there on this cold night. Maybe with nowhere to go.'

'I know.'

Ruth's muffled sob matched her own.

'Tell me again what she looked like, Ellen.'

'She was beautiful. She looked like you. Her clothes were

posh, but she talked like you.' Ellen went on giving all the details she could. Remembering for Ruth, but mostly for herself as she tried to hold on to the picture which sometimes faded. She didn't want it to, she wanted to remember.

A soft little snore told of Ruth sleeping. Ellen was glad for her. She closed her own eyes, but sleep eluded her. Her mind went from her mum to her gran and then to her dad, finally settling on her brother – Ruth's half-brother – and she wondered if he would ever really know them. She hoped he would. With all her heart, she hoped he would.

Chapter Eighteen

Ruth

The sun was beaming through the window the next morning.

Ruth couldn't believe the warmth from it that reflected through the glass, despite the usual smog haze of London hanging around the glistening-with-frost rooftops.

A sleepy Ellen asked, 'What time is it?'

'I don't know, luv, but it's light so it must have gone eight. We'd better get up. Come on, hop about a bit.'

Bett's voice came bellowing up the stairs. 'About time the pair of you were about. I've been up this good hour since. I've porridge on if you wants some.'

'Ooh, we don't half, Bett. Be down in a mo, mate.'

With the porridge filling them and being all wrapped up warm, they walked out into the cold air with Bett waving at the door.

When they reached the marketplace Ruth hailed a taxi. 'Bath Street, please, driver.'

'Where the eye 'ospital is, luv?'

'Yes, but we're going to the Red Cross office which is just across the road.'

'Ah, volunteering girls, eh?

'Yes, we go oversees next week.'

She felt Ellen tense beside her.

'Are you all right, Ellen?'

'My belly just tightened. I don't know if it was excitement or fear.'

'I know what you mean, luv. Mine's excitement now. I've got over all that I said last night.'

'Glad to hear it.'

Ruth sat back. *Brave words*, she thought, but she didn't really know if the feeling that clutched at her heart was fear or excitement.

Ellen sighed. 'I've dreamed of doing this since being a little girl. Now at last, even though I'm not very old, I'm attaining that dream.'

'Never mind about saying you're not very old,' Ruth told her. 'Just remember how old you're supposed to be!'

'I will.'

When they arrived, the driver looked at Ellen quizzically. For a moment Ruth thought he might say something of what he'd heard, but he just said, 'You'll pass, miss. And a very brave young girl you are. Good luck.'

'Phew. I thought we'd been rumbled then. Sorry, Ruth, I just forgot for a second.'

'Come on. Just don't when it's important not to!'

A poker-faced woman sat behind the desk when they walked into the clinically white office. 'Name?'

They gave their names.

'Wait in the corridor up there, please.'

As they climbed the four steps to the next level, Ruth's legs felt like lead. She was worried too that Alison wasn't here but didn't say anything as Ellen looked like a scared rabbit as they sat down in what looked more like a waiting room than a corridor.

In one wall was a frosted-glass window. Shadows moved around behind it, and she could hear muffled voices and now and then a cabinet drawer being opened and then slammed shut. Her nerves were on edge.

Suddenly the window slid open. 'Miss Faith and Miss Harpington? This way, please.'

She and Ellen stood to attention and marched off behind the stiff-backed woman.

'Where's Alison, Ruth?'

'I don't know. I can't understand it. Hope she ain't chickened out.'

But by the time they got to the office the woman was taking them to, an out-of-breath Alison came running up behind them. 'They let me through downstairs and told me to catch up with yer. Sorry I'm late!'

'Never mind, mate, you're here now. Let's see what they've got to say, eh?'

The next hour or two was a flurry of fittings and instructions that left Ruth feeling as though she was reeling with information.

They all carried bags when they left, packed with papers, and each had two long purple dresses, two long grey cloaks, two headdresses that flowed down their backs, and they were told to buy sensible shoes, white socks and thick stockings.

To Ruth, just to imagine herself wearing them filled her with excitement and the importance of what she'd taken on.

'Who would've thought, Ruth and Ellen from the orphanage and Alison from the poor end of east London would ever be nurses, and even less, would travel to exciting places like France and Belgium!'

'Not me! Come on, girls, let's go to Rose's caff. Ellen's

opening up me world and I don't even know her. And there's no better place to have a good chinwag than in Rosie's. Besides, I'm starving!'

Ellen and Ruth burst out laughing.

'Trust you, mate! All right, Alison, let's do it, shall we?'

Alison grinned as they jumped in a taxi but once seated, they all became quiet and Ruth knew that, like her, it had suddenly seemed to dawn on them that this was real, this was going to happen!

Ruth wanted to go to the station right now and jump on a train to see Adrian, to be in his arms once more, but there was still so much to do. The paperwork to register, tickets to be bought, the extra things she would need, and all kinds of arrangements to be made, even things like leaving a letter with the Red Cross to be sent to loved ones in the event of anything happening to them.

It was this bit of information that had opened her mind to the fact that what they were doing would mean they would be faced with dangerous situations. She'd never thought she'd be anything but safe and secure whilst she helped wounded young men.

But no one could stay solemn long in Rose's cafe.

Her, ''Ello there, 'ow yer doing? It seems ages since I saw you last, Alison,' and her cackling laugh at her own joke had them all laughing with her.

'Shurrup, Rosie, and get us a mug of tea, will yer? And I'll 'ave some of that mash and sausage this time with boiled carrots, luv.'

'Right yer are, Alison, I were just kidding you . . . Hello, Ruth, I really 'aven't seen you in a while, but then yer've been busy. I tell yer, girl, we're all that proud of you. Look on me wall.'

Ruth blushed when she looked up and saw a photo of herself in full costume.

'You'll sign it for me before yer leave, won't yer, girl?'

This astounded Ruth, but she said she would.

'And who's this, then? She has a similar look to you. Look like sisters, yer do, but I've never known you to have family, Ruth, girl.'

Ruth introduced Ellen and Ellen, with her usual charm, had Rosie in her pocket in no time telling the story they had rehearsed, and Alison knew and believed.

Rosie was enthralled. A local character, who busybodied into everyone's business and yet did no harm, she teetered off on high heels that Ruth would find painful after half an hour, let alone to work in them serving people all day. Her tight skirt made her bottom wiggle and her face was over made up, but pleasant.

When they sat down Ellen went a little quiet. She fiddled with her bags, and then took time to take her coat off.

Ruth understood. Ellen still hadn't had much time to get to know Alison and there was an awkward moment or two before Alison broke the ice. 'Well, mate, like I said to yer before, you're a diamond and I'm really looking forward to this trip with yer.'

'Thanks, Alison, and I am with you.'

Ruth sighed as that conversation came to an end but then Alison put a fear into her by asking Ellen, 'How old are yer really, Ellen?'

A shocked Ruth asked her, 'Whatever made you ask such a question, Alison?'

'I dunno, sometimes Ellen seems older than you and sometimes she seems so much younger. It just don't feel like she's the same age.'

'Look, mate, just accept it, will yer? It's none of your business.'

'Sorry, I didn't realize it was a sore point. You know what I'm like. I'm like a dog with a bone when I get a little query in me head. Me mum used to say I 'ad the curiosity of a cat.'

'Used to? Have yer lost your mum, Alison?'

Alison coloured at this question from Ellen and, for a moment, Ruth thought she was going to cry.

Ellen put her hand out and laid it over Alison's. 'It's all right, you don't have to tell us. I shouldn't have asked.'

'Me dad murdered her.'

A stunned silence fell at this. Ellen recovered first. 'Oh, Alison, no!' Ruth saw Ellen's hand tighten on Alison's.

'Do you have any brothers and sisters?'

'Yes. Four. We all live with me gran – me dad's mum, as he's in prison waiting to be hanged! Me mum didn't have any family . . . She were lovely. Me gran, well, she's all right with the little ones, but me? She sees me as the one to blame as me dad picked on me a lot and Mum stood up for me and that caused rows. But not as many as 'is drinking and womanizing and taking all the money me mum earned, leaving us starving 'alf the time.'

'So, that has led you to find food a comfort?'

'Blimey, are you a bleedin' psychiatrist now, then, Ellen?'

'I've been through a lot, Alison, and know a little of how the mind works.'

Ruth's heart ached for Alison and an understanding came to her with what Ellen had said, making her feel the guilt of teasing Alison about her eating.

She wanted to try to help her, as she knew Ellen did. She leaned forward and patted her arm. 'We'll look out for you, Ali. Miss Jaminson said that we will be posted together.'

'I suppose there won't be a lot to eat there?'

'I'm sure they'll feed us well, luv.'

'If not, you can have my rations, Ali, but the thing to do is to try to get to a place where you're well. It can be done. I did it.'

Ruth listened as Ellen told Alison how she had been in a nursing home, mentally ill, wanting to hurt herself and having screaming fits, and then, how she got well.

'Blimey, Ellen . . . And was it something bad that set you off? Something you couldn't cope with?'

As Ellen told of the incident in the wood near her home, Ruth listened with a feeling that her heart would break for this dear sister. She felt the horror of the story and knew what it must cost Ellen to tell it, but she also knew that Ellen chose to tell it instead of the nightmare of the orphanage as that would involve herself and Ellen wouldn't want to tell anything that wasn't her place to tell, so she chipped in, 'But that's not all. Ellen and me suffered a lot of that sort of stuff at the orphanage we were brought up in. I've had bad moments, but I had an amazing person rescue me. But it all comes to me now and again and I could scream and scream it away from me. We have to find some way of coping. For me, it's been me hat-making and the theatre.'

Alison was near to tears. 'How did yer both get over all of that? Me 'eart breaks for yer. But yer did, didn't yer? Yer fought back and I could too. That's what yer saying, ain't it? That me eating all the time is all down to me troubles and if I could learn to cope, I'd get better?'

Ellen leaned forward. 'Yes, but it isn't something you can do on your own, or overnight. We will help you, won't we, Ruth?'

'We will, luv. We'll always be there for you. The three of

us will help each other as we have a lot to face. This ain't going to be no picnic, yer know.'

'Be all right for me if it were, I'd eat the bleedin' lot!'

Ellen and Ruth burst out laughing. Alison beamed. Her happiness increased Ruth's. And for the first time, she saw a beauty in Alison. Always she'd looked sad and even though she'd made everyone laugh, the laughter hadn't touched herself. Now it did as her body began to shake, causing them all to go into a fit of giggling, dabbing their eyes, trying to stop, then looking at each other and exploding in laughter again.

''Ere, you lot, get this down yer, that'll quieten yer. You're disturbing me customers.'

Alison, through splutters and mopping her face, said, 'Sorry, Rosie, mate, but I'm so 'appy. These are the best friends I could ever 'ave and we're going to look out for one another. We'll quieten down now.'

When Rosie had put the steaming hot meal in front of them, she said to Alison, 'Stand up, luv, and let me give you a hug. You're a good girl, and easy to love, and I'm going to miss yer but I'm glad that you're going to be with others who love you as much as I do.'

Ruth and Ellen dabbed away tears at the sight of Rosie and Alison hugging. It was so lovely to see Alison realizing that she was valued.

'Right, sit down and eat yer meal, luv. And I were only kidding, your laughter warmed me little caff, and yer meals are on the 'ouse, as I'm proud of you – all three of you. Yer will keep in touch, won't you? A card now and then, eh?'

Alison's voice was thick with emotion as she said that she would.

Another woman who sat eating at a corner table shouted

211

out, 'Yer better 'ad as I'll be asking Rosie every day if she's 'eard from yer, Alison.'

A series of assenting noises could be heard, and then Rosie began to clap. All those in the cafe joined in and for Ruth, who knew the applause was for the three of them, it warmed her heart as she could see it had done for Ali and Ellen.

Their chatter was easy-going as they ate their food. Ruth all the while felt distracted by the thought of what they still had to do, realizing she wouldn't have time to see Adrian until Sunday.

There were their papers to register, and they had to get the necessary ones to allow them to travel. Then they had to shop for the rest of what they would need, not to mention her ordeal of leaving the theatre and saying goodbye to all her mates in the market.

The sadness of this last was helped by the sight of Ellen and Alison getting on so well. But she wished Sunday would come soon.

When at last it did arrive, they were all packed and the excitement seemed to zing in the air for Ruth as after the service they would catch the train and she would be on her way at last to see Adrian.

The small chapel was just as she remembered it – a rainbow of colour, happy chatter, hugs, jolliness, and love that had always surrounded her on a Sunday whenever she'd gone to this church with Rebekah. For a moment she thought she could see Rebekah sitting in her usual place but now she realized it was Ebony. She and Abdi stood and turned as she, Ellen and Bett walked into the church. Abdi put out his hand, but Ebony grabbed them each in turn and gave them a big hug. Then Ellen did something that Ruth had never done – she went towards Abdi with her arms open. At first it was a stiff embrace but then Abdi relaxed and hugged her back. Feeling shy, even though Abdi had breached the gap that held him aloft from them, Ruth didn't go forward as her feeling of being in awe of Abdi had returned. But then he turned to her with his arms open, and she went into them.

'Well, Ruth, so you begin another adventure. Our prayers go with you, and I know that Rebekah will protect you.'

She smiled up at him. 'She's always with me – me mum.'

'She was honoured when you called her that, but she so deserved the title.'

'She did, she was me saviour.'

'Can't we bleedin' well sit down, Ruth? Me legs are aching from the walk, let alone standing around.'

Ruth knew that Bett was feeling a bit left out but was embarrassed at how she'd shown this. She felt her cheeks colour, but then a voice behind them bellowed out a huge laugh. Turning, she saw Reverend Jafari.

'Welcome, welcome. Come on, dear lady, I've reserved the best seats in the house for you and I'm very pleased to meet you.'

What followed amazed Ruth as both Ellen and Bett threw themselves into the service. They sang as loudly as the others, and danced in the aisle with her and Ebony, though Bett's dancing was more a sway of her hips as she held Ruth's hands, but her face shone with happiness.

After the service was ended Reverend Jafari came over to them. 'Now, ladies, I've heard all about everything from Abdi, and like what I hear. I must say, too, that it is good to see you again, Ruth.'

'Hello, Reverend. I'm sorry I haven't been for a long time. I've been so very busy and I'm always tired on Sundays.'

'You should never be too tired for God, Ruth.'

'I know. I realize now how much I've missed coming here. But I always say me prayers, so perhaps I can be forgiven?'

She didn't add that those prayers were mostly to the Holy Mary. That may not have gone down very well.

'Good. And there's nothing to forgive as long as you keep God in your heart . . . Well now, what's all this about a soup kitchen in my hall?'

'It's come from something me sister, Ellen, wants to do.'

'God blessed you and us when he sent her back to you, Ruth. It's a lovely story that Abdi told me about you both – good coming from evil.'

'Ta, Reverend. You don't object to the plan, then?'

'Object? I think it's a wonderful idea and I will be there every day that it's open to give a hand and hopefully to convert some of those little ragamuffins and their parents!'

Everybody around laughed at this. The Reverend Jafari was a huge, jolly man.

'So, now, I believe this lady will be in charge?' He smiled at Bett. 'From what I can see, this project couldn't be in better hands, Bett. With Ebony supporting you and volunteers from my congregation, I think this will be a wonderful and much-needed project . . . And, Ellen, I understand this was your idea and you are going to provide the initial funding?'

The reverend was full of praise for Ellen and Ruth was glad to see that she was happy and relaxed because this place had done that for her many years ago, and she wanted it to do the same for Ellen too.

214

After arranging to meet with Bett and Ebony and any volunteers to finalize the details, Ruth told him that they really had to go as they had a train to catch.

'Come on then, let's get you a taxi.'

The whole congregation waved them off, leaving Ruth in tears. But as they all went out of sight, her happiness returned, for after they had dropped Bett back home, she would be on her way to see her beloved Adrian.

The few days they had together went all too quickly. She'd been in Adrian's arms a lot during that time. But not out in the cold, always in his apartment, as she was so afraid of him having another asthma attack. As it was, she'd noticed him wheezing, which she'd never noticed before.

And now she was in his arms again, standing on King's Cross station surrounded by a crowd of excited young women, all dressed in Red Cross uniforms. Her own excitement was tinged with deep sadness.

'I'll miss you so much, darling.'

'Oh, Adrian, we only just found each other, and now we don't know when we'll see each other again.'

'You'll be so busy, the time will pass.'

'You'll take care of yerself, won't yer? And promise me yer'll do everything the specialist tells yer to.'

'I promise I will, darling. I think at the moment I've just got a bit of a cold. I'll be fine, and I'll be busy too, as it won't be long now before I have to report for duty.'

'I'll write often.'

'I'll look forward to your mail coming and will write back every day, darling.'

His kiss held an urgency. She knew his feelings – had them herself as she was consumed with an urge to just take his

215

hand and run with him as far away from here as they could. This was a cold, empty place of goodbyes.

A voice broke them apart. 'Come along, everyone. The train's coming in now. Line up. Make sure you have all your belongings. Those of you with carriages have the number of the one you're to be in.'

They boarded, Ellen and Alison encouraging her along. A banging of doors and then a shrill whistle heralded the movement of the train. Ruth hung out of the window waving, hardly seeing Adrian's disappearing figure through her tears and the clouds of smoke that billowed around him.

A little prayer came to her: *Holy Mary mother of God, take care of my Adrian.*

Now he was just a little dot on the platform, and she was being told to put her head inside at once or she might be decapitated. This was from Alison who was making an attempt to keep her happy, but it wasn't really working.

The three of them sat together on their cases in the draughty corridor as all the nurses and sisters had taken up the carriages. They held hands and watched London go whizzing by as the train chugged them towards an unknown future.

Chapter Nineteen

Ellen

When the chatter between the three of them stopped and each was left with their own thoughts, Ellen's were of Dilly, how she'd cried and cuddled her, and of Cook too, who'd waved her hanky as they'd left Rose Cottage. But despite the tears, she'd found that the two were very happy and had all they needed. They lived together as friends, no longer in their roles as servants, but sharing the chores, and the house, and enjoying playing cards in the evening.

This had made it so much easier to leave them, though she wondered when she would ever see them again. These thoughts made her realize that her time in Leeds hadn't been all bad; she'd been happy and loved. But now it was time to go forward to her future.

It didn't seem long before the brakes of the train screeched to a halt, initiating a flurry of activity. 'Gather your things and line up on the platform, girls!'

'Right, everyone, see that everything is loaded onto the porters' trolleys, please.'

This was the first of a series of instructions till Ellen began to feel like a lackey.

And then like a second-class citizen when they boarded

the ship, and they were given blankets and told to sit up on deck as there was little room reserved for them inside.

But she enjoyed the feel of the breeze through her hair and watching the activity on the dock below. It was a wonder to her that the ship could float with what was being loaded – trucks, huge crates, which she could only guess contained tents, equipment and food. Not to mention that it was already weighed down with what looked like an army of servicemen, Red Cross personnel and their luggage.

Sighing as she sat next to Ruth and Ali, she asked, 'Do you think this is how things are going to be, Ruth? Are we just here to do the donkey work?'

'I don't know, mate, but I think we're at the bottom of the pecking order. I mean, the fancy name of VADs is only a title. We ain't nurses, are we? Miss Jaminson did warn us that we'd find ourselves doing a variety of jobs.'

'I ain't bothered, meself. I'm just so excited to be 'ere.'

'I know, Ali, but I want to be more than a dogsbody.'

'I think there'll be plenty of other stuff for us to help with, Ellen, luv. But we're here now and we have to accept and obey orders or else we're going to be very unhappy. We always knew we were just going to assist the medical staff, so as I see it, that means letting them have the best seats on the train and on the boat too.'

This all shocked Ellen. It wasn't at all how she imagined it, but if Ruth and Alison were accepting of it, then she thought she must be too.

When they were only a short distance from the shore, the rough sea began to take its toll. Girls came up on deck heaving their hearts out over the side of the boat. Ali joined them, but this didn't surprise Ellen as she had tucked into huge doughnuts from a vender on the docks.

She and Ruth moved between the girls, trying to soothe them. 'Ruth, can you find Sister and ask her for some water for everyone? Surely she cannot be unaware of what's happening?'

'I will if the waves let me get as far as the steps, luv. Hold on.'

Suddenly, the young woman Ellen was helping collapsed onto the deck.

'Help me! Someone, help me to lift her.'

Ali, still looking a bit under the weather, came across and together they managed to get the young woman onto the bench.

''Ere you are, luv. I couldn't find the sister, but one of the crew gave me this jug full of fresh water.'

'We must get some down her, Ruth, I think she's dehydrated.'

They helped the young woman to sip the water. Gradually she came to. 'Thank . . . thank you.' She took a deep breath. 'That's better. Sorry, was I awful?'

'No, no, don't worry. You were being a little bit seasick, and we think you got dehydrated.'

The young woman looked up at Ellen. 'Who are you? I don't remember seeing you with the other nurses.'

'We're volunteers.'

'Oh? Really? I thought you were just here to help do the cleaning, et cetera. Are you nurses, then?'

'We want to be, but we never got our training. However, I'm going to be a doctor in the future. For now, though, I just want to do my bit.'

'Well, you've made a very good start. You did a very good job and you've certainly helped me. Thank you. What's your name?'

'Ellen Hartington and this is my sister, Ruth Faith . . . We – we're twins. We have different names because, we were . . . orphaned and brought up separately and haven't long found each other.'

Almost fully recovered now, the young woman said, 'Pleased to meet you both. I'm Sister Mary Beckwith, known as Sister Mary. Ha! I'm supposed to be in charge here but I'm not doing a very good job of it, am I?'

'These things happen, Sister. We none of us know if we have sea legs or not. The important thing is to not eat too much – or not at all on a short sea trip, and to drink plenty of water . . . Sorry, I'm beginning to preach.'

'She's good at anything medical, Sister. She knows all there is about nursing or anything to do with the body and mind. She's a whizz.'

Ellen felt herself blush at Ruth's words. 'No, really I don't. I have a lot to learn.'

'We'll see how things go, shall we? I will certainly use the talent you have, Ellen . . . Ruth, did you say? Ruth Faith?'

'Yes, Sister.'

'*The* Ruth Faith of West End theatre?'

'She is the very one, aren't you, mate?'

Sister Mary seemed to see Ali for the first time as she said this. She smiled at her then addressed Ruth again. 'Well! This is marvellous. I have been to see you and enjoyed your performances many times. I love the theatre. It would be wonderful if you could entertain us from time to time – well, that's if we do get any time . . . Oh dear, that's a lot of *times*!'

The sister giggled at her own joke.

'I'd love to. It would be an honour, mate . . . I mean, Sister.'

The sister giggled again, and Ellen thought she could really like Sister Mary. She was nice – human, whereas she'd been led to believe that most were tartars.

'Well, once we get settled, we must talk, Ruth. And you, Ellen. I will see you later. For now, though, I'd like to go down and get some rest on my bunk bed, if only I could stand.'

'Do you want us to help you, Sister?'

'No, thanks, that wouldn't look good, would it? I'll take a deep breath and make an extreme effort, and with my fingers crossed, I might just make it to my cabin. Thank you again, Ellen, and I won't forget you and what you want to do. You made a good impression. From what I've seen you're more than capable of helping out on the medical side. And if you other two have similar skills, then we will use them, I'm sure. I just need time to get sorted and see what situation I find.'

Ali piped up then. 'Well, I don't mind what I do. I'd consider anything as 'elping, Sister, so don't worry about what role you give me. I'm just happy to be going there and getting something different 'appening in me life. But Ellen and Ruth, well, it'd be a travesty to put them to cleaning and stuff. They're good at this nursing thing.'

The sister smiled. She'd stood now, and it was obvious that she'd already put her plan into action to determinedly walk back to her cabin. Ellen watched her as she stiffly took a few steps, then a few to the side as the boat lurched, before she righted herself again. She had her fingers crossed behind her back for Sister Mary as she turned and grinned at Ali. 'Bless you, Ali. That was a nice thing to say. Are you feeling better now, love?'

'Yeah, I'm okay. You were right, yer know. I shouldn't have 'ad them doughnuts!'

221

'Never mind, they're over the side of the boat now!'

The three of them laughed.

'Come here and let me give you a hug.' Ellen put her arms out and Ali came into them. It wasn't easy to get her arms around Alison's bulk but it felt good to hold her. It seemed to cement their new friendship. More than that as she found she loved Ali and wanted to comfort her and didn't want her always to think she was doing the wrong thing, or should be subservient.

Hours later they arrived at Calais and once more there was a rush to do this and that at the bidding of Sister Mary, who seemed to have recovered and to be in fine fettle, shouting orders at everyone in a way that brooked no argument.

By the time they disembarked, there was a hive of activity on the dock. The trucks were almost loaded, ambulances were being loaded with medical equipment and Sister Mary, clipboard in hand, was directing personnel.

Some of the girls and young men in the Medical Corps were assigned to the ambulances. Ellen envied them as she would have loved to do that job – to be the first to the patient, giving vital assistance and comforting them as they got them to hospital. But then she smiled to herself. She wanted to do every job going, and she couldn't do them all!

By the time they were ready to set off on the next leg of their journey, it surprised Ellen that herself, Ruth, Ali, Sister Mary and two others, who appeared to be very best friends and didn't seem to want to chat much, were the only ones left of the medical crew standing on the dock. Besides them there were a couple of trucks and four servicemen. Everyone else had now been dispatched in different directions.

'Now then, nurses and volunteers.' Sister Mary consulted

her clipboard, crossing things off as she told them, 'We're going to billet in Dunkirk for the first night and then set off early in the morning. We're assigned to a hospital that lies between Furnes and Ypres at a place called Hoogstade. I'm afraid it could be a bit hairy but be brave. We will all be together, and we will have these servicemen with us who will protect us. We are in the first truck and the second one will carry supplies for our hospital.'

They all piled into the truck.

'Blimey, this is as bad as the ship!'

'Hold on to the strap, Ali, it'll steady you, mate. Are you all right, Ellen, luv?'

Ellen nodded, but inside she felt scared. She reached for Ruth's hand. Ruth held it and tucked it under her arm. Never had she felt more in need of a big sister than she did now.

It didn't take long to get to Dunkirk. They'd passed the time watching the countryside appear at the back of the truck and slowly go into the distance. For the most part it looked like England, which was comforting.

The peacefulness of it calmed her till it didn't seem possible they were going to a warzone. When the truck pulled up and they climbed out, they were outside a three-storey-high grey-coloured building.

Ruth gave her a look which said just what she was thinking: that the place was very gloomy. Its windows were all closed off by shutters, which didn't help and gave the impression it would be dark and dingy inside, but to Sister's rap on the door a little old lady appeared, her face creased in a sunny smile.

In French she beckoned them in. Sister Mary spoke in hesitant French. Ellen understood the lady to say, 'Ah, the English saviours. Come on in, we're all ready for you.'

Sister Mary thanked her before turning and indicating they should follow her inside.

Ellen could see that this house had once been a boarding house. In the dusky hall a board on the wall held many keys with a painted number above each one.

A musty smell met them, as if it had been closed for a while. She could imagine why with the troubles being so near and the fear of them coming this far as everybody knew it was Germany's aim to invade France.

The lady told them their room numbers, the floor they were on and gave them a key each. 'There's only one room that is a private single room, the others will house two or three.'

Without thinking, Ellen said in French, 'Me and my sister and friend will take a three, please.'

Sister Mary looked astonished and then annoyed. 'I will thank you to leave the organization to me, Ellen.'

'I'm sorry, Sister Mary.' Mortified, Ellen lowered her head. Ruth's hand came into hers.

The moment passed as Madame Courtney, as the lady had told them to call her, explained, 'The rooms all have a pitcher of hot water for each person, and a commode behind a screen. Please place the lid on this and bring it down in the morning. Take it through there to the drain in the yard and wash it well under the tap. Now, I will show you where we will have our dinner and breakfast.' She took them through to a back room.

A little nod told them that she was finished and dismissed them.

Sister Mary thanked her. 'Now, Ellen, I gather you would have understood all of that, so you three volunteers can leave us and go to your room. The rest of you gather around and I will explain.'

Ellen couldn't tell if Sister was still cross with her or not but hoped that she wasn't.

'Bloomin hell, Ellen, is there no end to your talents?' Ruth giggled and squeezed her arm as she said this.

Ali chipped in. 'I'd say you'd better watch out, though, luv. You don't want to step on Sister's toes.'

'I didn't know you could even speak French, sis. I was so proud of you.'

'Adrian's responsible for that. My ex-tutor also taught me languages, but Adrian opened a different world for me. He taught me German too, but I don't have such a good grasp of that. We had whole days when he would only speak one or the other language to me . . . I didn't think when I spoke out.'

'Don't worry, Sister don't seem the kind to 'old a grudge. I'd say she'll never mention it again, as she's let yer know how she felt about it.'

Ali needn't have spelled this out as Ellen certainly knew that. Her body quivered a little.

'Hey, it'll be fine.'

'It was the cold, Ruth, it's freezing in here!'

Ruth gave her a look, which told of her knowing the truth, but she didn't say any more.

The room was dark and cold-feeling, but when Ruth opened the shutters and the room flooded with light, they were pleasantly surprised to see three crisp, clean beds, with their bulky feather mattresses looking so welcoming.

'Well, there are our bowls of water all steaming. I can't wait for a wash; I don't know about you two? So, how are we going to do it? Who's going first, then?'

'I don't have to go behind any screen, Ellen. I'm used to getting ready in a crowded dressing room, so if you two want to take turns, that's all right by me.'

Ellen saw a blush creep over Ali's face and guessed that she wanted privacy. 'I'll get ready out here with you, Ruth. You have the screened area, Ali.'

'If you're sure none of yer mind?'

'Get on with it, mate. 'Course we don't mind, we're sisters and that's a bit different, though I reckon you might have to get used to washing in front of others in the future, Ali.'

Ali didn't answer this, but grabbed her bowl and scurried for the screen, making one more journey to collect fresh clothes from her case.

Ruth lightened the moment by singing. Soon all three were joining in:

> '*You made me love you*
> *I didn't want to do it*
> *I didn't want to do it*
> *You made me want you*
> *And all the time you knew it*
> *I guess you always knew it*
> *You made me happy sometimes*
> *You made me glad*
> *But there were times*
> *You made me feel so bad*
> *You made me cry for*
> *I didn't want to tell you*
> *I didn't want to tell you*
> *I want some love that's true*
> *Yes, I do, 'deed I do*
> *You know I do . . .*'

They were all giggling by the time the long song came to an end. Ellen had been surprised, as she knew Ruth had, at

Ali's lovely tone. And it was good to see her appear in only her liberty bodice and long petticoat and stand as if coming through a stage curtain to belt out the chorus. This is when they collapsed in giggles.

When Ali went back behind the screen, Ruth winked and put her thumb up. And yes, Ellen felt it too. They'd just had a small victory where Ali was concerned.

'I'm staying in me undies to lie down for a bit.'

'Me too, Ruth. I'm glad to get these clothes off, though. They smell from poor Sister Mary being ill on the boat.'

'I saw that. It went all over you, but you never flinched.'

'I got used to it in the home where I was. I helped out a lot on the sick bays.'

Ruth came over to her. 'Yer've been through so much, Ellen, luv, but here yer are, stronger than any of us.'

As she went into Ruth's arms, she didn't feel strong. She was just so glad to have Ruth with her as, like when back at the orphanage, Ruth made her feel safe, and as if she was protected.

'Flipping 'eck, you're all wet!' They both laughed. 'Not that I mind, I just love hugging you.'

Ellen squeezed her extra hard before coming out of her arms. She somehow felt bereft when she did. Ruth was everything to her, sister, mother and friend. Ellen felt the tension leave her body – she could cope and *would* cope.

When they were refreshed, they all chose a bed and lay down, though Ruth closed the shutters before she retired, which made the room very peaceful.

Ellen couldn't go off to sleep but lay still, thinking. How she wished she could write home to her gran to tell her how she was getting on and how far they'd come. This threatened to bring the tears, so she just quietly whispered, 'I hope you're proud of me, Gran,' and, 'I love, you, Gran,' before making herself think of something else.

Her little brother Christopher came into her mind, and she wondered if she would ever get to know him. This thought was interrupted as into the silence came little snores. With her eyes now used to the dimness, she looked over at Ali lying fast asleep, contentedly blowing out little bubbles with her lips as she let the snore go. She smiled to herself, suddenly feeling better, and pleased that she'd met Ali. She was a loveable tonic.

Descending the stairs a couple of hours later, the smell of delicious food hit them.

'I'm starving!'

They grinned at Ali but didn't comment, just stepped aside so that she could get to the table first. The long table laid out just in front of an archway gave a view of the huge stove in the room behind, on which pots bubbled away.

Madame Courtney indicated the bottles of wine on the table. 'Drink,' she said in English, but then in French that it was her finest and had been laid down many years ago. 'Back in the days when I had the top-class people here.'

They all looked at Sister, but she shrugged. 'Not in my limited vocabulary, I'm afraid. What about you, Ellen, can you translate?'

Ellen nodded, unsure if she should or shouldn't, but as Sister smiled, she went ahead and translated what Madame had said.

'So, you have a talent for languages as well as nursing, Ellen, I think you're going to be very useful to us in the camp. Where did you learn all of that?'

'I had an excellent tutor, Sister.'

'Oh? So, you didn't go to any of the schools I know?'

'No, I've never been to school. I was always taught at home.'

Sister Mary didn't pass comment on this, but she did look a bit bemused.

The meal was delicious. A stew for which Madame apologized as it hadn't much meat in.

'Oh, don't worry about that,' Ellen told her. 'Everyone is enjoying it and we're used to not having a lot of meat at home.'

As Madame told them her story of having had the finest guest house in Dunkirk, Ellen related it to the others. It became hard work as all of them wanted to tell Madame something, but she did her best with the help of Sister Mary, who knew a lot more French than she'd first indicated. This allowed Ellen to tuck in as she really was feeling hungry. She wasn't sure about the wine, though, as she'd never tasted it before, or ever been offered it, other than a small sip of sherry. Not wanting to bring attention to herself by having some, she took a tentative sip.

The soldier next to her nudged her. 'Not your cup of tea, love?'

'No, but I don't like to offend, which it can. The French offer their best wine to honoured guests; it's like a slight to have it refused – at least, I think so. I sometimes don't know if what my tutor told me was right or if he was having me on because he did like to have a joke about things.'

'Oh, I see. Well, just in case, while no one's looking, I'll swap my empty for your full. How's that? By the way, my name's Jim. I know yours now as it's been said often enough. Pleased to meet you, Ellen. I'm going to be stationed very near to the hospital. I'm a mechanic. I'll be keeping the ambulances and any machinery going. I'm a whizz with generators. We've got all the equipment in our lorry that's needed out there. They tell me it's not a very well-equipped place but hopefully we can make it better. Mind, our sergeant told us they've been doing a sterling job, especially during the wave of attacks from the Germans.'

'Is it really bad in war?'

'It's not pleasant. I'm scared out of my wits!'

The way he said this made Ellen laugh. 'Where are you from?'

'Coventry in the Midlands. Now, don't you be afraid. There's nothing to be afraid of really. Not that I know, as us mechanics are usually in the background, not in the firing line. Though I wouldn't mind killing a few Germans. What about you?'

Ellen didn't know what to say to this because she didn't like the thought of killing anybody, but the evening was going so well, and she didn't want to spoil that so she laughed with him.

But the snippet of conversation had made her think that yes, there would be death. Not peaceful deaths like her Gran's, but mangled bodies of young men blown up. A shiver went through her, and as she had done so many times since leaving Bett's home, she felt her true age. She did what she always wanted to at times like this and reached out for Ruth's hand. The squeezing of hers in Ruth's clasp steadied her once more, as she knew it always would.

Chapter Twenty

Ellen

The next day, Ellen found out just what being in a war really meant.

Intelligence reached them that the main road was under siege a few miles from their destination. Their route to avoid this took them along country lanes that were sometimes almost impossible to navigate as they had sustained bomb damage or were swamped in mud.

The girls huddled together as the sky lit with flashes and crashing explosions that seemed to be within yards of them, hurt their ears and rocked the truck, making it feel as though it would topple over.

This went on for hours and hours till eventually they came to a small village and Sister ordered that they stop. 'It's getting dark now. We will have to bed down for the night.' She asked the soldiers to go and scout out somewhere.

The bitter cold that had ached her bones cut even deeper now they were at a halt. Ruth's arm came around her. She snuggled into her.

'I'll hotch up to you, Ellen, luv,' Ali said. 'Yer should be more like me and have a bit of padding on yer!'

Despite the cold and feeling desolate, Ellen giggled. She didn't think you could ever be with Ali for long and not do so.

When the soldiers returned, they had been told of a convent nearby that would take them. 'We could have done with you, Ellen. It took a while to understand and to make them understand. We frightened a poor farmhand to death! Poor lad hid in a wet ditch till we convinced him we were British.'

The convent was far from anywhere and seemed to lack any comfort. The nuns were kindly and, with their help, did manage to cook up a meal for them all of potatoes, some kind of meat, which Ellen had never tasted before but which someone said was rabbit, and topped with a really nice white sauce.

When it came to them getting the sleeping arrangements sorted, there were only the chapel benches, though not enough of them and some would have to sleep on the floor.

'At least we're with the Holy Mary, Ellen, look.'

The little statue of an innocent young girl looked down on them. Her arms were spread open wide; her face, though not smiling, had a gentle expression and as Ellen gazed at her, she understood why Ruth loved her so much. She made you feel you weren't alone.

'Come on, let's help get the sleeping bags off the truck. Sister's trying to form a line of us to make it easier to pass them along.'

This turned out to be fun as the soldiers kept throwing them deliberately high, trying to make the girls drop them. Everyone, even Sister, ended in up in fits of laughter and Ellen began to feel stronger and as if she really could do this surrounded by such stalwart folk.

She, Ruth and Ali chose a corner under the stairs that led to the belfry. For the first half an hour they just held each other's hands as now the jollity of the human chain was over, the reality of sleeping on the floor with a room full of near strangers hit them.

'Are you all right, Ruth?'

'I've been better, Ali, luv.'

'I'm so cold.'

Ellen could hear the tremble in Ali's voice. She sat up. 'I'll come the other side of you, Ali. Between us, me and Ruth will warm you.'

Alarm set up in Ellen when she felt how hot Ali's body was and yet she was shivering all over. 'Ali? Are you feeling unwell?'

'Ye-es. I – I've had a headache all day.'

'Ali? Ali, mate, how bad do you feel?'

Ali didn't answer.

Throwing her own sleeping bag over Ali, Ellen called out, 'Sister, Sister, Alison is ill!'

Sister came running.

'I need some light over here!'

The sound of a striking match, then a glow turned into a bright light as Ellen saw that Jim had lit a lamp. He came over and held it up. Now Ellen could see Alison, her worry increased. Sweat was pouring from her. Her eyes were closed.

'Have you any pain, Alison?'

When Alison answered it was in a croaky voice. 'It – it hurts when I breathe.'

'Ellen, over there, my bag, bring it to me.'

Sister examined Ali with a stethoscope and took her temperature. 'It's difficult to say what it is, but she is very unwell. Someone go and wake the nuns. We need a bed for her, and water to cool her down.'

'I'll go!' Ruth, who was on her knees looking over Ali, jumped up and ran for the door.

'Wait, take Ellen. You won't be able to make them understand . . . Private, take another soldier and fetch a stretcher from the truck.'

Not speaking to each other, Ellen and Ruth ran for all they were worth across the courtyard. A banging and German voices stopped them in their tracks. Two figures were lit up by a light coming on in the huge hall of the convent.

The voices shouting in German continued. The nun who had opened the door was shoved back with the butt of a gun in her chest.

Frozen to the spot and still in the shadows, Ellen made out that they were saying, 'You have English soldiers here. Where are they? Tell us!'

The nun didn't speak.

Another sharp push with the butt of the gun sent her reeling. The soldier stood over her pointing the rifle in her face. 'Tell me or I will shoot!'

Ellen went to step forward, but Ruth grabbed her arm and pulled her nearer to the wall. When there, Ellen felt Ruth's finger come onto her lips in a gesture that told her not to make a sound.

A tug on her sleeve beckoned her to follow. On tiptoes they crept back the way they had come. Once in the nave of the chapel Ruth whispered, 'Go and warn Sister and the others. I'm going round to where we have the lorries parked to warn Jim.'

'No, Ruth! It's too dangerous.'

'I have to. Now go!'

'Let's go together. Jim and his mate will have guns. I can't let you go alone.'

Ruth didn't argue.

Jim and the other soldier were making the noise of a factory as they moved equipment in an attempt to get to the stretchers. The lights of one of the trucks shone in the still night on the one they were working in. Seeing this, Ellen's fear gave her wings, as she knew Ruth's had since her running matched her own.

When they came up to the men, Ruth gasped, 'Germans! Germans are at the door of the convent! They've seen your trucks!'

Jim jumped down and was in the other vehicle switching off the lights before he spoke. The other soldier grabbed his gun which had been casually laid against the truck. He picked Jim's up and threw it to him.

When they were all close enough, Ruth told them what they'd seen.

Jim instructed them: 'Right, run back to the chapel and tell them to douse the light. Then tell everyone to remain still and not make a sound. Oh, and lock the chapel door. Come on, Ron, we're going to kill us some Germans!'

Ellen and Ruth were halfway back to the chapel when a voice called out, '*Halt!*'

A trickle of water ran down Ellen's leg. She grabbed hold of Ruth's hand. It was icy cold.

'Keep calm, Ellen, luv.'

'I – I've wet myself, Ruth.'

'Oh, luv.' Ruth's hand tightened on hers. The trembling of it somehow gave Ellen courage. She couldn't bear for Ruth to be afraid. Nor was she going to let anyone hurt her. In French and a steady voice that surprised herself, she asked, 'Who are you?'

One of the soldiers answered in English. 'Who are you? is the question. Don't try to make us think you are French. You have on the Red Cross dress of English ladies. Where are the rest of you?'

The other soldier spoke in German. 'There, look, I can see a light. In the chapel. Are there soldiers in there?' He came closer, his gun pointing at them. 'Tell me!'

Ellen swallowed hard. In German she said, 'No. Only nurses. We are on our way to—'

'Shut up! Liar! Nurses do not drive trucks and lug heavy equipment about. You have soldiers with you. Where are they?'

He'd stepped forward.

An involuntary 'No!' came from Ruth as the soldier's gun shoved into her breast. 'Tell me or I shoot your friend!'

A deafening crack resounded around them. The English-speaking German crumpled to the floor, his screams adding to the unreal state that had gripped Ellen. The soldier threatening Ruth turned, but another crack and he too fell to his knees before landing in a moaning heap.

It seemed to Ellen that the world had come to an end as she stood staring, unable to take in the sight in front of her.

'Ron, fetch a light. Ellen, see what you can do for them.'

As he spoke, Jim collected the guns the two soldiers had dropped. Ellen hadn't moved. 'ELLEN! Do what you're out here to do, save the lives of these men!'

Not believing what she'd heard but propelled by the command, Ellen started to run. As she did, she heard Ruth's gasping, shocked-sounding voice, 'I must see if the nun is all right first.'

'No, Ruth. She will only be stunned; the sisters will see to her. You must stop the bleeding. We can't let them die. Ellen, Ruth, please don't let them die.'

Ellen was glad to hear this. Glad that Jim wanted to save a German after what he'd said about wanting to kill them.

Now he just needed the confidence to do it. 'You can help them, Jim. Take off your belt and make a tourniquet above the wound. Ruth is already attending to the other one. And here's Ron with the light. I'll go and fetch Sister.'

She ran to the chapel door but found it locked. At the sound of gunfire, Sister must have ordered it so. Banging for all she was worth and yelling at the top of her voice, she begged them to open the door. Suddenly, it did open. Another one of the soldiers stood there, his rifle pointing at her. 'Are you alone?'

'Yes, Jim and Ron shot the Germans. There are two of them. They're badly hurt, they need help. Ruth and Jim are doing what they can.'

Sister came running. The soldier barred her. 'No! It may be a trap. Wait while I check it out.'

'There's no more soldiers, I promise. There were only two.'

'But others may be alerted by the shooting. We have to be careful.' He beckoned to the last remaining soldier. 'Follow me. Sister, stay here and lock the door. If there are only two and they need your help, then we'll get them back here to you.'

'But Ruth's out there! I'm not leaving Ruth!'

'Ellen, please. We must do as the soldiers tell us in any war situation. Come in at once! I am ordering you!'

Torn, Ellen looked at the backs of the retrieving soldiers. 'Ellen!'

'I can't. I can't leave her!' Turning, she ran after the soldiers.

When they came to the scene, shock zinged through Ellen. Jim had his hands in the air, a German's gun trained on him. Ruth was bending over one of the injured soldiers. Another crack resounded louder than any of the others, and the German fell.

Ellen's gasp alerted a second British soldier to her. He turned, then fell at her feet as another shot rang out.

A hand grabbed her. She looked up. Another one of their own soldiers stood glaring down at her. His words came through angry closed teeth, 'You killed him, you stupid bitch!'

Ellen's terror increased with the sound of his gun exploding over and over as he turned from her, firing shot after shot into the body of the German on the ground, who'd found enough strength to shoot one last shot.

The realization that she'd taken the attention of one of their own soldiers, leaving him vulnerable, zinged through her. She fell on her knees next to him.

'No! No! Don't die. I didn't mean to. Please. I'm sorry, I—'

His voice croaked as he said on a moan of pain, 'My shoulder.'

'I'm sorry, I'm so sorry.'

'Help me.'

She looked up, wanting someone, anyone, to come to her aid as her mind had gone blank as to what to do.

'Ellen, Ellen, luv?'

'I did this! Oh, Ruth, I caused him to get shot!'

'What? How?' Ruth was ripping lengths off her already ragged frock to use as a tourniquet as she spoke.

'I gasped and he looked around at me.'

'Huh, I'd say it was his own fault. Can you 'ear me, mate? Surely you were taught to keep yer eye on the enemy at all times.'

'I – I was. Sh-she's right . . . I – it wasn't your fault. I'm sorry that me sarge spoke to you like that . . . Ooh, the pain, 'elp me.'

'Bring some light over 'ere, will you? Ellen, go and bring Sister and check on Ali. Make sure she's all right.'

With the soldier's words, Ellen felt herself calming. She ran and banged on the chapel door. 'All clear. We need help out here.'

When Sister appeared, all seemed to be in order in no time. Instructions were given and obeyed. Ali and the two injured German soldiers were taken inside the convent. The third German, who'd appeared from nowhere, was declared dead and taken out into the field across the road and left.

Ruth and Ellen were set the task of fetching everything that was needed as Sister tried to do all she could to ease the pain of the injuries.

On their last trip to bring bandages, Sister told them all, 'We'll have to take them with us to the hospital, they both need operating on. And I think we should go now. They need attention very soon and others may have heard the commotion and be on their way. Get everything packed up, please, everyone, and Ruth, Ellen and Barbara, I need you to squeeze in the front with the soldiers so we can get the patients laid down.'

One of the wounded German soldiers called out to Ellen, 'What is happening?'

Ellen told him, trying to reassure him the best she could.

'You speak German, too, Ellen?'

'Not as well as I do French, Sister.'

'Well, you had better stay inside the lorry with them. Theresa, you go with Barbara and Ruth.'

Not wanting to leave Ruth, Ellen said, 'The other soldier speaks English, Sister.'

'Well, he won't be speaking in any language for a while as he was shot in the neck . . . Sergeant, we must get going as quickly as possible. Can you organize your men, please?'

'It's in hand, Sister. They are loading the sleeping bags as we speak and will load the patients next.'

While this was going on, Ellen wandered over to Ali. 'How are you feeling, Ali?'

'A bit better. Sister gave me aspirin. I ain't felt right since the sickness on the boat.'

'You gave us a scare. I thought you had pneumonia, but your shaking has stopped and you're not sweating now, so it's maybe a heavy chill.'

Ali managed a weak smile. Ellen worried about her. Despite her making light of it, she really did think something was going on and it was more than a chill.

Ruth came over then. 'I'll see the pair of you when we get there, then, eh?'

'Ruth, was the nun all right? The one the German shoved over?'

'Yes. Once the danger had passed the nuns took care of her. I'd say she'll have a few bruises, and maybe a lot of nightmares, but I'm sure she'll be fine.'

'Right, girls, come on, let's get going. Everyone back in the trucks.'

When they were on the road once more and there was just herself and Sister besides the patients, Sister told her, 'I am very cross with you, Ellen. You have to learn discipline. What I say goes. Do you understand?'

'Yes, Sister, I'm sorry.'

'Sorry doesn't always cut it. You behaved like a child! Someone more the age of fourteen or fifteen, rather than a sensible grown-up. How old are you, anyway?'

'Twenty-three-ish, Sister. I – I couldn't leave me sister.'

'Oh, Lord! This is why I am against relatives serving together. There is a potential to put family feeling above sense . . . but, well, what's this "ish" business?'

Ellen explained.

'Well, that's amazing and very moving. I understand now, but I want you both to train yourselves to always put the good of everyone before the good of each other in the kind of situation we found ourselves in today. Ruth was in danger, I accept that, but you could do nothing about that. What you should have done is obey my orders and helped to keep the rest of us safe, not to mention our soldiers, who you put in grave danger today. You gave them the extra responsibility of keeping you safe when they had enough on their plate!'

Ellen felt ashamed of herself, not least because of the poor soldier lying on the bench in agony. She knew she'd learned a valuable lesson. She must learn to think and act like someone much older than herself.

The journey seemed interminable. Ellen had a headache with the strain of trying to decipher everything the German soldier said. And worse, she was beginning to like him as a person when she thought she should hate him and all he stood for.

The other German soldier had given a lot of concern as his condition had deteriorated, but thankfully their own soldier seemed a lot more comfortable, since Sister had, with her help, tugged his shoulder back into its socket. He'd been lucky, though, as his bullet wound was very near to his neck but seemed to be giving him little trouble. He'd made them laugh as he'd asked, 'Am I for being shipped back to Blighty, Sister? Only, I'd rather not. Facing me old man before the job's done will be worse than coming in close contact with the Kaiser!'

Sister had told him it wasn't up to her, that they would do their best to patch him up at the hospital and then it would be up to his commanding officer if he felt him fit for duty.

With the dawn, the war erupted around them once more as suddenly the air filled with a crushing noise of explosions and gunfire being exchanged.

'We must be nearly there. They said this hospital was very near to the front line.'

Still Sister remained calm, when Ellen felt like screaming with the knot of fear inside her.

'Take deep breaths, Ellen. This is what we have come for. To be on hand to help the wounded and to try to save lives.'

Ellen did just that and felt better for it. *Yes*, she thought, *this is what I want to do – I must make myself up to doing it.*

When the lorries came to a halt and they alighted from the vehicles, the sky was lit with flashes and the air spluttered with the sound of rifle fire. It seemed, too, that the earth shook with the explosion of shells being fired. Ellen wanted to cover her ears and run screaming into hiding, but as she saw her own fear manifested on the faces of the others, and more particularly on Ruth's, she pulled herself together.

'This is it, Ruth. Nothing can be as bad as last night, love. Then we were in the thick of the reality of it, but now we're protected by our status as Red Cross personnel. Remember? Miss Jaminson told us that all nations respect our flag and our work?'

'She did, but blimey, Ellen, I didn't know it would be like this! How's Ali?'

Her words went into the firing of huge guns and the screams of men. Ellen wanted to run and run in the opposite direction it was all coming from, but she knew she had to get used to it, so she prayed. *Please, God, help them and help us . . . Make me brave. Make me up to doing what is needed. Amen.*

'Are you praying, Ellen?'

Sister's kindly tones cut into her prayer. She nodded.

'Well, that helps, but what helps more is to get on with the practical side of things . . . Now, everyone, I have met Sister Margaret Baker. She also likes to be known by her Christian name, so Sister Margaret. And she tells me that they are already inundated with casualties, and the ambulances are out collecting more. I want you all to scrub up and be ready to help . . . Ruth, you will be on cleaning duty as they have qualified nurses doing that who can be put to better use. Just keep everywhere as clean as you can – wash down, mop floors, anything that needs doing to keep a sanitary area for the medical staff while they work. Ellen, I have seen what you can do, and your language skills will be useful, so I want you to assist wherever you see a need. Alison seems to be recovering, but isn't well enough to work, nor do we know yet if she is infectious – that is something you can pray for, Ellen, as it is the last thing we need. I want you both to help her up to the sleeping quarters and to get her into bed to rest. But please, hurry.'

They found the quarters were in a room that went the whole length of all the adjoining buildings. Sheets had been pegged up between beds to give some privacy.

'I think we should pull a couple of these down, luv, so that we're all together.'

'Yes, let's, Ruth. Look, the unoccupied ones have a note

on saying "vacant". Let's hope we can find three together.'

'I – I have to sit down, mate. I – I can 'ardly breathe after climbing them bloomin' stairs.'

'Hang on to me for a mo, luv. Ellen's going along to check out some beds for us.'

As Ruth said this, Ellen found three. 'Here, we're in luck, girls.'

'Come and give me an 'and, luv. Ali can barely hold herself up.'

When they had Ali comfortable and had pulled down two sheets, they scurried around to get ready, finding a closet with sinks at the end of the room.

'Well, the Ritz it ain't, luv,' Ruth said as she washed herself.

Ellen giggled at her. 'No, but we're all together, love, and that's something.'

'It is.'

When Ruth had dried her hands, she held out her arms. Enclosing her in love, Ruth told her, 'Wherever you are is the Ritz to me. I love yer, Ellen. You're part of me. And I'm proud of yer. So, just remember to keep calm, use the knowledge yer have and don't give the game away. I know it ain't easy for yer, but we're here now and it's where yer want to be.'

'Thanks, Ruth. I love you too. So very much. It's like I'm whole since you came back into my life.'

Ruth sighed. 'There's just one thing missing – Amy. But we'll never give up on finding her, will we?'

'We won't. We will find her. We will.'

As they went downstairs, leaving Ali snoring away, Ellen told herself that she needed to toughen up and not have anyone question her age again as she was sure Sister had doubts already.

Chapter Twenty-One

Ruth and Ellen

Hell visited earth the moment they left their quarters. The shelling took all the space around them, drowning out the screams and sobs of the young men lying mangled and bleeding in every spare inch of the ward.

'Which way is the sluice?'

To Ruth shouting this, a nurse pointed, then asked, 'Are you the cleaners? For God's sake, hurry up! We're slipping and sliding in blood.'

Ruth ran towards where the girl had pointed, found a mop bucket, filled it and hurried back, but her efforts were useless against the river of blood.

A doctor tending to a young man shouted over, 'There's a drain over there. Get a brush and get rid of the worst of it first.'

Feeling stupid and worthless amidst all the help being given by others, Ruth did as he said to the background of the agonizing cries of the wounded men she so wanted to help.

Near to the drain four stretchers were laid on the floor.

A voice with an accent cried out to her. 'Help me, Nurse.'

Ruth couldn't ignore him but couldn't do anything for him. ''Elp is on the way, mate. Just be strong and hang in there, eh?'

'Tell me ma I love her.'

'Where are yer from, luv?'

'A-a small town outside Toronto, on the shores of Ontario.'

'Is that up north? Yer sound American?'

'Can-Canadian . . . Ple-e-ase stop the pain.'

Ruth pulled back the rough grey blanket covering him. Shock made her gasp. The middle part of his body had no skin covering it, and that which he did have left around the area was blistered and black. She looked around her. There wasn't anyone free for her to call. 'I'll be back, luv.'

Running over to the doctor who'd directed her, she asked, 'How can I best help someone who is burned so badly his skin has gone and his fat layer is affected?'

The doctor, busy stitching a gaping wound, didn't look up. 'Gently pour cool water over it, then bandage him. Take one of those phials of morphine and give it to him and then pray for him.'

Ruth had never given an injection in her life, but she didn't say so. She grabbed the phial. Going back to the young man, she didn't stop to think but, knowing her hands weren't clean, took care not to touch him, or the needle, but jabbed it straight into his upper arm. 'That'll help yer, luv. I'll just go and get some bandages.' These she'd seen in an open cupboard next to the sluice. Hurrying as fast as she could, she scrubbed her hands and stuffed gauze and a bandage into her apron pocket, before filling a kidney-shaped bowl with cool water.

As she gently poured the water over the affected area she prayed, *Holy Mary, help me to help him. Please help me!*

The soldier moaned as the water hit him, but mercifully, it was a drowsy sound, and she hoped the morphine was taking effect. By the time she'd bandaged him, he was asleep. A gladness filled her, as did a sense of euphoria at having helped him.

Turning, she picked up her brush and continued to sweep away the tide of blood. Her tears wet her cheeks at the hopelessness of the task, but at the meaning of it too. All around her young men were dying. Boys not much older than herself. Body after body carried past her to be laid on the ground outside. *Holy Mary, stop this carnage . . . Please, please, stop it!*

Feeling her strength ebb from her, she heard a cry . . . Ellen? Bringing her attention back to the happenings around her, she looked across to where the sound had come from. Ellen was with a soldier. His screams filled the air. Ellen's desperate cry of 'I need help!' sent her running over to her, wondering how it was that – out of all the cries from the nurses shouting, 'Someone come here, I need help', and doctors shouting for a nurse – she'd only taken notice when it was Ellen who had called out.

'Are you all right, luv?'

'The world's gone mad, Ruth.' Ruth could see Ellen was shaking all over. She looked at the young man – he had no face. His crying was a soft, pitiful sound.

Thinking the best way to help Ellen was to take charge, Ruth said, 'I'll fetch water, Ellen. I've just treated a burn in that way. The doctor over there has morphine – go and get some.'

This calmed Ellen.

When Ruth came back she heard her say, 'You're all right. My name's Ellen, I'm going to help you.' The soldier answered in German. This shocked Ruth. She wanted to get hold of him and ask, 'Why? Why are you doing this?'

247

But then, as Ellen spoke gently to him in his own tongue, he didn't become German, French, English, or anything. He just became a man who was in great pain and needed help.

Ellen did her best with the little German she knew. She told him not to worry, that he would be fine, they would take care of him. She took the bowl of water from Ruth, not having to ask what to do now. She was steadied again, and drew on the knowledge she'd gleaned from all her medical books. She administered the injection, before seeing to his wounds as best she could while asking him, 'Are you hurt anywhere else?'

'My arm.'

'Check his arm, Ruth.'

'It's broken, luv. We'll have to set it. You know what Miss Jaminson said about the blood flow being stopped when a limb is broken.'

'Well, not really, as I didn't attend classes with her, but I have read about it.' Addressing the soldier in his own language, she told him, 'We'll do what we can, don't worry.'

Ellen looked around her. Still there was no one more experienced than her and Ruth who she could call to for help. 'Look, I'm going to hurt you, more than you are hurting already, but I have to do it.'

'He's getting drowsy. What are you going to do, Ellen?'

'I have to try to set it, like you said. There's no one else.'

As gently as possible she manoeuvred his arm into place. His screams of agony, despite the morphine, frightened and sickened her stomach with nerves. Sweat poured from her, but she carried on – knew that this was the best way to help him. 'Ruth, fetch a splint and bandages!'

When she thought she had the arm straight she nodded

at Ruth, who applied the splint and began to bandage it into place.

The soldier had slipped into an unconscious state. Not knowing if he could hear her or not, she told him, 'You must fight for your life, for your mum, dad and sisters and brothers,' whilst hoping that she was using all the correct words.

'I think he's all right, Ellen. You did an amazing job, luv. The best thing to do now is to leave him and go and see if yer can 'elp someone else.'

The next time Ellen saw Ruth, she was busy mopping up the blood next to a table from where surgery was in progress. The sound of the saw going through bone made Ellen shiver. She went over to ask Ruth if she was all right, but was stopped by the doctor. 'Are you familiar with surgical procedures?'

'I haven't done any of that kind of work, but I could help if you tell me what to do, Doctor.'

'Hold this leg. The nerves are making it jump and I can't saw straight.'

Ellen took a deep breath and held on to the foot. Though it was a sickening procedure and her stomach knotted with the fear of what was happening, a little part of her was fascinated to see the inside of the leg appearing as the doctor got through the bone.

'Put the leg down now. It's detached.'

Ellen hadn't realized she was still holding the limb. She felt the pity of that, when all she'd thought of before was how much she wanted to be able to carry out such surgery, but then it came to her that horrific as this was, the boy's life would have been saved by it. And she knew that she could do such a thing as she wanted to be the one who made a difference between life and death.

'Pass me what I ask for, and quickly!'

Ellen obeyed every instruction, knowing the implements from her studies.

'Wipe my brow.'

Taking a swab, Ellen obeyed, shocked to realize that the doctor was going through hell, that he didn't do this every day and, more especially, in these circumstances.

'You've done wonders, I'm in awe.'

He looked up over his mask, his dark eyes seeming to look into her soul. 'And so have you . . . Oh, you're a VAD!'

'Yes, but one day, when I'm old enough, I want to be a doctor like you.'

He put his head down and carried on stitching. When it was done, he said, 'Come outside a moment. Things are quietening down now, and he'll be fine. The orderlies will take him to the ward. I need some air.'

'I'll fetch you a drink of water.'

Outside, she could now see his face. He was the most handsome man she'd ever seen. His dark hair curled a little where his sweat had wet it. His features were chiselled and perfect. She wanted to tell him he was beautiful, but was stopped in her tracks as he said, 'Just how old are you? You said when you are old enough? Surely you are?'

Ellen panicked. Why had she said that? Frantic, she sought some sort of cover-up. 'That was just a joke . . .' She hated lying to him. 'It's to do with me being a woman . . . They make it harder for us . . . I – I'm in my twenties . . . twenty-three.'

He looked at her quizzically. All traces of the make-up she'd learned to apply must have gone by now – washed off with the sweat that had dripped from her face.

But then he shrugged his shoulders. 'Oh? Well, if that's the age you want to be, then I'm not the one to protest.

You certainly have the sense and capability of someone that age. And I suppose you know that is the acceptance age?'

'Yes, we were told when me and my twin sister volunteered to come out here with the Red Cross.'

'Well, you should go on and do your medical training, but it isn't cheap. And getting in isn't easy. You will need a referee. I'll help you with that when the time comes. I'm Bernard Holbeck, and you are?'

'Ellen Hartington. Ruth and I have different surnames.' She explained why. He didn't flinch at the story or seem to look down at her for her humble beginnings and this made her grow in confidence. 'Thanks for that offer, that's so good of you that you'd be willing to do that for me . . . Strangely, I met someone with the same surname as you before I came out here. Frederick Holbeck.'

'My older brother – well, I say older. Actually, there are only ten months between us. How was he?'

'Pompous . . . oh, I mean . . .'

His laugh cut her off. 'That's Freddie all right.'

'You don't look alike.'

'No, different in every way. He takes after our father, and me, our mother. Sorry he came over like that, he's a good sort. My only worry with him is that he will be a hero. What was he up to?'

She told him about Frederick going to Sandhurst and mentioned Adrian.

'Well, I never! Fancy, out here in the middle of hell, I meet someone who knows my brother and one of our best friends.'

He was smiling now, and he looked more than beautiful.

A voice stopped her dreaming. 'Doctor, we need you, quickly!'

Ellen followed him inside and over to a man whose stomach was ripped open, his innards lying on his lap.

'I'll see to him, Sister, with the help of Ellen.'

'Don't you need someone more experienced, Doctor?'

'No, Ellen has shown her competence.'

Ellen immediately thought that the best thing to do was to clean the wound and intestines. 'You'll need sterile water. I'll fetch some, Bernard.'

'And a tray of implements. There should be fresh ones made up.'

Ellen met Ruth on the way. She looked tired and forlorn.

'Ruth, what is it?'

'I feel useless.'

'Grab a clean pinny and scrub up, we're going to need someone. Bring bandages, and more water.'

When Ruth joined them Ellen was holding the man's stomach.

'What can I do?'

Without looking up, Bernard told her to run the water gently over his hands as he worked.

What followed was like a miracle to Ellen as Bernard niftily sewed every muscle back into its rightful place while Ellen gently manoeuvred it all, marvelling at how much of it there was and at seeing so many organs in real life instead of in pictures.

When at last all calmed down, Ruth took her hand. They didn't speak.

Ellen steered her over to where they had left the German soldier and found him still in the same place. His eyes were open. 'Are you all right?' she asked him in German. He shook his head.

'In pain?

He nodded.

'Hold on a moment.' She turned and waved Bernard over.

Though visibly tired, Bernard came to her. It warmed her heart that he didn't question treating a German soldier but just asked, 'Did you set this arm, Ellen?'

For a moment she felt afraid to admit she did.

Seeing her hesitation, Ruth said, 'She did, mate, and she did a bloody good job!'

'No need to defend her. I agree. I only wish we could tell him that he is in the best shape possible and that I will write up painkillers for him and arrange to have him sent to Paris for plastic surgery as the poor fellow looks scared out of his wits.'

Ellen could see what he meant. Even though most of his face had gone, the German's eyes were expressive.

She told him what would happen as best she could.

'You have a good heart. You treat me . . . the enemy?'

'Yes, of course. This war isn't your fault. You're only following orders like our soldiers.'

'Thank you, miss. I don't want to follow orders to kill, or even to be here, but I have to for the honour of my family and my country.'

'I know, don't worry about it.'

'Will I be a prisoner now?'

'I don't know. I haven't long arrived here, so don't know the procedure . . . Maybe. But I'm sure you'll be treated well.'

'I want to go home.'

'I know, everybody does.'

'Thank you for what you did for me. What's your name?'

'Ellen.'

'I'll never forget you, Ellen.'

'You're welcome. Just get well. That's the best way to thank any nurse.'

'Is he all right, Ellen?'

'He is, Bernard . . . Well, afraid, like us all, but I think he will cope.'

'You're a marvel. Adrian taught you well. He was always a whizz at languages. I expect he's gone to be an officer?'

'Yes. Only, not a fighting one. He has asthma. He has bad attacks that are frightening.'

'Sorry to hear that. He was never strong as a boy. But asthma . . . That's not good.'

Ruth interrupted. 'Could he die?'

Bernard looked quizzically at her as if seeing her for the first time. 'You're Ellen's sister?'

'I am, and yes, I know, we're different, mate, but there's a reason for that.'

'I know, Ellen explained, and I'm sorry you've both had it so rough and glad you've found each other now.'

'Ta. But tell me, how bad can asthma get?'

'I'm tired. Sorry. Will you excuse me?'

'Please. Please tell me that Adrian will be all right.'

Bernard looked astonished.

'He will, Ruth, love, I promise you.'

'I want to hear a doctor say it, Ellen.'

'I can't, Ruth. Not without examining him and knowing his history and progression. I take it you and Adrian are close?'

'We are. We love each other.'

Again, Bernard showed his surprise. 'I'm happy for you. Adrian's a top fellow. I am sure he'll be fine; his doctor will look after him and if he does as he is told, then he will have a long life.'

Ruth sighed. Tears streamed down her face. 'I – I'm sorry, so sorry.'

'There's no need to be. Look, we're all overwrought. Go and get a cup of tea and some rest. It's what we all need. The next shift will take over from us soon.'

Bernard patted Ruth's arm. She smiled up at him. 'Ta, Doctor.'

When she'd left them the German took Ellen's attention. 'Will you do something for me?'

'I'll try.'

'Would you write to my sister?'

'I will have to ask the sister in charge, but if she says yes, I'll do it for you. Only, I don't know a lot of German. I know more French.'

'My address is in my pocket. There is a letter there too, the one we all have to write, but I want you to tell her I am all right. She may get a message that I am missing. She knows English.'

'All right. If Sister Mary says I can, I will. I hope the painkillers give you some ease.'

'Thank you, Ellen.'

Ellen smiled down at him. The pity of what was happening came to her. This boy was probably not a lot older than herself. He didn't want to be fighting, he wanted to be with his family, to carry on his career, and yet here he was by command of others lying badly wounded on a filthy floor in Belgium. Her heart went out to him, and she told herself not to hate the Germans. They were just like their own boys.

Ruth's sigh brought her attention back to her. 'Just look at this bloomin' place and I've to clean it before the next lot come on duty!'

'Oh, I thought you'd gone for a rest and a cuppa . . .

255

Look, I'll help, love. We'll soon get it done together. I'll gather all the instruments up and get them boiling on the stove. You wash down all the trolleys and the operating beds – I saw disinfectant in the cupboard next to the sluice – then we'll tackle the floor together.'

'Oh, sis. We didn't know what we were taking on, did we?'

'No, but we're all right, aren't we?'

Ruth hugged her.

'We'll always be all right while we're together, luv.'

Ellen knew this had been said many times between them, but never before had it meant quite as much as it did right now.

Ellen was overjoyed when Sister gave her permission to send the letter for the German soldier, who'd told her his name was Gus.

Tired and aching after such a gruelling day, she couldn't rest until she'd written it, putting in it the love she could feel Gus had for his sister and telling her that though he was badly injured, she was sure he would recover and come home to her when the war ended.

After finishing it, she went and found Gus in a ward and told him. She could feel his joy as he weakly took her hand.

'Good luck, Gus. I think you will be gone from here by the time I rise in the morning.'

A tear ran down her face as she left him.

After they'd all had a good wash, dinner was a surprisingly jolly affair with everyone laughing and acting the fool. The chef was a marvel and Ellen learned that he was well loved by the local farmers who made sure he had plenty of produce for his nurses.

At first, Ellen couldn't join in. She had been so traumatized by the day's happenings, but then she realized that these people deserved what little fun they could get – no one deserved it more. And she did too. She'd given her all as they had. She'd helped to save lives. No one would begrudge them a giggle or two. Tomorrow was a new day – not that it would stop during the night, but she had heard that night shifts were a lot quieter as the fighting mostly came to an end after dark till dawn – how long it seemed since dawn this morning. But at least now their concern for Ali had lifted. She was sat up in bed tucking into a huge dinner and would be fit to help them the next day, but their fears hadn't all gone, and Ellen knew that each day would bring fresh ones. More injured, more dead and she asked herself, *When will it all end?*

At last, they settled down for the night after another giggling session between the three of them was quietened by someone calling out for them to please shut up.

Ellen knew a little shame at this. She lay back in the silence, feeling partly happy, partly fulfilled. She didn't know whether it was wrong to feel like that, but she did. She was doing what she knew she'd been put on this earth to do and though heart-wrenching and not easy, she couldn't think of anything she would rather be doing.

Bernard came into her mind, as did his brother Frederick, the strangeness of meeting them both as she had, but it was Bernard who occupied her mind as she drifted off to sleep.

Chapter Twenty-Two

Ruth

Ruth's head ached when she woke the next morning. It had been a strange night of dreams – some horrific which had awoken her, leaving her trembling with anxiety, and others all mixed up with Ellen turning into Amy. And then the Canadian soldier she'd treated coming in and out of the waves of what felt like cotton wool in her brain to tell her something, but she never did know what.

Startled from this dreamlike state by a bell ringing, Ruth sat up, glad to be truly awake and to realize that the experience was nothing more than dreams. There was no reality in any of it.

But as they dressed the idea came to her that it wouldn't hurt to ask the Canadian if he knew of children being shipped into his country. That's if the poor man had survived.

In the bed on the right of her, Ellen stretched, then shot up to a sitting position. 'You look wide awake, Ruth! Did you sleep well?'

Ruth didn't voice the lingering night terrors. 'Not bad, as good as I could in the strangeness of it all and after all we went through and witnessed.'

'I know, I had a bit of tossing and turning, but was so exhausted . . . Come on, sleepyhead, Ali.'

Ruth looked over to Ali's bed. She hadn't moved. Picking up her pillow, she threw it over at her. 'Ali! Time to get up . . . Unless . . . you're not feeling worse, are yer, luv?'

Ali still didn't stir. Ruth looked at Ellen. A trickle of fear clutched her stomach. Ellen's face showed the same concern. For a moment it was as if neither could move. There was something about the stillness of the huddled form of Ali that held them in limbo.

It was Ellen who moved first. She threw the covers off her legs and hurried over to Ali. This spurred Ruth on.

One look at Ali and her gasp joined Ellen's. There was a moment that they just stood and stared, then Ellen's cry of 'Ali! Ali! Someone, help us!' brought a hush to the chatter that had been going on around them. Then they were surrounded by some girls still in their nightwear, others half dressed.

Sister was amongst them and the only one fully dressed. 'What is it? What's the matter?'

'I – It's . . . Oh God! She . . . she's dead!'

'What? How? Let me get near, Ellen . . . Someone fetch one of the doctors and hurry! The rest of you, please continue to get ready. We will be needed to take over on time. The night staff have had a gruelling shift . . . Hurry now.' Sister clapped her hands.

To Ruth, the sound seemed alien and not fitting to the horror unfolding. It took her back to the theatre and normality, but she didn't want to go there. She didn't want Ali to be dead. She wanted someone to tell her that it was a prank. She wanted Ali to sit up and laugh at them all, but she knew that wasn't going to happen.

'Ruth! Ellen! Do as the others are. Come on, snap out of it! I know this is a shock, it is to us all, but we have to keep ourselves on track no matter what happens. Take your clothes and go in with one of the other girls and get dressed and ready for the day. There is nothing you can do here, but there is a lot you can do downstairs in the receiving ward, as you did yesterday.'

Ruth's legs felt like lead as she did as Sister Mary bid them to. Ellen helped; she slipped her hand into hers. She didn't speak, but the gesture spoke volumes. When they needed anyone, they were there for each other.

'I – I can't believe it. What could have happened, Ruth?'

'I don't know, luv. I can't take it in.' Bits of her dreams revisited her. Someone was gasping. She shook her head. No! That had been Amy, she was sure of it.

As more of her dream became vivid, she saw herself reaching out to Amy, but every time she did there was nothing there, just the horror of the faceless German, and the mangled bodies of others, and yet the Canadian wasn't hurt at times; he was smiling, telling her about Amy.

'Ruth . . . Ruth!'

Seeing the anguish and despair on her young sister's face gave Ruth strength. 'It's all right, Ellen, luv. You're all right. Let's do as Sister has told us to, eh?'

They dressed in a mechanical way. Ruth could see that Ellen was shaking as much as she was, but they didn't speak again. Behind the hanging sheet they could see movements and hear whispered words. 'I'm at a loss, Sister. I can see no obvious signs of why death should have occurred. Was she unwell?'

'Yes.' The sister went on to tell how Ali had been on the journey. 'But when I checked on her last night, she was fine and sitting up eating. She said she felt a lot better. I just cannot understand this.'

'The three girls came together, didn't they? Maybe they can throw light on any conditions she may have had. Otherwise I'm afraid, without an autopsy, we won't know.'

'We must do one, Doctor. We owe it to her family.'

'How? Be realistic, Sister. If there isn't anything obvious, we have no lab to test anything in, and no microscopes. I know it is a terrible thing to put "Cause of Death Unknown" on the certificate, but we have no option.'

'I'll speak to the other two VADs who she came with . . . Then if there is nothing known, I reluctantly agree with you.'

'If Marie Curie was here now, instead of coming soon, we may stand some chance of seeing something, but the X-ray equipment we do have isn't adequate and we have no one properly trained.'

'I heard that she had reached Belgium and should be here in a month's time.'

'As should some better weather. I'm sick of this mud.'

'At least it does deter this second wave of attacks a little.'

Ellen was staring at Ruth with something of a look of glee on her face. Ruth was mystified. How could she find anything to look happy about?

The words Ellen whispered to her gave her the reason:

'Marie Curie! I can't believe it! She's a scientist who discovered radium, and she has applied that to X-rays, making it possible to see much more of the inside of the body! She's amazing and she's actually coming here! . . . Oh, I – I shouldn't have reacted like that. Forgive me.'

'It's all right.' As she took Ellen into her arms, she spoke quietly as she tried to reassure her. 'Sometimes, you have to let yourself be the young girl you are – we both are, really. Life shoved us into adulthood before our time, luv, but now and again, the child in us comes to the fore. This lady is someone you greatly admire, that's obvious, mate. Don't be sorry for that.'

They clung to one another; Ruth could feel the trembling of Ellen's body matching her own. The shock was deep. The incomprehension of it too much to take. A tear slid down her cheek and wet Ellen's hair. She felt Ellen's body jolt with a sob. The reality was hitting them. Ali, lovely Ali, was gone.

They weren't able to tell Sister or the doctor anything, other than that Ali was always hungry, which neither of them felt could have any bearing on her death and there wasn't a sign of the anxiety they related that Ali suffered from having contributed. 'The doctor is adamant that she didn't take her own life,' Sister told them.

This relieved and yet shocked Ruth as she went reeling back in time and her lovely friend Hettie came to mind.

'Ruth, I know this has been a terrible shock, dear, but I am going to put you to work. It is the best thing for you – for both of you . . . Now, the doctor has reminded me that the wonderful Marie Curie will visit soon. That amazing lady has a team of volunteers visiting hospitals with up-to-date X-ray equipment in little vans, which I am told are called Little Curies!'

Always the enthusiast, Ellen chipped in, 'I cannot believe she is coming; I have studied all her work.'

'Ellen, Ellen, is there nothing that you don't know? Well, what you do know is very useful in the receiving ward. You did an excellent job yesterday, and so I am keeping you in there. Doctor Bernard said you gave invaluable assistance to him, and your command of French and German brought comfort as well as helping the medical staff to understand the patients from these countries . . . Now, Ruth, I am going to put you into the X-ray room . . .'

For a moment, Ruth thought she was to be given a job of responsibility, but then Sister said, 'I want it spic and span.'

'Oh . . . I – I'll see to that, Sister.'

'Now, don't look so downhearted. Your diligence on your first day, and the help you gave medically and on your own initiative wasn't missed. While you are sorting out the X-ray room, I want you to watch and learn, and help if you can. I could do with freeing up all qualified staff from jobs of that nature. The Germans have attacked in earnest, and intelligence is that they intend victory this time. We will most likely be inundated with casualties. It has to be all hands on deck. I hope to get some local women in to clean for us. So, off you go . . . and girls, my sincere condolences. I am very saddened to have lost such a young girl as Ali. Keep yourselves busy to help you to cope with her loss.'

'Yes, Sister.'

They said this in chorus and didn't speak as they left Sister's office.

Once they came to the end of the corridor and were to go their different ways, they hugged before leaving each other.

The X-ray room was along another corridor. Ruth couldn't imagine what it would be like. She had heard about the amazing invention of a machine that could take pictures of the inside of the body, but that seemed impossible to her. Nevertheless, Ruth made her mind up to concentrate fully on learning all about it, thinking that doing so was just what she needed to distract her. *Oh, Ali, Ali, how did it happen that you left us?* Her mind went once more to Hettie, and she realized how similar they were to each other and how both had had their demons. Hettie's death had been horrendous, but Ali's, with no known cause, was just as heart-wrenching. She didn't want either of them to be gone.

To her knocking on the door clearly marked 'X-ray', a girl's voice bid her to enter.

'Ah, Ruth, isn't it? I've been told about you coming to help me and possibly taking over from me. My name's Jean. Pleased to meet you.'

Ruth nodded. She found herself tongue-tied. What she'd been experiencing didn't fit with the matter-of-fact Jean as she hadn't yet let go of all the emotions her dreams had given her. Her body trembled.

'Are you all right, Ruth?'

Still unable to speak, Ruth just stared.

'Come and sit down. We've a good hour before we have a few minors booked in. The night staff have been busy, though . . . I can make you a cuppa if you like? We've got our own kitchen. It isn't big but with that and our own loo, it makes life comfortable.'

At last Ruth found her voice. 'Ta, I'd like a drink of tea.'

'Has something happened? You look in shock to me.'

Ruth found the words tumbled out. She told of how they'd found Ali and all about Hettie. She couldn't stop herself.

By the time she finished, Jean had her arm on her shoulder. 'Poor you. And poor Alison. I've never heard of anyone just dying. There're all sorts that could have caused it, but like the doctor says, without an autopsy we will never know. But Sister is right. Far better that you get on with the necessary work than you sit and mope. I'll make that tea.'

Jean, a plain sort of a girl with mousy hair and a long nose, but nice hazel eyes that held kindness and friendship, was tall and slim. Ruth knew she would like her and that helped as when she'd walked the corridor, she'd worried that she might be looked down on if whoever manned the X-ray unit was one of the snobbish lot, who hadn't yet given her and Ellen the time of day. But then, all nurses were from families who could afford to pay their way to be trained, not like herself. She was a bit of an oddity as even Ellen fitted in with her posh voice and her education.

'Here, drink this.'

'Ta, Jean. And thanks for giving me this minute to gather meself.'

'Where are you from, Ruth?'

'Bethnal, London . . . I know, I ain't yer usual run of nursing staff, but I've dedicated what time I could to learning from the Red Cross.'

'It's not who you are, it's what you can give. And if you give yourself to this work, you'll be doing a great service as it is valuable work, but also you will free me up. I am fully qualified and before the war was up for a promotion to become a sister. But as soon as everything kicked off, I volunteered. I've been through some hairy times as I began my war career in Brussels before the invasion and had to escape.'

They'd sipped their tea as they'd been talking, and Ruth began to feel steadier. She wondered how Ellen was fairing and marvelled again at a fifteen-year-old being so strong. Would this all be too much for her and tip her over the edge? How she wished they could have been together at least for today.

'Right, this is the main controls.'

Jean took her to a stand with a panel protruding. The knobs and switches looked confusing to Ruth.

'And this is it, the X-ray plate. At least the holder of the plates. It is very flexible so that with your patient lying down you can X-ray from head to toe. For chest X-rays they stand up – that's if they can – against that screen over there.'

And so, the day went on. Information coming at her at a pace. It was a relief when Jean set her the task of organizing the sheets, as a clean one was used on the bed for every patient. Used ones were dumped into a large bag and came back in a similar one from the laundry which was housed in the cellar and operated by local women.

'We haven't many shelves but do your best. How are you feeling about it all?'

'I find it fascinating. I ain't took it all in yet, but I'm willing to keep trying.'

'That's good. I think after a week working with me, you'll be up to scratch. Think of it as being a photographer, as that's all you're doing, taking pictures.'

The morning flew by after that as patient after patient was wheeled in, and all to the background of crushing explosive noise and shell fire.

'The Germans mean business this time. I shouldn't think we'll be here long as once they are nearing victory, we'll have to evacuate.'

Jean was so matter-of-fact about this that Ruth took it as all in a day's work for her and that made her feel safer.

When at last the shift came to an end, Jean was full of praise for Ruth. 'I can't believe how you have picked up so much. Well done, you! And, Ruth, I'm so sorry about your friend.'

'Thanks, Jean. See you tomorrow.'

As she was leaving, Jean called after her. 'Hey, if we get a day off together, we could go and have a coffee at a place I know. It's in the next village . . . that's if the Germans don't reach there first.'

266

'Ta, Jean, I'd like that.'

Jean's way of joking about the war had helped Ruth. She didn't see it all as something to be terrified of any more, but something that was there, a couple of fields or more away, and they had to deal with it.

Ellen stood at the end of the corridor when Ruth walked along it. Her pinny was splattered with blood, her hair wet with sweat and as Ruth neared, she could see tears streaming down Ellen's face.

Quickening her steps, Ruth held out her arms. They didn't speak, just hugged, Ellen's quiet sobs wracking her body.

As she became calm, Ruth asked, 'Want to talk about it, luv?'

'They buried Ali!'

'What? No! When?'

'This afternoon. They . . . they lay her on the ground wrapped in a sheet alongside . . . the dead soldiers and then when the ambulances were finished doing their runs to the front, they loaded the dead and took them.'

'Oh, Ellen. Do you know where to?'

'It seems we have a burial ground not far from here, but Sister said they will mark each one. They use a little wooden cross with their name on.'

Ruth's heart felt as though it was being torn in two. She clung on to Ellen.

'We'll visit her, eh, Ruth? Take her some flowers, when we get some time off.'

Ruth wanted to go this minute. To her, it felt as though they'd abandoned Ali to be put in the ground by strangers.

'Don't cry, Ruth. When you cry it makes me despair.'

Ruth wiped her face on her pinny. 'Shall we go somewhere private and say some prayers? Praying to Holy Mary always makes me feel better.'

'Sister told me that there is a room set aside for quiet moments. She found out about it yesterday. It's at the other end of the building. I'd like to go.'

They found the room. It had one wall lined with books, which Ellen clapped her hands at, forgetting her grief for a moment as she perused the shelves.

'Oh, look, a whole section of medical books!'

This made Ruth smile as Ellen hadn't even glanced at the novels. She'd never been a reader herself, but now, as she looked at the titles, she wondered if it would be a pastime that would take her out of herself, just as her stage work had done. She gazed along the shelf, and picked up a book by Jane Austen. The first sentence, 'It is a truth universally acknowledged, that a single man in possession of a good fortune, must be in want of a wife,' caught her attention.

'Did Sister say we could take the books to read, Ellen?'

'She did. Ooh, I don't know which one to borrow first.'

'What, even the medical ones? Wouldn't the doctors want them to be here in case they want to refer to them?'

'Yes, you're right.' On a big sigh, Ellen admitted, 'She did say the novels and poetry only.'

Ruth clutched the book to her. She had a strange sensation of being on the stage, that she was whoever had said the line and was projecting it out to the audience. The language had set the era in her mind as she saw herself in a rose-coloured silk frock that swept the floor as she walked and had a small bustle at the back.

'Ruth?'

'Oh . . . sorry, I drifted off into me thoughts then. Shall we sit a minute and say our prayers, eh?'

They sat in the corner on the window seat. The room wasn't large and housed a round table with chairs around it, one armchair and a cushioned bench set into a bay window. One wall was taken up with a huge fireplace. The books filled the whole of the wall opposite the window. Ruth liked the room. There was no particular colour scheme, mostly cream and brown, but it had the restful air such a room would need.

Once both were seated, she took Ellen's hand and bowed her head. In the silence that followed, she found a kind of peace as she talked in her mind with her beloved Holy Mary, telling her of her sadness and her fears. Pouring out her worries over whether she was good enough to help others and asking – no, begging – for the war to end. Her thoughts drifted after this until she felt Ellen fidget beside her.

They were both a lot brighter when they left the room.

'Let's visit there often, Ruth. I felt my cares leave me as we sat there together.'

'I did too, and yes, I'd like to spend time there. I prayed, but then I began to think about Adrian. I don't let meself do that often, as it only gives me pain and a longing to be with him. But this time . . . well, I sort of felt connected to him, as if he was thinking of me too.'

'I expect he is. He's a great thinker is Adrian.'

Ruth didn't know why but this tickled her and she burst out laughing. Ellen linked arms with her and giggled along and suddenly, the gloom lifted from her heart. Ali was at peace. Far too young, but whatever was wrong with her might have got worse and worse till she was crippled with it.

Thinking this lifted her further. She tightened the arm that Ellen was linked into to bring her closer. They smiled at each other, and Ruth felt blessed to have Ellen by her side.

Chapter Twenty-Three

Ellen

Ellen lay staring at the ceiling. Though tired, she couldn't sleep. Everything that seemed just routine – the death, the terrible injuries, the destruction – still affected her badly, even though the number of cases had lessened as the war in their area had abated for a few weeks now.

She and Ruth had been settled into their new roles for two months and both loved what they did. Ruth had practically taken over the X-ray hall, though Jean still gave her a hand with the more complicated cases.

Ellen knew that she had grown in confidence too, and Sister Mary's – and, more importantly, Bernard's – confidence had grown in her ability.

She couldn't believe it was almost May, though the warmer and drier weather was welcome, as were the lighter nights, giving them a chance to walk in the evenings and get some fresh air into their lungs.

They'd found Ali's grave and visited it regularly, taking flowers that grew wild in the garden that had been emerging around the hospital as the mud had dried and grass shoots had pushed their way through. The shoots had become a rich carpet of grass and had grown to such an extent that Jim – the fixer of everything – had set about repairing and oiling an old rusty mower they'd found in one of the barns and begun to cut it regularly, now a lawn was taking shape.

Today they had been given an afternoon off and had sat a while on the lawn before deciding to go for a walk to the small village in the area of Bellestraat where Jean had introduced them to a cafe which sold bitter-tasting coffee. It wasn't for the coffee they went, but for the change in scenery and the folk that gathered there. Amongst them farmers, seemingly unperturbed by the war around them, chatting in a jolly fashion.

Neither she nor Ruth had realized how something so ordinary could become so lovely a sound and so refreshing from cries of pain and medical procedures and talk. It relaxed them both, helped them to have a giggle and forget, just for an hour, the horrors of war.

The village lay in the direction of the French border – the only route they were allowed to go as others took them further into Belgium. But even then, they had to cross fields rather than take the road, which would bring them too far towards where the odd battle could suddenly erupt, before turning off to the left in the safe direction.

It was what they'd seen on their way this afternoon that was keeping Ellen awake. The field they'd crossed wasn't cultivated. It housed a ramshackle barn that had obviously been neglected for a long time as it had a tree growing through its collapsed roof at the back, though the front seemed in not too bad a condition.

Ruth had wanted to pee and so they'd gone around the back of the barn. When they'd got there, Ruth had said, 'I'll go just inside. Keep a look out, Ellen. I don't want the farmer to suddenly appear and take a pot shot at me bum!'

They'd gone into a fit of giggles, made worse as the laughing increased Ruth's urgency and she did a wriggly dance as she went to stop herself peeing her knickers.

Ellen was bent double with her laughter as Ruth had opened the creaking barn door, saying, 'Eek, there'll be spiders!' But that laughter had frozen when Ruth had gasped and then in a horrified tone had cried, 'Oh my God!'

Dashing to Ruth's side, she saw what Ruth had seen – the camouflaged shape of a huge gun! Closing the door, they'd run for all they were worth back in the direction of the hospital. Hardly able to speak when they got there, they'd somehow managed to tell Sister Mary.

They'd been sitting on the lawn, beginning to feel calm, when Sister had come out to them and told them that word had been sent to the officer in charge of their nearest troops. She hadn't said where that was and they both knew they mustn't ask, but she'd added that from now on everyone was confined to the hospital grounds.

This had set Ellen wondering if it was a German gun, and she asked herself, were they planning another offensive? How could they have got the gun there, so near to the hospital, without anyone knowing?

The more she thought about it, the more the danger of their position became real, setting up trickles of fear inside her.

Always the fighting had been over the hills somewhere. They heard it, and dealt with the consequences, but this . . .

Her thoughts halted suddenly as a long boom filled the air and seemed to roar as it travelled into the distance, shaking the hospital's old and crumbling foundations.

She sat up, thinking that it must be an earthquake. With

this thought came a sheer terror as she imagined the building crumbling and crushing them all to death.

Pandemonium broke out as everyone, catapulted from sleep, must have felt the same terror. Some screamed, some called out in shocked voices, 'What's happening?' while others who'd been here for a long time seemed to take it in their stride. Jean was one of these.

Bunked a few beds away, she shouted, 'Calm down, everyone! This is obviously the second wave we've all been expecting. Behave as you did for the first, in a professional manner.'

As the noise in the room settled, the warlike sounds they were more used to became apparent.

Someone in the end cubicle must have stood on her bed and looked out of the window, a precarious thing to do on the canvas beds, as she shouted, 'Oh my God! The skies are lit!'

Ruth, who hadn't spoken, whispered, 'Let's go outside and take a look!'

Ellen didn't have a second thought. She leaped out of bed, grabbed her housecoat and they were out of the door, followed by many others.

In the distance they could see flares, which one of the nurses shouted were magnesium flares, and a male voice piped up that they were used for signalling. These lit up the night and were quickly followed by the crackle of what sounded like a million rifles, though soon these were drowned out by the explosions of heavy artillery.

But none of it could drown out the booming voice of Sister as she bid them all to come in, dress and to start thinking about and preparing for manning stations in readiness.

Just as they all re-entered the building, like a playground

load of naughty children, the biggest bang of all happened. Once more the building shook, bringing down clouds of dust onto them and a rush of people as the laundry maids came screaming up from the cellars, many of them crying and saying that the Germans were going to kill them all.

Ellen felt fear deeper than any she'd felt before, but Ruth's reassuring grabbing of her hand helped her, as it had done before and always would do.

'Come on, mate, we'll do as Sister says. Don't forget we have the Red Cross flying above us, nothing'll be aimed at us. We'll be fine. And we have a job to do, so let's get ready to do it, eh?'

Feeling like the child she was, Ellen just nodded and went with Ruth.

It seemed to Ellen now as she and Ruth sat together on a bench in Calais port that that night had set in motion a horror she could hardly believe had happened.

For here it was October, soon to be her sixteenth birthday, and they were going home.

They sat, Ellen's mind giving her horrific memories; Ruth quieter than usual, staring into space.

As Ellen relived the past months, she thought of how sometimes they'd worked day and night. How terrible the gas attacks had been! So many awful deaths – physically fit men, choking their last breaths. The funerals – how the English paraded slowly behind the ambulances of any English soldiers as they took them to the cemetery.

But there'd been highlights too: the visit of Marie Curie, and of the Belgian king and queen. The taking over of the hospital by the Belgian general, that had meant more surgeons arriving and made getting supplies easier. The concert Ruth had put on and how well it went down as so many realized who she really was and some of those had seen her on stage but hadn't recognized her out of costume.

And when the summer heat blasted their bedroom, the fun they had when all took their beds out onto the lawn to sleep under the stars.

It was a time that she would never forget, but now couldn't be happier to leave behind and to be going home.

'You're quiet, Ruth.'

'I have something on me mind, Ellen.'

'Tell me about it. Maybe I can help?'

'I don't want you to get your hopes up, luv.'

'Why, has something happened? What is it, Ruth? Tell me.'

'It's news on Amy.'

'That's wonderful . . . It is good news, isn't it?'

'It could be. As you know, we've dealt with a few Canadians during the summer, but I have had more time to talk to them. I've asked about Amy, and they've all talked in a derogatory tone about the kids that came from homes here, calling them Home Children, but saying things like, "You aren't bothered about one of them, are you? Lazy buggers. We give them everything and they'll run away at the drop of a hat. They won't work. They expect everything on a plate . . ." Oh, Ellen, I've learned that most go straight to a home when they get there, and then are collected by farmers to help them in busy seasons, and that some of them are never returned as they're useful. And I was told that some throw themselves at the farmers' sons and become pregnant, hoping to get a foot in the door . . . Well, we know what that really means, don't we?'

Ellen shuddered. Yes, she knew. 'Oh, Ruth, poor Amy . . . We'll find her, we will.'

'I've also learned that Canada's a vast country. It'll be like looking for a needle in a haystack, except . . . well, one I asked – a bloke called Johnny Wanderman – knew of a girl from London, called Amy . . .'

'What? Could it be our Amy? Is it possible?'

'It is. Very, luv.'

'Why, what did he say?'

'I asked him to describe her, but he said she'd only been pointed out to him once when he was in town. He was having a drink with a bloke from the farm where she is and they had a laugh about the Home Children. This bloke said to Johnny, "Amy's one of them – her out there, standing by me cart. She works for me brother. She's one of the better ones and takes care of me sick sister-in-law." I asked him what she looked like and he said she had mousy-coloured hair and freckles. That she was small and didn't look like she could pick a needle up, let alone a bale of hay!'

Excitement tickled Ellen's stomach muscles. 'Oh, Ruth, that so sounds like Amy.'

'I know. And that's not all he said. He said the farm she was working on ain't far from his pa's – they call their dad pa over there.'

'But is this Amy all right? Did he say?'

'He said he thought so. He said the bloke she works for is a decent bloke.'

'Oh, Ruth, did you find out where this was?'

'It was in Ontario. He said that's a huge area, but he was being cagey then as if he had something to hide, so I checked his address. I've got it written down in my notebook in my trunk.'

'Do you think it could really be our Amy?'

'I don't know. It's a chance in a million, but it is a starting point for us, that's if you're still up for going to look for her one day?'

'I am. But when that will be we just don't know. We can't till this war ends, and our commitment to the Red Cross, but we will, Ruth . . . How about we write to the address? We could say we have been nursing his son and thought we would update him, and would he be kind enough to forward the enclosed letter to the nearest farm to his as we think that our friend is working there.'

'What if it isn't our Amy?'

'Well, we could still help whoever it is, couldn't we? She's obviously an English orphan – one of us.'

'Oh, Ellen, luv, you've a heart of gold to go with the head of wisdom, which makes it seem as if you are much older.'

'Well, I will be in a few days' time. I'll be sixteen!'

Ruth burst out laughing. 'Ha, you said that as if you were going to suddenly be twenty! Sixteen! You'll be bloomin' ancient then.'

Ellen laughed with her. The laughter helped her to cope with all she'd heard but didn't settle her mind as she knew it wouldn't Ruth's. Finding Amy truly would be like finding a needle in a haystack. She'd known this for a long time through her studies in geography but had wanted to keep hope alive for Ruth. But now, maybe, just maybe, they had something that might help them.

When they reached English soil, they couldn't believe their eyes. Adrian stood on the dock waiting for them. Ruth ran to him and was soon enclosed in his arms.

As Ellen got closer, she saw Frederick was with him.

Frederick stepped forward. 'Well, well, little Ellen.'

Ellen felt an immediate annoyance. What was it with him? She could slap his smug face. 'I am not "little Ellen"!'

'Oh, just as feisty, I see. Anyway, it's good to see you, even if I am on your most hated list.'

'You're not . . . you just say the most stupid things!'

'Well, I'm sorry, can I be forgiven? Adrian's working in the War Office and has a list of passengers on our ships. That's how we knew you were coming in today. When he told me – not breaking any secrets act, of course, as I am his senior officer in rank – I begged to be able to come as I need to make amends to you. How can I do that?'

His face looked so sad, she felt herself softening. 'Thank you. I can't understand why you haven't forgotten all about me, but it's good to see you as long as you promise not to patronize me . . . Anyway, I have news for you. We've been working with your brother, Bernard.'

She didn't say that she'd secretly admired Bernard all these months, nor that it had been a wrench to leave him.

'Bernard! Well, well, how is he? He didn't steal your heart from me, did he?'

This time she could see he was teasing, so laughed with him. At this, he took her arm and tucked it in his. 'Seriously, how is my brother? I do worry about him.'

'Tired, extremely overworked. Very dedicated. An excellent doctor and surgeon, and a very nice man.'

'He has stolen your heart!'

Ellen looked away. Adrian caught her eye and, having released Ruth, put his arms out to her. She ran into them. Adrian had moved from being her tutor to being her friend – more even, as she now looked on him as an older brother.

'Any news of Dilly and Cook, Adrian?'

'Well, say a proper "hello" first, eh?'

'Sorry, how are you? How's your asthma been?'

'I've had no more attacks, and have taken daily exercise as advised, so you could say very good.'

He'd put his arm around Ruth once more. 'We've been more worried about you two. Especially when we heard of the gas attacks.'

It was Ruth who answered. 'They were awful. Me eyes smarted as me throat did. Poor Ellen had blisters on her hands and cheeks. It must have blown over to us as we were coughing a lot. But apart from us, we saw so much horror. Men dying . . .'

'Oh, my Ruth, you're crying. I'm sorry, so sorry. It was insensitive of me to bring it up. You both must be traumatized.'

'Did Bernard suffer?'

'We all did, Frederick,' Ellen told him gently. 'Bernard had blisters too, but we all got over it. Most of the poor men didn't. It was a wicked act.'

Frederick's face fell.

'But he's all right now, I promise. He told me that if I saw you, I was to give you his love.' This was true in part, as Bernard had said that if she ran into Frederick, she was to give his best to him. Well, 'best' meant love, didn't it? This thought made her feel justified in saying the words she had.

Frederick looked touched.

Adrian changed the subject. 'Well, what will happen with your luggage? Are you to wait to pick it up?'

Ruth told him, 'No, we have a small case each and that will be given to us if we wait around, but our main trunks will be sent on to us. We gave Bett's address.'

'Oh, I thought you'd go straight up to Leeds, Ellen?'

Ellen suddenly felt alarmed. 'Why? Should I? Is there something wrong?'

Adrian looked uncomfortable.

'There is, isn't there? Is it Dilly?'

'Well, my dear, she has been failing in health . . . I'm sorry. Cook is looking after her, but she's very tired. When I was up there three weeks ago, I employed a woman from nearby to be a daily help for them.'

'Oh, Adrian, no!'

Adrian pulled her into his arms. How easily they'd fallen into this new relationship, but then Adrian was such a big part of her life and had been for a long time now.

'You must prepare yourself, my dear. You know that Dilly is a very old lady.'

'But she was always so healthy! I don't want anything to happen to her.'

'Will you come up to Leeds?'

'Yes, I'll go straight away. Are you going up?'

'I am. I have a couple of days' leave, I thought I could accompany you.'

Ellen turned to Ruth. 'Oh, Ruth, will it be all right?'

'Of course it will, luv. If we're needed, the Red Cross will contact Bett's address and I can get in touch with you, but we won't be for at least a week, I'd say.'

'You mean, you aren't coming? Oh, Ruth, I wanted to spend my birthday with you!'

'I can't straight away, luv. I need to see Bett, and we have to be on hand for any duty we are called to. My address is the one they have.' Ruth stepped forward and hugged her. 'But my heart will go with you, and I hope you find Dilly improved from what Adrian has seen. Hopefully I will see you in a few days.'

When she let Ellen free, Ruth turned to Adrian and went into his arms again. 'Drive carefully. Look after me Ellen for me. I so wish you both didn't have to go.'

Frederick caught hold of Ellen's arm. 'Shall we give them a moment, Ellen?'

Ellen understood but didn't want to leave Ruth. She turned to see her and Adrian in a deep kiss and knew that there was a part of Ruth that belonged to him. But she would always be her big sis, and she knew they would always look out for each other.

Chapter Twenty-Four

Ruth

Life felt empty for Ruth as Adrian and Ellen left her. Frederick took her arm.

'I will see you into a taxi, Ruth. You must be exhausted. Poor Ellen, having to go so much further after an already long journey and with the worry of her friend's health on her shoulders.'

The way he said this shocked Ruth into the realization that he had feelings for Ellen. She wanted to shout at him that he was too old, that Ellen was just a child, but then she remembered, Frederick didn't know that. Adrian wouldn't have told him. He, like everyone, would be taking her to be much older.

Her thoughts went to Bernard, Frederick's brother. She'd accepted a long time ago that he and Ellen were attracted to one another. She sighed. Things could get very complicated in the future.

'Ta, Frederick. That's kind of yer, mate.'

As she waved to him, she saw him call another cab and forgot all about him.

Her heart raced with joy as she left the train that had taken her to Paddington and boarded her second taxi, bringing her closer to Bett's, though it all seemed so surreal that everything looked just as she'd left it. No sign of the horror happening over the Channel, no blood running under everyone's feet, but no clear skies either, just the usual grey, misted-by-smog London sky of this time of year.

But this was the place in her soul and it would always be.

Bett was out when she arrived. She guessed she'd be at the soup kitchen. Her letter had been full of its success and how much she loved it.

Dumping her bag inside Bett's flat, she hurried along to the church. A steady stream of people stood outside waiting to enter. All looked down-and-out, poor things. Women carrying babies with several others at their hips, old people shuffling along and ragamuffin kids.

'I ain't jumping the queue, everyone. I've come to help.'

'You go ahead, Nurse.'

This remark reminded Ruth that she still wore her Red Cross uniform. She held her head up with the pride she felt at being taken for a nurse.

As soon as she opened the door, Bett spotted her. 'Ruth! Ruth, me luv!'

She dropped the ladle she had in her hand and came waddling over. Sweat stood out on her brow. Her pinny, though clean, was splashed with soup, and her hair was escaping her mop cap.

'Bett . . . Oh, Bett. It's good to see you.'

Two chubby arms enclosed her. The familiar smell of cooking assailed her and gave her the thought that she was truly home.

'Ruth. It's good to see you, girl!'

This from Ebony took Ruth from Bett's arms and into Ebony's. 'Oh, it's good to be home, mate.'

Ebony held her at arm's length and grinned her lovely grin that made her eyes sparkle. 'How long are you home for, Ruth, girl?'

'I don't know, we can be called at any time.' She told them why she hadn't got Ellen with her. 'So, can I give a hand here? How's everything been going?'

It was Bett who answered. 'So bloomin' well, we can hardly keep up, Ruth. Ebony's curries are famous near and wide and we've folk coming across London to get a decent meal and a taste of the wonderful stews that originate from her own country – I can't pronounce their names but love them. It's a stew today, in fact, but it ain't nothing like the stews we make. This one is so bleedin' delicious it knocks yer socks off!'

'Well, I hope it fills them first!'

They all laughed. When they calmed, Ruth told them, 'I saw the crowd and thought the whole of Bethnal must be starving. Well, let me take me cape off and wash me hands and I'll be willing to do anything you ask.'

The afternoon went by quickly with Ruth hardly noticing it, but now that the last hungry mouth was fed, she felt the sheer exhaustion of the whole day wash over her.

Bett noticed. 'Get yerself off, luv. I'll be along just as soon as we get these pots washed and the floor mopped.'

'I should help.'

'No! Yer all done in. Get the kettle on for me when yer get back and then yer can tell me all about yer adventures when I get there.'

This was the last thing Ruth wanted to do, nor would she call what she'd experienced adventures. She just wanted a bath in front of the fire and to laze in it for hours, letting the 'all' that Bett wanted to know leave her and then she could face whatever came to her in the future.

After lighting a fire in the sitting room of her own second-floor flat above Bett's, she lugged the tin bath in out of the yard and dragged it up the stairs. Those months in Belgium hauling grown men from bed to bed had made her strong as showed in how quickly she filled four huge pans and got two of them boiling on her own stove and two on Bett's. Though these last she would only warm as it would be too dangerous to carry them upstairs.

In no time, she had her wish. She slid her naked body under the silky soft hot water and rested her head on the cushion she'd propped up at the head of the bath. Closing her eyes, she let herself relax. That didn't work for long as images assailed her mind and tears began to stream down her cheeks. So much destruction. So much death. So many young men lamed, or left with one arm, or one eye, or no eyes; some even with no face. What would life in the future hold for them – strong, young engineers, dock workers and factory workers, all too weak to pick up those occupations when they returned? How would they support their families . . . or, horror of horrors, would they even be welcomed home by the young women they loved who had sent off a handsome young man? Would these women reject what in a lot of cases would be their ugly, maimed returning husband and, in others, a man they would have to care for?

The more these thoughts assailed her, the more Ruth cried. 'Why? Why, why?'

The word repeated itself over and over in her head. But she could see no reason. Sometimes the most horrific injuries or death count had been after a battle that had gained the victor no more than a field!

She didn't hear Bett come up the stairs, so her voice made her jump. 'That's a good idea, luv. Yer'll feel better for a good soak. I wouldn't mind one meself. I might put the pots on in readiness . . . Ruth . . . Oh, Ruth, girl, what is it?'

'Oh, Bett, it was awful.'

'Now, come on, girl. Let it all out, luv. I'm yer mate, you can tell me anything.'

As Ruth began to relate her thoughts, Bett listened. Ruth's body shook with sobs. When it was all out of her, Bett grabbed the towel and held it open. 'Come on, luv, let's get you dry.'

Ruth stepped out onto the old towel she'd put down and as she did, Bett wrapped her in the warmth of the huge one and held her close. Her big, soft body comforting her; her podgy hands, as they patted her back, soothing her.

'Yer'll feel better now, mate. Yer'll never forget. We must never do that, but yer'll be able to cope, I promise, luv.'

For the second time in her life, Ruth felt as though she'd found a mum. She squeezed Bett. 'Ta, Bett. I will while I have you. Yer like a mum to me.'

'That's a lovely thing to say, mate. I always wanted a daughter, instead of the law-breaking lumps I got. Mind, if I could have them back as young boys, I would. They loved their mum. They still do, but they give me a lot of heartache. I fear that day when they're caught and brought up in front of the beak.'

'Bett, did they ever find me real mum?'

'They did, luv, but then they bleedin' lost her again, useless idiots. She must have got wind they were after her, but maybe thought she were in trouble as most are that my boys are after. If they'd had an ounce of brain, they'd have made sure she didn't think that.'

'Are they sure it was her?'

'Yes, luv. They say she was the image of you on the photo I gave them. But don't you give up, we'll find her. In the meantime, yer've got me, ain't yer, girl?'

Ruth smiled. She could see that she couldn't have said a better thing to Bett than to liken her to being a mum to her. Though Rebekah would always be her first sort-of-mum and she had a real mum, Bett would forever have that place in her heart too.

Feeling better, she said, 'Right, give me the towel and let me get dry and dressed, then I'll help you fill it for your own bath. Have you got a fire going downstairs?'

'I have, girl. A cracker. I threw a couple of logs onto the embers as soon as I came in – it'll be up the chimney by now.'

Getting the bath ready, Ruth felt the last of her cares leave her. She supposed she'd always have these moments. How could she not, after seeing what she'd seen? But she knew she would get stronger. 'Right, I'll leave you to it, Bett.'

'Ain't yer going to wash me back for me, then?'

'I bloomin' well ain't!'

'Well, yer ungrateful sod!'

Ruth laughed as she hurried through the door. Then as she heard Bett let wind as she got into the bath, laughed even louder and was glad that she'd escaped when she had!

Snuggled in her chair next to the fire, she began to think about Adrian. Not that he was ever far from her thoughts, but a niggly worry had begun inside her when she'd seen him after so long. He seemed to have lost weight and was looking just a bit too thin. She wondered if he'd overdone the exercise. He'd told her the specialist had recommended that he expand his chest.

As her thoughts went on, she wondered for the hundredth time at how they had come together – him a well-educated man, not of means as such, but certainly from a better off background than herself, and her a cockney girl from an orphanage, and a showgirl. They didn't seem to have anything in common and yet, they had everything. But could such a relationship work?

Ruth sighed as she prayed to Holy Mary that it would. Then she smiled as she told the keeper of her secrets and her support, 'Come to think of it, luv, no one was more mismatched than you and your Joseph were, and you made it work.' She concluded that Joseph's kindness contributed to that. *Well, no one is kinder than me Adrian, so we're off to a good start there, Holy Mary. What do you say, eh?*

With this, she cheered up and allowed her natural confidence in herself to surface once more. With it came a longing to be with Adrian and her dear sister. She hoped beyond hope that they found Dilly to be all right.

When she woke the next day, she felt excited at the thought of visiting the market and the theatre. She decided the theatre should be her first port of call.

Randal, the director of the musical she had starred in, greeted her. 'Ruth, Ruth, my darling girl. You made it home!' With a flourish he gathered her in his arms in a weak cuddle that made her want to giggle. He smelled of the stage. An aroma that encompassed the stuffy, musty costumes, the make-up that was painted onto the actors' and actresses' faces, the fusty wigs they wore, and the paint used for the sets.

'So, have you done your bit, darling girl? Are you home for good? Can you take up your role again? We're still running, you know! But it isn't the same to me without you.'

An idea came to Ruth. 'I can't . . . well, not full time. I could be called back to duty at any time, but . . . well, I wonder if you would consider something?'

'Anything for you, my darling.'

'How about I do a turn at the end of the performance one evening? I could come on in my Red Cross uniform and do a wartime song, and then make an appeal for the Red Cross who are desperate for funds.'

She held her breath, unable to read Randal's thoughts. Then she could see the idea taking shape. 'Yes! It's marvellous. I could bill it as an exclusive appearance by our war hero, Ruth Faith, still serving in the depths of war to save our soldiers' lives!' He clapped his hands. 'I love it!'

'I will have to check with the Red Cross HQ, but if it isn't a problem with them, how shall we turn that into cash for them?'

'Have you many nurse friends? They could go and stand with a collection plate or bag as the audience retire! Oh, I simply love it. The theatre should do more for the war effort than keep up morale at home.'

'Ta, Randal, you're a luv.'

She was treated to one of his slack-arm cuddles again and kissed on the cheek. On an impulse she grabbed him. 'Oh, I've missed you. I've missed all of you.'

After the initial shock on his face, he said, 'My dear, you are crying. Was it so terrible?'

'It was. As was missing you all and my life as it was. But not just for me, for all those suffering and for all the nurses and doctors trying to help them.'

He was quiet, then he shocked her as he said, 'I know. I have lost my dear nephew; my sister is broken-hearted.'

'Oh, Randal, I shouldn't have been so heartless and self-centred, forgive me. I am so sorry, mate.'

He shook his head and smiled, but she didn't miss how his eyes had suddenly reddened as a tear played in the corner of one of them. But as he always did, he brushed everything aside. 'Well, that seems to be life at the moment, and we all have to get on with it. So, find out as quickly as you can about our fundraising idea, my dear, as we have limited time to fit it in.'

Taking her cue from him, she answered in a voice just as jolly as his, 'Not before I see all the cast. I won't hinder them, I promise.'

'Go on, then. They're all getting ready for rehearsals.'

The next hour was an excited flurry of hugs and kisses, which placed her in the world she loved. She so wanted to be here going out on stage to rehearse, and even more so when she stood in the wings and waited for the young girl who'd taken her place to go through the familiar routine.

A hand touched her arm. She turned. 'Ted! Oh, Ted, it's good to see you, mate.'

Memories assailed her as she looked into his tear-filled eyes of the first days when she ran away from the orphanage and Ted was one of the down-and-outs who helped her. And how he used to play his flute to get money to buy them all a hot potato. Now, he played in the theatre orchestra. She flung her arms around him. 'How have you been, luv?'

He smiled. 'Better than I've ever been, but no better than at this moment. 'Ave yer heard from Robbie?'

'Only once. He seemed to have a cushy number, but oh, I miss him.'

'We all do. Well, we got a letter from him a few days ago, and yer right, luv, he's doing all right, but he was devastated as his mate's . . . well, I think more than a mate, has copped it.'

'Not Abraham?' Ruth's throat tightened.

'Yes, could be. He called him Abe.'

'You mean, Abe's dead?'

'No. But badly injured. Very. Lost both his legs. Do yer know him, luv?'

Ruth could hardly get the word 'yes' out. Her heart went out to Abe. How terrible that this should happen to him. She made her mind up that she would try to find out where he was and visit him and she would write to Robbie later that day too.

After leaving, Ruth went immediately to the Red Cross headquarters and asked for an interview.

This was granted. The lady in charge was a different one to the last time. This one was a motherly character, with a warm way about her that made it easy for Ruth to put across her idea.

'It sounds wonderful, my dear. And there are nurses on leave like yourself who could help to collect the money . . . Oh, we are so badly in need of funds, this could be a real boost. Thank you, my dear. I trust it will all be done in good taste?'

'It will, Miss Darlington. I won't let any part of it be gimmicky or trashy. I am honoured to be a volunteer with the Red Cross and have seen service first-hand. I will be in all the correct uniform – no fancy take-off of it, I promise.'

'Thank you. I know you will do us proud and bring in lots of needed funds, Ruth. Please may I have a ticket for the show that night?'

'I will bring you as many tickets as you need as soon as I know all the details, Miss Darlington, and thank you again.'

'No. *Thank you*, my dear, I look forward to it very much.'

'Miss Darlington . . . May I ask something else of you? I – I, well, I've heard that a mate has been injured and is in a hospital in the Midlands. I'd like to know where so I can write to him . . . I mean, well, if I ain't allowed the information, then that's fine.'

'It is unconventional. If you give me his name, I can find out, but I will need to ask his family if I can give you the information.'

Ruth gave Abe's name and rank. She didn't say that the family might well refuse to let her have any details as she thought this might stop Miss Darlington from even trying. But she didn't hold out much hope.

With the good news that she had the permission she needed, Ruth felt like skipping to the market, as besides the element of raising money for the lovely Red Cross, she couldn't wait to get back on stage!

When she jumped off the bus, having enjoyed seeing so much of London again through its mucky windows, and had her bones shaken as it had trudged along, she allowed herself to skip to the market and felt like a kid again as she did.

Laughing at the gaping passers-by and calling out to those she knew, she felt as though she'd received a tonic – something to help her to forget the terrible injury Abe had received for a while, and to look forward once more. At least he would be home in a hospital in England and he was safe. What he had to face was dreadful, but knowing Abe, he would. He'd rise above it. She knew that.

'Hey, girl! Good to see yer!' Ruby's voice cut into these

thoughts. 'And full of the joys of spring even though bleedin' winter is just around the corner! Come 'ere, I need a hug.'

Ruby's arms enclosed her. Even through her coat Ruth could feel the cold of her blue-tipped fingers that poked out of her gloves.

'You shouldn't still stand market, Ruby. You retired once, luv, can't you again?'

'I will soon, mate. I've a nice little nest egg now. But what would I do with me bleedin' time, eh?'

'Lots of things. Women like you are needed, luv. Have you seen Bett lately?'

'Only a couple of times. She's busy with some charity work, feeding the hungry.'

'There you go. You could do that. And you have contacts to get them cheap fruit and veg. Or, if you don't fancy that, a lot of groups are knitting scarves and warm socks for our men on the front.'

'I could do that. I'm a good knitter. But ain't these groups made up of posh ladies? They're not for the likes of me.'

'Then start one of your own, Ruby, luv. Yer could do it at the same church Bett has her kitchen. There's a few of them as go there for a daily meal that could do with some warm knitted clothing. No one should be short of something to do these days. But whatever yer choose, yer need to think about getting off the freezing corner.'

'I know. It ain't even bloomin' winter proper yet, and I'm shivering. I'll do it, luv. I will.'

'Good. How's business been, then?'

'Not good but ticking over. Anyway, I want to 'ear all about what you're getting up to, never mind me.'

'Shut up shop a while then, mate, and let's go over to the cafe, eh? I see it's open again.'

'Good idea. 'Arry'll look after it for me.' Ruby shouted over to the stallholder next to hers.

He replied that he would, though he didn't like getting his hands dirty with handling the spuds.

'Sherrup, yer great oaf! I 'elp you out, don't I?'

All of this was friendly banter and made Ruth long for the days when she stood here with her hats and joined in it all.

As she and Ruby drank their mugs of hot tea she told as much as she thought Ruby could take. Some things couldn't be shared with everyone.

Her last call of the day was back to the theatre. Here all was excitedly arranged to take place at the next Saturday's performance.

'Rehearsal tomorrow, darling,' Randel told her. 'Bring along the song you chose. I'm sure the orchestra have the music to them all.'

'Randel, can I have a favour, luv? Can you see if Ted can do a solo on his flute with me? We go back a long way, me and him, and that would be very special to me.'

'Sounds good. Leave it with me . . . Yes. The flute would sound wonderful. We'll see what arrangement he can come up with. See you tomorrow. Get some beauty sleep. As you are, it'll take all the make-up we have on the premises to restore your beauty and hide your puffy eyes.'

Ruth laughed at him, but did know what he meant as she caught sight of her features. She'd done a lot of crying today and knew she had more in store when it truly sank in about poor Abe. But she was a trooper, so was up for the task she'd set herself and couldn't wait.

When she arrived home, Bett welcomed her with open arms. 'I've a nice fire going, luv, and as always, me kettle's on and already spluttering. Sit a while and tell me all about your day.'

As she came to the part about Abe, Bett looked down. 'I know. We all do but were waiting for the right moment. Abe's been writing to Abdi. So, Ebony told me all about it. He's in an 'ospital in a village in Leicestershire.'

'You know where he is? Oh, Bett, that's good news after all the bad as now I can go to visit him.'

'Shouldn't yer ask Adrian if it's all right, luv?'

This shocked Ruth. 'No, I know it will be. He might even take me.'

'Does he know how close you and Abe were?'

'Stop worrying, Bett, of course he does.'

Bett looked mystified and Ruth wanted to laugh. But she knew that Bett had had a volatile marriage with rows and fights fuelled by jealousy so understood her concern.

As her tired legs climbed the stairs to her own flat half an hour later, Ruth had a mixture of emotions.

She wanted to be with Ellen and Adrian, and yet, she wanted to be with Abe to bring him comfort. But also, she was filled with joy at her coming stage appearance and was glad that she had this to look forward to.

Chapter Twenty-Five

Ellen

As soon as they arrived at Rose Cottage, Ellen dashed inside. Memories flooded her of her gran – the house looked as though time had stood still and everything was where it always was.

Cook let them in. Ellen saw immediately how tired she looked. After a short hug, Ellen bid her to sit down.

'But I've to get you a pot of tea, Ellen. You've had such a long journey, lass.'

'I don't need tea, thank you, Cook. We stopped at a cafe for refreshments about an hour ago, I'm fine. Sit down and tell me, how's Dilly? Is she in bed?'

'She is. She's too weak to come down.'

Ellen jumped up and ran up the stairs. 'I'm here, Dilly . . . Oh, Dilly.'

Dilly lay back on her pillow, her eyes closed. She seemed to have shrunk to half her normal size, and Ellen knew she was near to the end of her life.

Taking a deep breath, she went to her. 'Dilly . . . Oh, my dearest Dilly. Are you in pain?'

Dilly opened her eyes. The dullness of them lit with a little twinkling light. A smile played around her lips. 'You . . . you came, me little lass.'

'Yes, I'm here, Dilly. I won't leave you . . . Dilly! Oh, Dilly . . . No!'

Dilly had released a long breath and didn't draw it back in again. Ellen bent her head and lay it on Dilly's gnarled hands. Her tears flooded her face. Her sobs were for Dilly, her gran and for all the dead and hurt soldiers she'd dealt with.

She knew Adrian was in the room, but he didn't try to stop her. She'd told him about a lot of what she'd experienced on the journey here, so he must realize that she needed this release. But after a moment, his hands came on her shoulders. 'Ellen, we must call the doctor. You know Dilly is at peace, my dear. Poor you. You always had this sadness to face as both your gran and Dilly were in their later years when you came to them. So much heartache for you. But you must be strong. Draw on the strength that got you through all that you faced in Flanders, my dear. Make yourself a professional nurse again, for Dilly and for the sake of poor Cook, who has lost her best friend.'

This steadied Ellen. She lifted her head, leaned forward to kiss Dilly's cheek and rose. Adrian steered her out of the bedroom and followed close behind her as she went down the stairs.

Cook was where they had left her, sat trembling in a chair next to the fire. 'Has she gone?'

Ellen nodded. 'She was so peaceful, Cook, and she knew that I was with her.'

'Ah, that's good.'

Ellen was at a loss as to what to say next. But Adrian said he would fetch the doctor, and would she, in the meantime, make a hot sweet tea for herself and Cook.

Glad to have something to do, Ellen leaped up and went

into the cosy kitchen. The kettle was already steaming on the stove, and a tray was laid out with three cups.

Taking the tea back through, she told Cook, 'Nothing will change your position, Cook, so please don't worry. Though I know you will be lonely without Dilly.'

'She were everything to me, Ellen.'

'I know. How long has she been ill?'

'She's been ailing a good few months now. I've looked after her as best I could and that cleaning lady – Prue – she helped me to give Dilly a bed bath twice a week.'

'I'm so sorry. If I had known, I would have put a nurse in for Dilly. That must have been very difficult for you?'

'I'd do it all again for Dilly, lass.'

'I know.'

There was a silence except for the sound of Cook slurping her tea until slowly she replaced the cup on the saucer and quite directly said, 'I have plans, thou knaws.'

'Oh?'

'Aye. I have a younger brother. He and me sister-in-law have wanted me to go to them for a long time. They live in Scarborough. They've run a boarding house for them as wanted to go to take the sea air, but now they have a few permanent lodgers, and plenty of rooms. I'd love to go there if it's all reet with you?'

'Of course it is. I'm pleased for you, Cook. My mind will be at rest knowing you are being cared for and with loved ones. I may not be able to take you myself, but I will see you get there safely.'

'Me brother will fetch me. He has a car. He's done all right 'as our Arthur. I just need to write to him, and he'll be here like a shot.'

'He sounds like a good brother.'

As Cook went on praising the brother that had been born when she was fourteen years old, Ellen thought of little Christopher. How she longed for him to know her – to be able to be a big sister to him and just to be in his life.

'By, that were a big sigh, lass. I must be boring you, sorry, but once I start on telling of me Arthur, there's naw stopping me. Dilly used to say I made the sun shine out of his backside.' Cook gave a little laugh, which turned into a sob.

Getting up from her chair, Ellen went over to her and crouched on her haunches at Cook's knee. 'You did all any friend could be asked to do for Dilly, Cook . . . Look, I can't keep calling you Cook. May I use your name?'

'Aye, you can, lass. Though it'll seem strange as I've allus been Cook to everyone. Me name's Rhoda.'

'Well, Rhoda, tomorrow is my birthday. I lost my Dilly the day before my birthday.'

Ellen had no idea why she said that. Rhoda didn't query it, but as a tear trickled down Ellen's cheek, she felt Rhoda's hand gently stroke her hair.

When Adrian entered with the doctor they were both crying – Ellen with her head on Rhoda's lap.

The doctor was a stranger to her, and Ellen was glad it wasn't the same one who'd become like a monster in her head for treating her like a mad person, when she'd just been a distressed and traumatized child. She'd never wanted to see him again.

Once he'd left, Rhoda said, 'Shall we go and lay our Dilly out, Ellen?'

The process of laying a dead body out was new to Ellen. They'd never had to do that for the dead at Hoogstade. They'd just wrapped them, tied a tag with their name onto their toe and left them in a row for burial.

Though not wanting to do this for Dilly as it would be a sure admission that she had truly gone, Ellen knew she must. So, she just nodded her head.

Adrian gave her a look of sympathy before saying, 'I'll just go over to my apartment for a while, check that everything's all right.'

Ellen found herself trembling at the coming ordeal as she and Rhoda climbed the stairs, but far from being anything to dread, the act of washing Dilly, dressing her in her best frock and changing all the sheets helped her. And then to see Dilly looking so peaceful and pretty, as Rhoda had put a little rouge on her high cheekbones, gave her a peaceful feeling. Dilly had lived a good life and a long one and now she was at peace.

Three days later they stood looking down at what seemed such a tiny coffin being lowered into the open grave when a beam of sunlight broke through the murky clouds and lit the brass plate on the coffin lid. Ellen looked up and she fancied she saw her gran reaching her hand out to Dilly. In her heart, she waved to them both as it seemed to her they floated away together. A lovely feeling settled in her, stopping the turmoil of grief and filling her with a warm glow. Both the women she loved so much were all right. They were together once more and happy.

'Are you all right, Ellen, dear?'

'I am, Adrian. I'm fine.' Taking a deep breath, she walked away from the graveside with Adrian by her side.

Rhoda followed on the arm of her brother, a nice man in his early sixties and fourteen years younger than Rhoda. He'd come the next day after Dilly died, to look after Rhoda and to help her to pack her things. They were leaving after the funeral wake.

As the little party of them sat in Gran's sitting room drinking tea, Adrian asked, 'I know we've spoken a little about the house, but have you made your mind up what you're going to do with it, Ellen?'

'Not really. Prue has said she'll clear Dilly's things and close the house down for me. I will continue to employ her to keep it clean and fresh, but it's all too much for me to think further than that.'

'I think you should talk to your solicitor. He can handle everything for you. I know he does already oversee the rental of the schoolroom, but there will be upkeep expenses.'

'He already sees to paying Prue and for a gardener coming in regularly. Any other maintenance, Dilly only had to report it to him and he saw it was fixed. I'll ask him to carry on with that, only Prue will keep him informed. Other than that, there's not much I can do yet.'

'You are a marvel, and I take pride in that, having been your tutor. But I worry about you. You may feel capable of all you do and of coping with all of your responsibilities, but you are only sixteen, and I fear the pressure of everything may tell on you again.'

'Not while I have Ruth and you. You're there to guide me like a big brother, and Ruth to love me like a big sis and mum rolled into one. I'll be all right. And as for my work, it's what I was born to do.'

'It is, and that shines from you.'

'What I lack in years, I have more than enough in experience. Most girls wouldn't go through in a lifetime what I have in my sixteen years.' A shudder involuntarily trembled through her body. Adrian's hand came onto hers. The gesture helped. She dared not think about it all. It had to stay in the box she'd shut it all in.

'I want to go home tomorrow. I want to be with Ruth.'

'We can and we will. You've everything arranged. And I have another couple of days' leave, so will be around for you.'

'No. You and Ruth have to spend some time together. I'll be fine.'

'I could ask Frederick to spend time with you. He has to return to France next week. His training is over, and he has to take command of a small battalion.'

Not sure on this, Ellen just said, 'We'll see. The important thing is that you and Ruth have some time alone. She's been longing for you all these months and then when she returns, I whisk you away from her.'

'Has she really been longing for me? I – I, well, I was afraid that she'd look on me as something that happened in a whirl and that was that.'

'You dafty. Her heart has been aching to be with you. She is dreading having to go away again.'

The hollows in his cheeks that had reappeared when they saw him again, filled out as his face stretched into a smile. But seeing this brought to Ellen's mind how worried she'd felt at first seeing him. 'Adrian, how's your health been?'

'Ha, don't play the doctor on me now. I'm all right. I lost weight pining for Ruth and missing you, not to mention worrying myself sick about you both. But other than that, my specialist is really pleased with me.'

Ellen wasn't so sure about this answer, but she didn't press him.

Seeing Rhoda off half an hour later was a touching affair. Rhoda had always been just Cook. Someone there, depend-able and with a ready piece of advice, or praise, but now she was Rhoda, a person who meant a lot more to Ellen than she'd realized.

'I'll write to you, Rhoda. Thank you for all you've done and all you've been to my gran, Dilly and me.'

Tears flowed freely down Rhoda's face. 'I'll await every letter, lass. Come and see me when this is all over . . . And, lass, I'm as proud of you as Dilly was, if that's possible. She loved you, thou knaws. She loved you with all her heart.'

Ellen swallowed hard. 'And I loved her. And you, Rhoda. Both in different ways, but I do love you.'

'Oh, Ellen, lass.' Rhoda put out her arms and took Ellen into her soft, squidgy body to hug her. Ellen found a peace there. She hugged Rhoda back. 'I'll come and see you when I can.'

Over Rhoda's shoulder she saw Arthur gleaming to see his sister so loved. Ellen liked him and knew he adored Rhoda and would take care of her. With this thought, she came out of the hug, kissed Rhoda's cheek, and stepped back to allow Arthur to help Rhoda into his car.

Within minutes they were waving her off till the car turned a bend and went out of sight.

As she turned to go back into the house, Ellen knew an era of her life had truly come to an end.

Back in London they found an excited Ruth. It was sad to take that excitement away from her as she imparted her news.

'Oh, Ellen, luv, I'm so sorry. If I'd have known, I'd have come up to you.'

'I know. But there was no time anyway. I'm fine. I know Dilly is at rest and hope she is holding Gran's hand. I never believed before about it being the natural progression in life to die when we are old, as that still leaves the loved ones heartbroken, but we have seen the terrible destruction of life and the painful ghastly deaths that can happen to the young, long before their time, and now count myself lucky that three of the people I loved have died peacefully and naturally, as I count Alison in that, and not in the brutal way my lovely Aggie was taken, or our lovely Hettie, and the countless young men we tried to save. And this helps . . . Now, why were you looking fit to burst when you saw us?'

Ruth's news thrilled Ellen. 'And I'm to be one of the nurses collecting in the money? Oh, Ruth, it's a wonderful idea. I cannot wait to see you on the stage again.'

'We're rehearsing every day; you can both come and watch if you like. My part is only a short one as I only have one song and a speech. I've been staying longer to help out with mending costumes, and anything needed, but now you're home I won't.'

Ellen could see a new glow lighting Ruth up. This was what she was supposed to be doing – her stage work. It was her life. She felt the sadness of this, and at how many young people were doing totally different things than they should, or wanted to. How the war was turning young men into killers, and young women into an army of workers. For her, the work they did was her life, but for Ruth and thousands of women, most of whom were working in factories, or on the farms, and even on the railways, their lives had been so disrupted. They were heroes too, in her eyes.

Finding how busy Bett was gave Ellen something to do so she could leave Ruth and Adrian to each other's company. She loved helping, and didn't mind that, not having many domestic skills, she was put to the task of dishing up the food.

The more she got to know Ebony and her husband Abdi, the more she liked them, especially Ebony who was full of fun, a far cry from the downtrodden maid Ruth had told her that she had been when they had first met.

'Well, girl, you're giving generous portions there. My, you'll fatten all the kids up for Christmas! I can't cook it fast enough to keep up with you.'

'Oh, I'm sorry. Is anyone leaving some on their plates?'

'No, you won't see that. Even if them kids are full to bursting, if there's food, they will eat it, as they don't know when their next meal will be. Probably not until they come here again.'

The thought of this hurt Ellen. 'What can we do to make that better, Ebony?'

'There ain't nothing more you can do, Ellen, girl. You've set all this up and that's a miracle in itself.'

It didn't feel like a miracle, not her part in it all. It was easy to give money, she thought, but to give all this time and work, as the others were, that was the real miracle.

As she helped to clean up, she thought about having money. It still seemed surreal that she could afford everything she needed and could help others, the latter being the best part of it all for her. But she began to wonder just how much she was worth, with the house, the schoolroom, and what was left of her legacy. Would it be enough to put her through medical school? Would she even be accepted? It was all a long way in the future; for now, she was content to be a Red Cross volunteer and wondered where they would send her and Ruth next. She prayed it was together again. She couldn't bear to be without Ruth.

Ellen put the broom she'd been using away in the cupboard. Tonight she would write to Amy. She knew exactly what she was going to say and do. She'd make sure she made all the arrangements that Amy would need to get in touch if the letter got to her. After all, it could be that she and Ruth might have left the country again by the time Amy replied. She'd give Amy her address at the cottage as well as Ruth's address at Bett's, instruct her solicitor to look out for the letter and to deal with it by helping Amy to get home if she wanted to before she and Ruth could go to Canada to fetch her.

She prayed the farmer she was going to write to would be able to help. She hoped so. She hoped with all her heart.

Chapter Twenty-Six

Ruth

The wind howled around the centre of London. The plumes of the horses danced on their necks as they trotted along, pulling the landau that Adrian had hired to pick her up from the theatre.

Ruth shivered. Snuggling her close, under the half-canvas roof that covered them, Adrian tucked the blanket tighter around their knees with his free hand. 'Sorry, darling, I thought this would be a nice treat for you.'

Ruth smiled. It wasn't and not all due to the weather, but her memories. She huddled in close to Adrian, trying to block out the image of losing her lovely Hettie and the heartache of seeing Ellen being taken away from her. She had Ellen back, but she could never have Hettie with her again. And now Abe, who'd hired the landau that fateful day many moons ago, was in a sorry state and Robbie was far away and in danger.

Feeling Adrian's body so close to hers helped. She looked up into his eyes and saw a look there that she'd never seen before. For a moment, she recoiled as she recognized his desire. But then tried to make herself not do so. This was Adrian. He loved her, of course he would desire her. And him doing so had nothing to do with the filth she'd known as a child.

Suddenly, wanting that desire, wanting to know how different it would be, she offered her lips to him.

Adrian's kiss started as the gentle kind he'd mostly given her, but then deepened, awakening a spark in her that she had no understanding of but wanted with all her heart. The feeling promised to wipe all others away – to take her to something she couldn't let herself dream as possible but knew existed.

As Adrian pulled away from her, he looked quizzically into her eyes as if asking a question. This was a different Adrian. A passionate man. A man who wanted her completely.

Ruth hesitated; knew that if she gave in, Adrian would regret putting her in this position and yet, knew that if she didn't, the unrequited feelings would torture her. She nodded her consent to the unspoken question.

Adrian leaned forward, his husky voice shouting to the driver to take them to Audley House, St Margaret Street. This building housed the apartment that went with his job with the War Office. Ruth had never seen it.

The nerves in her stomach clenched. *What am I doing?*

Adrian leaned towards her. 'Don't worry, darling. You can just come in and get warm if you like and to see where I live.'

His voice was gentle. Undemanding. Ruth found this strangely seductive.

The apartment wasn't fancy, but what she would call serviceable, and very much a man's home with brown leather wing-backed chairs, a huge brown leather chesterfield and a polished wooden floor covered by a plain cream rug. In the corner of the living room stood a desk with many files on it and a chart on the wall. Ruth glanced away from these, not wanting to look inquisitive.

Now they were here the moment became awkward. Adrian coughed. 'Let me take your coat. The fire is still glowing. I'll put some coal on it and liven it up . . . Oh, Ruth. Have I done wrong bringing you here?'

She lifted her head. Her shyness left her. 'No, me darlin'. I wanted to come. Yer ain't forced nothing on me.'

As he took her coat off her shoulders, he bent and kissed her neck. A shiver ran through her. It bore no relation to any feeling she'd ever experienced. This was a delicious awakening.

She turned. He dropped her coat and took her in his arms. 'My darling.'

His lips covered hers. Anticipation zinged through her. But then, the ugly face of Belton came to her, and she drew away.

'Darling?'

Looking up into his eyes and seeing his expression of concern, she said, 'Help me, Adrian, luv. Help me to forget.'

'Oh, my Ruth. Let's sit down.' He ushered her to the couch, then picked up her coat and took it through to the hall. When he came back, he'd taken his own coat off.

She felt the couch take his weight beside her. 'Ruth, I love you. I will try to help you, but I understand. No one can go through what you and Ellen went through at that home and be unscathed.' He slipped off the couch and kneeled in front of her. 'Will you do me the honour of becoming my wife, Ruth? I love you with all my heart.'

'I will! Oh, Adrian, me darlin'. I will.'

Tears glistened in Adrian's eyes. 'Thank you . . . When? Make it soon, then we can be together. You can move in here, I can come home to you every evening, and sometimes work just over there with you close by me.'

'But what about Ellen?'

'Ellen is stronger than you know, darling. She will be all right. She can be with us as often as her work allows.'

'But she needs me.'

'Yes, I know you need each other, but you won't be able to go with her to medical school, will you? And if she doesn't get in here in London – and believe me, it isn't easy for women; if there are ten places and eleven candidates, they will choose the male applicants. It is so difficult for women and may mean she has to go as far as Edinburgh.'

'Scotland!'

'Yes. There's a college of medicine for women there. Its founder – a lady called Elsie Inglis – is a doctor serving in Serbia. Sadly, there are fears for her safety as Serbia has been invaded . . . A remarkable woman. But what I'm trying to say is that if Edinburgh, or any other faraway place, is the only chance for Ellen to pursue her dream of being a doctor, she would go. And you would be the one making her go . . . In a nutshell, darling, the two of you cannot live in each other's pockets for ever.'

'As things are now, with me having found you, no, but we did plan that I would get a rental near to her so she could come home every evening, wherever she went.'

'Ah, that has changed, darling? You are thinking of marrying me . . . Look, before you decide, I want you to know that you can continue your stage career if you live here.'

'Really? You wouldn't mind?'

'No. I would love it. Now, can you please make up your mind, madam, as my knees are hurting!'

Ruth burst out laughing. Adrian laughed with her before grabbing her and pulling her onto the floor with him. 'There,

I can lie beside you now and look into your beautiful face and await my answer.'

She looked into his too-thin face and saw the beauty of him and felt her love for him swell. 'Yes, me darlin', the answer's yes!'

His lips came on hers and as his kiss deepened, his hands caressed her. The feeling she'd had earlier returned and expressed itself in a small moan escaping from her lips.

Adrian's breathing deepened. His own deep moan thrilled her as his hand found her breast.

Nothing in her wanted to stop this happening. She wanted to be Adrian's – completely his. No demons visited her as she gave herself to the slow, delicious sensation of having him undress her, kissing every part of her as he did, before slipping his own clothes off.

His body, though slim, was a surprise to her as his muscles gave him a lovely strong, masculine contour.

His voice croaked as he asked, 'Here? Are you sure, my darling?'

She could only nod as she thrilled at how he gazed on her.

'You're beautiful, my darling Ruth.'

The words caressed her soul. For a long time, she'd thought of herself as ugly with the sins that had been done to her body, but now she knew she was going to be cleansed – loved and cherished.

When the moment came, she accepted her Adrian with a cry of joy. All fear left her as she clung to him, moved with his movements, cried out her love, and felt sensation after sensation build inside her till they burst into a crescendo of exquisite, almost pain-filled feelings that had her hollering his name and begging him to stay still.

When the feeling subsided, she was left almost lifeless beneath him – his urgency allowed without protest, his love accepted, his body held in a vice-like grip as he truly made her his own.

They lay there for a moment, declaring their love, kissing each other, thanking each other, until they came to a calm place and Adrian rolled off her. He didn't leave her, though, but gathered her into his arms, stroked her hair and declared his love for her over and over.

'Let's marry very soon, Ruth. We can put up the banns in your parish and be married in three weeks. Please say you will, my darling, as I can't bear to be apart from you, not even for a minute.'

'You don't know what it means to me, me darlin', to be loved how you love me. I feel . . . well, whole . . . me . . . I mean, I feel that I am a person.'

'You are, my darling. Try to forget all you've been through . . . Though if ever you do want to talk, you can, but let's look to the future. Our future. A future of loving each other and having lots of babies.'

Ruth sat up. She hadn't given it a thought. 'Oh, Adrian, we might have done that already . . . made a baby, I mean!' She didn't feel alarmed, just full of love. 'I think we'd better get those banns up, and today!'

Adrian laughed out loud. A lovely sound. Ruth laughed with him. Never had she felt as happy as she did at this moment. Bending over him, she kissed him. His arms came around her, and he pulled her down beside him. She knew he wanted to make love again. She wanted that too. She went willingly to him.

Again, they drank in each other, taking their time, exploring all they had to give and needed, coming to a peak, thinking themselves spent, only to build the urgency again and again, until finally, crying with joy and exhaustion, they lay still in each other's arms. Ruth gazed into Adrian's eyes – her lovely man, her soon-to-be husband.

When they got up off the floor, Ruth shivered.

'The fire's gone down. Let's dress quickly, darling, and I'll take you for something to eat.'

'Can we go to me home, first?'

'Yes, we can tell Ellen together and then she can come to dinner with us.'

Ruth thought this a lovely idea, but how would Ellen take their sudden decision to marry? Would she feel abandoned?

Suddenly Ruth felt her loyalties divided between the two people she loved. She shared Adrian's happiness and knew being married to him was what she wanted most in all the world, but Ellen depended so much on her and would be upset to have to go off on her own to wherever the Red Cross sent her. They'd always supported one another since they'd been brought together again. They needed each other.

'I can see you are troubled, darling. Do you want to break the news to Ellen yourself?'

'I'm sorry, luv, it's just that—'

He stepped forward and put his finger on her lips. 'You don't have to explain. I know the bond between you. I'll hail a cab for you – they run up and down this road regularly – and then I'll come and pick you both up later.'

'Oh, Adrian, ta, luv. It's best I talk to Ellen first. I owe her that much. You see, it isn't just not being with her, but we had a plan to go to Canada to try to find Amy.'

'Canada! Good lord! That's a vast country, darling, and

it takes weeks to get there. You really haven't much chance of finding anyone there . . . Amy? Is that one of the other girls that was with you in the orphanage?'

'Yes, they shipped her off with loads of others.' She told him what she'd learned from the Canadian soldier.

'But there must be a hundred Amys that had that awful fate, darling, and why is she so special to you?'

'I don't know why, I just feel that she's a part of me, and so does Ellen. We love her and want to save her . . . And, well, I quizzed the soldier and his description of her – well, everything he knew about her – could be our Amy.'

Adrian was quiet for a moment, then said, 'But your journey wouldn't be until after the war, would it? It can't be as it is too dangerous. Look what happened earlier this year to the *Lusitania*!'

'No, but we are going to write to the address that I have and hope that will give us more information. But it is something we both must do, and Ellen can afford our fares.'

'I will come too. We will go as a family, and I will pay your fare, darling.'

'Oh, Adrian, ta, luv . . . Oh, I do love you.'

He held her close for a moment. With her head on his chest, she could hear him wheezing. A fear grasped her. 'Are you feeling all right, me darlin'?'

'Yes, fine. I got a bit anxious and that doesn't help me, but all's well now. I'll go and get a taxi for you.'

When he came back, he was very breathless. Ruth's heart sank. 'Do you need a doctor, luv?'

'No, I'll be fine. Let's get you down and into the taxi before someone else grabs it. I've paid him, so don't worry about that.'

314

'Don't come down with me, luv. The stairs are too much for you.'

Adrian readily agreed, which told her just how poorly he was feeling. 'Should I stay, luv? I'm worried about you.'

'No . . . honestly . . . this happens a lot . . . I've over-exerted myself.' He grinned. 'It's . . . it's your fault.' His laugh and the meaning behind it made her laugh too. It put her mind at rest and helped her to leave.

When Ruth told Ellen her news, Ellen's expression showed the many emotions she was going through. At first it was a look that said, 'No, you can't leave me.' Then a smile covered this as if she was forcing herself to accept. It was when a tear rolled down her face that Ruth felt undone.

'Oh, Ellen, luv, I'm sorry.'

'No! No, don't be sorry! It's amazing . . . beautiful. I-I'm crying out of happiness for you and Adrian. It's the best news. Can I be a bridesmaid? Ooh, we . . . we have a lot of shopping to do, and we don't know how much time we have to do it in!'

Ruth instinctively knew this wasn't why the tears had appeared and loved Ellen all the more for her pretence and bravery. She would allow it, not question it.

'I know, it's so exciting, but first we have to get ready as Adrian is taking us out for dinner!'

'Ooh, like proper ladies. Eek, what shall we wear?'

'You check your outfits and I'll run down and tell Bett . . . I'll tell you what, it ain't just shopping we have to do, I'll have to make Bett, Ruby and Ebony new hats!'

They both giggled. Ruth ran down the stairs. 'Bett, Bett!'

'Bleedin' 'ell! Is there a bleedin' fire, girl?'

'Ha, no, only in me heart. I'm getting married, Bett!'

Bett's expression was a picture. When the astonishment left her, she boomed, ''As he made yer bleedin' pregnant, girl?'

Ruth felt herself blush, and then felt silly. 'He's hardly had time, mate. I've only been home a few days!'

'They don't need much time, girl.' Bett laughed loudly at her own joke. 'Come 'ere and give us a cuddle. This is the best news I've 'ad in a good while!'

Ruth went into one of Bett's lovely cuddles.

'So, you won't be going away again? Well, that's worth the price of a new outfit. I'll get on to me boys to fix it. And while I'm about it, they can fix a nice car to take yer to the church too. Anything else yer need, Ruth, luv?'

'No. A nice car will be lovely. I've enough savings to get a wedding frock.'

'Don't yer go buying one, Ebony'd be put out. She'll want to make yer frock for yer. You buy the material, 'ave a style in mind and go and see her, but make it snappy, she's up to her eyes, poor girl.'

'That would be lovely, but ain't it too much to ask of her, with her business and her charity work?'

'Let her be the judge of that, but at least give her the bleedin' chance, girl.'

Ruth agreed. She'd never want to hurt Ebony, and she might if she bypassed her. Ebony's skills in dressmaking were a match to what lovely Rebekah's used to be.

This thought conjured up Rebekah in her frocks of many colours. The beautiful memory brought a tear to her eye. How happy Rebekah would be for her.

Sighing, she told Bett, 'Well, I'll have to go and get ready, luv. Adrian's taking me and Ellen to dinner.'

'Oooh, swanky pants – well, you just watch out yer don't get too big for yer boots, lady, with marrying well.'

'Oh, I will. The likes of you won't be good enough for Mrs Adrian Vale, Bett.'

Bett put her head back and roared.

When they were ready, Ellen stood back and admired Ruth's appearance. 'You look beautiful, Ruth. That deep blue really suits you. There's a glow about you. There was when Adrian and I came home and found you all excited, but now it's more intense.'

Ruth turned away, afraid that her naughty secret would show on her face. 'Ta, luv, I feel nice in this frock. I wore it when I was in the chorus of a stage production. We were allowed to keep them as part payment.'

Fitted to just beneath the bust, the peacock-blue frock flowed to the floor. The lace overdress was black with little roses around the edge of the hem and the sleeves. Ruth felt wonderful in it.

Able to face Ellen again, Ruth told her, 'Yours is perfect for you. I ain't seen it before. It's lovely.'

'I kept it in my case. It's one of a couple of Gran's that I love. She was the same size as me and had some lovely, elegant clothes, even though she never went anywhere.'

'Ah, that's lovely.'

Ellen's frock was a pale grey silk. Plain in style, but as she'd said, very elegant. It hung to Ellen's calf and gave her a sophisticated look.

They'd each helped the other to clip their hair up, Ellen with a fringe left to frame her face, and Ruth with a few tendrils of curls kissing her forehead and cheeks.

As Adrian hadn't arrived, they went downstairs to wait

and to the praise of Bett. 'My, yer both look beautiful, me darlin's. But Adrian's bleedin' late, ain't he?'

Ruth looked at the clock. A small dismay trickled a worry into her.

'Are you all right, Ruth?'

'It-it's just that Adrian wasn't too well when I left him . . . His asthma . . . He was wheezing and got out of breath on the stairs. Oh, Ellen, I hope he's all right!'

But as she said this, a knock came on the door. The sound of its urgency made her gasp in fear.

Ellen opened it. Her 'Frederick! What are you doing here? I thought you'd left!' compounded Ruth's fear.

She listened, not wanting to hear. 'May I come in? I – I have some bad news.'

Ellen stepped back in a mechanical way. The door opened slowly. Frederick, his face white as a sheet, stepped inside. His eyes found hers. 'Ruth . . . I . . . Adrian telephoned me, he told me your news . . . he invited me tonight . . . he could hardly speak . . . I – I went around to his straight away . . . I found him collapsed . . . I took him to hospital . . . but . . .'

Frederick's face creased in the agony of grief. Ruth felt her legs go from under her. Strong arms caught her.

'Put her on the couch, luv . . . Ruth . . . Oh, Ruth, me little darlin'. I'm 'ere, luv, I'm 'ere.'

Ruth's world fell apart. 'No . . . No! Not me Adrian. No-oo-oo!'

She felt Ellen's hand come into hers and clung to it. 'Help me, Ellen. Help me.'

Through her sobs, Ellen whispered, 'Always, my lovely Ruth . . . Oh, Ruth, Ruth, why?'

Ruth couldn't answer. Her mind gave her a turmoil of

thoughts. Some filled her with guilt as she heard again Adrian say, 'It's your fault.' Some left her remembering the feel of his love, and others told her that she could not go on living.

'Ruth, Ruth!'

The desperate plea in Ellen's voice steadied her a little. She was needed. Her lovely sister needed her. She had to find a way to carry on.

Chapter Twenty-Seven

Ruth

Adrian's funeral was set for the following Tuesday. Frederick had said in the absence of family he would make all the arrangements. He knew Adrian's solicitor as he used the same one. He believed there was an aunt still living but told her that the solicitor would know all of that.

Frederick was kindness itself to Ruth, and to Ellen, who Ruth knew was suffering too. He'd taken Ellen to the Red Cross office to explain and to ask when they might be expected to return and could it be delayed for at least another two weeks. Ruth had instructed her to let Miss Darlington know that the show would go on and that the tickets requested were on the way to the office.

She, Bett and Ellen had shed bucketloads of tears. Her for her deep loss, which hadn't really sunk in yet, of her beloved – her soulmate, as that's what Adrian had been to her, even though they were from different worlds. And never, even if there were consequences, would she ever regret their last couple of hours together. Any guilt she'd felt about that had gone. Adrian had made a silly joke. The kind that all couples share, and she would keep it in her memory as the last time they had laughed together. The whole afternoon would be locked in her heart. Her special treasure to visit when the pain became too deep to bear.

Saturday came all too soon.

Ruth stood in the wings, her crisp uniform making her hot under the glare of the backstage lights. The time was nearly on her. All the crew were rooting for her. She'd been hugged, kissed, told she was loved and now she was ready.

'All right, mate?'

Ted's voice coming from behind her sounded concerned. She turned. 'Yes, Ted. I'm doing this for so many. For Adrian, and for all those who so badly need the help of the Red Cross.'

'I'll be by yer side, luv . . . There's our cue. Deep breath, me darlin'.'

Ruth did just that, saying to herself that the show must go on. Never had the words meant so much as they did tonight.

She swept onto the stage as her introduction hailed her, to the roar of applause and the audience standing on their feet. This reception lifted her to a place where she knew she could do this – for the Red Cross, for those willing her on, for all the young men in the hospitals in France, and in the trenches, for all those who loved her, and most of all for Adrian.

'Thank you, everyone. Thank you. I am here to make a plea for your help on behalf of the Red Cross . . .'

As she spoke her voice got stronger. To Ted softly playing beside her, she told them of the conditions in which the Red Cross worked, being mindful not to tell gory stories, but uplifting ones of them saving young heroes, as she knew many in the theatre would have loved ones fighting abroad.

'These gallant doctors, nurses, ambulance drivers and orderlies give their all. Our men need them, and they need your help. Without funds they cannot exist. Please give generously as you leave. Please put your donation on the plates or in the bags the Red Cross nurses, standing at the back, are holding.'

When the clapping had died down, Ruth told them, 'I'm going to sing a song written by Ivor Novello and originally sung by a Mr James F. Harrison. In it there are a couple of moving lines which say: *Overseas there came a pleading, Help a nation in distress. And we gave our glorious laddies . . .* Ladies and gentlemen, remember, the Red Cross gave our glorious medical staff and much more too. I give you "Keep the Home Fires Burning, Till the Boys Come Home".'

Ted's own composition of an intro began. The strength that had begun to ebb away from Ruth came back into her as she listened to the melodious intro. The sound was amazingly beautiful.

She would keep the home fires burning for her Adrian. Her heart tumbled at this thought, but then she took a deep breath and sang out.

When it was over, once more there was a standing ovation. This lifted Ruth to the heights of the magic of the stage.

Exhausted, Ruth sat staring into the mirror in her dressing room.

A knock on her door made her jump.

'May I come in, me darlin'?' Ted bounced in. 'You were amazing, luv. Well done! The performance of a lifetime! I'm so proud of yer. And I've news. I've at last 'eard from Reg. I'm going to write to him and tell him about you, what yer doing and about tonight. He's out there somewhere. I can't pronounce the name, but he's all right and tells me he will get my letters if I send them to his regiment.'

'Oh, that's good news, luv. Give him me best, won't you? And, Ted, you were brilliant.'

'Ta for the chance, luv. The conductor shook me 'and after and told me there'll be more solos coming my way.'

Ted beamed. Ruth stood and held her arms to him. They hugged. 'I'm so pleased for you, Ted. This recognition has been a long time coming, but so deserved, luv.'

Ted wiped a tear from his eyes. 'Now, get yerself gone, luv. Your Red Cross lot are waiting for you, me darlin'. Yer did them proud, and from what I saw, their collection was overflowing.'

Ellen met her with a hug. Then it was Bett's and Ruby's turn and finally Ebony's. Abdi and Frederick both did the gentlemanly thing and offered her their hand.

They were full of praise for her and pride in her. To Ruth, it all seemed to be going on without her. She'd wrapped herself in the same armour she used that had helped her to go on stage and that was helping her to cope.

'Ninety pounds, two shillings and threepence ha'penny. Oh, and one button, Ruth! Amazing. Well done, you! That will keep us going for a long time,' Miss Darlington's voice boomed out as she came up behind them. Her slap on Ruth's back was none too gentle. 'You're a trooper.' She lowered her voice. 'Especially under the circumstances, my dear.' She looked both ways in a furtive way. 'I have news on that matter that I needed permission on, my dear. I wasn't granted the permission to give you information on your friend's whereabouts, but the hospital where he is needs staff . . . I know you're not ready yet, but when you are, I think it will be a good posting for you and Ellen. It keeps you out of the thick of it for a time and there is nothing like work – well, the work that we do – to help you to cope with a broken heart, my dear. I know, I have been through it in the Boer War, believe me.'

Ruth didn't know what to say.

'Don't make your mind up now. Lay your young man to his rest and give yourself a few days, then contact me. I can't keep the position long as home hospitals are under pressure. All the nurses and doctors want to be on the front line and keep leaving us.'

Ruth nodded. 'Ta, Miss Darlington. I'll be in touch. I'm glad that we collected a good bit of money.'

'So am I, my dear. And you showed the true grit that a good nurse is made of. I will be thinking of you. Stay strong.'

With this she left with the rest of the nurses – all but Ellen.

'Oh, Ellen, I'm tired.'

'Me too, and hungry.'

Ruth didn't have time to answer as Bett grabbed her. 'Ebony and Abdi are going now, luv, they're dropping Ruby off. Shall we get a cab? I'm feeling dead on me feet. We 'ad a busy day in the church 'all today.'

'Yes, that's fine.'

To Ellen she said, 'I've some of that stew Ebony made, left on the cold slab. We'll heat that up, and we'll beg some of her homemade bread, eh?'

'That sounds lovely.'

After hugs all round, and Bett off in search of a cab, there was only Frederick left.

'Well, I'll see you on Tuesday, but then, I will have to catch a train straight after the funeral. Will you both be all right?'

'We will, ta, Frederick. And ta for all you've done.'

'Ellen . . . I – I wanted to ask, will you write to me? Just to let me know how you are, I mean.'

Ruth held her breath. She hoped Ellen would say yes.

'I'd like that, Frederick. And you can tell me all you remember of Adrian as a boy. He was my inspiration and helped me in many ways you can never dream of, though I may tell you one day.'

Frederick's face lit up. 'Here's the address to write to. I'll so look forward to your letters. I want to know everything you and Ruth get up to and how you are, what your work is like . . . oh, and where you are. Everything!'

'Nosy!'

At this unexpected quip from Ellen, Frederick burst out laughing. And as low as she felt, Ruth did too.

'I love your spirit, Ellen. You told me off the first time we met, and you're still doing it.'

Ellen grinned. 'Well, you deserve it. Anyway, I want news of you and please try to find out how Bernard is. And where he is.'

A cloud passed over Frederick's face. Ruth felt sorry for him. He was obviously smitten by Ellen. She felt guilty about this. She would tell Ellen that once Frederick was in France, she should admit to him how old she really was. For his sake, she must take the risk this would pose to her career with the Red Cross, as it was unfair to him to let him think he was flirting with someone a lot older.

As this thought came to her, she realized for the first time how shockingly they were treating Frederick. He was a gentleman and would be mortified that he had even thought of a young girl in the way she knew he thought of Ellen. But they had chosen their path and the lie had been necessary for them to achieve that.

As soon as they were in the warmth of their flat and were eating their bowls of stew with chunks of freshy baked bread, Ruth brought the subject up.

She needn't have worried. Ellen was well aware of the situation and trying to deal with it. 'That's why I am like I am with him, Ruth. I try to put him down at every hint of him showing a fancy for me. But I don't think we should tell him yet. Like you say, he's an honourable man and would think it his duty to report me.'

'I wonder that Adrian hasn't told him. He must have seen how the land lies.' As she finished saying this, Ruth realized she'd spoken as if Adrian was still here, and that is how it had been for her tonight, had to be for her to get through it. Her throat tightened. 'He . . . he's really gone, hasn't he, Ellen?'

Ellen put her fork down and stared at Ruth. Ruth watched her head nod, saw how the action toppled a tear from her eye. It was quickly followed by more. Ruth thought, *I want to cry. I want to cry and scream and throw things, but I can't. It hurts too much.*

Putting her own fork down, she held her arms out to Ellen.

They rocked backwards and forwards, Ellen sobbing, Ruth trapped in a cold knot of pain that wouldn't release her.

Ellen broke away first. 'Look at me, when you're being so brave. I'm sorry, Ruth, love.'

'Don't be. I so want to cry but the pain is too deep.'

'I know. I felt like that when Gran died. Not for my father, though. I broke the chain of love that held me wanting him to love me back and felt better for it. But after Gran and because I'd been through such pain of losing her, it was easier to cope with losing Dilly . . . And all we'd seen helped with that too. Hers and Gran's passing were natural endings of life. We have seen so much that isn't and now, Adrian . . . How are we to bear it?'

'We will . . . I've something to tell you.' Ruth told Ellen what Miss Darlington had said. 'I think it a good idea. I have to do something, Ellen, or I will go mad, and I can't go back onto the stage. I have me duty to the Red Cross.'

'Oh, I think that's a wonderful idea, Ruth, and yes, I'll come too. Seeing your old friend will help you. And I'd like to meet him. I need to work too. Everything is so horrible at the moment.'

They hugged again. As they did, Ellen asked, 'When will you be ready, Ruth?'

'Sooner rather than later. I can't stay around here, luv.'

'Let's go and see Miss Darlington on Wednesday.'

'Yes, we'll do that, Ellen, and hope she can arrange it sometime next week.'

The funeral was the worst day of Ruth's life. The pain dug in deeper than ever with no release. There were so few there. Ellen, Ted, Frederick, Bett, Ruby, Ebony and Abdi, besides a couple of men in uniform, who saluted the coffin and gave their condolences, and one other man who introduced himself as Adrian's solicitor.

As they walked away from the graveside, the solicitor was waiting at the gate. 'Miss Faith, may I have a word, please?'

Ruth went to one side with him.

'I need to speak to you. Can you come to my office tomorrow? Here's my card.'

Ruth looked at the address. 'Is it anywhere near to Bath Street? Me and me sister are going there tomorrow.'

'Not far, but you will need to take a cab between the two. Can you be there at around eleven a.m., please.'

'Yes, we haven't got to be at the Red Cross at any particular time.'

'I'll take my leave of you now. And I'm very, very sorry for your loss and the loss to many of the future generation of a brilliant teacher.'

As he left, others began to say their goodbyes too.

'Sorry we have to leave, Ruth. I have a lot of cooking to do for the restaurant. I do that in the evenings, and the dishes for the church hall in the mornings.'

'I understand, Ebony. Thank you for coming to support me.'

The hugs went on until there was only Frederick left. Even Bett, Ruby and Ted had to dash for various reasons.

Ruth hadn't wanted a wake. She'd just wanted to go back to her flat and be with Ellen.

'Well, girls . . . Poor old Adrian, eh?'

Ruth could see that Frederick was near to tears. She saw his Adam's apple go up and down as he swallowed several times.

She held out her hand to him, but he did a surprising thing and pulled her into a hug. 'I'm sorry, Ruth, truly sorry. You made Adrian happy and for that, I thank you from the bottom of my heart.'

Ruth felt his body jerk, and this time heard the sob that had caused it. She patted his back.

'He thought the world of you, Frederick.'

He stood straight. 'Thank you. Thank you. I did of him too.' With this he straightened even more into a soldier's stance befitting his uniform. 'Well, I'll say my goodbye to you both.'

He turned and hailed a cab. As he walked towards the taxi that had pulled up, Ellen shouted, 'Frederick.' And ran forward. He took her in his arms. For a moment, Ruth thought he was going to kiss her, but she stepped back. 'Good luck, Frederick. I'll write to you.'

He smiled. And then he was gone.

Ellen came over and linked arms with Ruth. She didn't speak – there was no need to. They walked and walked, till Ellen said, 'I can't walk much further, love.'

'Sorry, luv, I – I just didn't notice. We'll hop on the next bus at the stop just there. We're in the direction of home so bound to get one to the market square.'

'We can get a hot spud off Bett's old stall and go and sit in the park if you like.'

'It'll be a bit cold. Let's take them home with us . . . Funny how you've caught on to calling it Bett's old stall when you've never known it to be that.'

'It just seems to have that name whenever you or Ruby talk about it, and I like it. It's like Bett's feeding us.'

'Ha, don't tell her, but there were times when her spuds were a bit hard. You had to wait for the dripping to really soak into them to soften them a bit.'

Ellen laughed. 'Do you think I dare tell her that? She's a tyrant at times. A big softy of a tyrant, but I still feel scared of her, and I hope I never meet those boys of hers as long as I live.'

'No, they aren't nice. If Bett scares you, you'd be terrified of them. And yet, they're more scared of Bett than you are. They jump at her every command and shrivel when she starts on them.'

Ruth couldn't believe how easy it was to have this banter when inside she felt as though she had died.

This feeling prevailed when she woke after a surprisingly deep sleep, and it was accompanied by one of dread that something really bad had happened, until the awful truth flooded her, and she gasped against the added pain of remembering what it was that held her in this vice and kept her in a kind of no man's land.

She snuggled into Ellen's body as she heard muffled sobs. *Poor Ellen is suffering too and is trying to keep her grief away from me.*

But even though she gently held Ellen and felt her sorrow, her own wouldn't break to give her a release.

At the Red Cross they were assigned to Ullesthorpe Court. Owned by Mr and Mrs Goodacre, the large manor house had been given over to those returning wounded from the war.

'They have mostly used local VADs but they are in short supply and the need is great. It is run by Sister Hadden, who lives in, but accommodation is a bit scant as the family still occupy some of the house, and hasn't been needed till now with nurses living within travelling distance. But the family have very generously made over one more room to Sister Hadden as she is struggling to get staff since two of her girls married recently.'

The words 'married recently' twisted a knife into Ruth's pain.

'I'm informed that this room is in the attic where the household staff have their accommodation. I have your rail passes here. Conveniently there is a railway station in the village, which connects to Rugby. Trains from Euston go to Rugby, so getting there is not going to be a problem. The hospital is out of the village towards another village called Frolesworth. Here is a little map that Sister posted to me when requesting more staff. It looks as though getting there will be very simple, though I wouldn't take any heavy luggage – there are no taxis in the villages and the ambulances are based in Lutterworth, a market town, which is about four miles away, so I can't arrange transport from the station. Now, girls, I wish you well. You are being very brave, both of you, and I am sure you are doing the right thing.'

After thanking them again for the huge amount raised, Miss Darlington smiled and, in a kindly voice, said, 'Good luck, both of you.'

Outside, Ellen slipped her hand into Ruth's. 'It doesn't sound so bad, does it? And it'll be lovely to be in the countryside without the sound of bombs and guns.'

Ruth nodded.

At the solicitor's, Ruth got a shock. Adrian had left everything he had to her. This was, to her, a fortune – two hundred and seventy-five pounds. But on top of that a house in south London that his aunt had made over to him recently. 'She has gone into a nursing home as she was getting very forgetful. It's in Camberwell, off the Peckham Road, Southampton Way. A three-storey house of considerable value. Adrian's Aunt Theresa is quite well off, having married a stockbroker. When she instructed me to transfer the deeds, she told me that she didn't want her husband's family to get their hands on the house as they had never bothered with her. She loved Adrian and is very upset to hear of his death. She would like to meet you, and said that if Adrian loved you, then she would and was glad you were having her house.'

The knot of pain inside Ruth burst, leaving her crumbling into a sobbing heap. She reached towards Ellen. 'Help me.'

Ellen's hand grabbed hers. The room was silent, until the solicitor said, 'I will leave you a moment. I'll have my

331

secretary bring you a cup of tea . . . I will need you to sign some papers, my dear.'

When he'd gone, Ruth and Ellen clung to one another. Ruth's body heaved and shook. *Adrian, my Adrian, how am I to go on without you?*

After a moment, the door opened. No one spoke, but the girl who entered put a tray on the desk in front of them. Ellen poured the tea. The hot liquid helped to soothe Ruth, so she was able to sign the papers the solicitor needed her to.

When they left the office, all Ruth could say was that she wanted to go to the churchyard. There she fell on her knees on the damp, cold grass next to the mound of earth that held Adrian. Her body was wracked with sorrow, her tears flowed for the loss of her love, her soul cried out for him, until at last she was able to calm herself and join a sobbing Ellen on a bench nearby. They held each other, and Ruth thought, no matter what, she'd always have Ellen.

Chapter Twenty-Eight

Ruth

The hospital stood in its own grounds along a country lane that housed a farmhouse and cottages just up the road. Otherwise, it was surrounded by woodland and fields, though it only took a few minutes to walk to Ullesthorpe village where there was a store that seemed to sell everything. Besides this there were a couple of pubs. The people were lovely and welcoming, and Ruth felt she would find some peace here.

They were walking around the beautiful gardens of the hospital when she spoke for the first time about her new fortune.

'I still can't believe it, luv. Adrian said nothing about owning a house – let alone a posh one! He only talked of living in his flat after we were married.'

'Knowing Adrian, he'd want to keep that for later. He'd think that you would take it that he was saying he was a good catch. He was always humble. Gran knew more about him than I did and did once remark how it was that he'd gone to an expensive school. Maybe his aunt saw to that. It doesn't sound like she has any family of her own.'

'Yes, I can see that. But even him having such a vast amount in his savings shocked me. He was, like you say, such a humble man.'

'Yes, and he more than likely saved it over a long time as well as swelling it during his time with his own private schoolroom . . . I think it's all a lovely gift for you, Ruth. It's like he's saying that he can't take care of you in person, but he will make sure you are all right in the future.'

'Yer know, he told me that he wanted me to carry on in the theatre. I loved him for that, as some are snobbish about my profession.'

'Will you? I mean, when this is all over?'

'I don't know. At the moment, I just don't want to do anything, but, well, we'll see.'

'I'd like that for you . . . I mean, well, I may have to go away to study to be a doctor, and I would know then that you're surrounded by a family as that's what the theatre folk seem to be.'

'I know. Adrian warned me to prepare meself for that happening, but I told him it won't. Wherever you go, I'll rent a house that you can come home to in the evening. I can afford to do that now and I couldn't bear to be without you, Ellen.'

'Oh, Ruth. That's an amazing thing to do. Thank you. Ooh, you've made me long all the more to achieve it now. I have already planned to do as much studying as possible again, as I don't think this is a busy hospital.'

'We shall see tomorrow. I can't wait. I'm so looking forward to seeing Abe and to being involved in his care.'

'You said you were once in love with him?'

'Yes. And he still means a lot to me. But it wasn't to be and can never be. I told you about him and Robbie.'

'Yes, it must have been a shock to you.'

'It was at first . . . well, anyway, they're the same people and I love them both and it hurts that Abe is hurting.'

'We'll help him. He's going to love seeing you, Ruth. I wonder if he knows.'

'No. I wasn't allowed to know where he was as permission should have been sought. This was Miss Darlington's way of getting me to him without breaking any rules.'

'She's lovely. Anyway, I'm getting cold. Shall we go back inside?'

'Typical! If you're not hungry, you're cold.'

Ellen hit out at Ruth. 'Well, I'm not an old fuddy-duddy, we youngsters feel the cold.'

'Ha! Yer cheeky so-and-so, I'm all of three years older than you!'

They laughed together, and to Ruth it was a good moment, as a few days ago, she thought she would never laugh again. Not properly, not a belly laugh like now.

As they reported for duty the next day, Ruth felt sick with nerves. They'd both slept well although the room they had was only tiny with two beds and a cupboard.

It had felt strange not having Ellen in the same bed with her, but at the same time, as she'd teased Ellen when they'd awoken, she was able to keep the covers all to herself instead of having them pulled off her.

'Good morning, girls.'

Ruth noted that every one of the staff, except Sister, who was greeting them, were VADs – no qualified nurses in sight.

'And welcome to our two new members, Ellen and Ruth.' Sister then dismissed the others, after telling them what had occurred overnight and who she needed them to attend to first.

Turning to them, Sister told them, 'We are a happy bunch here, and whilst not a convalescent home as our patients still need a great deal of care, we aren't called upon to deal with immediate casualties. Our men have been through operations before being sent to us, but most still require a good deal of nursing – dressings changed, et cetera. And of course, some rehabilitation, as in helping them to build their strength to be able to regain skills – walking and doing things for themselves. For the first week you will take over the domestic and mundane chores till you get to know both the patients and the routine. So, helping the men to go to the toilet – some are using bedpans and bottles – washing them after and making their beds. Work quickly as we don't want them waiting too long. You can work together. You'll find the sluice and linen cupboard to the right of the wards. Any problems, just ask.'

As soon as they entered the ward, Ruth looked for Abe. She found him in a side ward. His eyes were closed, his face looked sallow and full of pain but what was most notable was that only half of the bed showed the shape of him. 'Abe . . . Abe.'

His eyes shot open. He stared in disbelief. 'Ruth . . . Oh, Ruth, Ruth . . .'

Tears streamed down his face. Ruth bent down and held him, her own tears joining his.

'Is it really you, Ruth?'

'It is. Why didn't you write to me? I would have visited. Oh, Abe, that this should happen to you. But I'm here now. You're going to be all right, luv . . . Though firstly, you've to get over me having to help you with all your personal needs. Just treat me the same as any nurse, then we can talk as I work. This is me sister, Ellen, just one of the things I have to tell yer about. Though I need to know how Robbie is. Do yer know?'

She and Ellen worked quickly and efficiently in making Abe comfortable. Ruth didn't let helping him onto the bedpan faze her and she thought Abe coped with that well, as he did the bed bath and them helping him into his wheelchair. She found that one leg had been amputated just above the knee and the other just below. She didn't ask him how it happened as she knew from experience that reliving everything wasn't easy. He'd tell her in good time if he wanted to.

But what he did tell her was that just before he was injured, he had a communication from Robbie. 'He was due some leave.'

'You mean, he might come home?'

'Yes, for six weeks. But I don't know when. Oh, Ruth, I can't tell you how good it is to see you.'

'And me you, luv. Like I say, I've a lot to tell yer.'

'I haven't much to tell, it was just war and more war. Gains and losses, and the pain of losing soldiers under me and writing to their parents. Fear, and good times, then the one with my name on got me, and that's that. Oh, except it's been a worse hell since the wounding of me than it was before.'

'Well, I've packed a lot more in. But I can't tell you it all now. When was it that you heard from Robbie?'

'I think he should be due leave about now by my calculations.'

'That would be wonderful. He's bound to go home. Bett'll tell him where we are. I can't believe that I'll be seeing yer both after all this time and just when I need you.' Her voice caught in her throat.

'Ruth, are you all right?'

She shook her head. Looking at Ellen, she told her, 'We've

finished here now. We'd better get on. I'll go into the next side ward; you make sure Abe's all right.'

Running out of the ward, Ruth found a wall to lean on. She took several deep breaths. Ellen would tell Abe about Adrian for her, she just couldn't do it herself.

The morning was hectic and flew by. As they'd worked, Ellen told her that she'd told Abe and that he was so sad for her. 'He said, "I just want to hold her, but I expect that will be against the rules." But I told him, "I'm sure we'll find a way," as that's what you need, Ruth, your friends to just hold you.'

'I do, Ellen. Ta for doing that for me. But bloomin' 'eck, I don't know when we'll have the time to be held by anyone, or even stand still long enough. To my mind they still haven't enough staff.'

'No, they haven't. But Sister told me when I met her in the sluice that ours was a baptism of fire. She needs to see our work and our efficiency. And once she has, she will vary our jobs and bedpans and baths will be shared amongst more of us. But then, so will other menial tasks like giving out meals, helping to feed patients, as well as keeping the ward tidy. But she has had a change of mind over keeping us on a week of this as she has seen our records now, so is going to put us on to dressings and taking temperatures tomorrow. As Sister said, all a bit tame after what we've coped with, but so welcome to me as it means doing medical stuff again.'

It was a week later that Sister praised them for their work. 'We've seen a marked difference in one patient in particular, Captain Peterson. And it has come to my notice that you knew him in a previous life, Ruth?'

'Yes, Sister. We were friends. Unlikely ones, but we got on well.'

'How fortunate for him that you landed here . . . Anyway . . .' – she turned to Ellen – 'your idea of getting the men outside has worked. It goes against all we are taught, and it is jolly cold, but wrapped up well, they seem to love it and it is putting some colour back into their cheeks.'

'Fresh air is a healer, Sister.'

'And you are very, very knowledgeable. Remarkably so.'

Ellen told her about her dream and how she had studied towards that.

'Good. Well, the path isn't going to be easy. Many a woman has wanted the same thing and has fallen at the hurdles, of which there are many. The men seem to think it's a man's occupation and not for women. A hard attitude to overcome. So, I wish you luck. I will also be putting you in charge of the care of some of our more severe injuries. You'll report to Doctor Alfred on anything at all. He will need meticulous records kept.'

'Oh, thanks, Sister.'

Ellen beamed at Ruth. Ruth felt so happy for her. But then, Sister addressed her. 'Ruth, you are proving to be a very good team member. Invaluable to us as everyone working in a team means a smoothly run hospital . . . I heard what happened to you, so to help you, I am going to allow you time with your friend, Captain Peterson. You may sit with him every afternoon and take him for walks when the weather allows.'

It was Ruth's turn to beam, and to thank Sister. She even managed a little jig as they left the office, which had Ellen in stitches.

*

The last six weeks had passed quickly and already they were beginning to decorate the wards for Christmas. Ruth joined in but couldn't get any enthusiasm for the task or the season. This would have been her first Christmas married to her beloved Adrian and her heart was heavy as she tried to imagine it all. Though, when she walked into Abe's ward, her sadness lifted a little as he held a letter aloft. 'He's coming! He's home and Bett told him about us both being here! He will be here later this afternoon. Oh, Ruth!'

Abe's cheeks were glowing. He looked so much better than he had when she arrived. He was stronger too and beginning to use his arms to move himself from his bed to his chair, which would give him much more independence.

Ruth clasped her hands to her chest. 'In time for Christmas!'

'Yes. And he's going to try to find lodgings nearby. Maybe one of the pubs will have a room?'

'I don't know but we can ask. Ooh, it feels like all me Christmases have come at once . . . only . . .'

'I know, Ruth. You never talk about it, and you should. I would have loved to have met Adrian. He sounds a nice chap. I'm so sorry.'

Ruth swallowed. 'It hurts too much to talk.'

'But that pain will get less if you do. Next time you take me for a walk, I want to know everything . . . I want to know Adrian.'

This touched Ruth. 'If only there weren't that hill up to Ullesthorpe, I'd walk you up to the station, luv. It's going to be wonderful to have Robbie here.'

'As you keep saying.' Abe laughed. 'And in a theatrical voice, too! Hey, how brilliant if you and Robbie could put a concert on for us patients! I can't believe you rose to such heights, and I didn't know about it, and wasn't here to share the moment with you. We have a lot of history with that theatre.'

'We do, good and bad.'

As Ruth stood on what to her was a tiny platform and looked around her at the sign which proudly proclaimed 'Ullesthorpe', and at the wintered and weathered garden that she'd heard was a wonderful sight in the summer, the stationmaster came up to her. 'Your boyfriend coming in, Nurse?'

Knowing Robbie would hug her when he arrived, Ruth thought she'd tell a little fib to give a reason for him doing so. 'My brother.'

'That's nice for you. You girls deserve more than you get, stuck down there out of contact with the world.'

'Oh, I've seen plenty of the world. I served in Belgium.'

This came out like a proud boast. She didn't expect his reaction. He offered her his hand, and as she took it a tear plopped onto his cheek. 'Me lad copped it out there. It's good to think you girls were there to take care of our boys.'

'I'm sorry. That's very sad, but yes, he would have had the best of care if he came to our hospital or any nearby. And a proper funeral too. We honoured our lads by holding a service and then parading behind the coffin to the burial plot and held prayers there for them too.'

'That's comforting to know. Thanks. We don't know the details of his death, only that he was a hero . . . Well, the train's about to arrive, so I've me job to do. Thanks for that, miss.'

He touched his cap.

Ruth thought about the sleepy village of Ullesthorpe and how even that, tucked away from anywhere but nearby similar villages, hadn't been unscathed by the war. She wished it would end – no, she wished it had never happened.

341

A cloud of smoke enveloped her as this thought died and the noise of the train coming to a halt, the opening and slamming of doors, and the sound of a whistle blowing took over her thoughts and rekindled her excitement. She peered up and down the train. Then suddenly, he was there, carrying a rucksack, which he promptly dropped before running towards her, picking her up and swinging her around.

'Robbie, Robbie, put me down!' She could hardly speak for laughing. Joy filled her.

When he lowered her, he hugged her to him. They stayed like that for a few minutes till a cough behind them broke them apart. 'I need to lock the gate, sir.'

'Oh, sorry, yer can now. I'll just fetch me bag.'

As they walked to the hospital holding hands, they talked. Mostly about her, her career, and her loss of Adrian. At this point they stood still, and Robbie held her again. She couldn't help but notice his strength and how he'd filled out. Any trace of the boy she'd known had gone.

As he stroked her hair and soothed her tears, he whispered, 'Me poor Ruth. Life keeps kicking you in the teeth, mate. But like a true trooper, yer keep getting up again. I heard about your fundraising. I'm so proud of yer.'

'And I am of you.'

As she came out of his arms, he asked, 'How bad is Abe, Ruth?'

She told him, hoping he wouldn't be repelled as she made sure he knew all the facts.

'Me poor darling Abe. I'll look after him, when all this is done. I've been thinking about it. If he can get a place, then I can be passed off as his live-in nurse. I think that would be accepted as everyone has got used to male nurses during the war, as long as they are for other males only.'

'But what about your theatre work?'

'I'd give it up willingly if I have to, but if I can carry on, then I will. We will see how it all works. Abe is everything to me. All I want is to be with him and to take care of him.'

Ruth could only smile. She hoped it worked for them but wondered if they would have a lot to face from bigoted people. And how Robbie would fit in with Abe's friends as they were miles apart in background. But then, love can conquer most things, and with all her heart she wanted it to conquer the prejudices out there against the love these two very special men had for each other.

To see their reunion was very touching, and to witness Robbie greeting Ellen. They had an immediate affinity as each knew what the other had been through at the orphanage.

Already, Ellen and Abe got on well, and held what Ruth called intellectual conversations of the kind she would never be comfortable having.

When Sister came into the ward, she stared at Robbie. 'I know you! I saw you on stage in London! Well, well, how lovely to have you here.'

'Nice to meet you, Sister. I bet you don't know that Ruth here is also an actress?'

Sister looked at Ruth. 'No, I didn't. Well, well, we're plucked from all walks of life to do our duty for our country. And it is occurring to me that it is now the duty of you two to put on a concert for our patients for Christmas!'

'We'd be honoured, wouldn't we, Ruth?'

Ruth felt a surprising lift from this as she nodded her consent. To be able to perform with Robbie again would be a dream.

Ellen clapped her hands as she said, 'That will be wonderful!' And Abe had a smile on his face that told of his

343

pride and his happiness. For a moment, Ruth forgot her pain as Sister left them to it and she lost herself in the planning. This was what she needed – not the routine of her nursing existence, but to be involved in the theatre, or anything to do with it. At this moment, she knew it would be possible to feel happiness again. Not true happiness for a long time, but a feeling that would sustain her into the future.

Chapter Twenty-Nine

Ellen

The next couple of weeks were busy. Ellen found herself roped into making costumes. People from the village donated what they could, and auditions were held amongst the patients to form a choir.

Cyril Chambers, a patient they knew to have a humorous outlook on life, admitted to working on stage as a comedian, and said he would do a turn. Another chirped up that he was good at reciting monologues, but he couldn't remember any now. This is when Abe surprised them as he told them that he enjoyed writing poetry, so could easily write a monologue.

His effort was a hilarious take on the war and the hospital, and even Sister didn't escape having a mention and was depicted as a bedpan-wielding tyrant with a golden heart. She loved it when they passed it by her.

None of the patients questioned Robbie's constant presence at the hospital. They all loved him and viewed him as a famous actor from the West End of London, spending his leave with his London friends. There wasn't a hint of anyone seeing him as anything else.

This pleased Ellen as she'd come to love Abe and Robbie and it would have hurt her badly to see them ridiculed.

Every day Robbie took Abe for a walk, come rain or shine, and this she knew was their private time together.

For herself, she didn't feel fulfilled in the work she did, compared to what she had been involved in in Belgium, but made herself happy for Ruth's sake.

Leaving them a couple of days later to their final rehearsal, Ellen made her way to her room. She felt tired, and knew it was the fault of her monthlies. This thought hit her with a shock as she realized that Ruth hadn't had her period since they got here. She would have known. They shared everything with each other, and this was Ellen's second.

She brushed the thought away as she remembered her first had happened just as they'd arrived here. With them being a few days apart in the timing of their monthlies, it could just be the shock Ruth went through that had stopped hers happening around that time. There was a reference to that possibly happening in the medical section she'd read on the female reproduction organs and Miss Roland had referred to it too.

As she walked past the hall table at the bottom of the stairs, she stopped to look at the letters that were piled up on it, wondering if Frederick had written to her. She hoped he hadn't and had forgotten all about her.

As she sifted through the envelopes, she found one with her name written in beautiful handwriting and addressed, like a lot of the others, to the Red Cross Headquarters, London.

Not feeling at all pleased, she took it upstairs, wanting more to visit the lav and to put her aching head on her pillow for an hour than to read a letter she was sure was from Frederick.

When she finally felt comfortable and sat on the bed, she

picked the letter up. *Please don't let him have declared his love for me. I don't want it!*

Noting the quality of the paper, she unfolded it and read, *Dear Ellen.* She sighed with relief, the address was formal, not at all that of a lover.

> *I hope you don't mind me writing to you. I have thought about you a lot and wondered how you were and what you were doing. I could really do with you assisting me with operations again . . .*

Shock – in a nice, surprised kind of way – zinged through Ellen as she hastily read the signature. *My kind regards, Bernard.*

Her heart sang out, all thoughts of her aching head and tummy leaving her. *It's from Bernard! He has written to me!*

A little laugh escaped her.

Laying the letter out on her pillow and lying on her front, she read on.

> *We are now in France and working in a field hospital in Abbeville. It is just as busy, and I fear the Germans, having broken through the French lines, are advancing swiftly towards us. Certainly, I can hear the guns becoming louder every night and the casualties are piling up. But we are just coping.*
>
> *Is there any chance you will join us once more? I understood you were going home on leave but thought you would be back.*
>
> *I hope you are still studying, as one day you are going to make an amazing doctor. As I said, I will help you all I can, and I mean to keep to that.*

Ellen gasped with the pleasure of his words. Yes, she knew he hadn't mentioned anything romantic, but to her, just receiving the letter was romance enough.

But then a dampener to her spirits came:

I have heard from my brother and was happy to hear that you and he are getting on so well. He let me into the secret you have together. I have to confess to mixed feelings – only because, well, maybe I shouldn't say this, but my brother's life is so different to how I see you leading yours.

Far from putting him down, I love him very much, but he isn't the type of gentleman that would take to letting his wife study – least of all becoming a doctor and going out to work. And I feel that would be a travesty and a loss to the medical profession.

Ellen's heart sank. *How dare Frederick make such assumptions about me! How dare he even discuss me with his brother!*

Wiping away her tears that she told herself were solely down to her anger and nothing to do with her aching heart, she read on.

But I wish you both well. I just hope that as nothing can happen before the war ends, you get out to serve with me once more as you are sorely needed. Many nurses are.

I hope you don't mind, but I have taken the liberty of requesting you to be sent out here, telling them at HQ that we are a good team, and I need help desperately. I don't know if it will work, and I don't know if you will mind. I really hope you don't.

Ellen lowered her head onto the letter. *Yes, yes, I so want to. Please let it happen.*

She cheered up at the thought that if she could get out there, she could explain about Frederick's unwanted attention to her.

Still feeling the anger of his assumptions, she grabbed her writing case from under her bed – a desk-shaped box that was made of cane. The lid lifted in the same way a school desk did. In it she found a wad of writing paper, a blotting pad, pen and ink pot.

With her movements all reflecting her mood she set about penning a letter to Frederick, only to rip it up as she realized it would be horrible for him to receive it while he was in the thick of the fighting. She'd ask Ruth's advice. If only she could ask Adrian's. Adrian would know what to do. *Oh, Adrian, Adrian, I miss you more than I dare say for fear of upsetting Ruth. Look down over Ruth, Adrian, and take care of her.*

As this thought left her, it came to her that she hoped he had done when they were together. How would Ruth cope with what might happen if he hadn't?

In place of the discarded letter to Frederick, she penned one to Bernard full of her love for him as she realized in the instant that she'd seen his name that her feelings were that deep. This one she didn't destroy but put at the bottom of all the sheets of paper and closed the box. She would write to Bernard, but not until she'd asked Ruth how the best way to do it was. With all her heart she hoped Ruth was all right, and that soon she would feel up to going out to France with her.

When Ruth came up to bed, Ellen woke with a start.

'Oh, I didn't mean to wake yer, mate. Are yer all right? You looked very pale when yer left us.'

'Not really, Ruth. I started my monthly this morning and you know how it knocks me about. I didn't have time to tell you.'

Ruth looked down to the floor.

'Ruth?'

'Oh, Ellen, I've done a bad thing. I let me heart lead me. And Adrian did . . . We-we were going to be married within weeks . . . We couldn't help ourselves.'

Ellen sat up. 'Oh, Ruth, no! Do you think . . . ?'

'I'm worried sick . . . I missed a period and am praying I come on this time.'

'I know.' Ellen tried to soothe her by telling her what she'd read on the reproductive system and how it can be disrupted by shock.

For a moment, Ruth looked relieved. 'Really? It could be nothing more than that?'

'Yes. Let's not worry, I'm sure your next one will arrive . . . Unless, well, how do you feel? Have you noticed any changes in your body?'

'A little. A sort of stretching feeling in my breasts and they seem larger and me nipples a little darker, but that's all . . . Oh, Ellen, do you remember we used to call what happened to us "that thing" when . . . when we were raped? Well, that didn't ever result in me being pregnant and I'd started having me periods then.'

'There's loads of reasons why it might not have happened then – the man's infertility, you not ovulating when it happened, are just two that I've read about. You see . . . well, I studied it all as I needed to know after that . . . well, what happened to me in the woods . . .'

Ruth's hands took hers. Ruth's were cold and trembling. 'What me and Adrian shared was nothing like that, or any of the other times, Ellen. I don't ever want yer to be afraid to give yer love when the time's right, but . . . Oh, Ellen, I'm so scared.'

Suddenly, it occurred to Ellen to turn this around. She didn't want Ruth worried and afraid.

'Ruth, if it has happened, just think how wonderful that would be? Adrian's baby! A part of him for ever with you.'

Ruth's beautiful smile lit her face. 'I never thought of it that way, luv.'

'I'll help you. You have that lovely house and I have mine. We can live in either and we'll pass you off as a war widow, which you are really, and we'll bring the baby up together.'

'Oh, Ellen, I – I want it to be now. That sounds wonderful . . . though would the Red Cross release you?'

Not wanting to be released, but wanting to go to Bernard, it took a lot of courage for Ellen to say, 'I'll confess to my true age. They'll have to release me then.'

The hug she got from Ruth more than made up for the pain she felt at not being with Bernard.

The next morning, as if to seal as a truth what they had been thinking, Ruth dashed out of bed, grabbed the chamber pot from under the bed, bent over it and retched.

Ellen jumped out of her nice warm covers and was by her side in a shot, rubbing her back and making soothing noises as she began to explain why this was happening.

To her surprise, Ruth snapped, 'Shurrup, Ellen, yer like a walking medical encyclopaedia!'

Ellen stepped back, her hurt at the words that had cut through her bringing hot tears to her eyes. 'I'm . . . I'm sorry, Ruth.'

Ruth straightened, wiped her mouth with her hand and

burst into tears. 'No, I am. Oh, Ellen, how could I have spoken to yer like that? Forgive me, me darlin'.'

Ellen went into Ruth's open arms. 'You smell of vomit!'

Ruth's body jolted up and down, then her giggle escaped her, and she was laughing with her head back. The laugh worried Ellen, but she dared not say anything. Ruth was like an overstrung violin whose strings could snap at any moment. And then all of a sudden, they did. She crumbled into a heap on her bed and sobbed, 'I want Adrian! ADRIAN!'

Her scream cut through Ellen. 'Don't, Ruth, please don't.'

'I – I need him!'

Ruth's beauty turned to an ugly mask as her face contorted. Hoarse sounds came from her as she tried to breathe between rasping sobs. 'I – I need him, Ellen.'

This last was a pitiful sound. Ellen's tight throat gave way to gulping sobs as the pity of the awful situation became real to her. Yes, it was lovely that a piece of Adrian was growing and was going to live again, but what would that do to Ruth's life with no man to support her? 'Oh, Ruth, I'm here for you, love. I'll never leave you to cope alone, I promise. We can do this together, we can.'

Ruth calmed. Her rebound sobs wracked her body as Ellen held her, rubbed her back and stroked her hair. 'We'll get through this, Ruth, we will.'

In a voice that spoke of Ruth's acceptance she said, 'We will. While I have you by me side, we will cope, luv. I – I'm so sorry about what I said. Don't change, please don't change. Carry on with yer studying and relating it to everyday situations. I'm so proud of yer. That weren't me speaking, it was me desperation of the moment.'

'I know, sis. But you do still stink, so come on, get yer

wash, and let's get ready to go and break the news to Sister, eh?'

'We can't! No, Ellen, she might send me away. I couldn't bear that. I have to stay with you.'

'Look, let me go down and have a word with her. It's the best thing as . . . well, look, I'm going to be preaching again . . . but I've read that it ain't good for a woman to do heavy lifting when she's pregnant.'

Ruth gave a little laugh. 'Oh, Ellen, how could I have said such a thing? I don't even know where it came from, luv.'

'I think you'll say a lot more in the coming weeks as your hormones go through drastic changes, but I won't take any notice . . . Look, I'll tell Sister what we suspect and that you'll be leaving, and that I will too, but that you want to stay for as long as you can, and definitely until the concert and Christmas is over. I'll ask if, in the meantime, she could put you on light duties.' Ellen was on her haunches now looking up into Ruth's face. 'As Christmas is nearly here, I'll write to confess to Miss Darlington and tell her the truth about my age, and then we could be released at the same time.'

Ruth nodded. A tear fell onto her cheek. Ellen wiped it away with her thumb. 'We can do this, Ruth, we can.'

'But what about your future, going to college?'

'That will happen. I have at least three to four years in which to study to gain my entrance exams. And, if we live in London, I can have a tutor to help me. I won't give up on that, Ruth, as I know you don't want me to, nor will we give up on finding Amy and our mum. We can achieve everything we want to. Nothing will change as we'll always support one another.'

Ruth shook her head from side to side as she smiled down

at Ellen. 'I just don't know where yer came from, girl. Yer like a wise old woman at times.'

'Well, I grew up with two of the best, and everyone in my young life was much older than me, except Aggie. I was never allowed to be a child. I just don't know what one feels like or how they're supposed to act.'

Ruth's expression changed. 'No, nor me, nor any of us who were placed in that bloody awful orphanage – our childhood was stolen . . . But we can't do anything about it, luv . . . I'm so sorry about all of this, but I know, as always happens and happened when we were kids, we'll get through it together.'

Her smile lit her face again. Ellen knew it was genuine. 'Ruth, you get a wash and get back into bed, I'll get ready and go to see Sister.'

On her way, Ellen's heart thudded the pain of her sacrifice around her body. To give all of this up – never to work beside Bernard when he most needed her – broke her heart.

Sister was shocked rigid. She didn't seem able to speak for a moment. When finally she released her breath and lowered her eyebrows, she shook her head. 'Well! I can't . . . No! don't want to believe it . . . But, oh dear, poor Ruth.'

This last gave Ellen a small relief. Sister wasn't condemning.

'I shall be so sorry to lose her, and so will you. How will she manage? Will she go to one of those convents that take care of women in her condition?'

'No . . . she has friends.' Now wasn't the time to reveal her plans, Ellen thought. She needed to stay until Ruth left, and she needed that order to come from Miss Darlington, and not to rock the boat until then.

'She's going to need some very good friends as even those

you rely on most can turn their back on you over something like this. It carries such a stigma . . . Look, run up and tell her to come down when she's ready. Staying in her room isn't going to do her any good. I will put her on light duties – though I will do it discreetly so as not to arouse suspicion. And, Ellen, tell her that if ever she wants to prove herself an actress, she needs to brace herself to tell herself that no matter what, the show must go on. As this one must.' At this, Sister clapped her hands. 'To your post, Ellen! To your post!'

Ellen scooted out of the room and up the stairs. When she reached their bedroom and opened the door, she was shocked to see Ruth there in her uniform and standing tall. 'I've decided that the show must go on, Ellen. What did Sister say? Am I allowed to carry on?'

'Ha, not only that, but you took Sister's very words!' Ellen told her what the sister had said.

Ruth giggled at this. 'She's a good sort, Ellen, and I won't let her down.'

'I know, but remember what I said.'

'Yes, Doctor!'

They both laughed as this wasn't said anything like the last remark about her vocation which, though forgiven, still hurt a little. But then, Ellen thought, that's sisters for you, and that had been the first time they'd had a little discord, so they were lucky.

Ellen had no time to write to headquarters as several of the staff suddenly went down with a sickness bug and those left were run off their feet for a few days as many of the patients caught it too. Ruth, to be contrary, was now asking her to pray that her sickness wasn't due to the same thing, but truly was a new life – an extension of Adrian's life growing inside her.

Ellen knew other signs were there that this was a pregnancy. She pointed these out to Ruth, to reassure her.

The concert did masses to lift Ruth. Ellen saw a glow about her as she sang and danced with Robbie and, together, they had the audience enraptured before they laughed till the bedridden patients nearly fell out of their beds and others looked as though they'd be in less pain if they could roll on the floor at the near-the-mark jokes of Cyril. This continued at the excellent rendition of Abe's monologue.

Communal carols followed, after which there wasn't a dry eye in the place as staff and patients showed their love for one another in hugs and kisses.

It was as they were outside on the stone patio with Robbie and Abe, all of them wrapped up against the frosty night – the men smoking, and it looking as if she and Ruth were too, as their breath formed plumes of white vapour – that Ruth told the men what was happening with her.

Robbie took her in his arms and held her. 'Oh, Ruth, mate . . . This bloody war! I have to start my journey back tomorrow, luv, or I'd look after yer.'

They were near enough to Abe for him to hold Ruth's hand at the same time and in that moonlit moment, Ellen envied Ruth the friends she'd made. Yes, her own life had been materially better than Ruth's, but she'd have given it all up for a penneth of what Ruth had found in hers.

As this thought left her, she heard Robbie say, 'How're yer going to manage? Will yer stay with Bett?'

'No, I'm going to take care of her, Robbie,' Ellen piped up, only to be shocked as Ruth said a vehement, 'No!'

'But, Ruth—'

Ruth broke away from Robbie and came to Ellen's side once more. 'Ellen, luv, it will break me heart to be parted from yer, but you have a job to do. You're needed by the wounded. The country needs yer more than I do. And you're too bloody good a nurse to be lost to it. I – I know you want to go to France to rejoin our team, and I want you to. I'll be all right with Bett, luv, I promise yer.'

'Oh, Ruth . . . I can't leave you.'

'You can and you will. I'm pulling big-sis rank now.'

Ellen saw the sincerity in Ruth's eyes and felt torn.

'Please do this for me, Ellen. I will feel terrible taking you away from those who need you so badly.'

Ellen thought a moment. 'Only if Miss Darlington agrees to me going back. If she doesn't and insists that I stay here, then I am going to tell her the truth.'

'What truth?'

Ellen reeled around at Abe's voice. She'd thought that Ruth had told him about her age and that they were pretending to be twins. Or surely that he would have guessed.

Robbie coughed. 'It's something we have to keep a secret, Abe. I never thought I'd have anything like that from yer, but your sense of honour wouldn't let yer say nothing.'

Abe looked at Robbie for a moment, then at them before he said, 'Well, whatever it is, I know you're keeping it for honourable reasons, so I won't insist on knowing.'

Ellen felt the tension leave Ruth. She looked at her sister and could see that she really did want this to happen and knew that though she would miss her as if part of her was torn from her, she was right. There was a duty to be done . . . Notwithstanding the duty to her own heart too.

Epilogue

Summer 1919

The sun beamed through the glass roof as Ellen stepped onto Paddington station amidst a babble of excited nurses, still unable to believe that it was all over and finding themselves happy, despite everything.

She looked along the train, waiting to catch a glimpse of Bernard getting out of the officers' carriage.

Exhaustion plagued her. The last months had been long and harrowing as they had battled against not terrible injuries, as the patients with those had all been dispatched long ago, but influenza. Losing so many men and working in terrible conditions to try to save lives. They had done so, but very few.

How they had been saved from catching the virus, Ellen put down to the lint masks given to them by a local French hospital and often made by themselves if supply ran out. Though still they lost two lovely nurses who'd been through so much during the fighting.

She imagined that this station had seen many returning soldiers and joyful family reunions. But how many of them had survived for long after returning as the world was just coming out of the ferocious pandemic? She didn't even know if all her loved ones were safe as she hadn't heard from Ruth for months – very few letters had got through in that time.

She didn't even know if Ruth still lived with Bett, though that was where she would head for, praying that no news was good news.

Catching a glimpse of Bernard stepping down onto the platform, her heart jumped. He didn't know how much she loved him. He'd not been surprised by his brother's assumptions about her being supposedly in love with him; he'd just said that was typical of Frederick. But he had never spoken up about having feelings for her himself.

Frederick had long forgotten her as Bernard had received mail from him that told of his engagement to be married. Ellen had been relieved and happy for him. But oh, how she yearned for Bernard to show even a glimpse of what she had read into his words in his letter all those years ago.

'Ellen! Ellen!'

A desperate voice calling out lifted her heart from the doldrums that these thoughts had plunged her into. She turned in the direction of the sound.

'Ruth! Ruth, oh, Ruth.'

Within seconds she was enclosed in a wonderful hug that she never wanted to come out of. Her voice cracked as she asked, 'Where did you come from? How did you know I was coming home . . . ? Oh, Ruth, it's good to see you.' Tears flowed down her cheeks as she asked, 'Is . . . is everyone all right?'

Ruth shook her head. 'We lost dear Bett and Ruby. I-I've been heartbroken, Ellen. Bett were like a mum to me.'

They clung to one another. Ellen wanted to ask about Ruth's son, Archie, but dared not. Then suddenly she saw them as a few yards away stood Robbie with Abe in a wheelchair and on Abe's knee an adorable little boy who looked the image of Adrian. As they came up to them, Archie said, 'Welcome home, Aunty,' in a very grown-up voice and for a moment she saw herself, knowing only adults and mimicking them.

She laughed out loud. 'My, you're very grown-up, Archie. I'm so pleased to meet you.'

Archie giggled in a very ungrown-up, little boy way.

'Don't be fooled. He's a little rogue. He's been practising those lines for weeks now.'

'Weeks? How did you know I was coming home? I haven't been able to get a letter to you for ages.'

'Miss Darlington has kept me informed. You've had it rough, haven't yer, luv?'

Before she could answer, Robbie spoke. 'Hey, leave all the catching up for another time. I ain't had a hug yet.' With this, he swept her into his arms. Ellen had forgotten what it was like to be held in a loving way by another human being, let alone a loved one. She just wanted to hug them all and never stop.

At that moment she opened her tightly closed eyes and caught sight of Bernard. He looked as though he was about to approach them, but then on seeing Robbie hug her turned around to walk in the opposite direction.

Oh no! Why? He can't think Robbie is anything to me! Oh, Bernard, Bernard, my love.

'Are yer all right, luv?'

'No, Ruth, I – I . . .'

Ruth looked in the direction of Bernard. 'Oh, he's going. Has he never returned your feelings, luv?'

'Yes . . . well, I mean, in glances and gestures, but never spoken of them . . . Oh, Ruth, I'm going to lose him.'

The words trembled through her. She couldn't let that happen. On an impulse she left Ruth, called out to Abe that she hadn't forgotten him and left them to run after Bernard.

'Bernard!'

He turned. His face lit in a smile. 'I – I didn't want to intrude.'

'You can never do that, Bernard.' As she said the words, Ellen marvelled at her own boldness.

Bernard looked surprised, then composed himself. 'Well, I didn't want to leave without saying goodbye, and thank you. And to make sure you have my address and will call if you need that proposal to launch you into medical school.'

'Thanks. I would give you mine, but I don't know yet where I am going to live.'

'Oh? You do have somewhere?'

'Yes, a place of my own and my sister owns a place, but I don't know what has been happening in their lives yet . . . By them, I mean my sister and our two friends.'

'They are just friends? Both of them?'

'Yes. Just friends.'

'Oh . . . I thought . . . Ellen, as we are no longer working with each other . . . I wonder, well, would you consider coming to dinner with me one evening?'

Ellen's heart soared. 'Yes, yes, I would, thank you . . . I'll let you know where I am. I'll drop a note to you.'

His face held an expression she'd never seen. His eyes held hers.

'Ellen, I – I . . .'

Whatever he was going to say, he didn't. Ellen didn't know what came over her as she blurted out, 'I love you, Bernard.'

He dropped his case. His face took on many expressions in those few seconds that he neared her – astonishment, bewilderment and, finally, love. 'Oh, Ellen, really?'

'Really, you goose! I just wasn't prepared to wait for you ever telling me how you feel about me.'

'I love you . . . I've always loved you, darling Ellen. Oh, Ellen.'

A round of applause began as he took her into his arms. With his lips coming onto hers, her world inflamed into a happy bubble. The cheers around her became louder. When they parted, they were surrounded by their colleagues, many of whom had become their friends, but as well as these, Ruth, Robbie and Abe were clapping just as loud as everyone else.

Ruth stepped forward. 'About time, Bernard. And nice to see you again.'

'Ruth! I – I don't know how that happened.' Bernard was laughing.

'You were about to walk away from my sister, mate. She's been in love with yer since she first met yer and wasn't having it!'

Bernard laughed the laugh Ellen had come to love amongst all the million other things she loved about him. Her heart soared as she told herself, *And he loves me! Bernard actually loves me!*

'Let me give you me address, Bernard,' Ruth told him. 'It's Southampton Way, off the Peckham Road in Camberwell, luv. Number seven. You're welcome anytime. We all live there together, me and me son, Archie, Robbie, me mate, and Abe, another mate, and now she's home, Ellen too.'

'Oh, quite a houseful.'

'Yes. We like it that way, and all are welcome. The house is three storeys so there's an apartment downstairs that Abe and Robbie share and I live above in a two-storey apartment that's for me and Ellen and me son.'

'Sounds wonderful. A sort of commune.'

'Yes, a bit like that. Well, we'll leave you and Ellen alone a moment. We have a cab outside the station, Ellen.'

Most people had gone now and with all the fuss having died down, Ellen suddenly felt very shy and couldn't believe what she'd done but was so glad she had at last declared her love.

They stood a moment, gazing at each other.

'Oh, Ellen, I wanted so much to tell you of my love for you, but while we worked together and under such pressure and conditions, I just couldn't, and then when I saw you greet your friends, I thought . . . Well, we've never really got to know one another, have we? So, I didn't know about your friends, only your sister.'

'No, not in all the time we've worked together did we talk about our lives outside work.'

'We have a lot of catching up to do. Can we sit a moment? Look, there's an empty bench over there.'

When they sat, Ellen knew that this was the time for the truth. 'I've lived a lie for a lot of the time that we've known each other, Bernard . . . You see, I'm not Ruth's twin but her younger sister. I was only almost sixteen when we first came out to Belgium.'

'What? Oh my God, Ellen, how brave you were and how capable too. So, now you are . . . twenty?'

'I will be in October.'

'I can't take that in. I never dreamed. I just accepted that you were older to even be a VAD and with all the knowledge you had . . . Though, there was a moment when I suspected, I remember. It was when we first met and you said that when you were old enough you wanted to be a doctor . . . Speaking of which, I know you have never given up on your dream, and that doesn't change. I can wait for you, my darling. You must still do as you have always said you would and apply for medical school. I just know you will pass the entrance exam. How is your science?'

This was not what she wanted to talk about but answered by telling him it was one of her best subjects. 'I just need to brush up on it a little.'

'I'll help you . . . I know you're tired, as I am, but I also know this is what you want most in the world. I don't want to get in the way of that, darling.'

He'd called her darling.

'I have something I need to do first.' She told him about Canada.

He took her hands. 'Life gets in the way sometimes of everything we want to do . . . Look, go home now, darling, and I will call for you tomorrow night. We'll go out to dinner and have this talk then. I'll be in Southampton Way, at seven on the dot!'

'Ha, always precise! Well, I'll be ready . . . I – I love you, Bernard. I just want to keep telling you now that I have at last done so.'

'And I love you. We have a lot to figure out. We'll talk, we'll sort everything, Ellen, my love.'

Leaving him wrenched at her heart. Tomorrow evening seemed a million years away.

When she reached the cab, they were all settled in, with Abe in the front and a space for her in the back with Robbie, who had Archie on his knee and was next to her beloved Ruth.

She and Ruth snuggled into one another. It felt so good. Ruth didn't seem as though she could stop looking at her and smiling. Though behind the smile, Ellen could see the heartache. 'Has it been awful, Ruth, love?'

'Yes. It ain't been easy, luv. Bett caught the flu early last year. We reckon it was from the people she was helping – the homeless who were joined by returning soldiers who found themselves out on the streets with their families. We all worked tirelessly to help them. I caught it too, but got over it, as did Ebony, but Bett . . . Oh, Ellen, she was so ill. I – I couldn't help her. I did try, but she just didn't respond.'

Ellen put her arm around her beloved sister. Her own tears for the lovely Bett mingled with Ruth's.

'Mummy, don't cry.'

'It's all right, son,' Robbie told Archie. 'Mummies need to cry sometimes when they hurt, mate, just like you do.'

'I don't want Mummy to be hurt.'

'I know. Oh, look, there's a clown! Ha ha, he's acting the fool!'

Archie laughed out loud as they looked out at a street entertainer. 'Why is he doing that, Robbie?'

'To get some pennies to eat, I expect.'

Ellen felt the pity of this, and as she looked out of the window, shock at how, though it was a lovely sunny day, everything around her looked sad and neglected. Men slumped on the floor – injured men, some with only one leg or arm, or disfigured faces. She hadn't thought this would be how it was back home. London had stayed in her mind as a bustling, vibrant, colourful city, with everyone thriving and seemingly rich.

'Life has changed so much, Ellen. We all do what we can, but it's like trying to plug a bucket with a million holes in it.'

They were quiet for a moment. Ellen wanted to ask about Ruby, but Ruth seemed to just want to talk about Bett. The pain in her voice was awful to hear.

'She had a huge funeral, Ellen. Her sons saw to it. They carried her through the streets and to the marketplace where there was a minute's silence. It was all very moving, luv, and fitting for lovely Bett.'

'I'm sorry, darling Ruth. I wish I'd been here for you. I could have come home. They did offer us the chance, but not many did as the situation there was so dire. Our boys, who'd come through so much, dying of this rotten influenza. They needed us.'

Ruth just patted her hand.

'I missed you so much, Ruth.'

'And me you, luv. I can't tell yer how I longed for yer to be with me. If it weren't for Bett, Robbie and Abe, I'd have never got through having Archie.'

'When did you move to your house? And what about Adrian's aunt – have you met her?'

'She, too, died of the influenza, poor soul. She was a lovely lady. I often visited her in her nursing home. She loved little Archie and left what money she had to him. I loved her, Ellen. It was so hard to lose her. She told me so much about Adrian's life. I wanted him back to hug him and to give him happiness.'

Once more they clung to each other. Ellen found it difficult to hang on to any of the joy she'd felt at being home and finding Bernard's love at long last.

As if she'd sensed this, Ruth suddenly cheered up. 'Look at us, mate! We've longed to be with each other, and now we are, we're like a couple of wet weekends!'

Her watery giggle made Ellen giggle too. This was the Ruth she knew. The Ruth who never stayed down long but bounced back and overcame her inner sadness.

'We're going to be all right, mate, I promise. And, I have news!'

'Oh? Don't tell me. You've fallen in love with a man on a white charger!'

'What? No, yer daft thing. I've heard from that farmer in Canada!'

It was Ellen's turn to exclaim, 'What? Oh, Ruth, is Amy all right? Do you know where she is?'

'I do. Oh, Ellen, we need to go to her. We have to . . . but, well, yer've put yer dream on hold for so long, I'm thinking that I'll go and bring her home, while yer get on with what yer have to do to become a doctor.'

'No! We'll go together, Ruth, I'll—'

The cab pulling up and little Archie shouting, 'We're home!' stopped their conversation.

Ruth patted her knee. 'We'll talk about it. It can't happen overnight . . . but, Ellen . . . it will happen, won't it?'

'It will. Nothing's as sure as that. We'll go to Canada, and we'll bring our dear Amy home.'

As she said this, Ellen was torn with mixed emotions. She wanted to get on with her life – a proper life without war and fear. She wanted to be with Bernard. She wanted to be near to Ruth to be able to see her whenever she could, and she wanted Amy home.

It surprised her that nowhere on that list came wanting to be a doctor. Was that even important to her any more? This very question shocked her. But then, she thought, Bernard had talked of going into general practice when he was home. He'd made her laugh as he'd said, 'I want to deal with ingrowing toenails, kids with earache and mums having babies. I've had enough blood and gore to last me a lifetime.'

Suddenly, she knew. That's what she wanted too. And not necessarily as the doctor, but as the doctor's wife – the nurse he would need to assist him. She couldn't believe this ambition was completely wiping out the dream of her lifetime, but it was. She didn't need to be a doctor to heal people. She just needed to be the other half of the man that could do that as she knew that, through him, she could do that too. For Bernard would let her be much more than his assistant. He knew her skills. She didn't have to have a pass in medical studies to prove anything to him. Nor, she realized, to herself.

The house was lovely. After hugging Abe, which she hadn't had time to do at the station and finding him cheerfully accepting of his disability and skilful in getting around in his wheelchair, a specially adapted one for him with large wheels that he could turn to manoeuvre himself, and a second one she was told about that was for outdoors. 'I propel it by turning handles on the steering column. Robbie can hardly keep up with me!'

'Ah, but it keeps me fit for me dancing.'

'Oh, I never asked. Are you still working as an actor and dancer, Robbie?'

'I am, Ellen. Yer must bring your doctor friend to see a production, luv.'

'I will, that would be lovely . . . And you, Ruth? Are you back on the stage?'

'No. I lost the need to be when I had Archie. He keeps me busy, but I do have something I ain't told yer of. I've took up me hat-making again!'

'Oh, Ruth! That's wonderful. Do you stand the market?'

'No, I sell to a few shops, but . . . well, an old dream has come back into me, and I want to have me own milliner's shop, Ellen. And I've seen a place . . . Oh, we've so much to talk about, sis. So much of our lives to knit together again.'

They hugged again and into the hug poured the pain of their separation and all they'd been through.

When they at last dried their eyes, they found Abe and Robbie's sitting room where they'd all been gathered was empty.

'They'll have taken little Archie outside into the garden. Well, it's more of a courtyard, but Abe is a skilful gardener and has turned it into a peaceful haven of flower and rose beds.'

'That sounds wonderful. And reminds me of my cottage . . . I'll have to visit there soon. It should be fine, though, as my solicitor has seen to its upkeep. I think the time has come to sell it as London has become my home . . . Oh, but I'm gabbling on and you must be worried about Archie, love.'

'I am, bless him. He must be afraid seeing his mum like this. But I can't help it, Ellen, it's like all me sad bits, and me longing to be with you, and me happy bits have crowded me.'

'I know. We're going to need a few days to find each other again, Ruth . . . Not that we were lost to each other, but we've had almost four years of our time together taken away from us, and whereas my life stood still, you have been through so many changes.'

'Yes. Huge ones. Having Archie, losing Bett and Ruby, giving up the idea of the stage, starting me hat business again, and even where I live and me circumstances. All have changed. And it's like I want yer to know it all in one big rush so that you know me again. Can yer understand that?'

'I can. It happened when we first found each other. But it can be a gradual process. One thing hasn't changed, or ever will, and that's our love for one another.'

'You're right, me darlin'. Nothing can ever change or break that. We're those two little orphans who loved each other from the start, reunited once more.'

This time the hug they went into was a gentle holding of each other and a healing of the gulf that had intruded on their lives, but never on their love. Their love wasn't touchable by anything life could throw at them. It was a forever guarantee – a gift given to them as children in a stinking hell that scarred them for life but had never beaten them and never would.

She and Ruth were reunited.

Acknowledgements

Many people are involved in getting my book to the shelves and presenting it in the very best way to my readers:

My commissioning editor, Wayne Brookes, who works tirelessly, overseeing umpteen processes my book goes through and keeps me going with his cheerful encouragement – always optimistic, a joy to work with.

My editorial team headed by Samantha Fletcher, whose work brings out the very best of my story to make it shine. And Victoria Hughes-Williams, who is responsible for the structural edit and makes sure the story flows.

My publicist, Philippa McEwan, and her team, who seek out many opportunities for me to showcase my work. My cover designers, who do an amazing job in bringing my story alive in picture form, producing covers that stand out from the crowd. And the sales team, who find outlets across the country for my books.

My son, James Wood, who reads so many versions of my work, to help and advise me, and works alongside me on the edits that come in.

And last but not least, my readers, who encourage me as they await another book, supporting me every step of the way and who warm my heart with praise in their reviews. My heartfelt thanks to you all.

But no one person stands alone. My family are amazing. They give me an abundance of love and support and when one of them says they are proud of me, then my world is complete. My special thanks to my darling Roy, my husband and very best friend. My children, grandchildren and great-grandchildren who light up my life, and my Olley and Wood families. You are all my rock and help me to climb my mountain. Thank you. I love you with all my heart.

Letter to Readers

Dear reader,

Hi. I hope you enjoyed reading *The Orphanage Girls Reunited* – the second in the Orphanage Girls trilogy – as much as I enjoyed writing it.

Thank you from the bottom of my heart for choosing my work to curl up with.

I would so appreciate if you would kindly leave me a review on Amazon, Goodreads, or any online bookstore or book group. Reviews are like being hugged by the reader and they help to encourage me to write the next book – they further my career as they advise other readers about the book, and hopefully whet their appetite to also buy the book.

Coming next, in springtime 2023, is the third and last of the series – *The Orphanage Girls Come Home*.

This will be Amy's story, which we pick up as she boards the ship to Canada – remember Ruth saying goodbye to her on the dock in book one?

Amy, at eleven years old, is led to believe she is going to a wonderful new life, but as history now tells us, these children of the early 1900s, sent to many countries in the Commonwealth, were badly treated.

Those who landed in Canada were called the 'Home Children' and were looked down on and treated as second-class citizens. Only recently, prominent figures, both here and in Canada, have apologized to their surviving families for the suffering and for them ever being sent away in the first place – many taken from their families due to poverty and over-crowding of dwellings.

Ruth and Ellen will play a huge part in this book too, as we pick up their lives and continue on their journey with them – many surprises along the way, and as always, emotional times as well as happy ones – tissues at the ready for both.

Lastly, I am always available to be contacted personally, if you have any queries or just want to say hello, or maybe book me for a talk to a group you belong to. I love to interact with readers and would welcome your comments, your emails, and messages through:

My Facebook page: facebook.com/MaryWoodAuthor

My Twitter: @Authormary

My website: www.authormarywood.com

I will always reply. And if you subscribe to my newsletter on my website, you will be entered in a draw to win my latest book personally signed to you and will receive a three-monthly newsletter giving all the updates on my books and author life, and many chances of winning lovely prizes.

Love to hear from you. Take care of yourself and others.

Much love

Mary xxx

Their adventure begins in

The Orphanage Girls

Children deserve a family to call their own.

Ruth dares to dream of another life – far away from the horrors within the walls of Bethnal Green's infamous orphanage. Luckily she has her friends, Amy and Ellen, but she can't keep them safe, and the suffering is only getting worse. Surely there must be a way out?

But when Ruth breaks free from the shackles of confinement and sets out into East London, hoping to make a new life for herself, she finds that, for a girl with nowhere to turn, life can be just as tough on the outside.

Bett keeps order in this unruly part of the East End and she takes Ruth under her wing alongside fellow orphanage escapee Robbie. But it is Rebekah, a kindly woman, who offers Ruth and Robbie a home – something neither has ever known. Yet even these two stalwart women cannot protect them when the police learn of an orphan on the run. It is then that Ruth must do everything in her power to hide. Her life – and those of the friends she left behind at the orphanage – depend on it.

Available now

If you enjoyed

The Orphanage Girls Reunited

then you'll love

The Jam Factory Girls

**Whatever life throws at them,
they will face it together**

Life for Elsie is difficult as she struggles to cope with her alcoholic mother. Caring for her siblings and working long hours at Swift's Jam Factory in London's Bermondsey is exhausting. Thankfully her lifelong friendship with Dot helps to smooth over life's rough edges.

When Elsie and Dot meet Millie Hawkesfield, the boss's daughter, they are nervous to be in her presence. Over time, they are surprised to feel so drawn to her, but should two cockney girls be socializing in such circles?

When disaster strikes, it binds the women in ways they could never have imagined. And long-held secrets are revealed that will change all their lives . . .

The Jam Factory Girls series continues with
Secrets of the Jam Factory Girls and *The Jam Factory Girls Fight Back*, all available to read now.

The Forgotten Daughter

Book one in
The Girls Who Went to War series

From a tender age, Flora felt unloved and unwanted by her parents, but she finds safety in the arms of caring Nanny Pru. But when Pru is cast out of the family home, under a shadow of secrets and with a baby boy of her own on the way, it shatters little Flora.

Over the years, however, Flora and Pru meet in secret – unbeknown to Flora's parents. Pru becomes the mother she never had, and Flora grows into a fine young woman. When she signs up as a volunteer with St John Ambulance, she begins to shape her life. But the drum of war beats loudly and her world is turned upside down when she receives a letter asking her to join the Red Cross in Belgium.

With the fate of the country in the balance, it is a time for bravery. Flora's determined to be the strong woman she was destined to be. But with horror, loss and heartache on her horizon, there's a lot for young Flora to learn . . .

The Girls Who Went to War series continues with
The Abandoned Daughter, *The Wronged Daughter* and
The Brave Daughters, all available to read now.